HEATHER FOXTON

THE SECRETS OF GODOLPHIN PARK

13
ELEMENTS

For more information on the adventures of Heather Foxton,
visit www.heatherfoxton.com

THE SECRETS OF GODOLPHIN PARK

M.N.SMITH

ELEMENTS

First published in 2013 by 13 Elements

Third Edition published in 2018 by 13 Elements

Copyright © M.N. Smith 2018

Interior illustrations copyright © M.N. Smith 2013

The right of M.N. Smith to be identified as the author of this work has been asserted in accordance with the Copyright, Designs and Patent Act 1988.

This book is a work of fiction and, except in the case of historical fact, any resemblance to actual persons, living or dead, is purely coincidental.

13 Elements, c/o: http://www.heatherfoxton.com

A CIP catalogue record for this book is available from the British Library.

ISBN 978-0-9927378-4-9 Paperback

Typeset by
Chandler Book Design.

Printed by Createspace

For Ting. My BB!

In loving memory of Kristen Dennis.
Now in a better place, but in our
thoughts forever.

'. . . are advised to exercise particular caution with recruits who serve not for financial gain, vanity, ego or idealism, but solely in the pursuit of adventure and excitement . . .'

British Secret Intelligence Service Instructor's
Handbook: Section 1.3

'And ye shall know the truth, and the truth shall set you free.'

John VIII–XXXII

CONTENTS

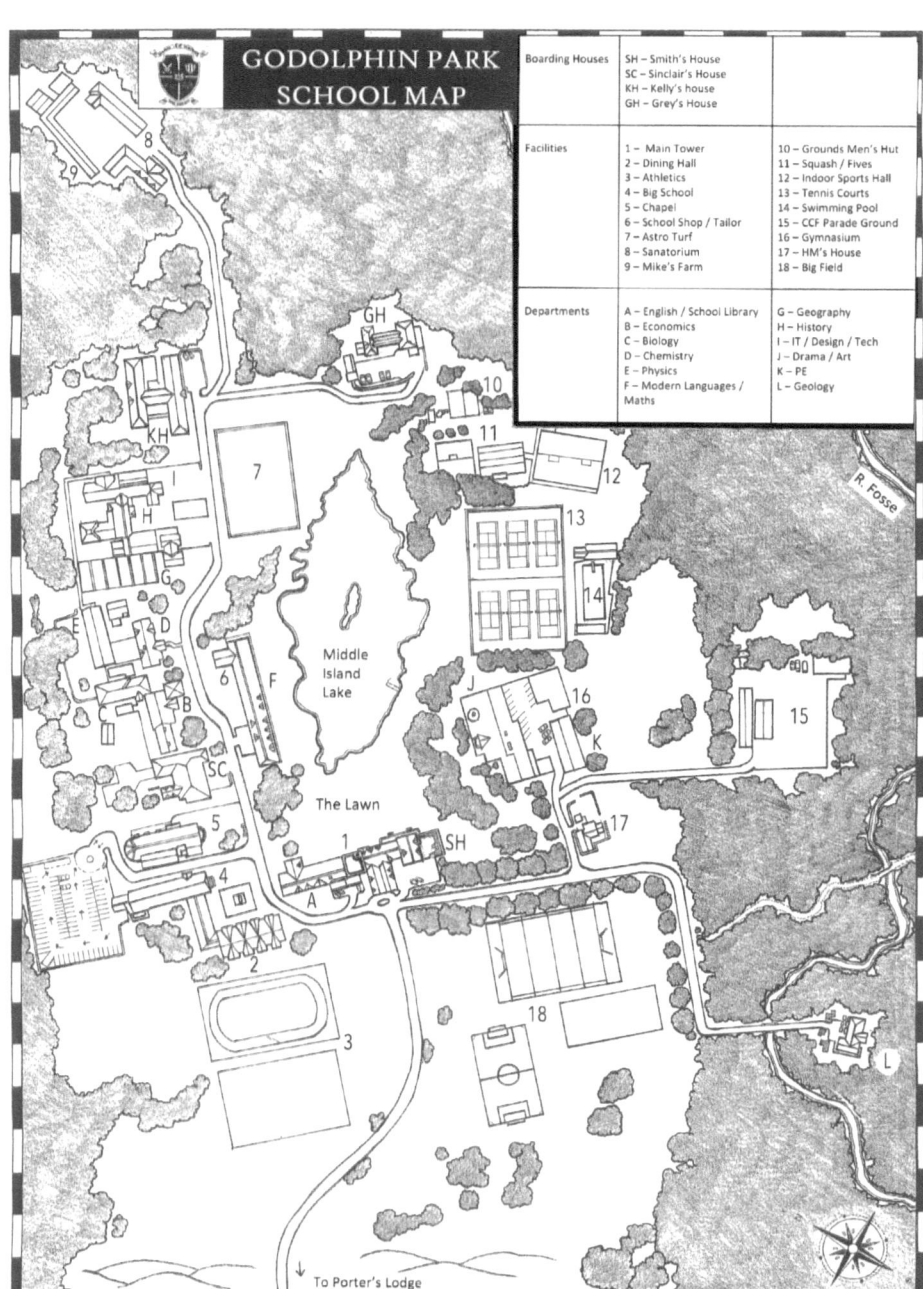

GODOLPHIN PARK
SCHOOL MAP

Boarding Houses	SH – Smith's House SC – Sinclair's House KH – Kelly's house GH – Grey's House	
Facilities	1 – Main Tower 2 – Dining Hall 3 – Athletics 4 – Big School 5 – Chapel 6 – School Shop / Tailor 7 – Astro Turf 8 – Sanatorium 9 – Mike's Farm	10 – Grounds Men's Hut 11 – Squash / Fives 12 – Indoor Sports Hall 13 – Tennis Courts 14 – Swimming Pool 15 – CCF Parade Ground 16 – Gymnasium 17 – HM's House 18 – Big Field
Departments	A – English / School Library B – Economics C – Biology D – Chemistry E – Physics F – Modern Languages / Maths	G – Geography H – History I – IT / Design / Tech J – Drama / Art K – PE L – Geology

Middle Island Lake

The Lawn

R. Fosse

To Porter's Lodge

THE PRICE OF BEING DIFFERENT

This'll all go a whole lot easier if you just trust me when I say I'm not like you. And yes, I know that's probably what everyone likes to think. That somehow they too are different from the rest of humanity in some unique sort of way. Just in my case it's actually true.

I suppose I've always known, deep down. For as far back as I can remember, my parents would tell people how I was always getting into these impossible places when I was young. But it was only when I started exploring my boundaries for myself that I really began to grasp how true this was. Like the time I first tried holding my breath underwater at bath time. By some miracle no one was around to freak out as the minutes ticked by. And when I finally came up for air, some three and a half minutes later … well, you get my point. And that was at a time when most of my friends could barely make a width of the school pool on one breath.

But it never truly hit home until I was a little older and it got me into a whole heap of trouble. I remember it vividly, even though it was so long ago. It was sports day and somehow I'd managed to get roped into doing the mixed hundred metres. I can't recall why I bothered trying as hard as I did. But, suffice to say, I won. And not by a stride or two either. We're talking the kind of margin that you just don't see in races between eight-year-olds. Like ever.

At that age I was completely unprepared for what happened next. The dreadful, lingering silence; those wary, uncertain stares; not to mention the shock of discovering that no one wanted to sit next to me anymore in class or at lunchtime. Yet, even then, it still never occurred to ask myself why, or how, I could do these things. That was just how the world was, I suppose. Though it did make me a lot more hesitant about letting people get close to me, lest they ever accidentally discover what a freak I was. I mean, if I didn't understand who, or what, I was, then how was I ever to expect anyone else to? Besides, all I really wanted back then was just to be like all the other kids.

Of course, that kind of naive innocence couldn't last forever, and the older I got, the more I came to understand why people react the way they do to things they don't understand. But that's life, I guess. Very quickly I became more of a loner, not in an anti-social, reclusive sort of way, but I found myself increasingly happy in my own company. Not exactly hard, being an only child. When company came my way, I'd gladly make the most of it, but I could also happily then move on and enjoy my own.

With maturity came an ever greater comprehension of the rapidly widening gap between my friends' physical abilities and my own. The only snag was constantly having to be on-guard, ever vigilant, lest I absent-mindedly do something stupid which caught someone's attention. But don't get me wrong, if that's the price to be paid for what I can do, then, hey, that's fine by me. I wouldn't give it up for the world.

What I didn't know back then, however, was quite how it would change my life. And change it, it did. Completely, utterly, in every way possible. And all it took was a holiday I'd gladly forget, an old man who made a few lucky guesses and my overwhelming desire for a life less ordinary. And that's precisely what I got!

This, then, is my story ...

CHAPTER 1

POST HOC, ERGO PROPTER HOC

Marrakech, Morocco, North Africa

'm Woken, Not by my alarm clock, nor a noise from outside, but by the faint ticking coming from my watch, a large, white Omega Seamaster, perched beside the bed. And this isn't the first time it's happened, either. But seeing as my dad gave it to me for my sixteenth birthday, back in February, I'm willing to forgive it for disturbing my sleep. What I like about it is, given that it isn't even remotely feminine or elegant, it flies in the face of everything my mother stands for. And anything which can do that should be encouraged, in my book.

With a groan, I roll over and try to ignore the incessant tick-tick-tick reverberating through the wooden bedside table. Unfortunately any hope I have of getting back to sleep disappears the moment every mosque across the city starts broadcasting its call to morning prayer.

'Oh, you've got to be joking,' I mumble in dismay, seeing that it's only just gone half past six in the morning. I try burying myself under the cover in the hope that it won't last long. But after a few minutes I realise that's wishful thinking and eventually have little choice but to admit defeat. With a laugh of despair, I throw the sheets back and wander out onto the balcony, cursing myself for having left the doors open last night.

Far off in the distance, the sun has just begun to creep up over the hazy red mountains to the east. Leaning against the railing, I inhale deeply and savour the rich blend of aromatic spices that almost give the dry desert air a tangible taste. As I watch the city wake, my thoughts turn to my friends and all the fun we're going to have here. Especially as there's only one teacher to supervise the lot of us!

Eventually bored, I turn to go back indoors. But, not paying attention, I end up stubbing my toe on the step. Cursing and grimacing in pain, I hobble inside and make my way more carefully into my en-suite bathroom. The tired, dishevelled-looking mess that stares back at me earns itself a weary frown. My unruly, long blonde hair resembles a bird's nest and my eyes look tired and puffy. But, then again, I guess it's about as flattering as could be expected at this time of the morning. That's not to imply I'm blasé about my appearance. Are you kidding? Show me a girl my age who is. What with everything we have to deal with, it would be some kind of miracle if I wasn't concerned. If it isn't about not being pretty enough, or perfect enough, or popular enough, it's any one of a hundred other pressures which boys, the media or our parents dump on us. Though, curiously, it was my mother who, despite all her faults, probably put it the nicest when she said I'm one of those girls who's pretty enough that boys shouldn't be a problem, but not so pretty that other girls will resent me for it. I'm fairly sure she was trying to be complimentary. At least, I like to think so, because then it'd rank as one of the only nice things she's ever said to me.

With a despondent sigh, I reach for a strip of paper to wipe the seat. But as I pull, the whole roll pops from its flimsy holder and falls straight into the toilet.

Barely ten minutes in and today's already shaping up to be one of those days.

*

It is just gone seven o'clock in the morning when the small private jet comes to a halt on its designated slot, far off on an outlying corner of Marrakech's Menara Airport. Before the engines have wound down, the side door opens and four Asian men quickly descend the steps. Without speaking, each loads his bags into the rear of the people carrier waiting on the tarmac. Then, as the last door slams, the vehicle accelerates off towards the nearby executive immigration building.

Upon their arrival at the quiet residential villa on the outskirts of the city, they troop inside in the same contemplative silence as they have been for the whole trip. Each is in this purely for the money, so conversation doesn't rank high on their list of needs. All are lean, fit and intensely serious. They exude the same quiet menace that comes from having spent most of their adult lives learning how to kill people in new and imaginative ways. Only the leader speaks; his orders quiet but authoritative. The others busy themselves with assembling their gear in the villa's front room.

Satisfied that their tactical radios and specialised tranquiliser guns are all in good working order, the leader retires to the traditionally decorated kitchen. There, he opens his laptop and logs it on. While it boots up, he absent-mindedly takes out his wallet and gazes affectionately at the picture of his daughter.

A daughter who, after this mission, will be financially set to go to any school she pleases. Sighing deeply, he pockets the wallet, in direct contravention of the orders he'll soon give his men that they should have no forms of identification on them during the mission. Ah, the privileges of command, he thinks with a smile. With the internet up and running, he navigates to a Canadian florist's website. Upon entering his password, a new page appears. One that merely contains a passport photo and nothing more. But it's all he needs to know.

A career soldier, the former major is used to not questioning his orders, but even he would love to know the logic behind the selection of this, their latest target. Nonplussed, he leans back and calmly interlocks his fingers behind his head. Now begins the all-too-familiar wait until their contact calls to inform them that their target is on the move.

*

The trip was our school's idea to help take our minds off of our soon-to-be-released exam results. Which suits me rather well. The longer I can stave off having to deal with them, so much the better. I'm not exactly holding my breath.

I start the day, along with two of my girlfriends, Mary and Frances, by having a massage and scrub treatment in our riad's cosy little spa. It turns out to be anything but relaxing. More like an exfoliation session with a power sander. But, once done, we emerge with possibly the softest, smoothest skin we've ever had.

A quick dash upstairs to make ourselves presentable and then we head out to meet two of the boys, James and Peter, for lunch in the city's main square.

In contrast to the peace and quiet of our riad—with its terracotta walls, billowing white drapes and local rustic charm—the narrow street outside is a pulsating, noisy, chaotic scrum of locals, tourists and mopeds. We have only just joined the procession when a pale-looking Asian man rudely pushes past me. He doesn't even bother to apologise. I make to shout after him in protest, but he's already gone.

*

Nearby, comfortably ensconced inside an air-conditioned people carrier, the major is relieved as the red blip he's been expecting finally appears on his portable tracking device. On his command, the driver puts the vehicle into gear and slowly moves off into the flow of traffic. Two men sit in the back, quietly checking and rechecking their weapons. A third rides alongside on a cheap, local moped.

The major nods in satisfaction. Everything is going nicely to plan, which is usually, he ponders cynically, when things start going wrong.

*

We all come to a sudden halt, in awe of the sight before us. Marrakech's bustling central marketplace, the Djemaa el-Fna. In fact, it's more L-shaped than anything. It's surrounded by a ring of quaint little cafés, numerous shops selling a mixture of 'antiques' and knock-off tat, a few hotels and some public gardens. But we're really after what lies on the far side. The old souk. From here it's lost in a hazy mirage that's rippling up off the flat, open expanse of baking concrete.

'Oh my God,' I exclaim, grabbing Frances's arm in excitement. 'It's huge!'

James struts past us cockily.

'Why thank you,' he says, turning with a suggestive smile. 'I know!'

Mary rolls her eyes and I burst into laughter. Then I punch him on the arm in disgust.

'Ew, you're so gross!'

Frances merely sighs and leads us off across the square. It is hot. Almost unbearably so. Even in my white vest, little khaki shorts and beige canvas Palladium boots, I'm not spared as the midday sun tries its best to roast us.

There are tourists quite literally everywhere. All aimlessly meandering around amidst the army of street vendors and local performers. Every tent we pass has either a performing monkey on a leash; someone in a colourful costume, armed with traditional leather bags, offering brass cups of what looks like water, but which I'm doubting is Evian; or snake charmers with their asps and a flute. All are pandering like crazy for our money. Instead, we make for a nearby stall selling freshly chilled orange juice. It only takes five minutes before I feel the first ominous lurch from my stomach. If ever I could have done without an Imodium moment, now would be it. Twenty to one it was the ice, something which my dad explicitly warned me about. But did I listen? Time to start looking out for a bathroom, I think.

As a girl you quickly learn to differentiate between the guys who're checking you out because they think you're kind of cute and the real fruitcakes who're only a couple of morals short of ripping open their trench coat and flashing you. So when I spot a lone Asian man with a big, chunky SLR, standing about forty feet away, there's no doubt in my mind as to which he is. He's so clearly pretending to look off in the other direction, but his camera isn't, and even from here I can see his index finger firing off shot after shot in my direction. Worse still, he's mumbling incoherently to himself. Somewhat perturbed, I suggest to my friends that now might not be such a bad time to go check out the souk.

My dad says it's one of the best in the world, next to the Kahn in Cairo and the Bazaar in Istanbul. Like them, it's a crazy-big maze of shops—literally thousands of them, he said, selling everything one could possibly want—all connected by narrow alleyways, hidden courtyards and other secret hideaways. At which point he'd quipped, 'It's shopping, Pumpkin, but not as we know it.'

When I finally remember the creepy man with the camera, I dart a wary look over my shoulder, only to find he's disappeared.

*

The major smiles as the message he's been waiting for comes in over the radio. He looks up from his tracker device and peers out through the windscreen. Quickly spotting what he's looking for, he points for the benefit of the driver, then speaks rapidly into his radio.

Behind him, his men jump up and ready themselves by the sliding door.

*

I'm not sure what puts me on edge. Just a sudden, indescribable sense that something isn't quite right. It's reinforced further when we join the crowd waiting to cross the road to the souk.

With my brow furrowed and senses piqued, I look around for any clue as to what's spooked me, and immediately spot the man with the camera hiding in the crowd, about ten feet away. Only this time he stares challengingly back at me.

'Hey, guys,' I say softly. 'Take a look over there, will you? See that guy with the camera? The Asian-looking one.'

As unsubtle as ever, James and Peter both crane their necks to see.

'Nope,' says Peter.

I point in irritation, only to find he's right: the man is gone.

'But he was just there. I swear. I'm positive he's following me.'

My eyes dart left and right. Then I catch a glimpse of him scurrying through the crowd off to our right. I point, but again the boys are too slow. Instead Peter laughs disparagingly.

'Why'd anyone want to follow you—'

With no warning, James suddenly rushes forward and drags him back as a black people carrier screeches to a halt before us. The sliding door is already half-open and before I know it a man lunges out at me. Too stunned, I'm not fast enough to react before he's grabbed my arm and is pulling me towards the vehicle. My voice fails me, but somehow my foot finds the lower door runner. Braced, it gives me the leverage I need to pull back. His grip tightens, fiercely determined, much like his ugly, pockmarked expression. With a violent lunge, this time accompanied by a scream, I wrench myself backwards as hard as I can. My arm, slick with perspiration, glides effortlessly from his grasp.

Foiled, he lunges forward again and I instinctively lash out. It's an uncoordinated sideswipe, driven more by fear than aggression, yet miraculously it connects with the side of his jaw.

There's a sickening crack, and it's not from my hand, even though it hurts like hell. The blow snaps his head sideways and deposits him gracelessly back into the people carrier. There he stays, slumped between two seats, showing no signs of life. I freeze, hands to my mouth, suddenly terrified at what I might've done. It's only the sight of a second man rounding the back of the vehicle, a pistol in hand, which refocuses my attention. At the same time my friends take one look at him and then flee into the crowd.

I watch them go with horrified disbelief; my attacker, with an unimpressed sneer. Turning his eyes back to me, he spots the figure inside the people carrier and I notice a flicker of hesitation register. For a moment, neither of us moves; like a matador and a bull sizing each other up before the inevitable clash.

Then someone shouts from inside the vehicle. It's a language I don't recognise. The gunman quickly blinks away his doubts and raises his pistol. Not the smartest move. At the sight of it everyone close by panics and scatters in all directions, screaming and jostling. The commotion unnerves him. But it's the break I need and this time I don't squander it.

Reeling backwards, I run blindly into the road and weave through the oncoming traffic. Brakes screech, but too late as several cars pile into the back of those in front of them. All I can think of is to reach the souk. At least there I might find somewhere to hide. I glance back to see the gunman push past several terrified tourists and set off after me. Following behind him is the creepy-looking man with the camera.

My breathing is already ragged, my pulse pounding as I reach the entrance. There's no time for pleasantries. With fists and elbows, I frantically barge my way inside and wade through the infuriatingly slow-moving crowd. I ignore their angry shouts as I dart from one narrow alleyway to another. With every turn my hope grows that I might have lost them.

I rush on towards an old archway and duck in behind a small bric-a-brac shop to catch my breath. Sweat pours from me in a way I didn't think possible outside of a hot yoga studio. I try to make sense of my thoughts, but they're all jumbled. A grizzled old storekeeper looks up from his newspaper on the other side of the passage. He follows my anguished gaze, but seeing nothing of concern, shrugs and goes back to his paper. The minutes tick by and slowly my breathing calms and my hope grows that maybe they've given up. Surely they couldn't follow me after all the twists and turns I took.

But then, suddenly, inexplicably, there they are. Leading the way is Pistol-guy with Camera-man right behind him. But now an older, more serious-looking man has joined them. About twenty metres away they stop and confer over something the older man is holding. It looks like a mobile phone.

I edge backwards, pressing myself against the wall as I go. As if the horrible sense of foreboding I have about this isn't bad enough, my stomach now decides to give another ominous rumble.

Oh please, not now.

Clenching my lower abs, I dearly hope I can hold on long enough. A blur of theories about what they want races through my mind. None is particularly pleasant. This can't be about money: I barely have any. So it has to be something else. I shudder at the next thought.

'Over my dead body,' I hiss defiantly through gritted teeth.

Despite my best efforts, I simply can't clear my mind sufficiently to recall the map from my guidebook. Not that it matters. Because at that moment, Camera-man looks up and points towards the archway. My stomach lurches again, but with no time to worry about it I break into a sprint and head ever deeper into the old city.

Before long, the crowds thin and the stalls become noticeably more domestic. Pretty soon the air is filled with the heady aromas of spices, leathers and, occasionally, the more pungent stench from a local open-air butcher. With every twist and turn I become ever more hopelessly lost. Finally, exhausted, covered in sweat and with an increasingly acute pressure in my tummy, I slow to a walk. Panting hard, I wipe the sweat from my forehead and take my phone from my thigh pocket. I can't ignore how let down I feel by my friends' actions, which, while probably smart, don't really fit with what I think friendship is about. Nonetheless, without our teacher's number, I have little choice but to dial James.

'H! Jesus, are you okay?' he stammers. 'Where are you?'

'I don't know,' I snap, angrily wiping tears from my eyes. 'I'm so lost.'

'Listen, we found a couple of tourist police guys. Here, tell them where you are.'

Before I can respond, a new and more authoritative voice comes onto the line.

'Hello, Miss. I am Mohammed with the Marrakech Brigade Touristique. Tell me, please, where is you?'

'I—I don't know …'

'Is there landmark, or special building? What route you take in the souk?'

'I don't know,' I snap anxiously, all too aware of how useless I'm being. 'I just ran into it …'

My voice catches as the three Asian men round the last corner and break into a sprint. Is there no getting away from them? Spinning on my heel, I flee down the nearest alley. Carrying far too much speed into the next corner, I slam painfully into the opposite wall. Somewhere to my right I can hear a motorbike of some sort. Perhaps I can hitch a ride with the owner. I round the corner and only just manage to jump back as it flies past, inches from me. Its brakes bite and the rider skids it to a ragged halt. He spins round, clearly excited to see me. I gasp and all hopes sink. He's one of them! With an anguished cry of despair, I dart back into the alleyway and sprint into another half-hidden passage.

I can hear the bike somewhere behind me, its engine amplified in the narrow confines of the winding, twisty alleys. As bad as the aches in my legs are, they're nothing compared to the urgent cramps building in my belly.

The bike surges into the alleyway behind me. A glance ahead reveals a straight stretch with no twists or turns to slow him. It rapidly dawns on me that unless I do something drastic, he's sure to catch me before I reach the end of it. He seems to know it too, and reaches back for his odd-looking gun.

At any other time I'd likely be wracked with doubts and worries and hesitance and indecision, fearful of the reactions and repercussions that will surely follow from all those about to witness what I have in mind. But not now. Without another thought, I surge forward, faster and faster.

No restraint ...

No holding back ...

All out ...

The world accelerates past at a dizzying pace. For a second, I'm so lost in the thrill of the moment that I forget what's happening. And when I do glance back, the rider's vengeful, cocky expression has been replaced by one of utter disbelief.

At this pace, by the time he recovers his wits and twists the throttle, I'm almost at the next bend. Too absorbed in the concentration required to weave at this speed in between startled bystanders and hurdle small walls, tables and anything else that gets in my way, I don't care anymore what people think. It feels like some kind of natural high. But how long can I keep it up for? Even in this twisty-turny section of the city, if his knack for finding me is anything like the others', then he's bound to catch me eventually. My only option is to get him off my back—and permanently.

As I round the next corner, I spot just what I need sitting outside a traditional Moroccan light fixture shop. I take a second to catch my breath before snatching up a particularly heavy-looking ornate light box. I turn and ready myself, feet apart, the casing slung up over my shoulder in readiness. It's time to take the fight to them, as my dad would say. Because, win or lose, at least then I go down with dignity. I'd hate for people to think I was a coward when my time came.

So I wait, pumped and primed, my heart pounding furiously as the bike approaches. My muscles tense in anticipation. He's mere seconds away. In that moment I realise how scared I am—terrified, in fact. But I keep my nerve and grasp the casing even tighter as he rounds the corner. With a scream, I swing the box at him with all my strength. His frantic attempt to swerve comes too late. The fitting slams into him with a force for which he's completely unprepared.

It sweeps him clean off the moped, which hurtles on towards a brick wall. Somehow he manages to land on his feet, but only for a fraction of a second before momentum catapults him on, headfirst, into a display of pots and pans stacked up outside the shop opposite. The wall of metal utensils disintegrates and collapses as he ploughs through it and disappears somewhere inside the shop. I let out a little laugh of disbelief and punch the air in amazement.

People come running from all directions, but I ignore them. My attention is already focused on the small device affixed to his handlebars. It's cracked, but still working and it unclips easily enough. On the screen is an overhead map of the souk. What worries me is the blinking red dot in the centre, because as I move, so does the blip. With a gasp of comprehension, I begin to panic. I frantically look myself up and down. But there's nothing there. Nor is there anything on the soles of my shoes, or along my shoulders or down my sides. Pausing, I spot a full-length mirror propped up outside another shop and run over to it. Amidst the chaos of the fallen rider and the ruined shop front, none of the gawping locals appears to pay me the least bit of interest. My vest is damp with perspiration, but otherwise it's fairly clean. So when I turn, the tiny, dark, round fleck between my shoulder blades is impossible to miss.

'How the hell ...?'

It's just beyond reach and I don't have time to start looking for somewhere more private. For all I know, the others might be just around the corner. Everyone still seems occupied by the 'accident'. So, with a muttered curse, I hastily pull my vest top off—all too aware just how inappropriate this is in an Islamic country. I have the dot off in a second and quickly redress, but not before a few observant locals shoot me rather scandalised looks.

Ignoring them, I peer closely at the small dot. I've never seen anything like it, except maybe in films, or on TV, if indeed it is what I think it is. It's barely five millimetres across and looks to be made of some carbon-fibre-like material. How it could have tracked me through all this is both amazing and at the same time truly scary. But it's the only explanation. How the hell did it get there, though? Then I remember the rude man from earlier. *Could it be?* If so, then I'm seriously worried, because it means none of this is a coincidence.

There's a rather inbred-looking cat sunning itself on a nearby table. It's amazingly tame and offers no protest as I stick the dot to its fur. But then I have to physically shout at it to get it to run off down a nearby alleyway. I permit myself a fleeting grin of congratulatory self-satisfaction. But before I can get out of sight, the three remaining men race around the corner. The fallen moped, the ruined shop front and the rubber-necking locals bring them to an abrupt stop. For a moment, I stand and glare challengingly back at them. There's no attempt on their part to hide their anger at my having complicated their plan like this. At the same moment my stomach gives a woeful lurch and my courage deserts me.

Self-preservation triumphs over foolish bravado and I take off down a passage into a covered square which is hosting a farmers' market. I spin left and right, clueless as to which way to go. Another rumble from down below says I'm almost out of time. This far north of the city there are no more tourists or police. Nor are there any bars into which I can dash to find a bathroom. The hopelessness of my situation threatens to overwhelm me. A quick glance backwards shows my pursuers are no longer hiding their intentions. All have their guns drawn. Yet no one cares. Barely anyone even looks up from their street-side board games or doorstep conversations as I run by. I've never felt so alone.

Halfway down the road, I'm overcome by the most awful rotting stench imaginable. It's thick and pungent, and seems to be coming from beyond the wall to my right. There's a small door there. Not thinking, I dart through it in the hope the smell might put the men off. It's worth a try, because until now, not much else seems to have worked.

I regret it immediately. The air in the narrow alley is even viler. But that's not the worst of it. A thick, slimy river of blood is slowly oozing out from beneath the back door of a small hut to my left. Already woozy at the sight, I retch at the intense, bitter, coppery smell. It comes too quickly and the rush of bile is up my throat before I know it. I try to hold it back, but, too powerful, it explodes from my mouth and through my nose. My eyes stream as I cough and splutter.

Half covered in vomit, I realise I've delayed too long to turn back now. Instead, I run on towards the wooden gate at the far end of the alleyway. Barely halfway there, I slip on the thick sludge underfoot and fall to my knees. Panicking, I race to get up, but too carelessly on a path as treacherous as this. With no grip, my boots sluice out from beneath me and I plunge, front first, to the ground. I recoil in revulsion, only to fall again in my haste. Terrified that they could arrive at any moment, I scramble to my feet but too late realise the sudden exertion is too much for my tired bowels to contain. Despite a last-ditch attempt to re-clench them, my muscles are simply too exhausted and fatigued to stop the torrid stream within from gushing out all down my inner thighs.

With the last of the vile expulsion goes all my strength, determination and resolve. My spirit collapses and I sink to the ground with a wet, defeated squelch. Aghast with humiliation and self-disgust, I want nothing more now than to curl into a ball and cry. Sod it. Let them come. I don't care anymore. What could they possibly do to me that's worse than *this*? I slap the ground in despair.

But as quickly as the sense of self pity overwhelmed me, so too is it driven back by a fierce spark of determination which ignites deep within me. I can't give up. Not now. Not after everything I've already been through.

With a grimace at the state I'm in, I heave myself to my feet. At least the cramps are gone. That I can make light of it is something, I guess. Flinging my filthy, matted hair from my face, I set off towards the gate—albeit more carefully than before.

It leads into a large open area full of small concrete pits. Those not covered by some kind of animal skin are filled with a variety of foul, coloured liquids. Beyond the high perimeter wall lies a sea of flat-roofed buildings, all in a similar state of general disrepair. A path cuts a swathe through the centre of the site. Halfway along it is a small hut. Beyond that, at the very end, is a little concrete building.

A dozen or so tannery workers stand here and there, either having a cigarette or sitting out in the sun. All now turn and stare at me. Ignoring them, I take the path towards the small hut, behind which I dart just as the Asian men enter the tannery. It's good to see they fared little better than I did. All are caked in filth and holding their noses. Perhaps they're not so tough after all. Not that it makes much difference. There are still three of them; they're armed and I'm not.

I look down to see a small pile of white powder by my foot. I can't imagine there is much around here that does you any good if touched or ingested. Taking no chances, I scoop a good handful of it up in a scrap of plastic sheeting. Now for a way out of here. I dart a glance around the corner. The leader has sent Pistol-guy off towards the far side but Camera-man is now coming my way. My only option appears to be a steep slope of the same white material, albeit one that is compacted and compressed, which leads up to the roof of the small stone building.

I press myself back against the wall as Camera-man's shadow appears on the path. Despite my attempt to hide, he spots me the instant he clears the hut. With no time to think better of it, I lunge forward and fling the powder at him. Its effect is instantaneous and is accompanied by a roar of pain and surprise. His hands fly to his face, where they rub furiously at his eyes. Seeing my chance, I lunge at him and, with all my weight, knock him backwards over the lip of the pit directly behind him. Arms and legs flailing, he plunges into the thick, white liquid below. His screams, when he resurfaces, are twice as agonised.

The others are already pounding up the path behind me as I gather my wits and set off towards the slope, and possible escape, as fast as I can. Without warning, something whizzes past, awfully close to my ear. I scream, but don't slow down. In seconds, I'm at the foot of the slope. Without pausing, I surge up it, driven on more by raw terror than anything else. They are so close now.

But then, almost within reach of the top, the slope breaks loose beneath me. I land heavily and lunge for the ledge, but it's too late: I'm already slipping back down the slope. I flail for grip, but find none.

Before I can turn, a hand grabs my ankle and pulls me roughly down into waiting arms. I lunge out, kicking and screaming, as Pistol-guy expertly twists me round and body-slams me to the ground. Too quick, he's on top of me and pins me face down with his whole weight on my back.

The older man runs up beside us and hurriedly sets his bag down. My eyes go wide and I struggle even more furiously as he removes a set of sterilised syringes, pulls off their wrappers and lays out a collection of small medical sample bottles. I fire a chain of expletives at him with the same venom my mother uses when angry. But he either doesn't understand or doesn't care.

Terror and fear completely take over as Pistol-guy pulls up my shirt, exposing my lower back. I bring everything I have to bear on the man: heels, elbows and nails. A lucky strike elicits a shout of anger and leaves three long, ragged scratches across his cheek. He shifts his weight—just as I give an almighty buck. Caught by surprise, he stumbles forwards, allowing me to scramble out from under him and right into the older man, sending him tumbling backwards. His little bottles scatter in all directions. He catches himself with one hand, while protecting the syringe with the other. As he gets to his feet, a small leather wallet falls from his hip pocket.

Quickly back into the fray, Pistol-guy grabs my hair and pulls me, screaming, off balance. Before I can lash out, the older man is also upon me and together they wrestle me back to the ground. Then, with Pistol-guy holding my arm firmly, the older man readies himself to jab me with the empty syringe. Curiously he takes the effort to swab my skin first with an alcohol pad.

Before he can stick the needle in, there's a shout from the other end of the path. We all turn to see a tall, dark, rugged-looking Moroccan policeman standing there, his feet apart and his gun aimed, steady and menacing.

Pistol-guy is the first to move. Fast and fluid, he drops the odd-looking dart gun and snatches out a very real-looking black pistol from within his jacket. A fraction of a second is all he needs to have it up and aimed. But the policeman is already there and he doesn't hesitate. The whole tannery shudders with a massive, ear-deafening BOOM!

I shriek as Pistol-guy stumbles backwards. He looks down, almost in comical disbelief, to see a gushing red stain seep through his shirt. A second shot snaps his head backwards in a punch of red mist. Then gravity takes him, and he crumples lifelessly to the ground.

In a rush of panic, the older man grabs me from behind as a shield. Suddenly a knife is at my throat before the policeman can even adjust his aim. The Asian man shouts something that neither I nor the policeman understands.

Sensing the futility, he makes an exaggerated gesture to get the policeman to lay his gun down, before pressing the knife emphatically against my jugular for effect. I desperately want to say something to calm him down, to ask him what he wants, to find out why he is doing this and possibly even to beg him to let me go. But I can't find my voice. My eyes are as wide as they can go and I barely even dare to breathe.

The policeman doesn't move. His aim stays trained on us. I sense my attacker darting anxious looks left and right, searching for an exit. In a soft and pleading voice I finally find the courage to ask what he wants. He completely ignores me and simply presses the blade harder to my skin.

There's a commotion at the entrance and his grip tightens noticeably as several more policemen rush into the tannery. Off in the distance comes the familiar sound of approaching sirens.

Realising his chances of escape are growing ever less likely, he begins shouting again at the police. Then he pulls the knife away and waves it threateningly at them. In a moment of madness, I ram my elbow back into his ribs and jerk forwards, away from him.

That same instant, several things happen at once. The policeman fires and hits my attacker in the shoulder. Right behind it comes another sharp crack, but louder and from somewhere behind us, and my attacker thumps into me with a guttural grunt. Something warm splashes across my face as a geyser-like eruption of red explodes out over my shoulder. His grip goes limp and I scramble clear, screaming as he collapses to the ground. Horror and incomprehension completely overwhelm me as I take in the ragged, bloody mess where his face used to be. A last quick twitch of his foot and he goes still.

Thereafter, everything registers as a slow-motion blur of activity. The policemen all fan out with their guns drawn; the tannery workers flee; people on the surrounding roofs race to safety. For a moment I stare, numb and oddly entranced by the lazy flapping of several crisp white sheets put out to dry on a nearby rooftop, and watch as the dark-haired woman hanging them out also rushes for cover.

For a second none of my limbs respond and nothing makes any sense. I struggle to understand what just happened and only slowly do I become aware of how badly I'm shaking and hyperventilating.

Still unable to see properly, Camera-man scrambles from the pit. In a bid to wipe his eyes, he points his gun in the worst possible direction: that of the large policeman. There's no hesitation. A third and final shot sends him reeling back into the pit.

As silence finally descends on the tannery, the police begin to move up the path towards me. The last of my adrenaline rapidly bleeds away and I slump back onto my haunches, filthy, bedraggled and exhausted. But at least I'm alive. My eyes settle on the small leather wallet lying in the dust beside me. Almost without thinking, I reach out and take it. Glancing first at my attacker, bleeding out onto the ground a few feet away, then at his wallet, I see his name is John Wei. Then, for some reason, I slip the wallet into my pocket before anyone notices it.

When the tall officer reaches the two fallen men, he kicks their weapons a safe distance away. Only then does he finally holster his sidearm. He calls out to the others in Arabic. Several run to haul Camera-man from the pit with the aid of a few broomsticks. Others, their radios crackling and hissing, approach to inspect the two men at the foot of the slope. The tall policeman takes off his cap and turns to me.

'Is Miss Heather?' he asks.

I nod weakly.

'Yes, all over, all over,' he says with a calmly reassuring smile. 'I am Mohammed, from the phone. We are police. We are here.'

I nod wearily. Part of me wants nothing more right now than to douse myself under the rudimentary open-air shower I can see over in the corner, hopeful that the water might also wash away everything that's happened. But there is simply too much emotion welling up from within me, desperate for release. A sudden startled gasp is all it takes for me to burst into tears. With the tap now wide open, it pours from me: the entire spectrum of human emotion, from fear and anger to relief and gratitude; all stream down my filthy face and wrack my aching body with violent sobs until, finally, I'm spent and drained in every conceivable way, my eyes running dry and my throat croaking hoarse.

I can sense the loitering policemen's eyes on me, all hesitant and uncertain what to do with me. Frankly I would prefer it if everyone just left me alone. But it's not to be. Finally one of them lays a comforting hand on my shoulder. I glance up at him and suddenly find myself in fits of laughter. A moment later, I'm crying again.

* * *

CHAPTER 2

A GHOST FROM THE PAST

85 Vauxhall Cross, Central London

As the last faint rays of daylight fade outside the Lego-like headquarters of Britain's Secret Intelligence Service, its chief, commonly known as C, rounds off his hastily prepared presentation. Considering it was only this morning that his head of the North Africa desk brought him Interpol's request for information on three Asian men involvement in an attempted kidnapping, he is quietly impressed that it went as well as it did.

Of course, it's not every day you find out that former Chinese Special Forces are trying to kidnap British holidaymakers. Even less often for the apparent purposes of securing blood and bone marrow samples from the victim. But it quickly got him thinking and it wasn't long before he made the connection which really set off the alarm bells in Whitehall.

Considering the potential repercussions of his theory, the audience of senior government ministers sitting dotted around his office react exactly as he expected them to: badly. Several slump back in their chairs and groan. Others simply put their head into their hands. But only one sits frozen in stunned silence as he gazes up at the photos on the wall-mounted screens with a growing sense of unease.

The first to speak is Foreign Secretary Richard Rowley.

'So, let's see if I've got this straight, shall we?' he begins, shaking his head in disbelief. 'Besides the fact that this is the first I'm hearing about this whole God-forsaken espionage wet dream …' He jabs his finger accusingly at the screens. 'But I'll come to that in a minute, because I'm a little more concerned about how the hell they, *of all bloody people*, managed to find out about this. Jesus Christ,' he yells. '*We* didn't know!'

'In truth, we don't actually know who they were working for yet. We just know who they used to work for,' C chimes in, matter-of-factly.

The others remain silent. A few shift uncomfortably as the minister's sarcastic tirade continues.

'How is it that the only news *you people* ever seem to bring me is bad news? You're like the God-damned *Daily Mail*, is what you are.' Rowley turns to the others. 'Gentlemen, I don't know about you, but this has to rank as just about the biggest cock-and-bull story I've ever heard. C, please tell me you're joking? I mean, all this conjecture based on a syringe?'

'Dick,' the spymaster replies mellifluously, 'I assure you it came as quite a shock to me, too, when I worked it out. Yet, as outlandish as it sounds, I think you'll find it makes perfect sense, if you look at the timeline. And, as Sherlock Holmes pointed out, once you've eliminated the impossible, whatever remains, however improbable, must be the truth.' With a shrug he points at the screens. 'Only in this case it seems to be precisely what we thought *impossible* that now appears to be probable. And as to your other point, Richard, believe me, we're looking very seriously into who could be behind this. Don't you worry about that.'

'Right, well then,' the foreign secretary replies, clearing his throat dubiously. 'Could someone at least assure me that we know where this girl is and that we have a plan to get her home?'

'As usual,' C says with a wry chuckle, 'we're somewhat ahead of you.'

The foreign secretary nods, apparently pacified by his chief's grasp of the situation.

'Well, in that case, I apologise, gentlemen,' he says, looking around the room. 'All rather a lot to take in at once.'

C can't help but smile at the politician's sudden change of tone.

'Indeed it is.'

'For God's sake, C,' snaps a fat, balding man from the other end of the conference table. Prone to nervous bouts of perspiration, the head of Britain's domestic intelligence service, MI5, looks anything but happy. 'How can you be so bloody calm about all of this? If the press ever gets even so much as a whiff of it, this could well bring down the whole of His Majesty's Government! This would make everything from Phillby to WMD look like a slap on the hand.'

C ponders the thought.

'Yes, I suppose it probably would,' he replies. 'Certainly not our finest hour, if that's what you mean. But right now we have a far more pressing problem, so let's not get our knickers all in a twist about something we can't control, shall we? If I'm right, then it's imperative we agree on a course of action for when she is back in the country.'

'Well, I think it's obvious,' exclaims Guy Forbes, the tall, overbearingly arrogant and notoriously narcissistic defence minister, as he stands to pour himself another whiskey, in this case a glass of C's eighteen-year-old Bowmore. 'As it bloody well should be to everyone here.' He looks around the room and shrugs nonchalantly. 'We just make her disappear, and with her goes the whole blasted can of worms.'

'Now steady on, Guy, that's a bit excessive, even for you, don't you think?' interjects C's chief of staff, William Sanders. 'She's only a child. I don't think we're really in any position to make such a decision, do you?'

'Oh for crying out loud, Bill, stop being so naive. We make these decisions every day. Who lives and who dies. Do we bomb this village, or that one? God knows we all have more blood on our hands than we'd care to admit. And half of those poor bastards never posed any *real* danger to the country. But that—*that girl* ...' He glares up at the photos. 'She could destroy us all!'

'Speak for yourself, Guy,' one of the others mutters sarcastically.

'If I want your bloody opinion,' Forbes snaps back, 'I'll damned well ask for it.'

'Look, I'm sure I speak on behalf of everyone here when I say we appreciate the concern you have for our careers, Guy,' Richard Rowley says with a disingenuous smile. 'But I agree with Bill. Killing her would be excessive, and perhaps also a tad short-sighted.'

'I agree,' says C. With a sigh, he gets up and crosses over to the wall-mounted screens, where a banner is flashing the words 'Cardinal Classified'. He points to one of the photos. 'I knew her, once upon a time. And I don't think someone who sacrificed as much as she, or her team, did for this country is best honoured by this sort of talk. Frankly the suggestion alone is insulting.' He raises a finger in warning and surveys his audience, paying particular attention to the defence minister. 'Make no mistake, gentlemen, not on my watch! Besides, if it's true, then this could well be the break we've been looking for.'

'I'd watch my tone if I were you,' the defence minister replies. 'Remember who you're talking to.' He knocks back his whiskey before setting the glass down unnecessarily hard.

'I don't work for you, Guy,' C says calmly. 'I work for the Foreign Office with a direct line to the PM, so until that changes I'll address you any damned way I see fit.'

With little true leverage, Guy Forbes huffs dismissively and refills his glass. Seeing no other signs of disagreement from the others, C continues.

'Now, admittedly it may not be the smartest choice, strategically,' he concedes, nodding towards the defence minister, who merely rolls his eyes and turns to look out the window, 'but it is the right choice, morally speaking. Regardless of the risks, I believe it's our responsibility to ensure the girl's safety and wellbeing upon her return. Certainly until such time that we can determine what this is all about and whether Beijing is actively involved, and, if so, how to get them to back off.'

'And how exactly do you propose doing that?' Guy Forbes snaps. 'Because if you're right, then what's in her will be the holy bloody grail to them. They're not just going to give up and walk away because we ask them nicely.'

'Well, we can cross that bridge when we come to it.'

It's only now, as the argument escalates and the name-calling becomes, in her opinion at least, juvenile, that the tall, determined-looking woman who has so far been content to sit at the back, quietly observing, finally decides to speak. With her long blonde hair, dark Kathryn Sargent trouser suit,

Jimmy Choo stilettos and orange Hermès Berkin perched beside her, Katherine Sloan-Sinclair seems glaringly out of place amongst the others' more conservative civil servant attire. Yet, despite this—and only being in her early forties and therefore the youngest member of the Shepherd Committee, not to mention the only woman—none of it diminishes the respect the others accord her. For her job is by far the most clandestine of anyone's present. Having finally grown bored of the men's unproductive squabbling, she uncrosses her legs, leans forward and clears her throat, resolved to put the matter to rest. Silence falls over the room and everyone turns to her.

'Well, I want her,' she says matter-of-factly, as if there is no debate about the matter. She begins gathering her bag. 'Either way, she's going to need somewhere safe and secure to stay for a while. And I have somewhere perfect for the job.'

'Yes, I thought you might,' C says with a conspiratorial smile. 'Where were you thinking? Brambles?'

'Actually,' she says, glancing back at the screen. 'Given her background, I was thinking Godolphin Park. She'll be a better fit there.'

C mulls the observation over for a moment. Then he turns back to her with an amused look.

'You know, I think you're right. Very well, let's make it so. She's all yours, Katherine. Light the boilers up under it, and fast. Sound her out. Use whatever carrots you need to, but she has to accept, understood? And if you need some stick, use that, too. There's simply too much at stake to have her running around out there unsupervised. Talk to Gambon. Tell him to think seriously about who she rooms with. If all this,' he says, waving a file, 'comes out, as I fear it inevitably will, then she's going to need some pretty solid support.

We can't afford to lose her. I don't need to tell you how important she could be to the service. So let's try not to foul it up, alright?'

With a curt nod and a smile, Katherine Sloan-Sinclair stands and makes her way over to the large bay window overlooking the Thames. To the others it is abundantly clear the meeting is over and they quickly make their way to the parking level, where their chauffeurs are waiting to take them back to Westminster. As he closes the door on his way out, Richard Rowley gives C a conspiratorial thumbs-up. The spy chief nods and turns his attention back to Katherine as she takes a small mobile phone from her pocket.

'May I inquire who you intend to run this?' he asks from behind his desk.

She smiles coyly and turns back to the window.

'Hereford four-five-six. Mr Abbott, please.'

C can't help but laugh.

'What I wouldn't give to see this,' he says with a chuckle as he looks down at a photo on his desk. With a sigh, he taps it in deep contemplation. 'Why do I get the feeling, Missy, that you're about to seriously complicate our lives?'

* * *

CHAPTER 3

THE MEN FROM THE SHADOWS

26 Hertsmere Road, Canary Wharf, London

By the time I finally arrive home it's just gone nine-thirty in the evening. After the nightmare of the last few days, all I want now is the simple comfort of my own bed. And sleep. Lots of it.

Of course, things just wouldn't be complete without it pouring with rain as the taxi pulls up outside our building. Another typical British summer, then. I give the unusually humourless driver a scowl as I hand over the extortionate fare before dragging my battered, sticker-laden, aluminium suitcase out onto the pavement. By the time I reach the front door, I'm soaked through.

The doorman gets about as pleasant a smile as I can muster as I make for the lifts before he can ask how my trip went. As the doors close, I slump back against the mirror and breathe a deep sigh of relief to be alone again finally. The ride up to the twenty-ninth floor allows me a chance to reflect properly on the events of the last forty-eight hours, during which I have see-sawed erratically from moments of tear-filled hysteria to joyous levity.

It didn't come as a big surprise when the school said they had not been able to contact my parents. Yeah, welcome to my world, I thought. What I conveniently omitted to tell them was this was due to their being in New York on holiday. But it got me thinking, what if they were never to find out? It would certainly save them a tonne of anguish, especially my dad, but more importantly, it would save me from a lifetime of being grounded.

After several frustrated attempts with the useless key-card, I finally open the door, kick off my flip-flops and roll the suitcase on towards the living room. The flat is depressingly quiet. For a moment, I half wish I was back in Morocco. Not that it isn't a nice place; it's got two floors, both light and spacious, with floor-to-ceiling windows offering a spectacular view of Canary Wharf. I imagine it must have cost my parents a fortune. Shame, then, that they're home so little to enjoy it.

Stacked in the corner, beside a clothes rack loaded with haute-couture samples, is this month's delivery of Choos, Blahniks and Louboutins—known to my mother as the holy trinity—all awaiting her next editorial. I can't resist taking a quick nosey through what's on offer. Once in a while there's something here which I have no moral qualms about liberating. With a shrug, I head into the open-plan kitchen, just off to my right. I dump my bag onto the island and throw my sodden clothes in the general direction of the washing machine. Only now do I spot the handwritten note awaiting me atop the pile of mail.

My Darling Heather,

How was Morocco? I hope you had a wonderful time. Sadly we couldn't get the early flight, so we're back 2 days after you. Hope that's OK? We made sure the fridge is fully stocked. We're so sorry about this. We were really hoping to be with you when you opened your letter. See you soon—Big hugs and kisses,

Mum & Dad

x x x

P.S. Love you lots!

I roll my eyes. It's obviously my dad's handwriting. Bless him, he tries so hard. Though quite why he still bothers signing for my mother is beyond me. I've only just got home and already I'm preparing myself for the oh-so-inevitable argument that's bound to ensue within moments of her arrival. I'd love to know at what point she forgot what it's like to be my age.

Before I can dwell on it further, I'm reminded of something else. Something I was trying hard to forget. My exam results.

With an unenthusiastic sigh, I flick through the mail until I find the exam board's letter. Then, with one eye closed and squinting through the other, I tear the envelope open and unfold the paper. My shoulders drop and I curse. Without so much as a second glance, I toss the letter onto the countertop and head out into the living room. One thing's for sure, come two days' time it's going to be an awkward conversation explaining this disaster away to my father.

Tired and deflated, and with little inclination to do anything, I slump down onto one of the plush leather sofas and allow myself to sink into a world of self-inflicted recrimination. If only I'd stood up to my friends and their constant distractions from my revision. Ha! Who'm I kidding? *What revision?* I think ruefully. Well, too late to cry over it now. Curiously, after the experience of the last few days, it actually seems oddly unimportant now. Perhaps the best strategy might just be to be honest with them and deal with whatever comes.

Conflicted and distracted, I notice the answering machine blinking away in the darkness. With a petulant stab, I press Play.

'You have two new messages. To play messages—'

I push it again.

'Good afternoon, this is Jonathan Menzies for Mr and Mrs Foxton …' The sound of my headmaster's voice has me sitting bolt upright in an instant, a horrible tightness in my stomach. 'I'm afraid I've just been informed by Mr Phillips that there's been an … an incident in Morocco. I'd greatly appreciate it, therefore, if you could call me back as soon as you get this. My number is—'

Without thinking, I hit the Delete button … and immediately regret doing so. A horrible prickly heat washes over me as I realise what I've done. How stupid could I be? Once my parents find out, they're bound to ask about the message. The best I can hope for is that the headmaster simply never calls back. Though the chances of that are slim. Hanging my head, I groan in despair. How did everything get so badly messed up?

What I really need is to talk to one of my girlfriends. It won't solve my problems, but it'll certainly make me feel better. I fetch my phone and speed-dial Mary. An older woman answers almost immediately.

'Oh, hi, Mrs Andrews, it's Heather. I was wondering if I could speak with Mary, please?'

There's an awkward pause.

'Yes—erm, can you hold on a moment?' She tries to cover the mouthpiece, but the hushed conversation at the other end is easy to overhear. 'It's the Foxton girl. What do you want me to say?'

Before I can even fire an irked look at the phone, a deeper voice comes on the line. 'Good evening, Heather. It's Bill Andrews, Mary's father.' His tone suggests I'm not going to like what's coming next. 'There's no good way to say this, so I'll just get it over with, alright? I'm sure you can understand that we've spoken to the other parents. And, well, we feel it would be better if you weren't to socialise with our children in future.'

I want to swallow, but suddenly can't. I want to interrupt, to protest my innocence, to tell him what really happened, but I can't do that either because he seems intent on not letting me get a word in edgeways.

'I don't know what you are mixed up with, and frankly it's none of our business, but we don't want our daughter involved in it, you understand? So you are not to contact her outside of school. What you get up to during class is your business, but, in truth, I don't think Mary is particularly keen on that, either. Not after what happened.'

Now that I don't believe. Or do I?

'I'd hope you're mature enough to respect our wishes. Goodnight to you,' he says stiffly, before hurriedly hanging up.

For a moment I don't know whether to laugh or cry. I'm of half a mind to text Mary directly, but suddenly I'm scared what he said might be true. What if she really doesn't want to be friends with me anymore? I hesitate and try Frances instead.

Only it's engaged. Not a good sign. Paranoia immediately floods my head with all sort of worrying thoughts. Perhaps it's just coincidence? I give it another minute and then try again. This time she answers immediately, but her tone instantly puts me on guard.

'Heather, I'm so sorry,' she sobs. 'We had no choice. They all got together and decided we were never to see you again. Just in case ... you know. The boys, too. They've all somehow got it into their heads that we'll get killed, or worse, if we hang out with you.'

'I—I can't believe I'm hearing this,' I stammer, slumping back on the sofa. Then it dawns on me. 'Wait, how did you know what I was calling about? Did Mary just call you?'

She doesn't even try to deny it.

'Yeah, she said she overheard her parents talking to you.'

'And?'

'What do you mean "and"? And what? And I don't know. But we're scared, alright?' A sudden, noticeable edge has crept into her voice. 'I mean, those men had guns. They could've killed us.'

'*Us,*' I explode, suddenly aware that her sobs have conveniently stopped. 'Us! I'm sorry. Did you even listen to what happened to *me* that day?'

'Sure we did, but it's just ... Jesus, why'm I the one having to have this conversation!' Her exasperation is unmistakeable and I already sense what's coming. But, naive to the end, I close my eyes and pray it isn't. 'Look, it's just that, oh, I don't know. But you read about it all the time, don't you? Just you never expect it to actually happen to you, do you?

'Those guys didn't make a mistake, Heather. They didn't just happen upon us by accident. It was deliberate and planned.

And if it happened once, then it can happen again. I'm serious, so are they, and they're not kidding around this time. Daddy even threatened to take away my Gold Amex. And he's never done that before, like ever! Even that time, you know, with the clinic.

'Look, all I'm saying is I'm just not sure if it's really such a good idea to try to defy them this time. The others feel the same. Oh God, someone's coming. I've got to go. I'm really sorry.'

And with that, the line goes dead.

It takes me a few seconds to remember to breathe. I feel numb and hollow and suddenly so very foolish. Heather, the stupid little girl who didn't listen when everyone was warning me this might happen. How did I not see it coming? I stare at the phone for what feels like an age. I just can't believe they'd do this. And for a credit card! It's the pettiness which makes their rejection all the more painful and shocking.

Having never been one for large groups of friends, it suddenly dawns on me that I've pretty much just lost nearly all of mine in one go. Certainly those from school, anyway. With the choicest of expletives, I throw the phone at the opposite chair and sink back into the sofa. Then, with a sullen look, I huffily fold my arms and stare out through the rain-streaked windows at the lively, vibrant city beyond and ponder how my life managed to go quite so badly wrong.

*

I spend most of the next morning moping around the apartment, feeling thoroughly sorry for myself. I even spend a while running all manner of Google searches on the ID I took from the tannery, just to take my mind off things, but all to no avail. There seem to be hundreds of people called John Wei out there. I finally give up in frustration.

Of course, it was too much to hope that any of my friends might have called or sent me a text overnight. Instead, I find they've all gone and de-friended me online. Talk about childish, but it still stings bitterly. Yet, as the hours pass, my unhappiness slowly turns to resentment before gradually diluting into indifference and then hatred.

By around midday, I have pulled myself together enough to call the one remaining friend who I can always count on. Ben isn't like my friends from school. In fact, he isn't even in school. He's about eight years older than me and already has a proper job in the City. His parents are best friends with mine, so that kind of makes him the older brother I never had. After a bit of pushing, he relents and agrees to come over after work.

When he arrives, it's to find me in a far better mood, with music blaring and my eyes no longer all red and puffy.

'A bit loud, isn't it?' he calls humorously, gesturing to the sound system as he leaves his shoes by the door and slings his suit jacket over a chair.

'Who cares? It's not like there's anyone around to complain,' I shout back.

'Yeah? Go tell that to your new neighbours moving in across the hall.'

'Are you serious? I thought the place was still empty.'

'Well, I almost tripped over one of their big green packing crates coming out of the lift,' he says as he takes a beer from the fridge.

With all the bad news already awaiting my parents' return, a noise complaint is not what I need. So down it comes, but only by a little.

'Anyway, come on,' I say, pulling him towards the sofa, onto which I push him, before leaping onto the opposite armchair. 'I have so much to tell you.'

'Oh dear,' he says with a playful sigh as he loosens his tie. 'What's the big drama this time that has you dragging me all the way over here?'

'What do you mean?' I exclaim, pointing towards a nearby office tower. 'You only work over there!'

'Yeah, yeah. Okay, come on, let's hear it then.'

Turning my mind to everything I need to get off my chest, my temporary levity drains and he sees that this time it's serious. Keeping as brave a face as I can, and conveniently omitting the more embarrassing bits, not to mention anything that involves outrunning scrambler bikes or the like, I describe, in vivid, animated detail, just as I did during the slightly more hysterical police interviews, exactly what happened. I then go on to explain how all of my so-called friends have now decided to dump me like some kind of social cancer, and finally I round off my rant with how, as if all of that wasn't bad enough, my grades came out at the diametrically opposite end of the alphabet from where my dad wanted them to be.

'I know a lot of people have it worse than me. Alright, fine, a lot worse,' I concede, seeing the look on his face. 'But it all just seems so unfair. Okay, I admit the grades were my fault. Three years of dossing, what did I expect? I get that and can accept it. But my friends! How could they just ditch me like this? I didn't do *anything* to them!'

With a deep sigh, Ben leans forward and fixes me with a sympathetic gaze.

'Look, I agree, it's not fair. But then again, neither's life. And don't forget, some people live pretty ordinary lives.

Stuff like this is bound to throw them. Sure, it would've been nice if they'd shown a little more backbone, but let's face it, they were pretty much your average, flaky, Sloane-ranger types, weren't they? I'm sorry, but that's just the feeling I got those few times I met them. But in truth—and I know you're not going to like this, so sorry for saying it again—I always had the feeling that they were only in it for the perks they got from your mum.

'Hey, let me finish,' he says, seeing my dark look. 'I think they liked the bragging rights it gave them. Not to mention the free clothes and all those parties you invited them to. But, hey, it's only my opinion.'

I nod despondently, yet can't help but clench my jaw in annoyance, not at him, but at what he said. And not because it's untrue, either. In fact, quite the opposite. It's because it's always about *her*! My mother. Mrs Foxton, the fashion editor. It's not that I don't love her. I do, I think, in my own weird way. It's just that it's always Mrs Foxton this, Mrs Foxton that. How popular she is. How good looking she is. How elegant she is. All the famous people she knows. The jokes about her uncanny resemblance to Meryl Streep in *The Devil Wears Prada* wore thin a really long time ago. She's always setting this impossible standard. One I'll never be able to meet. I'm a straight C-grade girl. Always have been, probably always will be. Middle of the road, comfortable, never outstanding, never drawing unnecessary attention to myself. For pretty obvious reasons. I can do without the scrutiny. But living with her is like living in a permanent shadow. And the worst bit is it's a shadow she does her best to remind me of as often as she can.

'Look, at least now you know they were fair-weather friends,' Ben says with a shrug. 'I know it hurts, but everything happens for a reason. Maybe you'll only see the upside later, but trust me, you'll get over it.'

I nod, not entirely convinced, but thankful nevertheless for having been able to share it with somebody. And thankfully he's smart enough not to pry more into what happened on holiday.

'I have an idea,' he says as he returns to the kitchen for another beer. 'You can't just hang around here, sulking all day. So how about I take you out tonight? Maybe a movie or something?'

'How about a club?' I blurt, suddenly taken with the idea of doing something a little more energetic.

'Not exactly what I had in mind,' he retorts from over by the fridge.

'I heard that! Oh come on, it'll be fun. Please! Besides, I have a really good fake ID. It's even got a barcode.'

He grimaces.

'What would your parents say if they found out? They still seem to think I'm a decent, upstanding sort of guy.'

'They wouldn't if they knew about that *thing* you got me from Ann Summers for my birthday.'

He groans and I sense victory within grasp.

'So's that a yes?' I venture cautiously.

'Alright, it's a yes. But an *extortioned* one. And not a word of this to your parents, you hear!'

*

Getting ready without Mary or Frances with me, or at the end of the phone, is depressing. I feel a sharp pang of longing as I remember the fun we used to have, laughing and gossiping, sharing make-up, doing each other's hair and all the other stuff we would get up to before a night out. But I know I have to move on. After my vent to Ben, I've decided that enough is enough. And, as sad as that is, it's my only option, really, or else I'll go mad dwelling on it.

After my usual moan about having nothing good to wear, I eventually settle on a shimmery, cream-coloured top, which'll look great in the club later, some skinny jeans and a nice pair of black-patent, red-soled stilettos that I liberate from the pile by the front door.

*

After dinner, we stroll through the West End towards one of London's newest, hippest nightclubs, C-Turquoise. Ben leads me past the queue obediently lining up behind the rope cordon, right up to the burly, Middle-Eastern-looking bouncer. The man gives me a rather dubious look and for a horrible second I'm convinced he's going to turn me away. But after a few quiet words from Ben, and a slightly overemphasised handshake, he greets me like we're old friends and waves us on through.

I resist the temptation of asking what that was all about and meekly follow Ben downstairs to the club's main level. I come to an abrupt stop at the sight which greets us. The whole dance floor is made of Perspex. But that's not all. For beneath it is an enormous, real-life aquarium.

'No way! That's insane. Is that for real?' I point at the sandy seabed with its large corals, around which schools of brightly coloured fish are swimming lazily. My eyes go even wider as a fairly big shark glides effortlessly past, right beneath my feet. Patterns of dancing, wavy light ripple across the club's interior, giving it the distinct sensation of being underwater.

'Pretty cool, huh?' Ben says with a chuckle.

'You think they'd let you swim in there?'

'Somehow I'm doubting it.'

'Yeah, pity.'

*

It's only around midnight when I see Ben again. He hurries over with a worried look on his face. Taking my arm, he smiles briefly at the group I have attached myself to, and then shouts in my ear:

'Come on, I need to talk to you.'

I shrug and follow him towards the back of the club, where he turns on me with a scowl.

'Okay, what have you gone and done now?'

I laugh. 'What do you mean?'

'I mean them—the police!' he says, pointing accusingly towards the entrance. Puzzled, I stand on tiptoes. Sure enough, there are several uniformed police officers at the foot of the stairs.

With an indifferent shrug, I ask, 'Yeah, so what?'

'Well, they're looking for you is *what*.'

'W—what?' I stammer amidst a sudden rush of worry. My first concern is that something has happened to my parents. But that's unlikely. They don't send five cops for that. And certainly not to a club. No, this is something else. Something far more serious.

'I came out of the toilets and they were showing a photo to Jacko, the manager. I heard them say your name.'

'I—I don't know. I mean, I haven't done anything …'

'Hey, I'm not *implying* you have. But whatever it is, perhaps it's best they don't find you *here* is all I'm saying.'

'Yeah … Good thinking, Batman! That really would make my dad's day, wouldn't it?'

'I tell you what,' Ben shouts into my ear. 'Use the back door, over there. I'll get our things and meet you outside that burger joint just around the corner, say in about five minutes, okay?'

I nod and, with one last worried look over at the police, hurriedly make my way towards the fire exit. A swift push on the release bar and it opens to reveal a dimly lit flight of steps. With my drink in hand, I take them two at a time, landing on the balls of my feet as I go. The exit emerges out into a gloomy, rubbish-strewn alleyway. Not exactly the best place to hang around at this time of night, so I make for the road at the end of it as fast as my heels will allow. I get there only to find the street awash with blue flashing lights. Turning, I set off, head bowed, as fast as I can in the other direction. But I've barely got five paces before I jump in fright as someone clears their throat alarmingly close by in the darkness behind me. I spin around, and find myself confronted by a man's shadowy outline and the glowing tip of a cigarette.

'So you're the girl, huh?'

Already nervous, twitchy and thoroughly on-edge, I scream and lash out with my handbag. He swats it away effortlessly. Then, with an unimpressed scowl and a last, slightly exaggerated puff, he steps from the shadows.

'Oh yeah, you're definitely her. Hello, Heather Foxton.'

He's stocky, grumpy-looking, not as tall as me but is probably old enough to be my dad. He's got short, salt 'n' pepper hair, a prominent widow's peak and a severe-looking goatee, which makes his mouth look oddly downturned. Despite the warm weather, he's wearing a Barbour jacket and jeans. I can tell by his pissed off demeanour that he isn't what I initially feared him to be, so I quickly reappraise the situation. Nevertheless, I still take a couple of wary steps backwards.

'Who? What girl?'

'The one everyone's got their knickers all in a twist about. So do your parents know you're out this late?'

I watch, intrigued, as he drops the glowing butt and scrunches it out underfoot. Common sense is screaming at me to run, but there's something about his manner which prevents me from doing so.

'Who are you?' I demand. 'What do you want and how do you know my name?'

Still scowling, he steps forward and takes the drink from

me. A quick sniff and he unceremoniously dumps it into a nearby dustbin.

'Oi, you didn't answer my question,' I snap, annoyed at the waste and wary of his intrusion into my personal space.

'Relax,' he replies, unimpressed by my false bravado.

'Look, I don't know what you guys think I've done, but I only just got back fro—'

'Morocco?' he says, casting a disinterested look up the street. 'Yeah, that's kind of what I have to talk to you about.'

'Excuse *me?*' I say, scrutinising him more closely. 'Who did you say you were again?'

'I didn't.'

'Yeah, duh! I was being *sarcastic.*'

He fixes me with a penetrating look.

'Kid, I have a lot to tell you and not much time in which to do it. And, frankly, I'd prefer to do it someplace a little more private than here.'

'What's wrong with here?' I reply, now far enough away from him to be a little more confident. 'Look, no offense, Mister, but I'm not going anywhere with someone I don't know!'

'Uh-huh.' He reaches inside his jacket and withdraws a leather ID holder. I warily take it from him and withdraw a few paces. Apparently his name is Abbott and he works for the Foreign Office.

'So if I come with you, how do I know I won't just end up face down in some rubbish bin tomorrow morning?'

With an emphatic look he snatches his ID back. The briefest of smirks flickers across his face. 'You don't.' And with that he sets off at a brisk pace up the road.

I curse under my breath.

'Oi, hold on. What about my friend? I can't just leave him waiting for me. Can he come with us?'

'What do you think?'

'Well, I can't just leave him waiting!'

He stops and looks back, far from pleased. Seeing my reticence, he sighs, takes out a mobile phone and begins dialling.

'Where were you going to meet him?' he says.

'Around the corner. That big burger place.'

The conversation is quick and punchy.

'Right,' he says, hanging up, 'all taken care of. The police will drive him home. Satisfied?'

'What are you going to tell him about me?' Does he think I've been arrested?'

'No, he'll be told you're helping the police with their inquiries. Now come on.'

I huff in frustration, torn between curiosity and wariness. My brow furrows and I bite my bottom lip.

'Okay, fine, wait for me!'

Keeping a safe distance, I tail the odd, grumpy man through the crowds of West End revellers. For someone of limited stature he sure has a deliberate sense of purpose that people instinctively respond to by getting out of his way; in marked contrast to me, who's having to dodge between everyone just to keep up. All the while a voice tells me this is a really bad idea.

Regardless, within a few minutes we're at the gates to Green Park. A few words with the lone policeman there and in we go. I stop abruptly and frown, not at all happy, as Mr Abbott, whistling to himself, saunters off across the open expanse of poorly lit lawn.

'You've got to be kidding me,' I shout after him. 'You don't seriously think I'm gonna follow you out *there*, do you?'

'You want to know what all that was about in Morocco or not? Choice is yours, Princess,' he calls back. 'See you by that bench when you decide to grow a pair.'

I curse under my breath and glance around with frustration as I weigh up my options, or lack of them. Clasping my little perfume vaporiser defensively, I reluctantly set off after him. Seeing in the dark isn't such a problem. Still, I don't like this one little bit and keep my distance all the way across the lawn until we reach the path. Curiously all the street lamps there are off except for the one behind the bench on which he's sitting. Despite the light I make sure to sit as far away from him as I can.

Without a word, he takes a beige manila folder from inside his Barbour and passes it to me. Across the front, in big red letters, are the words 'Top Secret'. I look up with large, questioning eyes.

'Just read it,' he says with a dismissive wave of a hand. It's fairly obvious he'd prefer to be anywhere but here.

The folder isn't particularly thick, just a few stapled A4 pages. I flick through them quickly enough. It's some kind of personnel file. The top sheet has a small black and white photo in the upper right corner. A closer look and I gasp in recognition.

'That's the guy,' I exclaim, jabbing at the picture. 'From Marrakech.'

'Yeah. Keep reading.'

I skim over the text. Words like Major Li Chen, Chinese People's Liberation Army and Intel Division catch my attention. I look up at Mr Abbott, confused.

'I don't follow.'

'They're some serious people, those guys. Special Projects, Angola, Sierra Leone. Not the sorts of places they send amateurs.'

'I still don't understand,' I stammer.

'What's there to understand?' he says. 'The men who tried to kidnap you were Chinese Special Forces. The elite of their military. Or, at least, they used to be. We have no records for them after they abruptly left the Chinese Army several years back. But whoever they work for now, well, they seem to want you, or something you have, pretty badly, wouldn't you agree?' He says it so calmly, as if this is such an everyday occurrence.

'B—But why?'

'Ah, now there *your* guess is as good as ours ...'

His tone is unmistakeably loaded, almost as if he's expecting me to provide the answer. I just don't know whether that's really what he's after or not; however, something tells me not to volunteer anything until I know exactly what's going on. So I merely shrug and give him a blank look, which seems to throw him a little.

'Well, what do you expect me to do about it?'

'You? Nothing,' he says drolly. 'But perhaps we can.'

'Yeah, well I'm still a little fuzzy about who exactly you are.'

He ignores me. Tired of this, I lay the file down between us and fix him with an emphatic look.

'Mr Abbott, how about you tell me why you really brought me all the way out here? It can't have been simply to show me this.'

'Actually it's to offer you a choice. Right now we don't know who these men were working for. But, for some reason, someone is after you. And there are those who feel you might not be entirely safe until we can get to the bottom of this.'

With a deep sigh, I run my hands through my hair and stand up. The thoughts are coming so fast I can barely process one before the next arrives. It's always the way. Fear and anxiety quickly breed anger and aggression in me, and I can't help snapping:

'So, what are you saying? That I can't ever go out again?'

'In the short term that might not be such a bad idea. We have nothing on these people. The ones you didn't put into hospital—nice going with that, by the way—'

'Thanks,' I mumble absent-mindedly as I slump down onto the bench with a groan.

'The others refuse to say anything. And round-the-clock protection simply costs too much.'

For a second my mind returns to the men in Africa and I pick the folder up again. Something's niggling me and I don't like it. Glancing back over the first sheet, I stifle a little gasp of realisation. How could I have missed it? His name! It's different here from the one in the wallet I found in the tannery. I should know: I've re-examined it almost every day since the attack, hoping to glean something, anything, from it. For some reason it's only now that it occurs to me that I probably ought to do more to find out who these people were, and, more importantly, what they wanted. Perhaps with this information I actually have something this Abbott guy doesn't. But until I sense he's being completely honest with me, I have no intention of sharing it with him.

'I can't believe this is happening,' I mutter. 'I thought this nightmare was over.'

'Well, there is another possibility.' He lets the idea hang, waiting for me to bite.

This is just the kind of game I hate.

'Okay,' I relent finally. 'And what's that?'

'Before I answer that, I have a question for you. It's not one to be taken lightly. How you respond is crucial, so take your time. I'd like to know: what do you want to do with your life?'

I laugh. Not what I was expecting.

'What do you mean? Like in a job sort of way?'

He shrugs ambiguously.

'I'm not sure. I mean, I'm only sixteen. I haven't really thought about it properly. But I do know what I don't want to do, though.'

'And what's that?'

'Pretty much anything like what my parents do. Stuck in some boring office all day long, serving some soul-sapping corporation. That would kill me. I want to do something more exciting. Something adventurous, I suppose. Is that what you were looking for?'

'Adventurous, huh?' Abbott notes, raising an eyebrow. 'Okay.' He shrugs. 'Well, you see, there's a boarding school, just south of London, where we have a certain amount of influence. It's somewhere you'll be safe until we can find out what this is all about.'

'I'm sorry ... *what*?' I look at him in disbelief and shake my head. 'I—I can't just ... just start at a new school. I mean ... do you have *any* idea how big a deal that is? Besides, my family's here. And all my friends ...'

He looks perplexed.

'I'm confused. Your parents are hardly ever here, and after last night I don't think you'll be hearing much from your friends again, so what's the big deal?'

I round on him with a mixture of surprise and anger.

'How the hell do you know about any of that?'

He waves it away as inconsequential.

'Oh my God. Have you been listening to my calls?'

'Only since you got back from holiday. The rest we got from your doorman. Listen, I get there will be some upheaval, but in case you missed what happened in Morocco, you need this a lot more than I do, so that's the deal. Take it or leave it. I didn't come here to beg. But it's a nice school with big grounds and old buildings. And you'll soon make new friends. We'll even toss in a scholarship to sweeten the deal for your parents. Don't knock it till you've seen it.'

'I'm not particularly fussed about what my parents'll think. I'm more concerned about what going to boarding school means.'

'Why do I get the vibe you don't like your parents very much?'

'It's not as simple as that, Mr Abbott.'

'Oh yeah, why's that?'

'Because I'm adopted is why,' I snap, waving the manila file at him. 'I'd have thought you'd know. It adds, how shall I say … complexity to a relationship.'

For a moment he has no reply. He purses his lips and gives a lightly awkward nod of acknowledgement. Then his tone softens.

'I know what you're thinking. It's written all over your face. But trust me, I've been here myself. Admittedly a long time ago, I know.'

I force a smile and sigh.

'Look, I can't just make a decision like this on the spur of the moment.'

'Sure you can,' he says blithely. 'It isn't that hard. You probably just need a bit more convincing is all.' He turns and calls out into the darkness, 'Gentlemen, time for a field trip, I think.'

A rustle from the bush behind us makes me swing around to find myself face to face with two men, both clad head-to-toe in black fatigues, as they rise up from behind it. Their faces are also blackened, but more worrying are the very real-looking machine guns slung across their chests. I recoil visibly.

'Captain Lennox,' Mr Abbott says calmly. 'Perhaps *you'd* like to reassure the young lady here that she's in no immediate danger? You might have more luck than me.'

'Can do,' comes a new and more authoritative voice, but this time from behind me on the other side of the path. I spin again to see two more soldiers emerge from behind the trees there. The taller one steps forward with a smile as he unclips his weapon and lets it drop to his side. Then he extends his hand.

'Hi, I'm Captain Lennox. Don't worry, Heather, you're safe with us.'

'Uh-huh?' I reply dubiously, shooting an anxious look at his gun.

Mr Abbott points at the soldiers.

'They've been with us since we entered the park. And there was another team in civvies with us from that club of yours. Perhaps you've noticed you also have new neighbours? Right now you're safe. But we can't do this forever. Your best option, your only option, really, is to accept our offer.'

I nod somewhat resentfully, yet at the same time my brain races. It doesn't matter which angle I come at this from, I keep returning to the same question I had after Morocco. Why me? I can't believe they would offer this to just anybody. Seriously, why bother? So the only logical conclusion has to be that he's lying. But again, why? The more I hear, the more troubling all of this gets.

'I don't know,' I say. 'Can I even make a decision like this? Is it legal?'

'Yeah, I wouldn't worry too much about that,' Mr Abbott says, with a nod to Captain Lennox, who immediately turns away to talk into his radio. From the darkness beyond the treeline comes what sounds like a high-pitched turbine generator starting up. Without speaking, the soldiers all move off towards it.

'You coming?' Lennox enquires.

I fire him a baffled look.

'Coming where?'

'Well, no one knew when you'd be leaving your flat. Your little night out on the town caught us slightly by surprise, so we had to fast-hop it here from Credenhill.'

Frowning at the drought of proper answers tonight, I reluctantly set off after him. As I clear the trees, I stop dead in my tracks, my eyes wide and my mouth open at what I see before me.

Lennox looks back and smiles.

'A bit cooler than taking the train, wouldn't you say?'

His joke's lost on me as I stare past him at what's parked in the middle of the clearing. Speechless, all I can do is point at it and gawp like a goldfish.

* * *

CHAPTER 4

ON A WING AND A PRAYER

Then I laugh out loud.

'Are you serious?' I exclaim, my voice rising in excitement as I take in the dark, aggressive-looking helicopter that's parked in the middle of the clearing. Inside its cockpit, bathed in a dim red glow, the pilots are already preparing for take-off.

'Do I look like I'm joking?'

'Hmm, yeah, fair point,' I concede.

'So what do you say we go take a look around that school and see if it's all that it's cracked up to be, huh?'

The rear rotor has already begun to turn, and is quickly followed by the main one. I look at Lennox and ponder again just how dishonest they're being with me. No doubt these guys are lying through their teeth! I'm just waiting for the penny to drop, because there's simply no way in hell anyone would go to all this trouble, or be quite so openly desperate to get me to go and see this place otherwise. I just don't understand why they can't be upfront about it.

Taking my elbow, Lennox leads me towards the helicopter, making sure that I duck my head as we pass beneath the rotors. Inside, it's a bit like a big London taxi: two rows of seats set fore and aft, facing each other across a central divide. I follow the others' example and pull myself up into the cabin. Stooping, Lennox swiftly buckles me in and pops an enormous pair of green headphones onto my head. They immediately dull the rising noise. Through them I can hear the pilots running through their pre-flight checklist. The last soldier jumps in and the whole machine begins to vibrate as the rotors speed up. Wind gusts in through the open side doors. I take a hair bobble from my bag to stop my hair from blowing around in all directions. Over in the corner, Abbott sits and scowls to himself, probably imagining all the other things he could have been up to tonight.

'First time in one of these?' Lennox asks, far more friendly, over the intercom.

'Yeah!' I call back, too loudly, it appears, because several soldiers wince and reposition their headsets.

With an apologetic look, I swivel excitedly round to peer into the cockpit. One of the pilots gives me a nod, which I return with an excited smile. He pulls a lever beside him and everyone is slammed down into their seats as the helicopter leaps from the ground and powers up into the air. With a scream, I hold on tight, as if on a rollercoaster, as the park falls away with alarming speed. In seconds we're above the trees and suddenly the whole of London is spread out around us like a brightly coloured spider's web. The nose dips and we surge forwards over the canopy and on towards Piccadilly Circus. Faster and faster we go.

Captain Lennox comes over and clips on a safety line. He's quick to point out Nelson's Column and Trafalgar Square as we race past, then the Mall and Buckingham Palace, the London Eye and the Houses of Parliament, and finally, way off in the distance, the Dome and Docklands.

'Pretty cool view, huh?'

I shoot him a sideways glance and smile. I think I'm going to like Captain Lennox.

We speed on through the night, the air rushing past just inches from my face. Despite Lennox's efforts to introduce everyone, my excitement gets the better of me and I forget most of their names almost immediately.

We've only been airborne for about ten minutes when the pilots start preparing for landing. Curious to know where we are, I glance into the ridiculously complicated cockpit and soon find the airspeed indicator. A hundred and seventy-three miles per hour. Ten-minute flight. That'll put us somewhere about thirty miles south of London. Then, not entirely trusting my maths, I quickly confirm it with Google maps on my phone.

'LZ, nine o'clock,' one of the pilots says.

I follow the others' gazes and see that we're circling a sprawling country estate with numerous buildings scattered around a large, central lake. The silvery moonlight illuminates the grounds with a strange, eerie quality. Surrounding the school appears to be a dense belt of forest.

The helicopter banks hard and comes in low over the lake. From my seat I can see the huge, churning cloud of spray that's whipped up behind us. With dramatic flair, the machine sinks into a soft landing on a gently sloping lawn which stretches from the lake, behind us, up to a large, ivy-clad building at the top of the rise. Some way off to our left, a lone man stands waiting for us.

The air is decidedly cooler here and a lot crisper than it was up in London. The sky is also considerably blacker, and the view it offers of the stars is unlike anything to be found in the heavily light-polluted city.

Abbott quickly waves the man over and introduces him as Mr Patrick Lander, a teacher here and also the housemaster of Smith's house, which, I'm told, would be my house, *if* I accepted their offer.

Easily late fifties, he's got slightly greying hair and a pleasant enough face. He's obviously married, because he's constantly fiddling with his wedding band. Despite that, there's something distinctly no-nonsense about him.

'It's nice to meet you, Heather,' he says cheerfully, gesturing at the grounds around us. 'Welcome to Godolphin Park School.'

Without further ado, he excuses us from the others and leads me off up the lawn towards the main building. It has two identical wings extending out either side of a taller central tower, which is crowned by a ring of crenelated battlements and a flag flapping lazily in the breeze above it.

'Now this,' Mr Lander proudly explains, gesturing to the left-hand wing, 'is my, or perhaps rather, *our* house.' He flashes me a hopeful smile. 'SH for short. The tower is part of the main teaching block. It's also where the headmaster's office is. The wing on the other side contains more classrooms. And then beyond that is the school dining hall.'

I turn and marvel at the grounds, which stretch off almost as far as I can see. Overwhelming would be somewhat of an understatement.

'We have four boarding houses,' Mr Lander goes on as we climb a flight of stone steps which lead to a raised patio overlooking the lawn. 'Over there,' he says, pointing to a distant building beside a small chapel, 'that's Sinclair's. The one halfway around the lake is Kell's. And lastly, all the way off on the other side, is Grey's.'

I find myself nodding but paying him barely any real attention; the blizzard of questions within my head has simply become too pressing to ignore anymore. I turn to him with a puzzled expression.

'I'm sorry, Mr Lander, but please can I ask what this is all really about?

'I've done school visits before, but never at this time of night, and never in a helicopter with an escort of soldiers. I mean, first I get accosted by some guy who sounds and acts like a spy, and then ... all this. I just want to know what's really going on,' I say with a tired smile.

Mr Lander looks at me with a pitying expression and nods acceptingly.

'Yes, I imagine this must all appear a little odd. I must admit it's also a little unorthodox for us, too. Alright, take a seat, Heather.' He gestures to one of the wooden picnic tables set out on the patio. 'I'll be back in a moment.' He heads indoors and returns a minute later with a set of neatly stapled papers, which he places face down on the table between us.

'This is usually a far more drawn-out and rigorous process, but in your case we don't have the same luxury of time or ... delicacy.'

I narrow my eyes suspiciously, now at a complete loss as to where this could be going. But I'm intrigued. Very intrigued.

'I have two questions, Heather. And I'd really like you to consider them properly before answering. Let me start by asking whether you find life fulfilling at the moment?'

I shrug. 'Not really.' Then, with a rueful smile, I add, 'Actually pretty unfulfilling, if I'm being honest. I mean, besides school, which is a whole different issue, I'm kind of bored with what I do most of the time. The parties, getting dragged around the fashion scene all the time, all the gossip. It used to be fun, but now I just find it ...' I struggle for the word. 'Do you know what I mean?'

'Perhaps you feel you aren't rising to your full potential?' he suggests. 'That maybe you could do more with your life? That you're not making a difference to anything at the moment?'

I take a deep breath and sigh. But secretly I'm elated because he's hit the nail right on the head.

'It sounds bad, doesn't it? A lot of people would kill for what I have, and here I am saying I'm bored of it, but, yes, that's pretty much how I feel most of the time.'

'Well, maybe we can help with that. Now the second thing I'm interested in is whether you consider yourself to be patriotic?'

'I guess,' I reply earnestly. 'I mean, I support England if they're playing at Twickenham, if that helps?'

He smiles.

'Better, I suppose, than supporting Germany in the football.'

We share a laugh.

'So why's that important?'

'Because it's the foundation of everything we do here,' he replies. Seeing my confused look, he adds, 'What you said earlier about Mr Abbott. You might be surprised at just how astute an observation that was.' He fixes me with a penetrating look. 'Heather, this isn't exactly a normal school and this certainly isn't a normal interview. In fact, depending on what happens over the next few minutes, normal might very soon become rather hard to define. But before I get into any of that, I need you to read something I have here and decide if you want to sign it or not. Because I can't tell you any more until you do so.'

His ominous tone surprises me and I look down warily as he flips the stapled pages over. One glance at the title, though, and I begin to see why.

'Just read it,' he says, seeing my look of disbelief. 'But very carefully.' With that he sets off back down the stairs. 'I'll be with the others. Take your time. And when you're done, just shout.'

Official Secrets Act 1989 (c. 6)
1 Security and Intelligence

1.   A person who is or has been—

a.   a member of the security and intelligence services; or

b.   a person notified that he/she is subject to the provisions of this subsection, is guilty of an offence, if, without lawful authority, he/she discloses any information, document or other article relating to security or intelligence, which is, or has been in his/her possession, by virtue of his/her position as a member of any of those services, or in the course of his/her work while the notification is or was in force.

It takes me a good quarter of an hour to go through all sixteen sections, and then another to understand properly what it all means. But by the time I've signed it, I have an excited little tingle at the bottom of my spine.

'Do you have any idea what you just agreed to?' Mr Lander asks with a quizzical look as he gathers the papers up.

'Not really,' I reply with a smile. 'But it sounds fun.'

'It is. But it can also be dangerous as well.'

I shrug dismissively. 'Can't make an omelette without breaking some eggs, right?'

'Quite. And another thing. It's not strictly legal, either.'

My expression remains stoically unchanged.

'So last chance to change your mind. Because as clichéd as it sounds, your life may never be the same again.'

'I'll take my chances.'

'As you wish.'

'So now can you tell me what's going on?'

'Well, we want to give you a job, Heather.'

I fold my arms.

'Doing what?'

'Something that's of service to our country.'

I burst into laughter.

'What could I possibly do that's useful to anyone, let alone the country?' The last bit comes out more a snort of derision than anything.

'Well, not to put too fine a point on it, but you're different, Heather. I think you know that, and now so do we. The only difference maybe is how we think that's best put to use.'

A horrible sense of unease suddenly grips me. It obviously shows.

'Relax, we're the good guys,' he says with a reassuring laugh. 'Let's just say we think that some of the abilities mentioned in the witness statements from Marrakech might turn out to be quite useful around here ...'

He needn't finish the statement. I have a pretty good idea what he means.

'And what exactly is it that happens *around here*?'

He chuckles and takes the signed papers.

'Have you ever heard of MI5 or MI6?'

'Sure. Isn't that who James Bond works for?'

'In a manner of speaking, yes. But do you know what they do?'

'Sort of. But if you'd like to broaden my understanding, then I'm all ears.'

'Well, at its simplest,' he says, getting into his stride, 'most countries usually operate one or more clandestine intelligence services whose job it is to protect the country against internal and external threats. In the UK we have two main ones: MI5 and MI6. Five, or the Security Service, looks after internal threats. Counter-terrorism, organised crime, that sort of thing. Six, on the other hand, or the Secret Intelligence Service, spies on foreign governments and anyone whose activities could hurt the UK's interests globally. Supporting them is GCHQ, the Government Communications Head Quarters, who are based in Cheltenham. But rather than using spies and agents, like Five and Six, they instead rely on surveillance satellites and listening-posts dotted around the world to watch our enemies and monitor their communications. You with me so far?'

I nod eagerly, conscious not to betray the rapidly mounting sense of excitement that's coursing through me.

'Yes, all except how this,' I gesture to the school, 'fits in.'

'Just coming to that bit,' says Mr Lander. 'So back in 1919, at the end of the First World War, the then head of MI6, a man called Captain Sir George Mansfield Smith-Cumming, together with Director of Naval Intelligence Sir Hugh Sinclair, Foreign Secretary Sir Edward Grey and the founder of MI5 Vernan Kell all—'

Suddenly it clicks.

'The four houses ...' I whisper.

'So you were listening,' he notes with a surprised smile. 'Excellent, quite so. The four of them convened to analyse why British Intelligence had failed so miserably to infiltrate the German High Command during the war. Their conclusion was that if all one did was recruit well-spoken, civil servant types from Oxbridge, hand them a radio the size of a suitcase and send them off into Germany with little to no real training, then it shouldn't come as such a surprise when their officers get shot at the border. They realised that what they really needed were officers for whom the tricks of the trade were second nature. For whom tradecraft, as we call it, was instinctive. Who spoke the language of our enemy fluently, who weren't intimidated by the technology of the time and who had the training to survive behind enemy lines, to blend in and disappear.

'Now you can't teach all that to someone just out of university. It takes far too long. And by the time someone is that age they simply aren't receptive enough to carry it off like a native. But it occurred to Sir Mansfield that if you started the training earlier, then by the time the candidate was old enough for live operations, the likelihood was that these skills would have been so deeply ingrained by then as to have become instinct.'

'Why do I have a funny feeling I know what's coming?'

'Good. Then it won't come as a surprise. It all started rather unofficially. They secured these grounds from the late earl of Surrey, Lord John Godolphin. You'll see a picture of him later in the main atrium. But come the start of the Second World War in thirty-nine, British Intelligence was restructured into nineteen official Military Intelligence Sections. They ordained this one Section 13. The joke was that merely referred to the average age of its recruits. But joking aside, what you see here is the operational training facility for today's Directorate of

Military Intelligence Section 13. And we'd like to offer you a place here.'

It's not often that I find myself speechless. I clear my throat and try not to laugh.

'H—Hold on. Let me just make sure I follow. You want to train me to be a spy, is that what you're saying?'

'It's a little more complicated than that, but in essence—'

I can't help bursting into laughter and clapping my hands.

'Ha! That's insane!' Then, seeing his less-than-impressed expression, I compose myself and take a deep breath. 'Alright then,' I add, straight-faced, 'so what exactly do you do here, then?'

'Well, like I say, it all started as a training environment, which they called A-School. But it didn't take long to see its real potential. You see, there are a lot of situations where a teenager can get away with something which an adult would draw too much attention doing. For instance, why have a grown man stake out a suspect's house, sitting in a car or posing as a gardener across the road, when you could have a group of kids playing football right outside in the street? Or how many targets would suspect the rowdy group of school kids walking behind them down the street of being a surveillance team?'

I smile and shake my head. Yet as outlandish as it sounds I can't really fault their logic.

'For years we have had headmasters all across the country looking out for pupils with an aptitude for languages, mathematics or computer skills, or who exhibit certain other sought-after *characteristics*, like you demonstrated in Morocco. I don't know many girls your age who could incapacitate three highly trained Special Forces soldiers. And with no prior training, either. Skills like that are pretty rare and tend to come in rather useful around here. And for that reason they created B-School.'

I ponder what he has said before asking the really burning question.

'Aren't you just the least bit curious to know how I can do these things?'

'Not as curious as you are.'

'What's that supposed to mean?'

'It means that's your journey, and yours alone to discover. It's not for us to get involved.'

'Is that because you already know?'

'We might have an idea.'

'But you're not going to tell me, are you?'

'No.'

'Why not?'

'Because it's classified.'

I scratch my head. 'Well, apparently so's the rest of it. I don't quite follow.'

'One day you will.' He says it with a disarmingly genuine smile which makes it all the harder to get angry at his deliberate evasiveness.

'Mr Lander, with all due respect, I've tried really hard, for a really long time, to stop other people finding out about this. I'm not sure I'm particularly comfortable with everyone here suddenly knowing about it.'

'Good,' he replies pointedly. 'Because neither are we. In fact, the fewer people who know, so much the better. For reasons that will one day become clear.'

'Look, I don't know what you guys have in mind. I just don't want people to think I'm a freak.'

'Point taken, but that's not why we want to keep it a secret. Regardless, I think you'll soon find that there's no shortage of other pupils around here with equally impressive talents. Take your year group, for example. One is well beyond PhD level in special-purpose algorithms, large-number theory and cryptographic mathematics. The benefits, I imagine, of an eidetic memory.'

'Sorry. A what?'

'A photographic memory. Another of your year group breached the NSA's firewall when he was eleven and turned off all their spell checks for fun. No mean feat, I assure you.'

'Who's the NSA?'

'The American equivalent of our GCHQ. Then there's another of your year group who can speak Chinese, Arabic and Russian fluently. Believe me, Heather, this place isn't just about training field operatives. It also sources the next generation of senior service support officers.' He leans back and folds his arms. 'And that, in a nutshell, is what we do here.'

I can't say I even know what to begin thinking right now. Internally I'm shocked, amazed and thrilled all at once, not to mention excited beyond belief, but at the same time, I'm also a little scared. But in a good way ... *I think.*

'I'm impressed by how well you're taking this,' Mr Lander notes. 'Most people tend to get a bit wobbly by now.'

'Maybe I'm not like most people,' I reply, surprised at how rapidly I'm warming to the idea. 'So what happens now?'

'Well, assuming you accept our offer, we would look to complete the enrolment by getting your parents on-side—'

'I'm guessing you'd prefer they don't find out about all this, right? What this place really is?'

'Preferably not ...'

'Figured.'

'And that isn't a problem?'

'Not for me, it isn't. It's funny how no one ever seems to get this. I was even trying to explain it to the guy from earlier. I don't think he got it, either.'

Perhaps Mr Lander doesn't understand what I mean, or maybe he simply chooses not to pry into the intricacies of adoption. Either way, I'm grateful. Because as much as I love my dad, part of me relishes the opportunity to decide my future for myself.

'Each month you'll be paid a Civil Service salary appropriate to your grade. It goes into an Isle of Man account, where it will sit until you're eighteen. How you use it thereafter is your choice. Some use it to pay for university, if that interests you. Consider it a nice little thank-you from His Majesty's Government. In the meantime we will ensure that your formal academic record reflects a hardworking and diligent student. But no one stays in MI13 after they've left here. Some opt to go into one of the senior services. But if that's not the thing for you, then you're free to do as you wish at that point, subject, of course, to adherence with the Official Secrets Act.'

I take a deep breath as I try to digest everything. Then, with a little laugh, I add, 'This wasn't exactly how I saw the evening going.'

'Well, this isn't how we usually do things, either. But I take it, then, that you are interested?'

I nod enthusiastically.

'Good. Just be mindful not to lose sight of the fact that this is a serious place. No one is playing here. It costs a lot to train each candidate and it's not money spent lightly. What this service does plays a critical part in keeping the country safe. As does keeping its existence a secret. I just want to make sure you understand.'

Again I nod.

'Okay, lecture's over.' He clasps his hands together enthusiastically. 'How about that tour, then?'

We walk around the side of the house and on towards some of the teaching blocks. Most are locked but we get to peek inside a few of the wonderfully old-fashioned classrooms in what they call the science and history blocks. In reality, he says, rather different subjects are taught in each. Somehow, as we walk, we get into discussing the ethics of what goes on here.

'In truth, it's something they've wrestled with for a very long time indeed,' he admits. 'Ever since the place first went operational, in fact. But go back through history and you'll find moral struggle after moral struggle about who can and can't fight for their country. During the American Civil War the idea of African American *male* soldiers serving in the army was a contentious one. Nowadays it's women on the front lines that's the big issue. Yet go back to thirteenth-century France and we'd all have been taking orders from a girl, barely older than you, called Joan. So draw your own conclusions as to whether we've advanced in our thinking or not.'

I can't help but smile. I like his analogy.

Over the road we look around the fantastically modern language school. Then we follow the lake around, stopping off briefly in the art department, which in reality, Mr Lander explains, is their aerial reconnaissance analysis training school. In fact, the only things that actually turn out to be what they appear to be are the tennis courts and indoor sports halls. He doesn't seem to get the joke when I ask if the floor slides open so secret jets can take off.

Instead, in the interest of time, he turns us around and leads me back to SH.

The tour of the house begins downstairs in the rather cosy common room, where students can relax in front of the TV or by playing snooker. Upstairs we take in a couple of the bed-sits. All are empty for the summer holidays, with only stripped mattresses, bare desks and walls flecked with the scars of hastily removed Blu Tack to show for themselves. But it's still exciting to see them and imagine what life must be like here when it's teeming with activity.

By the time we arrive back on the lawn, I am completely sold. Of course, there is some undeniably daunting stuff to get my head around in the coming days and weeks before term starts, but the overwhelming sense of fun and adventure which I get from the place trumps that hands down. Also, the idea of having friends around me all day long and access to facilities which my current school could only dream about, coupled with the allure of now knowing what this place really is, all help to make up my mind. It isn't a hard decision.

'That's excellent news,' Mr Lander exclaims when I formally accept their offer. 'And, like we said, don't worry about your parents. We'll see that the news is broken to them properly.'

Unsure quite what that means but too tired to bother asking, I bid Mr Lander good night and climb back into the helicopter for the equally quick return trip to London.

I'm still in my own little world, dreaming about what life at Godolphin Park will be like, when the taxi pulls up outside my home. It's just gone four in the morning and bed is calling to me. Loudly.

'Now listen up,' Mr Abbott says, swivelling round in the passenger seat. 'There's something I need to give you.'

He removes a black credit-card-sized object from his wallet and hands it to me. It feels like it's made of some lightweight metal. Printed on the front is one word: EXCOM. Next to that is a small Union Jack with a telephone number beneath it. The rest of the card is taken up by a digital display, an On button and a little biometric scanner. He quickly programmes it to accept my thumbprint and then shows me how to use the device.

'It's for emergencies only,' he stresses gruffly as he hands it back to me. 'The first whiff of trouble, you don't dither, you don't phone a friend, you call that number. Understand?'

I nod and stow the card in my purse. Done or not, I'm tired of his near-constantly irritated attitude, and I gladly open the door and step out onto the pavement.

'And don't even think about losing it!' he shouts as the taxi pulls away into the night.

* * *

CHAPTER 5

THROUGH THE GATES OF TORRES VEDRAS

My euphoria lasts from the moment I get up the next morning until the moment I step, dripping, from the shower. I cast a critically scrutinising look at my reflection and then, with a sigh, reach for a towel. Mid-lean, I freeze, my eyes suddenly wide, all senses alert. I could have sworn I heard a faint, drifted fragment of an all-too-familiar voice. My pulse quickens and a half-formed prayer appears on my lips in the hope that I'm wrong. But no, there it is again, and a whole half day earlier than expected.

'Oh crap!'

I seize my dressing gown and fling it around me as I race for the landing. My mind is in sudden disarray as I try to remember where I left the results letter. I can only hope my parents haven't come across it yet, or, for that matter, found out what happened on holiday. I pause at the top of the stairs for a last calming breath. Then, just as I'm about to head down, I hear another voice, only it doesn't belong to either of my parents. A sharp, clipped accent. Obviously educated.

Possibly middle-aged. I listen a little longer and the penny soon drops. I was wondering what they meant when they said they'd handle my parents. I just never expected them to be this quick.

'... so if you are both free this afternoon, Mr Lander and our headmaster, Dr Gambon, would be very keen to meet you,' another voice says. This time, a woman's.

'Well, what do you think, darling?'

I smile at the reassuring and comforting sound of my father's voice.

'Well, I think we should have a good chat with Heather first,' my mum replies. 'This all sounds wonderful. I just can't believe she didn't tell us about it. And you're sure there hasn't been a mistake? Heather's report cards never painted her as being, how shall I say it, the most *engaged* pupil ...'

I roll my eyes. And so it starts! That there's a hint of humour in her tone, though, is a good sign, I suppose. Because if that's the worst she has to complain about, then maybe I'm in the clear on all the other stuff? But only one way to find out. Drawing the lapels of the fluffy white dressing gown closed, I set off downstairs.

There are two people with my parents. Both suited and smart. Spread out over the coffee table between them are all manner of brochures and forms.

My father is the first to his feet. All six foot two of him. He opens his arms and I rush to him. The archetypal banker, some might think. The reality, however, is very different. He's the prankster of the family and, frankly, a bit of a nerd at times. An avid movie buff, comic collector and keen historian with an interest in anything military, is my dad. How often we've found ourselves wandering the halls of the Imperial War Museum!

Not exactly what most girls would call fun, but for us it's win-win. He gets his kick from something that interests him and I get his company. A rare occurrence, given the demands of his job. And unlike most of my girlfriends, my dad is my rock, my sounding board and the shoulder I cry on when I need it.

My mother, on the other hand, is exactly what you'd expect a fashion editor to be. Blonde, elegant and glamorous. But beneath that all-too-easily underestimated exterior lies a ruthlessly ambitious and coldly driven woman who's utterly intolerant of failure or ineptitude. But it's worse than that. Unable to have her own children, essentially damned by biology, she does her level best to ensure the lives of all those around her are kept just as miserable as hers is, deep down. My dad doesn't stand for it but I'd hate to work for her. Something demonstrated as she takes a call and, within seconds, begins torching her poor, suffering assistant for some minor oversight. She quickly hangs up and looks over at me. Instantly I know something is wrong, for instead of her usual greeting—typically a complaint or criticism—she actually smiles. Then she, too, rises and approaches me, arms wide open.

A big grin appears on my father's face as he waves a horribly familiar piece of paper in the air. My eyes go wide and I freeze.

'I don't know how you did it, Pumpkin,' he says proudly. 'But these are excellent ... truly excellent!'

'Eh!'

'Yes and when exactly were you planning on telling us about your new school?' my mother chips in pointedly.

I look with confusion from one face to the next. Clearly amused, my father pulls me into an all-embracing hug. Over his shoulder I catch sight of what I'm presuming are the school's admissions staff. The woman gives me a conspiratorial nod and, like the village idiot, I finally catch on. It can't be the same letter. I take it and barely manage to contain my snort of disbelief. A royal flush of As and Bs across the board. No wonder Mum's sceptical. I would be, too. Somehow they've doctored my grades. But of course! It all makes sense. How else could they sell the story that I've won a scholarship? Certainly not with what I really scored, that's for sure. And they had to come today or else my parents might have found the original letter. I fight the urge to laugh at the audacious fraud that's being perpetrated right before my eyes. But now I get why my mother's being nice all of a sudden. She's excited I might finally be moving out.

'I know, it's great, isn't it?' I reply enthusiastically, amazed at how easily the lie tumbles from my mouth. 'I'm sorry, I should've told you sooner, but I wanted to save it until I was sure I'd got it.'

Still she eyes me suspiciously.

'Quite where you found the time to study enough to get these, I just don't know.'

'Mmm,' my father adds, turning to the suited couple. 'Now you *are* sure there hasn't been some sort of mistake? I mean, this is the girl who didn't learn to tell the time until she was nine and who—'

'Dad! I'm standing *right here!* God, why'd you always have to go and embarrass me like this?'

'Don't get yourself all in a tizz now, Pumpkin,' he says soothingly. 'I'm just pulling your leg. We're very proud of you. Aren't we?' He turns to my mother.

'Of course,' she replies, not quite as convincingly. For a second I catch a hint of unspoken argument between them; a shared look that embodies a long history of marital conflict, most of which, curiously, has tended to be about me in one way or another. He ignores it and pulls me into another hug, ruffling the top of my head as I squirm.

'Our Heather can be a bit sensitive at times,' he jokes to the admissions staff.

'Ugh!' I pull free and glare at him. But I can't stay mad for long, and in no time a depreciating little smile has crept back onto my face, glad of his praise and affection, even if I don't deserve an ounce of it.

*

One look at the school itself and the decision is a no-brainer for my parents. Whilst they make it clear, or at least my dad does, that they aren't happy to see me go, they admit that what the school can offer me is so much more that what they can, especially given their hectic schedules.

The rest of the enrolment process is smooth and painless. It is followed, a few days later, with a call from the school's administrator, a woman called Ms Culham, to book an appointment with their tailors in St James. It turns out to be a funny little shop called John Phillips, Jermyn Street (London), run by a funny little bespectacled man. The uniform is nice enough, consisting of an elegant, charcoal-grey, single-breasted jacket, along with a matching high-waisted pencil skirt and white, fitted shirts. The materials aren't cheap and the jacket's collar, waist pocket flaps and cuff-trim are all a lush black brushed-cotton. Stitched onto the left-hand breast pocket is a large embroidered shield, presumably the school's coat of arms. It all seems slightly excessive for a school uniform, but I'm not complaining. Very soon we have a full trunk at our feet with what seems like an awful lot of kit.

Uniform from School Shop—(F)

(Minimum requirement. Name tapes to be added with house initials.)

1 Charcoal grey blazer (Sixth Form—with trimming)
2 Charcoal grey skirts
7 White blouses (Sixth Form)
2 House ties
3 V-necked sweaters
3 Pairs navy or black tights/stockings (no socks)
2 Pairs black leather shoes—appropriate for everyday wear (must have substantial sole)
1 Lockable tuck box

In addition (for boarders)
3 Pairs jeans/trousers/jumpers
7 T-shirts/sweatshirts/blouses
7 Sets of undergarments
2 Nightwear
1 Pair slippers
1 Dressing gown
2 Towels
1 Duvet (with two sets of covers)
1 Dark coloured great coat
1 Trunk or large suitcase
1 Weekend bag/case
1 Scarf from school shop (optional)
1 Pair outdoor or Wellington boots (optional)
1 Wash bag with personal toiletries
1 Shoe polishing kit

Games kit from school shop
1   School tracksuit
2   Black and silver polo shirt with school logo
2   Hockey shirt for team players
2   Black games skirt
2   Pair black short shorts—for under games skirt
2   Pair black running shorts
2   Pairs silver and black hockey socks
2   Pairs short white socks
1   White skirt (for tennis players)
1   Black school swimsuit—one-piece only
1   Pair trainers—outdoor (suitable for artificial turf surfaces)
1   Pair trainers—indoor (non-marking soles)
1   Hockey stick
1   House rugby shirt
1   Pair house socks (optional)
1   Gum shield
1   Pair shin pads

*

As an only child, entertaining myself isn't such a big deal, but even I find the last few weeks before term starts mind-bogglingly boring. Despite some small, lingering doubts, it's with enormous relief when the fourth of September finally arrives.

I have just about enough time to make myself some toast with French butter and Frank Cooper's Vintage Oxford marmalade before Dad starts getting ready. My mother left late last night so she could be in New York in time for the start of fashion week. It wasn't a particularly emotional goodbye, so it's left to Dad to drive me down today.

It doesn't take long before we've left the city behind and are speeding out into the open rolling countryside. The roads soon narrow and the trees close in overhead, forming a tight canopy through which the sun only appears in brief flashes. I gaze up through the Mercedes's glass roof at the bursts of light with a smile of nervous excitement. The route is anything but intuitive and even with the SatNav we get lost a few times before we eventually find the right road. Soon we're deep in dense, tangled woodland as the single lane road snakes along the path of least resistance, bending left and right around the thickest copses and undulating up and down over the heavily contoured landscape.

'How is anyone ever supposed to find this place?' I ask humorously.

Dad laughs.

'Yeah, you'd almost think they don't want anyone to find it.'

I look out the window and smile. If only he knew, I muse to myself.

We spot the tiny, well-concealed access road as we shoot past it. Dad slams on the brakes, leaving ragged tyre marks on the asphalt behind us and the latent impression of the seatbelt forcefully imprinted across my chest. I'm not impressed. Nonplussed, he hurriedly reverses up and takes the turning. The road meanders its way through the trees for a good few minutes before finally emerging out into a wide, open grassy clearing. Up ahead stands a squat, castle-like gatehouse. A high perimeter wall extends out either side of it, marking the boundary of the school's grounds. I flick through the school brochure in my lap.

'They call that the Gate of Torres Vedras.'

'Interesting,' my father notes. 'Isn't that what the duke of Wellington called his fortifications north of Lisbon which held off the French army's siege in 1810?'

The building looms over us, imposing and deterring, as we drive into the tunnel beneath it. On the right-hand side is a glass window. On the other side of it the elderly school porter sits waiting to tick off arriving pupils. While Dad deals with him, I glance off into the corresponding room to our left. It's in darkness, save for a little light coming from the open doorway at the rear. Disinterested, I am about to turn away when someone walks past in the corridor beyond. I do a quick double-take. For unless my eyes are deceiving me, I could swear he was in full army uniform. But before I can think more of it, Dad buzzes his window and accelerates out into the sunshine.

Smiling at the possibilities that maybe they have the army guarding this place, something sure to keep the Chinese at bay, I relax a bit and edge forward, full of anticipation, as the full grandeur of the grounds slowly unfolds before us. The driveway meanders over the gently undulating grassland of the school's approach. Here and there, small clusters of trees break up the open landscape. After about a mile, the rolling grassland gives way to a patchwork of level playing fields on which a number of pupils are already kicking rugby balls around.

A small slip road takes us into the tree-lined car park of Smith's house. Once we are parked up, I sling my rucksack onto my shoulder and together we take hold of the trunk and make for the door through which everyone else is coming and going.

Inside it's absolute chaos, with crowds of parents, pupils and accompanying siblings everywhere. The corridors are already crammed with trunks and boxes and all manner of other stuff. We edge our way through the noisy scrum as best we can. Of course, new face, new school, I attract all the attention which the newbie always gets. From the typical checking-you-out glances from the boys to the slightly more appraising, and occasionally icy, stares from the girls.

'I'm all the way at the top,' I say apologetically as we pause at the foot of the main staircase. It's not going to take long before doing this several times a day will lose its novelty. Thankfully the top floor is a lot quieter than the ones we pass on the way up. We check the map and follow the corridor halfway down until we reach a short passage which branches off to the right. Supposedly my study is at the end on the left. Sure enough, outside it I find a small handwritten note affixed to the doorframe which reads 'K2: Butterworth and Foxton'.

I find myself suddenly quite nervous as to what kind of reception awaits me inside and dart a cautious glance into the room. It's big enough at about eighteen feet long by twelve or so wide. Not a bad size for two people. There are two windows: one at the far end, overlooking the lake, and another above the bed on the right which overlooks a small balcony and the house garden far below. Together they allow a good amount of natural light in. The furnishings are pretty basic and nothing to write home about. We each have a single bed, a desk, a chair, and wardrobes set either side of the door.

I peer at the names again. The Butterworths are already here and, from the look of things, it seems the girl with whom I'm to share has taken the left-hand side of the room. It's a bit late now to say anything, seeing as they are almost done unpacking. My roommate is kneeling on the floor, busy attaching a lens to a rather nice-looking SLR camera. I take a tentative step into the study and she looks up. With her fabulous milk chocolate complexion, she is, quite possibly, one of the prettiest girls I think I've ever seen. Quick to her feet, I'd say she's about four inches short of my five foot eight and a half inches. Her riotous, dark wavy hair is absurdly thick and luscious, and her massive lashes and dark eyebrows only serve to accentuate her large, dark-brown eyes all the more. Her cheeks dimple and her face breaks into a wide, open smile.

'Hi,' she exclaims brightly, her 'i' rising ever higher like a musical scale. 'I'm Milly. Milly Butterworth.'

'Hi, Milly,' I reply, slightly more reserved but glad the ice is broken. 'I'm Heather.'

Her personality seems to be perfectly complemented by her carefree boho-chic look. Her vibrant, floral maxi dress, with its intricate beadwork, billows lazily in the wake of her movements. The hang of her huge hoop earrings and her collection of ethnic necklaces, bangles and bracelets just top it off. But most fitting of all is the way she's padding around barefoot, with a pair of flip-flops casually discarded by the door.

A moment of slight awkwardness follows, as neither of us knows quite what to say next. Breaking the silence, my dad quickly introduces himself to what I presume to be Milly's parents. It's only after a couple of seconds that I notice they are both Caucasian.

'I hope you don't mind,' Milly says quietly while the adults talk, 'but I took this side. Is that okay?'

I cast an appraising look over what will be, I suppose now by default, my side of the room.

'If not, err, I can always …' she adds quickly, clearly embarrassed by her hasty presumption, especially, it seems, in front of her parents.

I turn to her with a smile.

'Nah, this side's absolutely fine.'

She appears greatly relieved.

It takes another trip to the car to bring all my stuff up. Neither of us wants to draw out the inevitable goodbye, so Dad and I make our way back down to the car park, where things get teary. When he finally drives off, after several hugs and a few last comforting words, it is not with his usual panache and it pains me to think that he's as upset by this as I am. I need a little bit of time to compose myself before venturing back upstairs.

The study is empty on my return, so I presume Milly is now also saying her goodbyes. From the look of her desk she seems to have two main interests, maths and photography. How she is with the first, I have no idea, but going by the pictures displayed around her desk, she could probably get a job with *National Geographic* with no trouble. I've just finished setting up my own desk when she reappears, obviously relieved that we are finally alone.

'Peace at last,' she sighs with a weary little laugh, as she falls onto her bed.

'So is this your first year as well?' I say, keen to start a conversation.

'Actually this'll be the start of my fourth.'

I nod and take a look at my trunk. Before I can open it, she takes a deep breath and says:

'Go on, you might as well ask the question.'

'I'm sorry?' I reply. 'What do you mean?'

'Well, now's usually when people tend to ask what the deal is with me looking like this and my parents, well, like that.'

'Actually,' I say cheerily, 'I think I already know. But that's only because I'm also adopted.'

She looks up, surprised yet relieved.

'Wow, I wouldn't have guessed. Not from your dad, anyway.'

'Yeah, I suppose I'm kind of fortunate that way. But I do have another question, though,' I add. 'I guess I just want to make sure you're cool with all this? You know, my sharing with you? I'm just hoping no one forced you to room with me, is all.'

'Actually it's totally fine. Really! And we seem to have loads in common already. Besides, I didn't know who to share with this year, so when Lander asked, I thought, why not? The girl I've shared with for the last three years, Anabel, wanted a single this year and I prefer to share. So, seeing as we can't share with the boys ...' She shrugs acceptingly. 'Besides, sometimes change can be fun, right?'

I nod, relieved to lay my biggest concern to rest.

'So is it normal to have boys and girls in the same house?'

'Not really, but they're kind of innovative that way around here. Don't worry, though, we get our own bathroom. So, would you like a tour?'

'For sure!' I reply, more than happy to leave my unpacking till later.

'Wizard—well, come on, then!'

Suddenly a whirlwind of energy, Milly jumps up, grabs my hand and pulls me towards the door.

'So all the studies up here are named after mountains, it being the top floor and all. Back down the corridor is the sprogs' dorm.' She sees my blank look. 'Oh sorry, it means newbie. Like first year. There's pretty much school-slang for everything here at GPS. Like fagging is the sprogs doing chores for the upper-sixth. We call teachers beaks, prefects monitors. Mufti is what we call your home clothes. Tuck is sweats and stuff. Don't worry, you'll soon get the hang of it. So that's the lower-fifth down there. But just the boys. The girls' is a floor down. Everyone else up here is lower-sixth, like us.'

We come to a T-junction at the end of the corridor.

'That's Anabel's,' Milly says, pointing to our right. 'She's really very sweet, but can be a little quiet at times.' She makes to say something else but then stops herself and simply nods in the other direction.

I'm not quite sure what to make of Milly. On the one hand she seems quite bookish, going by the quick look I had over her desk, but there's also a hint of a slightly wilder, more carefree side, going by her clothes and mannerisms. I'm just hoping she's up for a bit of a laugh from time to time.

'So is Anabel your best friend then?' I ask.

'Not exactly,' Milly replies cryptically. 'It was only ever the two of us girls in our year till now, so we didn't really have a whole lot of choice but to room together.' She leaves it at that, but it's good enough for me. Curiously part of me is actually glad to hear it.

'So how many are there in our year?'

'In SH or in total?'

'In the house.'

'Just the five of us. But then there's only about twenty-five or thirty in the whole house. Nice and cosy, but not surprising really when you consider, well, you know.'

We share a conspiratorial smile. Then, unable to hold her curiosity, she asks:

'So what field did they recruit you for?'

I laugh.

'In all honesty, I don't know. It's all been pretty rushed. I guess I'll find out soon enough. And you?'

'Cryptology. Nothing exciting.'

Now I know who in my year has the photographic memory.

'So whose room's that?' I ask, pointing to the door to our left. As if in answer, we both startle as the corridor erupts with an onslaught of hip-hop from behind the door. Milly rolls her eyes.

'Luther and Nigel's,' she says wearily. 'Come on.'

She doesn't bother knocking but walks straight in. Even though term only started a few hours ago, the two boys have already turned their room into a pigsty. Clothes are strewn everywhere and there is computer equipment all over the floor. The walls are plastered with posters of scantily clad girls. To the right, a lanky-looking, pale-skinned boy has his tongue between his teeth as he applies a delicate touch of paint to a Games Workshop miniature. His desk looks like some kind of industrial manufacturing workshop, with a magnification lamp and a soldering iron buried amongst the mess. On the other side of the large room, his Afro-Caribbean roommate seems equally focussed but with something on his computer. Probably surfing porn, I'm guessing. Best not to know. Both boys are so preoccupied that neither has noticed our arrival. Milly has to shout to get them to look up and come over.

The modeller introduces himself as Nigel Bromhead. He is tall and thin with dark hair. I try not to smile at the sight of his top button, which is firmly done up. God knows what my mother would say about that. But it's individual, I suppose, and I like that, even if it's not my style. That aside, he seems genuine and pretty down-to-earth.

Not that the same can be said about his roommate, Luther Glasgow. The complete opposite, in fact. He's short and grossly overweight. Yet once I get past the tightly cropped Afro, baggy trousers, loose-fitting American football shirt and wannabe gangster look, he turns out to be quite amusing and talkative. The strong Scottish accent helps.

'I was going to take Heather on a tour,' Milly says to the boys, both of whom seem quite happy to get back to whatever they were doing. 'So we'll see you at tea—'

She is interrupted as someone bellows at us from the other end of the corridor.

'WHAT THE DEVIL IS GOING ON HERE?'

* * *

CHAPTER 6
FRIENDS, ENEMIES AND THOSE IN-BETWEEN

'Glasgow!' The man shouts. 'What is that racket?'

My new friends share an alarmed look.

'So busted,' Milly mouths to Luther. *'Again!'*

He curses, apparently all too aware of what's coming. Nigel seems frozen. I peer around the doorframe to see Mr Lander marching up the corridor, looking none too amused.

'How often have I told you this house is not your own private ghetto of sin and inequity?'

The speed with which Luther makes it to the sound system is genuinely impressive for someone so rotund. The volume comes down, just as our housemaster barges into the study. He sighs and gives Luther a falsely appreciatively smile. Then, turning to me, his expression softens.

'Ah, Miss Foxton. I see you've had the misfortune of meeting what constitutes the remainder of your year group. Hopefully your presence might serve as a welcome contribution to their development into more civilised human beings.' Turning to Luther and Nigel, he adds, 'I trust all this rubbish will get the necessary sign-off from the school's electrician before you plug them in and burn my house down!' He doesn't wait for an answer. 'Excellent, well, if you'll excuse me I must now attend to our new lower-fifth.'

He turns and walks back towards the sprogs' dorm, whistling to himself as he goes. I look to the others, wide-eyed and amused.

'Is he always like that?'

'Yes!' they chime as one.

'He's just being nice because you're new,' Milly elaborates. 'Any other time, these two would've been royally busted and in detention.'

'Ai, that we would,' Luther notes with a scowl. 'He's easily th' tooghest hoosemaster haur. Aye knows what's gonnae oan. Makes daein' anythin' fin twice as hard. Jist wait, yoo'll see suin enaw.'

They all nod in resigned agreement, though I'm still struggling to understand him.

'Anyway, *c'est la vie*,' Milly reflects with a resigned shrug. 'Come on then, let's go see the rest of the school, shall we?'

*

I've only been here an hour, yet the school is buzzing, the sun is shining and somehow I already feel at home, despite our cantankerous housemaster. There is so much more to see by day than we were able to on my first whistle-stop tour. It is so quintessentially everything I expected a boarding school to be. Historic old buildings—some even dating back to the early sixteen-hundreds—quadrangles, or quads for short, playing fields stretching almost as far as the eye can see and teachers in long, flowing black gowns, all expecting to be addressed as Sir or Ma'am as you pass them by.

By the time we finish our walkabout and head over to the dining hall for tea, Milly's near constant running commentary has given me a pretty good idea of what to expect. Certainly who to watch out for—both teachers and pupils alike—and most importantly, of course, who all the fittest boys are. But what really intrigues me are her stories about what being part of MI13 is like. Of particular interest is what she calls the Data Room, or the Oracle, as it's nicknamed. Supposedly it's some sort of hi-tech system with access to no end of databases, both public and private, relating to almost anything you could ever think of searching. But especially people. I can't help but reflect on the utter lack of success I've had over the holidays trying to find out even the slightest tangible bit of information about the man from the tannery. But Google, as I already found out to my detriment, only goes so far, and Mr John Wei remains as much of an enigma as ever. What I really need, it seems, is something like what Milly is describing. Now I just need to find a way in to use it.

Like so many of the other buildings, the dining hall is something to behold. It is big and airy with floor-to-ceiling windows running down the entire left-hand side. The roof is vaulted, much like an old church's. There are two food counters on the right-hand side, and serving entrances at either end. Rows of stout wooden tables and matching benches are arranged down the length of the room.

The selection on offer is a lot better than I expected, and after a good deal of umm-ing and ah-ing, I load up a plateful of macaroni cheese, a small salad—to ease my dietary conscience—and a chocolate mousse. We reach our table to find the boys in the midst of a heated debate. I squeeze in next to a petite Asian girl, who Milly introduces as Anabel Heathcote-Wong. She's typically slim: the beneficiary, I suspect, of that fantastic Asian metabolism which they all seem to have. Introductions over, the boys immediately pick up where they left off.

'Hoo can ye e'en say 'at?' Luther blusters. 'It was utter *shite*!'

'No, it wasn't,' Nigel retorts wearily. 'It just wasn't original, but that doesn't mean it was shite.'

'What are they arguing about now?' Milly asks.

'Oh, Nigel said *Superman Returns* was a good movie,' Anabel replies, disinterested.

'Well, it's *true*!' he protests in exasperation, desperately looking for support.

'Whit ur ye, visually dyslexic?' Luther howls. For a second it's not clear if he's being serious or not. However, the others' amused expressions suggest this isn't unusual between the two of them.

'Look,' Luther says, carefully setting his knife and fork down. 'It was a friggin' travesty! Th' guy's selfless, okay? He's nae jist gonnae rin aff withit sayin' cheerio th' noo tae fowk. Bollocks! Onie real Superman fan woods ken 'at. An' th' bloke spent twalv years studyin' th' accumulated knowledge ay th' twenty-eecht knoon galaxies in th' fortress ay solitude, if ye believe *Superman: Th' Movie*. Ye hink, he's jist in th' wey o sit doon oan an islain gart ay kryptonite withit havin' come up wi' a better plan? Noo, *Man ay Steel*. 'At was a guid film.'

'There! You see what we have to deal with,' Milly whispers.

I smile and watch on, bemused as much by their nerdiness as by the others' disinterest. Before long, I too tune out and turn to look around the hall. The cliquey groups are easy to spot. Over there we have the sporty ones, there the nerds, then the too-cool-for-school crowd and the usual assortment of other clusters in-between. Quite where my new friends fit in, though, I'm unsure. They're not the 'cool' gang. That much is clear. But, then again, after my last lot of friends, that's fine by me. In fact, that's exactly what I was hoping for: normality.

Eventually, with their argument unresolved, Luther gets up for seconds and returns a minute later with another overflowing plateful. The bench creaks in weary protest as he sits down.

'Whit?' he exclaims, seeing Milly's less than impressed look. 'Aam a growin' boy, aw reit!'

'Yah!' she retorts. 'But in what direction?'

The table breaks into fits of laughter.

'Ai, jist envioos ay mah ample curves, is whit ye ur,' Luther chuckles knowingly, running his hands over his voluminous torso.

'Heads up,' Anabel whispers. 'Here they come.'

We turn to see a small group approaching. Front and centre is a distinctly hostile-looking, statuesque blonde girl. Her clothes are all high-end and she walks with an arrogant, overly confident strut. The disdainful looks she flashes left and right leave their recipients in no doubt as to what she thinks of them. But her most unpleasant glare is reserved for our table. I watch, baffled, as her friends all give us equally nasty looks before moving on towards another table.

'What was all that about?' I ask.

'Oh,' Milly replies without any attempt to disguise her contempt, 'they're the ones I was talking about. Victoria Farabee-Peacock and the rest of her inbred, racist friends from

Grey's. The red-haired one next to her is bum-chum number one, Augustus Cole.'

'She's only here because her father got her a place,' says Nigel.

'Hold on, I thought they don't tell parents?'

'Well, her dad's some bigwig in the Foreign Ministry, or something like that,' he explains. 'So, no surprise, she was born with a silver spoon stuck firmly in her mouth.'

'Mair likely somewhaur else,' Luther mutters darkly.

'Would explain why she walks that way,' Milly ponders aloud. That draws a collective laugh. 'We reckon her loser friends are just trying to get fast-track jobs through her dad.'

'Yeah, and they seem to find it ever so amusing to call us the FIPs,' Anabel chimes in with her quiet, mouse-like voice. 'It stands for Failed Immigration Policy.'

'Prime candidates fur th' Foreign Office, 'en,' Luther says with a shake of his head.

'Yeah, go figure,' Milly adds with a sigh. 'When they don't have their heads up her arse, they're trying their best to get us to leave. Pretty sad, really.'

I glance over, partly inclined to dislike them instantly, mainly because I have no love for racists or bullies, knowing personally all too well what it feels like to be on the receiving end of just this sort of stuff. I'm usually willing to give everyone the benefit of the doubt, but …

I get my answer as Farabee-Peacock catches my eye. Her expression hardens and she turns away, leaving just her middle finger sticking up at me.

*

Tea time over, we make our way out into SH's sunken garden, where the conversation turns to everyone's background.

Milly was born in Nepal, to parents who realised they either couldn't—or didn't want to—afford another child. As fate had it, a visiting British university professor and his wife came across her in one of the capital's many crowded orphanages and fell in love with her on the spot. Upon their return to the UK, she came too. They now live in the countryside up near Oxford, where her father teaches mathematics at the university, and her mother art.

Conversely, though born in the UK, Anabel has lived most of her life in Hong Kong, where her parents both work for the British Consulate. No big surprise, then, that she's fluent in both Mandarin and Cantonese. In the tranquil surroundings of the garden, she livens up a bit and even teaches me my first Cantonese phrases. Now I just need to work out where I'm ever going to use phrases like *yau mo gau-cho ah, moh mentai* and *or nor mng sik gong zhung mun*. And if that wasn't enough, thanks to short stints her parents did in Moscow and Morocco, she's also fluent in Russian, Arabic and French. No two guesses, then, why she's here.

Nigel's parents run a cider brewery in Somerset. They sound very down to earth and pleasant. So I can see where he got it from.

Ironically, given that his surname is Glasgow, Luther actually comes from Edinburgh, where his parents own a small computer software company, which, I suppose, explains where he gets his interest in all things techie.

When it comes to my turn, I keep it short and simple. Unlike Milly, I've never been very comfortable talking about my adoption. Partly because, given my similar appearance to my 'mother', I've never really had to. In truth, besides Milly, very few people actually know. We share a look, silent, but full of meaning and unnoticed by the others. So it's just a father in banking and a journalist for a mother. It's not a lie, just precautionary, especially after what Ben said about my last group of friends.

The conversation soon turns to the school rules. And there seems to be no end of them. Now knowing how strict Mr Lander is, I make sure to pay particular attention to what they say.

'It's a strange place,' Milly begins, 'because on the one hand they have all these petty little school rules, and then at the same time they're teaching us how to break no end of laws. It's a joke.'

'Yeah, but ye definitely don't want tae lit heem catch ye drinking,' says Luther, as he discreetly slips a hip flask from his pocket and takes a quick gulp, before hiding it away again.

'And for some reason he gets really wound up if you're late for class,' says Nigel.

'Perhaps if you two ever bothered being on time you wouldn't get into trouble, would you?' Milly notes dryly. The boys just ignore her.

'No smoking,' says Anabel.

'Nae sex, either,' adds Luther.

'Who'd want to have sex with you, anyway?' Milly teases.

'Och, that's cold,' he winces, play-lunging for her. She squeals and scrambles out of reach just in time. A nervous smile flickers across Nigel's face. Now I'm in no position to judge, but even I can recognise an awkward virgin hoping the conversation doesn't come to him. He quickly changes the subject.

'But what's absolutely guaranteed to land you every pun-
ishment in the book is if he ever catches you out of bed after
lights out.'

'Aye,' Luther notes drolly. 'God forbid anyain ever makes
it look like he doesn't hae his hoose under control.'

I look at him with a crafty smile.

'My dad has a saying. It goes: it's only wrong *if* you get
caught.'

'Aye, we'd gie oan weel, heem an' ah,' Luther says with
an approving nod. 'An' as chance woods hae it, th' first river
party ay term is comin' up at th' end ay th' month. Who's
interested?'

'What is it?'

'Every so often they go and throw a party down by the
river in the middle of the night. Usually on a Saturday,' says
Nigel. 'They're quite good fun, the few times we've been. It's
just getting out of the house unnoticed, which is easier said
than done.'

'Sounds like a challenge.'

I can sense Milly's hesitation as a couple of the others also
voice interest.

'This is so not a good idea,' she sighs. 'We know what's
going to happen. Lander will bust us, like he did you two the
last time, and we'll all end up in detention.'

I lean closer to Luther.

'Tell me more,' I say keenly.

For the next few minutes, the boys reminisce about the
parties they've been to, as well as some of the other daring
escapades they seem ever so proud of having pulled off right
under Mr Lander's nose over the years. The more I hear, the
more I know I made the right choice coming here. It's comical

how Milly's expression grows ever more unenthusiastic the longer the conversation goes on.

By the time we go back inside, things have calmed noticeably from their earlier state of chaos. The common room is packed for the evening film; likewise the small pantry, where small groups are busy cooking pasta and making toast. Here and there, shy, awkward and rather uncertain-looking lower-fifth formers huddle together, still very much ill at ease with their new surroundings and the towering senior pupils. Despite my earlier elation, I can't help but sympathise a little at what they must be feeling. I just choose not to let it show quite so obviously.

After lights out, Milly and I lie chatting in whispers for a while across the darkened room. When finally we bid each other good night, I find she's asleep in minutes. If only I were as fortunate.

Awake and alone, and with no distractions to keep them at bay, the first inklings of homesickness soon creep up on me. In no time, tears are rolling down my cheeks and I find myself seriously regretting having ever agreed to come here. I turn and face the wall, desperately hoping that my sobs don't wake Milly. How long I cry for I have no idea, but by the time I do eventually fall asleep, the pillow is properly damp on both sides.

*

It's three in the morning when Milly stirs. I look around from my perch on the deep window ledge at the far end of our room where I've been sitting, staring out over the grounds, for the last three hours or so. By now I must make for a sorry sight.

Knees drawn up to my chest and a half-empty box of tissues beside me. The only thing missing, I think ruefully, is a pint tub of ice cream and then the picture would be complete.

'You okay?' she whispers.

I give a despondent half-shake of my head.

'Not really,' I groan.

If the moon was any brighter, I'm sure it would betray my puffy, swollen eyes. I give a hollow laugh of despair. 'Who'd have thought it, huh? Me getting homesick?'

Milly sits up in bed, rubs her eyes and yawns.

'It passes soon enough. Just depends on how quickly you immerse yourself sufficiently in this place to forget about it. Pretty soon this'll be home.'

I give a deep sniff as my bottom lip threatens to tremble again.

'You can climb in with me for a bit, if that makes you feel any better,' she offers.

I nod numbly, unsure really what to say. She shimmies over to make room and I slip in next to her. Amazingly, everything does begin to feel so much better as I feel her warmth behind me in the narrow bed.

'Any time you want to talk, I'm here if you need it,' she whispers.

I nod, barely able to hold it together long enough to thank her.

* * *

CHAPTER 7

LIE OF THE LAND

The morning wake-up call is neither subtle nor delicate. It consists of a lower-fifth former running around the entire house as fast as they can at seven o'clock in the morning, whilst ringing a big naval bell as loudly as they can.

Thereafter, everyone heads in a mad rush down the stairs and into the changing rooms before the showers all get taken. A quick application of make-up, a vigorous towel dry and rough comb through of the hair and then it's a brisk walk across to the dining hall for breakfast before the queue there gets too long.

But it's worth it because breakfast here is good. A full English with bacon, eggs, sausages and baked beans—which might even be Heinz. Large bowls of butter and marmalade sit on each table. I grimace as Luther smears thick lashings of the latter onto his fried bread. It looks seriously gross, until he makes me try it. And to my surprise, it's not actually that bad.

*

It doesn't take long to discover that life here is really just about one thing: getting from one place to another as quickly as possible, without being late. I don't even have time to feel miserable because after breakfast, it's straight back to the house to brush our teeth and prepare for the day's classes. Then, at eight thirty, it's back across the road into the main auditorium for the headmaster's weekly address.

Much like an old gymnasium it's a large, wood-panelled hall with a row of big, old-fashioned windows up near the ceiling. A sea of interlocking plastic chairs is divided by a wide central aisle which leads up to a raised theatrical stage at the front.

Once the hall is full, the rear double doors open. First comes the headmaster, followed closely by the new head boy, who looks ever so pleased with his new, brightly coloured, one-of-a-kind school colours jacket. Then, two by two, come the rest of the teaching staff, all in their long, flowing black academic gowns. Once on the stage, each takes their seat, leaving just the headmaster standing by the lectern. From here, I'd say he is about sixty-ish, with shrewd, piercing eyes that glide over us, hawk-like and scrutinising. He looks like the kind of person who's been around, seen things, done things that others haven't. In a nutshell, someone not to be trifled with.

'Attention on deck,' he calls commandingly in a deep, no-nonsense baritone. He doesn't need to shout, yet an instant hush falls over the hall.

I give Milly an enquiring look. She smiles and leans in closer.

'He used to be an admiral in the Navy, so …'

'I thought he's a doctor?'

'Yeah, that too. He's got a PhD in International Relations.'

'Well, a very pleasant and good morning, boys and girls,' Dr Gambon begins. 'I hope everyone is well rested and ready for another term of hard work and, dare I say it, a little fun?' He pauses for effect. His voice has a soothing, slightly moist quality to it, especially on the consonants. Listening to it soon gives me a pleasant little tingling sensation at the bottom of my spine.

'A few notices. Firstly, would all new pupils remain behind to receive their timetables and school allocations, and to set electives, if joining the sixth forms. Secondly, Mr Ridder asks that I inform everyone that try-outs for the rugby and football teams begin this afternoon. A quarter past four on Big-Field, for those interested. Dr Cadogan also wishes to remind everyone not enrolled with B-School that the Geology block remains strictly out-of-bounds.'

He goes on like this for several minutes. Eventually, the head boy stands to read the Lord's Prayer in Latin. Upon the last syllable of his 'Amen', the teachers all rise and file out. Immediately after they're gone, the rest of the school rushes for the exit, just in a far less orderly manner. My housemates jostle past, waving briefly as they go, and soon it's just the lower-fifth and a handful of new sixth-formers remaining.

After much deliberation, and mindful of the wholly fictional relationship between my supposed grades and my actual academic ability, I settle on a cover syllabus of International Relations, History and Economics, with a minor in French.

Then the day takes a turn for the worse when I'm told that I am to be enrolled in A-School until such time as I prove myself suitable for a transfer to B-School. I look questioningly at the deputy headmaster, a tall, rather severe-looking man with pale skin and red hair called Mr Gibson Cuthbert, in the hope that there's been a mistake. After Mr Lander's talk I was expecting to go straight into B-School. Now it seems I have to wait even longer until I can begin to get to the bottom of what happened on holiday! Cuthbert's unfriendly expression leaves me in no doubt that any further protest would be a mistake. Annoyed, I grudgingly head over to the school's sanatorium with the others for our medicals.

*

Things only get worse on reaching the san. The hour and a half wait I can handle. Even the lack of magazines is okay. The medical itself starts straightforwardly enough until the slightly patronising doctor places a colour-sight booklet before me and then promptly declares me colour blind. Supposedly it's very rare in girls, the unfriendly looking female nurse says as she jots something down on my notes.

'But how is that possible? I can see all the different colours and could even cluster them together. I just don't see any patterns.'

The doctor chuckles.

'A lot of people say that. They're still colour blind.'

'Well ... well, how do you know that ... that, I dunno, that maybe my eyesight isn't like so good that maybe I can't make out any patterns between them because to me they look nothing alike?'

That gets an even bigger laugh.

'Well,' he says, trying to keep a straight face, 'as there is no box here for Superman vision, I suggest we just call it colour blindness and move on, shall we?' He smiles to himself, shaking his head as he absentmindedly also adds a note to my file.

I scowl at the two of them and huffily cross my arms. Typical adults, always ignoring what you say.

The doctor proceeds over to the eye chart on the far wall, where he removes a pen from his inside jacket pocket.

'If you could start here?' he says, indicating a line several rows up from the bottom. 'We can always begin higher up, if you're having trouble?'

In a flash of anger, I retort:

'Did you like the hotel?'

That earns me a baffled look.

'I beg your pardon?'

'Your pen says the Grand Hotel, Eastbourne. Was just curious.'

He looks at it, as if reading the tiny, faded writing along its length for the first time. Then his confusion crystallises as he tries to understand how I could have possibly read it from all the way over here. Point made, I stand up and give them both an emphatic look before moving towards the door.

'Can I go now?'

When neither of them replies, I nod and make my way out into the sunshine. There I stop on the grass and frown, more annoyed at my lack of control than anything else. Disappointed in myself, I head back towards Big-School for a lecture on the school's rules. A few minutes late, I apologise to Mr Cuthbert and quickly find a seat at the back. My reward: an unmistakeably venomous glare. It doesn't take long to notice I'm getting the same reproachful scowl after each rule has been outlined. Almost as if he expects me to be the first one to break it. Yet I'm not the only person here who's looking bored, so why the special attention? Petulantly, I decide not to bother listening anymore and slip out when his back is turned.

*

The grainy photocopied map they've given us proves to be of little use in helping me find my first class. It's not made any easier by the fact that my housemates all seem to have different timetables to mine.

I can't imagine the main block has changed much since it was built, back in the sixteen hundreds. It still has its original bare stone walls and ochre tiled flooring throughout. Even the 'newer' classrooms are pretty old-fashioned, with bare floorboards, high ceilings and draughty stone-framed windows. Each has a raised platform at the front on which the teacher's desk and a large revolving blackboard reside. Pupils' desks are all the old wooden ones with folding tops and inkwells in the corners. Not one hasn't been crudely engraved with the names of pupils from previous generations.

I quickly forget my earlier annoyances as I dash up the stairs to my first class, an induction to the workings of MI13. Just the thought alone that I am on the verge of becoming a spy seems ridiculous, yet it is the realisation of years of silent childhood fantasy. Taking the class is the notoriously unpredictable Mr Williams. Besides the fact that people seem to think he's mad, the joke is he's been around for almost as long as some of the buildings. In person, he is a curious little man who has taken to combing the last few sad strands of hair over his crown to try to hide the fact that there's almost none left. His wardrobe seems to consist entirely of ancient-looking three-piece tweed suits with brown leather elbow pads and ties that resemble old hemp sacks. Topping it off is his ridiculous little moustache that begins to resemble Hitler's the longer one stares at it. Given that this is an introduction, the rest of the class are predominantly first-years. No surprise then that I keep catching a number of the boys shooting me inquisitive sideways looks.

Twenty minutes into the lesson, just as he is concluding the syllabus, Mr Williams suddenly pauses from his monologue and appears to listen intently for a moment, but to what, I don't know, almost as if someone is whispering into his ear. Then, leaping into action, he grabs an old canvas and rubber gas mask from the shelf and dons it, all the while shouting: 'Don't panic, don't panic.'

Darting to the back of the classroom, he proceeds to climb out onto the window ledge which runs around the second floor. Oblivious to our stunned expressions and growing alarm, he walks off nonchalantly past the windows of the first-year class being taught next door, causing chaos to break out on the other side of the thin partition wall.

For a moment we share looks of disbelief. Then we crease into fits of laughter. He never does come back, so after five minutes, we gather our things and go to the next lesson, Basics of Agent Recruitment and Running. Our teacher, Professor Summerfield, is an expert in international relations and, being youthful, tall and curvy, is the polar opposite of Mr Williams.

And so the morning's classes go. Next I have Introduction to Field Craft, where we learn how to make and operate dead-letter drops—basically, secret hidey-holes to pass messages, documents and other things surreptitiously. After that it's into yet another classroom, where we are introduced to a polygraph machine, or lie detector, and are told that by the end of term, we should all be able to beat it.

*

By the time my new lower-fifth friends and I get to lunch, my head is swimming with all I've learnt already. We're speculating what Deception Studies promises to entail after lunch. Even being stuck with the lower-fifth wasn't so bad after all. A couple of the slightly more mature ones are actually quite amusing and we are now getting on alright. But the fact that I have no idea how long this arrangement will go on for before I am allowed into B-School is nonetheless annoying.

On entering the main corridor leading to the dining hall, my little friends run off to join some of their classmates. Their 'byes' are loud and overenthusiastic, leaving everyone in earshot in no doubt that they're on first-name terms with a lower-sixth girl. Apparently that's an achievement around here, it seems. Suppressing a smile, I turn to see Milly and Anabel in what looks like a hushed but heated argument at the end of the corridor. As I approach, they quickly separate and pretend nothing is wrong, though I sense a slight coldness in Anabel's manner. Sensing it's wiser not to pry, I fall in behind them and we all walk on in silence towards the canteen. I watch the two of them with interest. The weight of unspoken emotion between them right now is huge. Maybe it's about a boy or something, I think to myself.

Just as we reach the door, another, larger group comes out in the opposite direction. The lead girl roughly pushes past Anabel, sending her stumbling back into the door. Behind them come Farabee-Peacock, her ginger-headed friend Augustus and three other lower-sixth boys from Grey's.

'Hey, watch where you're going,' Milly snaps defensively.

The larger, far bigger girl rounds on her with a disbelieving look.

'What did you just say, swot? I'm sure I heard you say something.' She barges into Milly, driving her back against the wall.

'Nothing,' Milly says, ashamedly looking down at the ground and suddenly fidgeting nervously with the hem of her jacket. Anabel's no better. I can't believe my housemates are just going to stand there and take this.

'Yeah, that's what I thought,' the girl hisses, an inch from Milly's ear, before shoving her hard into the wall. 'Open your mouth again, swot, and I'll deck you.'

'Okay, look, that's enough,' I say, moving towards the group from Grey's to try to calm things down. 'She didn't do anything to you, so leave her alone.'

All eyes are suddenly on me. Even my friends'. Correction: especially theirs. A smirk appears on Farabee's face and the others from Grey's all start acting up in mock fright at my warning tone, baying for the bigger, mousey-haired girl with the badly done pig-tails to deck me instead. She turns slowly, almost as if in search of the source to some minor, irritating background noise. With a scowl, she puts her palm to my face and pushes roughly. Unprepared, I stumble back a few paces and shoot her a dark look.

'Touch me again,' I say quietly, 'and I promise you if anyone's going to get decked here, it's you.'

Before she can react, there's an angry shout from behind me.

'Oi, what's gonnae oan?'

I turn to see Luther approaching, with a nervous-looking Nigel tailing closely behind.

'Shut up, Pork Chop,' one of the Grey's boys shouts back. And he does.

With no warning, someone slaps my books from my arms, sending them all tumbling to the floor amid a gaggle of laughter. I sigh and turn to see the large, brutish girl standing defiantly before me, her arms folded and a taunting look on her face, daring me to respond.

'Seriously, what was that for?'

'What do you think!' she snaps back venomously. 'You've made your bed with the immigrants. This is just called sleeping in it.'

'What the hell have you got against them?'

'If it wasn't for them, all the bloody foreigners,' she snaps, shooting an unpleasant look at my friends, 'this country wouldn't be in the mess it is.'

'Oh, what a load of fascist crap,' I fire back. 'If you knew anything about it, you'd realise things are only the way they are because our parents' generation and their parents all thought they could live way beyond their means, without ever having to deal with any repercussions.'

'What idiot told you that?'

'My dad, if you must know.'

'Oh, and he's an expert is he?'

'Well, he's about to start a new job at the Bank of England, so what do you think?'

Obviously not liking that answer one little bit, she turns her nose up and scoffs. I'm all too aware of everyone's eyes on me, watching on expectantly. A crowd is rapidly gathering and most have a somewhat shocked look that anyone is daring enough, or stupid enough, to stand up to the Grey's lot. Even Anabel and Milly are silently willing me to back down—much like they probably always do, all in the hope that people will then leave them alone. Sadly, I learned a long time ago that

that isn't how you deal with bullies. The half-dozen Grey's lower-sixth formers laugh tauntingly as I squat down to pick up my books and put them into my rucksack.

'Why can't you just leave them alone?' I say, more to Farabee than the others.

'Because making their miserable lives even more miserable is one of the only things that passes for fun around here,' she replies with a bored look as she examines her fingernails. It's the first time I've heard her talk. Her accent, like most around here—including mine, I dare say—is one of money and privilege, albeit with a cold, hard, clipped edge. 'And now we have you to add to our little black book.'

'Yeah, well, now I'm warning you: leave us alone, or I'll ...'

For a moment they seem taken aback at being threatened so openly, or perhaps they're just pretending. Then they all burst into laughter.

'You'll *what*? You ever even think of touching *any* of us,' Farabee-Peacock sings airily, 'and my father will have you thrown out of here so fast you won't even have time to pack. Haven't you figured it out yet? We *own* this place.'

With that, they saunter off, laughing. As they go, the trollish-looking girl collides with me deliberately hard, spinning me around and sending me stumbling backwards. In an instant, my mood spikes to redline. I turn to Milly.

'What's her name?'

'Candice Hardcastle,' she replies quietly.

'Oi, Candice!' I shout.

She stops and turns. They all do. As I stride towards her, I tuck my hair casually behind my ear. Quite where this sudden rush of inner confidence or flagrant disregard for what's obviously about to be a pretty offensive breach of school rules comes from, I don't know, but new girl, new school: I'm only going to get one or two opportunities to show the bullies around here that I'm best left alone.

Candice already has the beginnings of some belittling putdown on her lips when, without warning, I lash out and sucker punch her squarely in the gut. The blow is harder than is probably either wise or necessary, but I don't care. She folds like a collapsing ironing board and falls to the floor, where she writhes, wheezing and gasping for air. Instantly, the others all back off—just as I expected them to. And now for the icing on the cake.

'No!' I shout, looking from Candice to a clearly shocked Farabee-Peacock. 'That's what I was talking about! I swear— you ever become my problem again and I will smash each and every one of your heads in with a brick and then bury you under the front lawn. And you know what, Farabee? Screw your dad, you spoilt little rich bitch.'

Fuming, I give some serious thought to kicking Candice in the side of her arrogant, piggy-faced head, just for good effect. Probably wisely, I think better of it and storm off, straight past my shocked friends.

'Bloody hell,' Luther mumbles in astonishment as I pass him. 'Hope ye ne'er gie mad at me.'

*

I would have been surprised had I not been sent to the head's office at some point—I just didn't expect it to happen quite this fast. Barely five minutes later, not even halfway through my first day here, and I am being frog-marched up to his office by a clearly livid Mr Lander. There he orders me, in no uncertain terms, not to move until such time as the headmaster can be bothered to deal with me. I slump into the chair and begin to curse my rash behaviour. This temper of mine and its dangerously short fuse is ... I sigh and shake my head regretfully.

A couple of minutes later, the door opens and another pupil emerges, looking none too happy himself. He casts me a rueful look and disappears down the stairs. A loud, gruff shout comes from inside, which makes even the headmaster's secretary flinch.

'Foxton, get your arse in here!'

I swallow awkwardly, take a deep breath and reluctantly head in. It's a nice office, tastefully decorated with a couple of sofas set either side of a small wooden coffee table in the centre. Several tall bookcases line the walls, with little side tables set here and there in between them. Just in front of the bay window, all the way on the other side of the room, is a desk, and behind it, seemingly none too pleased, is Dr Gambon. Without looking up from the file he is reading, he gestures to one of the chairs on the other side of the desk. Then he removes his gold-rimmed specs: as sure a sign as any that a really unpleasant bollocking is on its way. Nervously, I take a seat and wait, my knees together. Now it's me who's fiddling with the hem of my skirt. After a minute, he snaps the file shut and fixes me with a steely gaze.

'Well, it didn't take you long to make a mess, did it?'

'But, Sir—' I blurt.

He raises a hand, cutting me off.

'Foxton, I really don't care, and frankly I don't want to hear it. She annoyed you. You responded. Cause and effect. This isn't the Girl Guides. However, it's a team effort here and it does no bloody good if we're all at each other's throats. So I don't want to hear of a repeat of today's fracas, understood?'

I nod, not quite believing that this could possibly be the end of it. He sighs and leans back with a 'What am I going to do with you?' look.

'You of all people should know better than to draw attention to yourself like that. Above nearly everyone else here, you're actually here for a jolly good reason.' He pauses, considering his next words carefully.

'Sir …' I venture hesitantly. 'If we're going to be talking about that, then can I at least ask about the men in Morocco … You, the guys up in London. You all know what they were after, don't you?'

'Bloody right,' he says, twirling his specs.

'But you're not going to tell me?'

'Of course not. That would be like telling you the ending of a book before you've read it. No, that's your journey of discovery. But you now work for His Majesty's Secret Service, Foxton. There would be something severely amiss if you weren't able to work it out eventually by yourself.'

'Well, that's sort of what I'm trying to do.'

'Really, how so?'

'Well, by getting into B-School for starters.'

'Yes,' he notes with interest. 'Mr Cuthbert mentioned you were rather adamant about that earlier. What I'm curious to know is why?'

'Because I need to use that huge search engine they have down there.'

'The Oracle? What for?'

'So I can find out who the men in Marrakech were.'

'We already know who they are.'

'No, Sir, you know who they *were*. But the man in Green Park said they, or at least their leader, hadn't been seen or heard of for ages, so maybe he changed his name?'

His eyes narrow, intrigued.

'And what would make you say that?'

'Because I have this.' I take the faded leather wallet from my rucksack pocket and pass it across the desk to him. 'He's using a different name in that to the one you have in that file of yours. And your file looked pretty old. So I'm thinking maybe it's what he was going by more recently. I just figured it might lead to whoever he was working for.'

'How did you get this?' he asks, waving the wallet at me.

'It fell from his pocket just before someone blew his head off.'

With a considered nod, he passes it back to me.

'Interesting. Most interesting. But that alone isn't a good enough reason to get you a pass into B-School.'

'So what is?'

'Impressing Henri Cabal sufficiently that he'll let you in.'

'Sorry, who?'

He smiles and reaches for his phone.

'Doris, kindly ask Mr Cabal to come up, will you?' Then, turning back to me, he says, 'Henri Cabal is English, though you wouldn't know it by meeting him. His real name is Henry Cable. Interesting chap, though. Not the best of childhoods. He eventually decided to start over and joined the French Foreign Legion. Seems he rather liked their way of life. But he soon became too much for even them, so they booted him out. Right into the welcoming arms of MI6. After a rather illustrious career, he ended up here, running B-School. Brace yourself, though, he can be, well, somewhat abrasive.'

A few minutes later, the door opens and in walks a man with a narrow, supremely arrogant-looking face. He's tall and thin, with a wiry build, bristling with restless energy, though his movements are precise and graceful, like a dancer's. In his hand he holds a scrawny-looking, hand-rolled cigarette. He leans forward, arms wide, with an amused yet bluntly enquiring look, as if he's expecting an apology for having been dragged all the way up here, or, at the very least, a damned good explanation.

Dr Gambon smiles and points at me.

'Ms Foxton here wishes to enrol with B-School.'

'*Oui*, and I want to win zee lottery so I can stop doing zees sheet every day. What makes 'er so special?'

'Well, Henri. Partly because she is new here and has joined in the lower-sixth. It strikes me she might be better served by being fast-tracked into a speciality rather than trying to play catch up on the three years of generalist training which she's missed in A-School.' Dr Gambon passes me a printed list. 'Have a look if there's anything here that takes your fancy.'

I cast my eye over the list of specialist streams in B-School. There is Dept A—Watcher Section, Dept I—Imaging Intel, Dept H—Humint or Human Intel, Dept E—Elint or Electronic Intel, Dept P&P—Placement and Procurement. And on the list goes.

'What's this one?' I ask. 'P and P?'

'Oh, that's jolly good fun,' Dr Gambon says enthusiastically, firing a smile at Henri. 'Right up your street, I think. It's all about taking things from places and putting things in places. All without being caught.'

Instantly seeing where this is going, Cabal throws his arms into the air in protest.

'*Non! Absolutement non!* I am not 'aving some leetle gerl waste my time—'

'You surprise me, Henri,' Dr Gambon muses. 'For someone who has been given chances he probably didn't deserve, I'd have thought you, of all people, would give unto others as was given unto you. The second reason you should consider her is because you don't know what Ms Foxton here is capable of.'

Cabal drops onto one of the sofas and takes an exaggerated drag on his runty little cigarette. Then he waves it airily at me.

'Guilt trippin' Henri into sayin' yes ees not going to werk. She wants into Pee 'nd Pee, zen she 'as to earn eet. Let's see 'er get from zee door to your desk without touchin' zee ground. Hmm, zat is fair, *non*?'

Dr Gambon smiles, a little too knowingly for my liking. He offers no protest and turns to me.

'Well, there you have it, Ms Foxton.'

I cast a glance over the route I'll need to take. It's obvious why Cabal chose it because it's anything but easy, with slippery wooden surfaces for most of the way and an enormous seven- or eight-foot gap around the desk itself, but that's not to say it's impossible. Cabal folds his arms confidently and leans back, already assured of the likely outcome.

'Alright, then,' I say, rising to the challenge. 'But can I go change first?' I gesture at my school uniform.

'*Non,*' Cabal replies with a cheeky smile. 'Out in zee field you do not peek and chuuse what 'appens. Do it now, or don't. I don't care.'

With a shrug, I slip off my shoes and walk toward the door. Halfway there I stop and rub my foot on Gambon's coffee table. As I feared, the tights are going to be far too slippery, so I pull them off and equally cheekily hand them to Henri Cabal to look after. With a laugh, he shakes his head and gestures for me to hurry up.

I step outside and close the door behind me. Upon reopening it, I grasp the top edge and hop up onto the door handle. From there, I swing round and step off onto the side table behind it. It's a short stretch from there to a sideboard that takes me to the first bookcase. A small jump and I'm sitting on top of it. I shimmy along until it is only a four-foot gap to the nearest sofa. A jump I easily make. So far, so good. Barely even a challenge. But now I'm faced with either the huge leap onto the desk, or a far riskier, more circuitous route around the side of the room on some rather unsteady-looking side tables. And from there the jump is almost just as hard. It's clear to me that Cabal had no intention of letting me succeed. Except, unlike the headmaster, he's underestimated me.

Moving to the other end of the sofa, I ready myself for the coming jump. Seeing that I'm not giving up, Cabal stubs out his cigarette and shifts forward, no longer quite so convinced about his earlier foregone conclusion. Smiling at Dr Gambon, who's now moved over to join Henri, I bend to undo the small buttons on the side seam of my skirt, allowing it to open a longer slash all the way up to my hip. Now at least I can run properly. With a last deep breath, I power forwards and leap off the sturdy armrest. The distance was never really in doubt, but my landing is anything but elegant and I carry far too much speed across the narrow desk and am forced to leap on again with a squeal, right over his chair, to the wide window ledge beyond. From there, with an abashed shrug, I hop back onto the desk and drop into a crouch. My eyes fall to the file Gambon was reading. I try not to react, seeing that it's actually mine. Wow, what I'd give to see inside that.

Smiling, my point made, I look up at the adults.

'So, when can I start?'

'Ha!' Henri Cabal exclaims with a clap. 'I like zis gerl. Well, *que sera, sera. Non?*' With that, he tells me he'll be in touch, and then leaves, stopping only to throw my tights back at me.

Dr Gambon chuckles and heads back to his desk. While I make myself presentable again, he takes the files on his desk and proceeds to open his wall safe. I am just nosey enough to see the combination which he types in and then also quick enough to look away before he catches me watching.

'Don't for a moment think that what you've just got yourself into is going to be easy. It most certainly is not. Henri does not suffer fools and he looks after the P and P stream. And right now that stream consists of precisely you, and only you. He failed everyone else who tried out for it. So, enjoy. But, all that aside, I would be most intrigued to know what you find out about your Mr John Wei, there.'

I nod.

'So I'm not going to get into trouble for what happened earlier?'

He shrugs disinterestedly.

'Candice Hardcastle is many things, but a nice girl is not one of them. I imagine she's had this coming for a long time. Just try not to do it again, though, understood?'

'Yes, Sir.'

'Good, now get out. I have work to do.'

With an amused smile, I nod and make a hasty exit.

*

What kind of reaction I was expecting upon my return to the study, I'm not quite sure. While Milly's obviously grateful that I stepped in when I did, I suspect she's also worried that I've actually made things worse. I guess only time will tell. It was a fairly uncharacteristic outburst earlier, but hopefully it's put the Grey's crowd on notice that our year group isn't going to be quite the pushover from now on that maybe it once was. One thing we're all agreed on, however, is how amazed we are that not only did I get no obvious reprimand, but that I actually seem to have been allowed to switch schools: something which I'm told is almost unheard of this early into someone's first term.

The rest of the day passes as a blur, though I hear nothing more from Henri Cabal until halfway through prep time, when Milly announces she has to head over to the Geology school, a euphemism I now know to mean B-School. About forty seconds after she has left, my phone vibrates. It's a message from Cabal and it simply states:

Follow her. But don't be seen.

I curse and hurriedly cap my fountain pen, grab a training hoodie, wrench on my trainers and rush after Milly. She's obviously in a hurry because she's already long gone by the time I reach the bottom of the stairs. I turn to the small group of sprogs sitting on the bottom few steps.

'Hey, any of you see where Milly Butterworth just went?'

They point towards the back door, which I reach just in time to see her dart behind a hedge, some way off in the distance. I watch from the shadows, perplexed by how cautious she's being, constantly darting looks over her shoulder. Does she know I'm following her? She joins a narrow road leading into the woods, which tallies with where I remember the Geology school to be.

The woods are spookily quiet as I edge into them. The moon casts long, silvery beams of light across the road, so I hang back at a safe distance, darting from one tree to another for cover. After a couple of minutes, I come to a small bridge. Beside it, stuck firmly into the ground, is a very prominent signpost.

THE GEOLOGY DEPARTMENT AND ITS GROUNDS ARE STRICTLY OUT-OF-BOUNDS TO ALL STUDENTS NOT ENROLLED WITH THE FACULTY.

I hesitate—but only for a second. Then, with a wry smile, I run on until I reach the first of several shallow pits. Ribbons of yellow cordon tape stretch around the boundary of each. Standing in the centre of the clearing, just beyond, is the Geology block itself. It's an impressive Romanesque building with marble and sandstone pillars and balconies adorning it. Front and centre, a wide flight of steps leads up to its main entrance. So why is it then that Milly's sneaking off around the side of the building?

Intrigued, I creep after her, making sure to stay well in the shadows, hugging the wall. When I reach the far corner, I slow and ever so carefully peer around it. She has stopped twenty feet away in front of a back door. A small, underpowered, wall-mounted lamp illuminates her face. She seems wary and on edge and keeps darting paranoid glances left and right. I watch as she reaches up and takes hold of the lamp—and then, to my surprise, pulls it from the wall. Only it doesn't snap off, but rather is attached by some sort of lever, which, when released, returns the lamp to its original position. There's an audible click and she hurries inside.

I stare after her, dumbstruck and, not for the first time today, lost for words. The door closes again just as I reach it. Cursing, I gently reach for the lamp and slowly pull it from the wall. There comes the click. With a burst of excitement, I edge the door open.

Inside, a narrow flight of steps leads down to some kind of basement. A string of ungenerous bulbs provides just enough light not to trip. With a firm grip of the banister, I creep down the stairs, freezing at every scrape and scuff. Even my breathing sounds loud in the otherwise perfect silence. Once at the bottom, I peer around the corner to find myself in a crypt-like wine cellar. Aisle after aisle of dusty racks stretch off into the gloom.

Suddenly I jump as a loud, violent grinding noise shatters the silence. Just as quickly, everything then goes quiet again. With my heart in my mouth, I remain frozen, deadly still, barely daring even to move a muscle. What the hell am I doing here?

I give it a minute, and then tiptoe towards the end from which the noise came.

But all that greets me there is a dead end. No doors, no exit, just another wine rack bolted to the roughly hewn rock face. And neither of the end aisles offers up any clues, either.

Stumped, I'm on the verge of giving up when my eye catches a glint of light from one of the wine bottles. Unlike the others around it, all of which are covered with a thick layer of dust, this one's neck has been wiped clean. And pretty recently, too. The instant I take hold of it and pull, I yelp and jump back as it, and a large section of wall, rears back and slides sideways to reveal a tunnel hidden behind.

'No way!' I gasp in astonishment.

For a second I don't know what to do. But with little doubt that this is where Milly must have gone, I dart through after her, and just in time before a hiss of hydraulics closes the entrance again.

The tunnel turns out to be an old, disused railway track. Running alongside it, where I now stand, is a precarious maintenance ledge. Like the stairwell, the lighting in here is rudimentary at best. To my left the tunnel rapidly disappears into darkness. The other direction runs on for about fifty metres before curving into a left-hand bend. But at least there's light that way. I half-picture Milly coming here to partake in some sort of nerdy Dead Poets' Society. Amusing images of her dancing around a torch-lit chamber chanting, 'O Captain, my Captain' play in my mind.

Once clear of the bend, the track straightens and terminates at a small, underground railway platform. It looks vaguely reminiscent of an old London Tube station. Some place long since abandoned. It appears deserted but I can hear the faint whisper of voices from somewhere nearby. As quietly as I can, I hop down, nip across the tracks, and scramble up onto the opposite platform. An old, faded sign reads 'MOD-WD Nettledown'. I make my way past it towards an exit halfway along the platform. Just as I reach it, my phone vibrates, announcing a new message. It reads:

Now get past the guards. You have one minute.

I stare uncomprehendingly at the phone. How could Cabal possibly know where I am? A proper look around, however, reveals several cameras dotted along the platform. Okay, so that's how. I give one of them a chagrined wave and dart a glance around the corner.

The passage is about thirty feet long. At the far end it opens onto a huge, brightly lit underground cavern of some sort. But now I understand the message. For there, standing at the end of the tunnel, are two armed guards in camo fatigues, idly chatting away to one another. Both have their backs to me, which I guess will make my approach easier. But I still don't know how I'm actually going to get past them. Though I'm sure something will come to me. At least, I hope so.

I take a moment to psych myself up. Then with three deep breaths and a last look at the ground I have to cover, I push off from the wall and accelerate towards them. Landing softly on the edges of my trainers, I manage to cover well over half the distance before they hear me. Startled looks flash across their faces as they turn. For a second neither does anything. Then they spring into action. Their movements are fluid and precise. In the space of a heartbeat they've taken a couple of darting steps backwards. Then, like a slap to the face, everything becomes clear. I slow momentarily as panic sets in. They're going for their guns is what they're bloody doing!

* * *

CHAPTER 8

DOWN THE RABBIT HOLE

Too late to turn back, I have but one option. I surge on as fast as I possibly can. My acceleration is obviously not what they were expecting. One appears to freeze completely, taken aback, it would seem, by the sheer speed with which I'm now coming at him. The other guard, in his haste, fumbles the strap of his holster.

For all I know I could well be screaming by this point.

The sensible, rational part of my brain seems to have completely checked out. That, or I'm actually clinically insane, because they appear to have every intention of shooting me. But suddenly it dawns on me that I might actually make it.

In an instant I'm upon them. But now how to get past them? Any attempt to push past and they will surely grab me. Better, I realise, to go over them. I veer across the path and leap up at the wall, where my foot finds good grip four feet up the crudely hewn rock. From there, I push off with all the strength I can muster. Tucking into a ball, I somersault right over their heads. It's not the best of landings and I stumble into the cavern before tumbling to my hands and knees. With a swish, I fling my hair from my face and look up in disbelief. Whatever this place is, with its industrial lighting grid suspended overhead, large, matted gymnastics area in the middle and bare rock walls, it looks more like the Batcave than anything—it's just that Alfred left the lights on.

A look to my left reveals a row of rooms set into the rock itself. The door to one of them—a massive, bank-vault-like apparatus—rests ajar, allowing a good look inside. The room is bathed in a deep blue glow emanating from several large wall-mounted screens. My eyes dart past two ducted fans set into the wall, and on towards a cluster of computer work stations. And there, amongst a group who are all staring at me, mouths wide with disbelief, are my housemates, Milly, Luther, Nigel and Anabel.

Before I can move, several strong pairs of hands grab me from behind and wrench me to my feet. Instinctively I lunge out, but an urgent shout from the other side of the hall stops me just in time. I'd recognise that drawly Gallic accent anywhere now. And there he is, standing in the doorway to one of the rooms. And he's smiling. That alone unsettles me.

'*Pas mal*,' Henri says with a shrug.

Scowling, I turn to the guards and point at their guns.

'Were you actually intending to use those?'

Neither replies, but the confused looks they shoot in Henri Cabal's direction don't fill me with confidence.

'Come,' he calls. 'We should talk.'

'You *think*!' I mutter.

Everyone's eyes follow me as I make my way across the hall and into the office. The instant he closes the door, they all break out into excited chatter in the hall.

To the left is a security station where a lone guard sits watching a bank of TV monitors. It has feeds coming in from all over, including outside the Geology block, inside the wine cellar, as well as inside the railway tunnel.

'So this is B-School, huh?'

'*Oui.* You want a tour?'

'*Bien sûr,*' I reply, grinning.

Our first stop is the Data Room. Suitably impressive; to call it state-of-the-art would be an understatement. It looks like the bridge of the *Starship Enterprise*. All backlit white facades, raised platforms, touch-screen keyboard panels and aluminium and mesh chairs. Three enormous curved screens are fixed to the front wall.

'Once zey 'ave showed you how to oose eet, you can try finding your Chinaman een 'ere, *n'est-ce pas?*'

Conscious of time, Henri then drags me, almost literally, from room to room. First, into some of the B-School classrooms, all of which are far more hi-tech than what's on offer in A-School. Then down a ramp in the far corner to the chemistry and electronics labs. Just beyond them is an audio analysis studio, a library, and then, one level down, a firing range. The loud retorts sound even through the thick, breezeblock wall. My eagerness is probably a bit too apparent because Henri quickly detours us off towards the big submergence pool. At about twenty metres deep, it's where they teach people to scuba dive. Last up is their obstacle course, which is laid out around the large underground staff car park.

Upon our return to the security office, all I want to do is race home to share this with Milly and the others, all of whom have already gone back to the house. Instead, Henri sits me down and begins explaining what he has in mind. None of it seems particularly open to discussion. I am to become a thief, he says. Therefore, my timetable is now to include learning how to pick locks, open safes, disable alarm systems, scale buildings and evade security guards. Whilst my agility and athletic abilities are fairly good, there's always room for improvement, he says. I am therefore to start training with a friend of his who is a Parkour expert, who'll instruct me in the urban art of navigating and traversing obstacles in my environment. Further, I am to practise floor and vault gymnastics, and in whatever time I have left over I am to come and learn Capoeira from him. All, he explains, in an accelerated effort to make me as supple, flexible and cat-like as possible.

'Because 'ow else do you expect to become a cat-burglar?' he asks rhetorically.

Funnily enough, I don't actually recall ever saying this is what I wanted, but I'm not about to argue, either, because it actually sounds quite fun.

Their hope, he explains, as he begins opening up a black cardboard box, is that in as short a time as possible I can start working for MI13, stealing items of interest and planting anything from listening devices to who knows what else.

'*Bon*, so, your new phone.' He lays a dull-grey metal handset on the table. 'Eeet ees called a PADDLE. A Personal-Audio-Digital-Data-Leverage-Exchange, but zee kids 'ere mostly just call zem iSpys.'

'That's funny.'

From his frown I'm not so sure he agrees. It's a sturdy, yet surprisingly light handset with an all-glass touch-screen front. The ports all have rubber gasket seals and, he tells me, the internals are waterproof coated.

'Not exactly particularly feminine, though, is it?' I note with a teasing smile.

He snorts and snatches it back.

'Standard eesue to everyone in MI13. Eet will allow a surveillance team to connect via a single encrypted network, while still looking as eennocuous as any normal mobile. Eet also 'as 'igh-speed internet access and a voice command function which actually works, which ees good, *non*? Super 'igh-res camera, freunt and back. The rear one 'as un infra-red mode and zee flash ees also a projector to give briefings een zee field, eef needs be. Zere's a removable earpiece and eet all meets Mil-Spec 810 and IP54 standards, so ...'

I cast him a blank look.

'Eet ees waterproof and you can drop it down zee stairs.'

'Okay, well, good to know. So how deep can it go?'

'Deeper zan you.'

*

The next morning, as the rest of the school head off to their 'normal' classes, I follow my friends excitedly across Big-Field and into the woods. This time we use the Geology block's front entrance. There, in one of the back rooms, one of the boys shifts a large bookcase aside to reveal a service lift. I turn to Milly with a puzzled look.

'Hold on, if this is here, what were you doing skulking around out the back last night?'

'See, the school porter isn't in on it, so he always goes and locks up after class. If we need to get in, we just use the back door.'

Luther sniggers childishly and gets several unimpressed looks from us girls.

'I still can't believe you followed me,' says Milly.

'I can't believe you didn't spot me! Some spy you are,' I tease.

The lift slows and a melodic *ping* announces our arrival in the small lobby that serves as the entrance to B-School. A large mosaic of the school shield dominates the centre of the black marble floor. Sitting in the corner, behind a solid wooden desk, is an old lady wearing tinted glasses. Her eyes follow us like a hawk's and her hands remain firmly out of sight below the desk. One by one, we pass by a palm scanner before walking down a tunnel into the main hall.

Once there, Milly points to a pamphlet holder affixed to the wall beside the entrance. Every day, she explains, Professor Cadogan, the school's real Geology teacher, stocks it with a specially prepared 'nugget' covering a different Geology topic.

'Well, they can't have us sounding like complete idiots whenever someone asks what we actually learn here,' she explains.

Today's is entitled 'Igneous Rocks'.

Igneous rocks (etymology from Latin ignis, fire) are rocks formed by solidification of cooled magma (molten rock), with, or without crystallisation, below the surface, either as intrusive (plutonic) rocks or on the surface as extrusive (volcanic) rocks.

Over on the mats, the first class of the day is assembling. I watch with curiosity as a lithe, athletic-looking Eurasian woman brings them to order. She begins with a demonstration—namely how to take on four fully grown men all at once. Barely a few frenetic seconds later and all four are flat on their backs, groaning. She calmly puts a hair-band in and turns back to the class.

'So, whatcha think?'

I turn and my heart skips a beat as I find myself again face to face with Captain Lennox. I stammer, unable to find anything to say. He points at the woman.

'That's Ms Suntory, our Close Quarter Combat instructor.' I note his voice is tinged with a healthy mix of admiration and respect. 'Suntory is a cover name, obviously.'

Finally finding my voice, I smile and say, 'Obviously. I'm just not sure what to be more concerned about; her beating me up like that, or the fact you guys think it's even necessary to teach it.'

'Ha, don't over-think it. It's more of a precaution, really. Never hurts to be prepared, though, does it?'

'Nah, it'll just hurt learning it.'

He laughs and begins to move off, before turning back to me.

'Hey, stay put there for a sec. You're with us this morning while Cabal gets everything set up for you. Should be kind of fun, though.'

Seeing me watching her, Ms Suntory sets the class an exercise and makes her way over.

'You're Heather Foxton?' she asks stiffly. I nod and she extends her hand, which I take with an apprehensively wary look, half-expecting some kind of judo throw to come at any moment. Thankfully it doesn't.

'You waiting for something in particular?'

'I'm not sure. He just told me to wait here until he comes to get me.'

'Well, you want to learn something while you wait?'

'What, like some martial arts, you mean?'

She permits just the faintest trace of a smile to appear, before turning back to her class.

'Come. This lot aren't far ahead of you.' She calls them together. 'Who can tell me why we aren't teaching martial arts here?'

With an embarrassed look, I stare at my feet as a pupil raises his hand.

'Because they're too prescriptive, Miss. Anything built around a strict framework of rules and etiquette is a drawback in a real fight situation.'

'Exactly. So our aim is to teach something simple, yet robust enough that it can be adapted to suit nearly any situation. And few martial arts give you that flexibility. And why do we like to keep things simple?' She volunteers a slightly built, Middle-Eastern-looking girl in the front row.

'Because adrenaline clouds the mind, Miss.'

'Correct. I'm impressed,' Miss Suntory exclaims. 'What's made you all go and study so hard?'

'Yeah, *I wonder*,' I muse wryly to myself as she divides them into twos and begins demonstrating a series of techniques so simple that even I, a complete novice, grasp them almost immediately. All are incredibly fast, yet brutally efficient. And there seem to be no rules. Just whatever it takes to win, using whatever is at hand at the time, be it a Bic biro, a hardback book or a rolled-up magazine. I'm intrigued and edge closer as Miss Suntory stops one pair and gathers the class around.

'Remember, fast and fluid. Never hesitate, or it'll be used against you. And watch their feet! How someone shifts their weight will tell you all you need to know about where they intend to strike next.'

To demonstrate, she has one of the assistant instructors lunge at her with a rubber knife. I'm rather hoping they don't actually expect us to ever come up against someone with a real one! Effortlessly she snaps into action, deftly sidestepping his lunge. Suddenly his hands are in hers and in one fluid movement she pulls him forwards, off balance. A quick pivot backwards, a twist of the hands, and she sends him flying head over heels into a sprawling heap on the mat.

'And look where I am now,' she says. 'The right amount of pressure here and you dislocate not only the wrist but also the elbow and shoulder. Everyone follow? Good. Now you try.'

Somewhere behind me I hear my name being called. I turn to see Captain Lennox heading for the lift with a group of pupils hurriedly following to keep up.

'Foxton, you've got twenty minutes to go get into some civvies,' he shouts.

'Sorry, some what?'

'Civilian clothing, Foxton. Now move it.'

'Where are we going?' I ask.

'To put your arse in the grass. Field trip. Come on, strap it on, people. I ain't got all day!' he shouts, clapping, and we all run for the lift corridor.

*

An hour and a half later, we find ourselves in the middle of a rather grim housing estate, surrounded by a mass of derelict-looking tower blocks. The sky's a dark, threatening shade of grey. A perfect mirror for the atmosphere around here. The rubbish doesn't appear to have been collected in ages and the weeds have been allowed to grow unchecked between the paving stones.

'Right,' Lennox says, once everyone is assembled. 'I take it you all know about the recent race riots that happened here?' The burnt-out shell of a nearby car serves as the most obvious reminder of that. 'So it's not too hard to imagine that the residents might be a little wary of strangers. Your mission,' he says with obvious relish, 'is to get onto the balcony of one of these flats. You must have a drink in your hand and be accompanied by the property's owner, and all within the next ten minutes.'

I am not the only one to groan.

'Use whatever cover story you choose. This is all about getting what you want from those with absolutely no reason to help you. And, just to spice things up, you should know that we posted notices through their mailboxes yesterday, supposedly from the police, warning occupants of the dangers of letting strangers into their property.'

The group deflates even further with a few moans of, 'Oh, great,' and, 'Yeah, cheers for that.'

He flashes us a fabulously disingenuous smile and then hands out everyone's allotted flat number. Several pupils immediately run off towards their tower block. A minute later, I'm the only one still standing on the pavement. I just can't fathom why someone would let a complete stranger into their home. I mean, what idiot would do that?

After two minutes, I'm still at a complete loss for ideas. But then a small car drives past. For a moment I take it for a driving instructor. Then I see the distinctive logo plastered onto its side. And suddenly a flash of inspiration comes to me. To Lennox's surprise, I gasp and run off, but not towards the estate. Instead I run in the opposite direction, towards the nearby high street. Five minutes later, I'm back with a triumphant grin. He taps his watch in exasperation as I dash past him.

'Yeah, I know, I know,' I shout back reassuringly. 'I've got a cunning plan.'

'I should bloody well hope so,' he calls after me.

As I rush up the stairs, I pass a few of the others on their way back down. All look rather downcast and dejected. One floor up, I catch sight of another boy jumping back in alarm as a door is slammed in his face. Not a good sign. Unperturbed, I continue up to my floor and rush along the open walkway until I reach my designated flat. After a couple of deep, calming breaths, I whip my iSpy from my purse. Then I ring the bell and put on my warmest smile. It takes a moment before the door edges open, ever so slowly, on the chain. A nervous-looking old lady peers out through the gap.

'Hi,' I say enthusiastically. 'I'm Serena Nolens. I'm an intern with Foxton's estate agents, over on the high street.' I hand her the business card I swiped only minutes earlier from the trainee agent's desk. 'I was wondering …'

'No one's buyin' 'roun' 'ere,' she replies curtly. I'm just in time to catch the door before she closes it.

'Actually,' I say pleasantly, 'we're selling one down the end and my boss told me to put the ad in our window. But I forgot to get a shot of the communal gardens from the rear balcony and he'll kill me if I don't get it. I tried the neighbours, but no one's answering. I was hoping you might be so kind as to let me grab a quick snap from yours?'

I hold my camera phone up for effect. She glances warily up and down the walkway before re-examining the card. Her expression softens.

'And you're by yourself, are you, dear?'

'Yes, just me,' I say, flashing an innocent smile.

'Oh, all right then. Wouldn't want you getting into trouble, now would we?'

'That's awfully kind of you,' I gush as the chain comes off the hook. 'Wouldn't be able to trouble you for a quick glass of tap water while I'm at it, would I?'

*

I guess it would be too good to be true if it were all fun and games. Just after lunch Milly drags me back over to B-School for a guest lecture. She, Luther and Nigel have been buzzing about it all day.

'Oh great, nerds of the world unite,' I groan as she drags me to sit with her in the front row. My worst fears are confirmed the moment I lay eyes on the presenters. Receding hairlines, brown corduroy trousers and matching brown cardigans with elbow patches. What I wouldn't give for a sick note right about now.

'Good morning, boys and girls,' the first presenter begins in a nasal, sleep-inducing voice. 'My name is Neville King.'

'Yeah, king of nerds!' I sigh sarcastically under my breath. I roll my eyes at the filthy look Milly shoots me. 'Okay, fine,' I hiss. 'I'll try. But remember, you forced me to come. I told you this so wasn't my thing.'

She gives me the cold shoulder and swivels back towards Mr King. Turns out he is the director of signals interception at GCHQ. I shake my head. To my roommate that's clearly commensurate with having a celebrity in the house. I'm half-asleep by the time he gets to explaining how modern-day cyber-crime and its bastard cousin, cyber-espionage, have become vertically integrated components, not only of organised crime but also of national defence, and how its perpetration is no longer solely the remit of socially retarded youths locked away in their bedrooms.

'Takes one to know one,' I mumble. A moment later, a note lands in my lap telling me to shut up. I scribble the word 'Killjoy' and pass it back. Milly scrunches it up huffily and leans forward eagerly as Mr King turns on the projector and dims the lights. A black and white photo appears on the screen.

'Meet Owen Hamilton. American, this chap is. Almost shut down the UK's National Grid as part of a commodities trading fraud last year.'

Another photo appears and I stifle a yawn.

'Vadim Menyatov. Russian ...'

And so it goes on. Each time the projector whirs, a new face appears, accompanied by the same nauseatingly monotonous commentary. I start to wonder what's for lunch and whether I ought to clip my toenails before bed tonight. Thankfully, just as I'm about to fall asleep and, quite probably, off my chair, he switches off the machine and turns the lights back on. I'm relieved to see I'm not the only one pulling myself upright in my seat.

'... so if you ever see any of them down the supermarket, do let us know, won't you?' he drones, laughing cringingly at his own joke. I roll my eyes as both Milly and Luther throw their heads back and howl with laughter.

He then hands over to his colleague, David Simpson, the head of algorithmic large number analysis and research at GCHQ. The lecture goes from bad to worse as he launches into another mind-numbingly boring monologue, this one about the exploitable weaknesses within most commercially available operating systems.

As Milly and Luther edge forward keenly on their seats, notebooks poised at the ready, I ponder the chances that the ground beneath me might open up and swallow me.

'Please, Lord, make it end!'

*

That evening, while the others are all busy with their prep, I'm told to join another group of students outside the main school building. There we wait for someone called Frank Sable—who, I'm told, heads up the covert espionage school—to collect us.

Again our destination is a not-too-distant estate. Only this time, an industrial estate. We arrive to find it deserted and park on a crossroads junction near its centre. The whole place is bathed in a sickly artificial glow from the overhead street lamps.

'Right, gather round,' says Frank. 'What we're going to cover tonight are the basics of mobile field surveillance. This is one of the core activities that we assist Five and Six with, regardless of your primary speciality. It's the bread and butter of MI13, if you like. Right now about a dozen of your peers are out on live operations with Five's A4 watchers, so pay attention, yeah, because it could be any of you up next.'

That gets a few excited whispers going around the group. To think that had I stayed at my old school, right now I'd probably be writing some boring essay. Instead, here I am, being taught this.

'The whole point is, of course, to follow someone without being noticed. And if you're asking yourself how hard that could really be—well, pretty damn' hard is the answer. Because, done properly, it's a complicated and intricately coordinated dance that can be screwed up by even the smallest of mistakes. Drop the ball for a second and you risk months of work, not to mention your and your teammates' safety. So we're going to drill it and drill it until it's second nature. And then we're going to drill it some more.'

He divides us into groups of three and then allocates each group a more experienced pupil to act as the target.

'First, you need to understand all the roles and the lingo. So let's start with The Box. That's what we call the surveillance ring set up around the target's current location. Moment they leave, the point officer will broadcast a call of 'standby'. That's your signal to get ready at your initiation point, or IP. One by one, each team member falls in behind the target. Then we tail them to their next destination, where a new Box is set up. This continues until we either get what we want or they go home again. Sounds pretty easy, huh? *You think?* Ha! You *wish*!'

I'm starting to like Frank Sable and his dry, sarky attitude. With his long, mullet-like hairstyle and sloppy clothes, he's certainly nothing to look at. But maybe that's the point. He breaks into a wry smile and wags his finger at us reproachfully.

'Not even close. This stuff is like performing ballet whilst doing a crossword puzzle and having a telephone conversation with a call centre in India all at the same time. The trick, however, is to make it look effortless.

'Now typically we use larger groups, and you'll usually be in full school uniform, which we find works pretty well most of the time. But there will be occasions, like over school holidays, when we opt for more discrete surveillance techniques and smaller groups. But the principles remain the same.

'Okay, so the roles. For tonight's exercise we'll practise with groups of three. Number One is always the person closest to the target, whom they keep in sight all the time. So that means close, even up to a few feet behind them. Number Two follows behind Number One, but at a safer distance. Lastly Number Three, who is on the other side of the road, essentially opposite Number One.

'All clear so far?' says Frank, noticing a few puzzled faces. 'Don't worry, it will be in a minute.'

He moves us towards the junction and then takes the first group fifty yards up one of the tributary roads. There he puts them into their respective positions.

'So this,' he calls back, indicating two lower-fifth form boys staggered behind their target and a middle-fifth girl on the other side of the road, 'is your standard surveillance layout.'

We all nod.

'Right, there are a couple of scenarios which you'll need to be absolutely fluent with. These are when the target makes a left or right turn, enters a building or makes a sudden U-turn. The rest will come with time and practice.'

'Could be worse,' my neighbour whispers to me. I shrug, too intrigued to comment.

'Of course, the risk of having any one team member so close to the target for too long raises the chances of their being spotted. So we like to rotate positions from time to time. Okay, let's imagine for a moment then that the target's walking down the street, say on the right-hand side pavement, and they turn right onto another road. Here's what we do. Number One carries on across the road to become the new Number Three. Two speeds up to become the new Number One, right behind the target, and Three crosses over to become Number Two. Conversely if the suspect is on the left-hand side and turns left, these switches are mirrored.'

To demonstrate, Frank then has the demo group enact the moves.

'Okay, pretty simple, huh? Well, now let's suppose the target's on the right-hand side of the road, but this time they cross the street and go down a road branching off to the left. Number One will cross over diagonally onto the pavement opposite the target, thereby replacing Three, who in turn slows down as the target approaches and falls in behind them as Number One. Two just stays where they are.'

Again the demo group acts it out and again it all looks pretty straightforward.

'Now it's all well and good if the target doesn't suspect anything, but what if they keep making deliberately erratic moves to try to spot you? Don't forget, most of the people we're interested in will most likely suspect they're being watched. It's our job, therefore, to be there, but without them ever knowing it.'

I can't help but smile. I remember how, before term started, I would try to spot the team who were supposedly following me, but all to no avail. In the end I just gave up. They were like ghosts. But now I understand what they were doing. My mistake was always looking for the same person.

'... the worst case scenario is when you're right behind the target and they turn suddenly and come right back towards you. What do you think you do then?'

'I guess don't do anything,' someone suggests. 'Like, just keep going?'

'Yeah, that's pretty much all you can do. But easier said than done. Your instinct will be to stop just as suddenly or, worse, make an abrupt turn to go look in a shop window or something. But that's exactly what the target's hoping for. Because then it's game over; you're blown.

'So instead what we try to do is this: Number One, just keep going. Walk straight past the target. Don't even look at them. Cross the road to become Number Three. The old Three should cross over to slip in behind the target as Number One. And Two should have enough time to stop, make their own U-turn, and amble on slowly, allowing both the target and the new Number One to overtake them.

'But, like I said, it takes practice to have the presence of mind to get it right and in a manner smooth enough that no one will notice. But don't worry, that's precisely what we aim to do,' he adds encouragingly.

'Now, the last scenario is where things get tricky. This is when the target enters a building. Sod's law it'll be a department store or some large public area, and your team won't be big enough to cover all the exits quickly enough, so we just do the best we can. Number One keeps going and either waits farther on down the road or crosses over and waits there, with a wider field of view. Two follows the target into the shop or building, if it is safe to do so. Three comes across and waits on the opposite side of the entrance from where One is. This one's a little grey because there could also be a back exit. If there is then One goes around the back instead. Two still goes into the building and Three stays put opposite the front entrance. Whoever gets eyeball on the tango first radios the others.

'Now, to achieve all this, you'll need to use your iSpys to maintain an open channel with the rest of the team. You can do that in the menu. Select 'group forum' and then select the group name to patch yourself in. Any questions so far?'

No one has any so Frank assigns each of the teams a pavement approaching the junction. Then, one at a time, we begin practising each of these scenarios. At first it's all pretty straightforward. But then he goes and complicates things by instructing all the targets to approach the junction at the same time. Again and again we dissolve into fits of laughter as they pass by each other at the same time and the whole exercise collapses into chaos. Half of us lose our targets. Some end up reforming in the wrong teams, while others, seemingly in frustration, resort to calling out orders, thereby instantly blowing their cover.

'See, not so easy after all, is it?' Frank says after about twenty minutes of farce. 'That's why we'll drill this again and again until half-term. Then, when everyone's up to scratch, we'll take a trip into town and put this into practice on real life members of the public in a busy civilian environment.

'But before we finish for tonight, there are a couple of things I'd like you to bear in mind. First, don't be afraid to get close, and I mean really close, to your target. It's actually safer because people don't expect you to be that close.'

He takes someone's iSpy and holds it up. 'It's no coincidence that these things resemble commercially available smart-phones, but even so, be careful about unnecessary little movements, like repositioning your ear bud too often, or straining to hear what someone is saying. No one does that when they listen to music, so neither should you.

'But most importantly, always have a purpose. Know where you're going and why. Have a legitimate destination in mind at all times. It helps you blend in and look innocuous. Never just stand around aimlessly on a street corner. Only drug dealers and hookers can pull that one off without looking out of place.'

* * *

CHAPTER 9

BOYS, BEERS AND BRUISES

With everything I have on, the first real free time I get comes a couple of weeks later after Henri and I return from a day trip up to London. We spent it first in the National Gallery, just off Trafalgar Square, before wandering along the Mall towards Buckingham Palace. He wanted to get that one in before the summer tours stop at the end of September. But at no point were we there for the art, or to experience the splendour of the nineteen fabulous State Rooms on show. No, we were there to scope out their security and surveillance systems. Two very good and diametrically opposing examples, within easy walking distance of one another, of very different types of security systems: the museum's designed to stop people taking things out; the palace's to stop people even getting in.

The first part of being a thief isn't about learning to pick locks or crack safes, though I have already started those classes. It's about getting into the head of the professional security contractor who fitted the anti-intrusion system in the first place. And most of them follow the standard installation handbook play by play, Henri says.

As we toured the galleries and the lavish halls of the palace, he had me spot all the cameras, pressure pads, laser grid emitters, infra-red detectors and a host of other devices I'd never even considered or heard of. And all without attracting the attention of the museum guards or palace staff. Very quickly I began to spot the patterns. And some were obvious. But it was the unseen ones that Henri paid particular attention to. And some were truly ingenious. Who'd have ever thought that pressure pads are more often than not to be found about a foot into a carpet, not under the very edge? I certainly wouldn't have. Henri says that's to avoid some clumsy minimum wage cleaner sucking up the cables or damaging them with their vacuum cleaner. But that was the point of this whole exercise: to start getting me to think like that.

Over lunch in St James's Park we discussed some of history's greatest thieves. From American Bill Mason, who is thought to have stolen an astonishing thirty-five million dollars' worth of jewels from some of the most heavily secured houses in the world, to 'fellow' Frenchman Albert Spaggiari, Henri said proudly, and I had to try hard not to laugh, who pulled off one of the largest robberies in history by tunnelling into a Société Générale bank vault in Nice in 1976, from where he stole over sixty million francs. Most intriguing of all, however, was his story about Doris Payne from West Virginia, a glamorous African American lady, he said, who for five decades would enter jewellery stores, all dressed up to the nines, and through sheer charm and charisma would get the shop assistant to show her a number of pieces. Somehow she would get to the point where the assistant would forget exactly how many items she'd seen and then crafty old Doris would leave, having snuck a couple of them onto her person.

Finally back in B-School, though, and I am just crossing over to the elevator corridor when I notice the Data Room is empty. Perhaps this is the chance I've been waiting for, I think excitedly. I slip inside and settle myself down by the main control station. There I slip the Chinese man's wallet onto the console beside me. A flick of the touch-screen panel and the system jumps to life. I stare at the screens, utterly perplexed as to what to do next. Prodding several buttons does nothing. With a peeved look, I swivel to see if anyone is around who can help—just as the headmaster walks past. He stops and comes in with a curious look on his face.

'Having trouble?'

'Just a bit,' I say.

'Well, scoot over. If you're here for what I think you are then I am just as interested.'

In no time he has the system up and running. My excitement blossoms.

'Right, where to start?' he says, dancing his fingers above the keyboard in anticipation. 'This is your search. I'll help, but the direction we go in is up to you.'

I take a deep breath and think.

'Okay,' I say. 'Well, this thing can search government records, can't it? Alright, so how about seeing what records are attached to the UK driving licence in here.'

The search brings up an address. But when we look it up, we find it's now derelict. And records show that the car John Wei used to own in the UK has been crushed. Several other seemingly great ideas also all come to dead ends and disappointment. Though we do find that the name he travelled under to fly to Morocco was the same one as on the ID card. The travel documents also appear to be genuine, though beyond that we find no other evidence of Mr John Wei. It's only after I've exhausted nearly all of my good ideas that I go back through the sheets we've printed off and gasp.

'Hey, all these hits are pretty recent,' I say. 'So he'd have had to have arrived in the country in the last two years, right? Can you remember when they started using those bio thingies at the airport?'

Dr Gambon nods encouragingly.

'Well over two years ago,' he replies.

I ask him to run a photo comparison between the ID photo and UK Immigration's records. In no time we get an entry hit for an identical-looking man called Paul Wong. Finally something. I turn to Gambon with a look of excitement. It's funny, we're like two students doing a coursework project together.

'Okay, then,' I say, brimming with renewed confidence and enthusiasm. 'Let's run him.'

And now the real hits come up. With a few helpful prompts from Dr Gambon I soon find bank details and an address in Shirehills in Prestwich, Manchester. From there I find another driving licence and a registration number for a nice Audi.

In a little under ten minutes we've found the petrol stations he used to fill up his car, and a pattern soon emerges. While Greater Manchester City Council says they only keep their CCTV footage for thirty-one days, GCHQ and MI5 thankfully then store it all for considerably longer. Scarily quickly we trace John Wei/Paul Wong's regular drive to work and it leads us to an industrial estate called Chadkirk Business Park in Stockport. If you could even call it that, for it appears to be twenty acres of lovely-looking, two-storey buildings set in an old mill complex in the middle of the Cheshire countryside. But which building was he always going to? At this point I get stuck and Dr Gambon turns to me with an encouraging look.

'Well, you have tracked his movements to this complex. So how do you think you could narrow it down even further? What might help us pinpoint his movements more accurately?'

I furrow my brow and ponder deeply, wracking my brains as I tap a pencil on the console.

'Err, would his car have some kind of tracker, for breakdowns, maybe? Or for his SatNav?'

He shrugs and bobs his head, unconvinced.

'Ah, wait, what about his phone?'

'Now you're talking.'

'Can we do that?'

'Well, which carrier was he with?'

I riffle through my papers until I find Paul Wong's bank statements for the two years he appears to have been in the UK. I read out the name of his mobile service provider and Dr Gambon quickly brings up what looks like a backdoor entrance to the carrier's system. In moments, a map of the UK appears and it is quickly populated by a red line connecting all the places where Paul Wong's phone ever contacted a cellular tower. Zooming in on that part of Stockport, we quickly narrow the most frequent cluster of pings to a small collection of three buildings. A cross-reference against the complex's website list of current tenants in that area produces nothing that jumps out at us. One is a printer, another a fence manufacturer and the third a graphics company. Quick phone calls to each, asking if we could speak to Paul Wong, result in three people saying they've never heard of him. As I hang up the phone, I turn to Gambon and frown.

'What are we missing?' I ask. 'What would he have been doing coming here so often if not to work, or something? And how can no one know him?'

'There is an obvious answer,' he says. 'Think about it.'

'Oh, wait,' I gasp. 'What if they've moved?' Before he can reply I am redialling. He smiles and leaves me to it. Two firms have been there for some time, but the graphics house only moved in at the start of the month. I turn my iSpy to speaker and lay it on the console.

'Would you happen to know who used to rent your office space?' I ask.

'Not really,' the heavily accented girl at the other end of the line answers. 'Just that they were called Vanguard Logistics, or something like that. They left in a right hurry. Only know 'cause we found some of their headed letter paper still in the copier.'

I hurriedly thank the girl and hang up. Dr Gambon is already running a search through something called Companies House. The return lists Vanguard as having been dissolved, and coincidentally the day after I returned from holiday. The further details screen lists it as having been a private security consultancy. We share an excited look.

Bringing up another screen, Dr Gambon takes its company number and runs a search through a list of UK bank filings for a matching corporate account. Thanks to the UK banks regulator having recently demanded all account details from UK regulated institutions for anti-money laundering and tax evasion purposes, MI13 now also have access to that. In less than half a minute we have the company's entire financial history. Gambon looks anything but happy.

'This is most unusual,' he says with a deep frown. He sits back and rubs his chin. 'They have payments coming in and

151

out, some for very large sums indeed, yet not one transaction has a proper counterparty at the other end. All are simply between numbered accounts.'

In the end he proposes running the whole lot through a classified system, which he refers to as the Algorithmic Funds Origination Tracking System, or AFOTS for short. It all gets a little complicated, and I don't get half of what he explains, but from what I do catch, it was apparently set up by us and the Americans after 9/11 to allow the US Federal Reserve and the Bank of England to track terrorist funding payments—though quite how it does it, I am at a loss to explain.

'No saying how long it'll take,' he says, standing stiffly and rubbing his lower back. 'Maybe a couple of days. Possibly a few weeks, depending on how convoluted the trail of payments is between the company and whoever was ultimately bankrolling it.'

I glance at my watch, amazed.

'But that only took us like half an hour.'

He smiles and pats me on the shoulder.

'Welcome to the intelligence business in the twenty-first century.'

And with that he's off, leaving me staring at all the crumbs that John Wei/Paul Wong—or whoever he was—left behind him in the two years he was in the UK. What's amazing is that despite fake passports, cover names, and all that tradecraft, none of it made the slightest bit of difference when we really started looking for him. I can only assume he was either pretty sloppy, or, more likely, they were so confident that they'd never get caught after the Morocco incident they didn't feel the need to hide their activities any more than they had. Of course, once things went wrong, someone obviously panicked and hurriedly shut up shop and scarpered. I allow myself a proud little smile, buoyed by the thought that now we're onto them, it's only a matter of time before we find whoever was ultimately behind the attack. The game is indeed afoot.

*

With every passing day, my understanding of the lie of the land becomes that much clearer. And once I figure out the houses, everything else just sort of clicks.

Kell's is the biggest house and is obviously where the dossers are sent, for they don't seem to take anything seriously over there. But then again, their housemaster, whom everyone simply refers to as Jerry, seems so chilled out that it's not a great surprise. Grey's is without doubt the home of the rich and spoiled, and, as far as we in SH are concerned, it's also home to the galactically ignorant, right wing, white supremacist movement at Godolphin Park School. Sadly, they're also pretty good at sports, so they're generally treated like royalty by teachers and pupils alike. Sinclair's simply strikes me as being where the more academically minded pupils end up. Which just leaves SH, home of the not entirely untalented misfits, as I've fondly begun to regard us. But my friends here are warm and friendly, they look out for each other and they're inclusive of anyone new, which is great. It makes our social circle a little ramshackle and not the coolest crew in school, but none of them is worried about that, and, funnily enough, neither am I. With the exception of the Grey's crowd, our little clique doesn't seem to be particularly disliked by anyone, which is a plus. But then again, I realise, neither are we exactly embraced by any of them, either.

But despite this, life is good. The Parkour and P and P classes are fun but tough. The Capoeira and CQC, which I have also started, merely result in no end of painful bruises. This is the first time I have ever done anything like it and no one is more surprised than me by how quickly I pick it up. Somehow it just seems so intuitive to watch Ms Suntory demonstrate something and then be able to repeat it again almost immediately, and, where necessary, adapt it easily.

At the same time, I can't help but dwell on what really lies behind all of this, namely these odd yet apparently unique skills I have. Skills which I still have no good explanation for. Yet most of the adults around here obviously know more than they're letting on. So much for building trust.

Nonetheless, that irritation aside, what with so much happening, the first few weeks seem to fly by, the homesickness quickly passes, just as Milly said it would, and before I know it, the end of September is upon us.

*

Just before lunch, Luther barges into our study. He rubs his hands together eagerly and casts expectant looks at each of us in turn.

'Sae who's up fur th' end ay month brig party tonecht?'

'Me,' I shout, raising my hand.

'Aye, sae that's one,' he says, counting on his fingers. He turns to the others. 'Well ...?'

Nigel shrugs, knowing he doesn't really have a choice, and turns for support to Milly, who looks anything but enthusiastic.

'It's a dumb idea. Lander's bound to catch us,' she says warningly.

'Chill, Mill, we're nae gonnae gie caught,' Luther replies, a little too confidently, even for my liking.

Milly doesn't look convinced, but when Nigel caves, she finally nods reluctantly.

'Fine, but I'm telling you we have to be seriously subtle, okay?'

'Yeah, yeah, whatever. Laters, peeps.' Luther leaves with a cheery grin and a wave. Nigel follows right behind him. I turn to see Milly has put on her enormous headphones and is already back to her studying. I take a look at my own list of pending coursework, if I can even call it that, and decide instead to go and call my parents for our weekly chat.

*

We meet just after midnight at the top of the stairs. The house is in darkness and as quiet as a graveyard. At every creak underfoot we all freeze and clutch at each other, fearful of being heard. More often than not, it comes from under one of Luther's fat clods. The tension is taut and palpable as we creep along the main corridor towards the back door. At the forefront of all our minds is the horrible possibility that all the lights might suddenly come on to reveal Mr Lander standing there. Yet despite being nerve-wracking, it's also quite exciting as well. Outside of B-School, it's the most fun I've had since I got here.

We cast a wary look around before edging out into the car park. There we pause again with baited breath, checking to make sure there are no prowling teachers in sight. Satisfied, we tiptoe on towards the main path that leads to the treeline. We give the headmaster's house a wide berth and dart for the woods—or waddle, in Luther's case. From there it's easy to find the path that cuts through the woods to the small town of Sandford Abbey. It's only a few hundred metres to the bridge over the River Fosse. But in no time the canopy quickly thickens overhead and we find ourselves in near total darkness. Of course, no one remembered to bring a torch and soon the others are all tripping and stumbling in the dark. Well, all except me. I watch, puzzled and slightly bemused, as first Nigel, then Milly, trips over the same exposed root. Seriously, how did they not see it? It's like right *there*! Then Milly goes down again, this time into a large muddy puddle. I try desperately hard not to laugh as she curses Luther and his stupid idea.

'We should probably eat more carrots,' Nigel says quietly, as I help her up.

'Oh yeah, and why's that?' she snaps.

We round on her as one.

'Shhh!'

''Cause they help you see in the dark,' Nigel whispers.

'Nae they don't,' scoffs Luther. 'That's bollocks.'

'Is not! My nan told me so.'

'Yeah? Weel that's wa it's bollocks. Jeez, yoo're sic' a sucker. Dae ye e'en ken whaur 'at carrots story comes frae? It was jist somethin' th' RAF made up durin' th' Battle ay Britain tae hide hoo guid uir radar was. They put it out 'at aw their pilots ate was carrots an' 'at that was whit helped them fin' th' German bombers at necht.'

'You serious?' I ask. 'So how come then most people still believe Nigel's version?'

'Because most people are suckers. They'll believe whatever the government tells them to,' chimes Milly. 'And the government lies to the country pretty much all the time.'

'Really?' I say, turning in surprise. 'I'd never have pegged you for the conspiracy type.'

'There's nothing conspiratorial about it,' Nigel adds frankly. 'It's true.'

'Yeah, I'm serious,' says Milly. 'Governments change but the lies stay the same. They know most people in this country either pay no attention to what's really going on, or they're too thick to question it properly. Come on, it's the perfect set-up for them to get away with pretty much whatever they want to. Why else would they have let education standards slip so badly? Haven't you ever wondered why state schools are in the mess they are? It can't be that hard to provide good education, so it has to be because they're deliberately trying to create a voting public who're too thick and ignorant to question what's really going on.'

I stop abruptly, certain I just heard something. I grunt in annoyance as one of the boys walks straight into the back of me.

'Shhh, anyone else hear that? It sounds like ... music?'

No one answers. Not for the first time in my life I shake my head at how bad some people's hearing is.

'Whatever. Come on, I'm pretty sure it's this way,' I say, pointing to a narrow path which meanders off through the thick undergrowth. It emerges out into a small clearing by the riverside. There, off to our right, is the old stone bridge. And in front of us is a sunken bank where twenty or more pupils are gathered around a small fire. Everyone has a beer. Some are cooking sausages and marshmallows on sticks in the fire. Music plays quietly from a small docking station. A few couples have even slipped off into the dark bushes.

'It's brilliant!' I say to Milly. 'Now *this* is what I imagined boarding school would be like. How did it take them a month to organise one of these?'

Milly turns to me with a baffled look.

'How the hell did you hear this from all the way up there?'

I shrug evasively and set off quickly in search of something to drink, smiling to myself as I go. I seem to hear the sound of the approaching bikes before the others, too, and stop to watch. Half a minute later, three powerful motorbikes trundle to a halt up on the bridge. Their riders dismount and remove their helmets. When they reach the clearing I find my eyes lingering for longer than necessary on the leader, a tall boy with dark hair and chiselled good looks. As he walks past, he catches my eye for a few drawn-out seconds and smiles briefly. I'm not slow to return it. Then, embarrassed, I turn and gently bite my lower lip in excitement. That's when I hear *her* voice. Oh great, who invited Farabee-Peacock?

'Alex,' she calls commandingly without any attempt at subtlety.

As if her being here wasn't bad enough, she walks straight up to the biker boy, flings her arms around his neck and plants an unnecessarily smoochy kiss on his mouth. My smile rapidly turns to a scowl and I set off despondently towards the drinks stash. Why her? I mean, I wouldn't have minded if it was anyone but her!

I have just pulled a can free when I feel a tap on my shoulder. I turn and, much to my displeasure, see Augustus Cole standing before me. I sigh and make to pass by him.

'So I heard you're tight with Cabal,' he says aloofly. 'Seems he's taken you under his wing, is what I've heard.' He inhales deeply, causing his nostrils to flare unattractively. 'Maybe you might actually be worth getting to know, after all.'

'I'm sorry,' I say, turning back to him in disbelief. 'Is that really how you try to chat up girls? Wow, you're even more arrogant than I thought. Look, I don't know how to say this nicely, *Augustus*, but you're a two-faced turd. I see the crap you give my friends. If I thought that befriending you might put an end to it, I'd probably consider it. But I know what you're like. You're a snake, Augustus, and I wouldn't piss on you if you were on fire.'

'Suit yourself. But I'm not going to forget this.'

'Yeah? Well I'm not going to lose sleep over it.'

'Fine,' he snaps. 'Then go join your niggery-chink friends.'

'Oh, don't you worry, I will,' I fire back, before shoving past him and making my way towards my friends. What were they thinking, letting that lot into MI13? No one seems to have a good answer. Most just attribute it to the old boy network at its worst.

Half an hour and a couple of beers later, I've finally given in to the mouth-watering cravings I got each time a waft of cooking sausage drifted my way. And it is delicious. But then another familiar smell wafts my way and I turn to see Luther lighting up a huge spliff. He takes a long, lazy drag and a wide grin spreads across his face.

'Aye, thes is th' life,' he says dreamily, before leaning back and passing it on. The moment I take a drag, I instantly regret it and lurch forward, coughing violently, much to everyone's amusement. Worse, the good-looking boy with the motorbike is right behind me. I don't even need to look to know. I've been all too aware of where he's been all night long.

'God, it's strong!' I gasp, to a wise, knowing nod from Luther. Flushing red, I quickly pass it on, only too happy to go back to my beer.

'Aye, maan, everything be irie,' he drawls in a hilariously exaggerated but terrible Jamaican accent as he lights another. Behind me, I catch the tail end of a rather fraught conversation between Farabee and her boyfriend. I listen in keenly as he asks why she even bothered inviting him down if this was how she was feeling.

Without answering, she simply turns and walks off in a huff. The boy looks anything but pleased.

'What was that all about?' I whisper to Luther. He shrugs, far too stoned to be interested.

I look back to see the boy flick an unimpressed glance at his watch and sigh, obviously unsure now what to do. Farabee is already halfway up the path on her way back to Grey's. He catches me watching and, in a deflated sort of way, points to the empty seat next to me.

'Anyone sitting there?' he says.

'No. Take a seat. You look like you could do with one,' I say, beckoning him over. I'm not quite sure why I said yes. Chances are anyone dating *her* is likely to turn out to be just as big a twat as she is. Then again, were she ever to find out that I had been talking to him, it'd probably annoy the hell out of her, which would be worth it just for that.

Grateful, he sits down and, with a resigned shrug, pops the ring pull of his can of Coke.

'You're not drinking?' I say. 'There's loads, you know.'

'Thanks. But I have to drive back up to Eton tonight. What a joke. Coming down here was such a mistake.'

Eton. Well, that would certainly explain the accent. Desperately keen not to be nosey, but simply unable to resist, I ask, 'So you two ...' I point after Farabee. 'Are you ... you know?'

'Not really,' he replies, taking a swig. 'I'm not really sure what it is anymore. First she asks me to come down, so I do. I get here and she starts playing all offhand and weird. Then she just decides she's off to bed. No explanation, nothing. Nothing personal, but girls can be tough to understand at times.'

I fight the urge to let my satisfaction show and simply cheers his can with my own.

'Don't worry. The right girl won't be. I'm Heather, by the way.'

'Hey, Heather, I'm—'

'Alex,' I blurt. 'Yeah, I heard.'

He nods. 'I couldn't help overhear you put that idiot friend of hers in his place earlier on. Good for you,' he says. 'Sticking up for your friends like that.'

'Well, they're worth it,' I say proudly, introducing him to Luther and Nigel, both of whom seem equally stoned by now. 'Aren't you going to go after her?'

With a dismissive wave, Alex leans toward me and replies, 'Some people are more worth fighting for than others, wouldn't you say?'

I laugh and shrug innocently.

'Maybe ...'

'So tell me about yourself,' he says, turning keenly to face me. 'What's your story? Any dark secrets I should know about?'

'Oh, you have no idea,' I exclaim, before laughing out loud. My hand accidentally lands on his knee, though he doesn't seem to mind. That's a good sign. Because right now, with the warm, flickering glow of the fire lighting up his face, I suddenly feel ever so drawn to him. I don't think I hide the fact particularly well, not with my inhibitions already mellowed as they are by the beer.

It's about one in the morning and I'm finding myself getting along with Alex like a house on fire when, all of a sudden, a couple of boys up near the trees call for quiet. It takes a few more agitated 'hushes' before everyone falls silent.

'What is it?' Milly whispers urgently as she rushes over with Anabel in tow.

'I dunno,' one of the boys replies. 'I thought I saw something out there. Just keep quiet for a sec.'

Alex turns to me with an unsure look. I can tell he's thinking it's about time he leaves. I nod understandingly. Even though we've swapped numbers, I'm still gutted that he has to go already. With a smile, I go up on tiptoes and plant a quick kiss on his lips. My heart flutters when he returns the gesture, only his lingers a fraction longer than mine. Then he runs off up the hill. Milly flashes me a look that screams to know all the juicy details.

Where his two friends have been hiding all this time, I have no idea, but suddenly there they are again, right behind him. In seconds all three are on their bikes and speeding off into the woods, and not very subtly, either.

Milly turns and fires Luther a dark look, but he's too stoned to care.

'What happens if we get caught?' I ask her.

'What, you mean after I strangle fatso, here, for getting us into this mess? I don't know. If we're lucky, Lander will just get us to write pages of lines. But more likely, knowing him, we'll be in detention for weeks, or be restricted to house in our spare time. Take your pick. Either way, it's bad.'

Even in the half-light I can see Milly's attempt at casual bravado couldn't be further from the truth. She's genuinely scared and I feel kind of bad now for having pushed her to come out.

'Oh, cock! Not good, people,' one of the boys hisses as he jumps down into the clearing. 'Beaks in the woods.'

'How many?' someone asks.

'I dunno. All of them, I think. Quick, get the fire out, and someone stash all that,' he says, pointing urgently to the beer crates.

A bucket of water quickly goes over the fire, resulting in a loud and unsubtle hiss. The crates are soon hidden under the bridge and then we all stand in silence, waiting nervously to see what happens.

From within the woods a man's voice calls out, 'Over there!'

A few people immediately make a run for it along the riverbank. Once one goes, everyone does. Milly waves for me to follow her but in the panic and confusion that ensues I lose sight of her. With no other option but to retrace our steps from earlier, I sprint up the narrow track and burst onto the main path, only to find three teachers running towards me. With a colourful choice of expletive, I dart on into the woods on the other side. Quite where everyone else has gone, I have no idea, but I seem to be the only person over on this side. Regardless, I need to get back to SH before Mr Lander can lock the place down and do a roll-call.

To my right I see several torches flashing around erratically. Worse, somewhere off to my left someone has a dog. And, from the sound of it, it's not a small one, either. I run on even harder. The woods quickly thicken, slowing me considerably. I can't waste time like this. Thankfully the torches have now disappeared, and hopefully the dog has become someone else's problem. Though I half-expect it to leap out from behind a thick patch of shrubbery at any moment.

I make a ninety degree turn to the right and push on, praying this direction will bring me out onto Big-Field. I haven't gone far, though, when I find my path blocked by a wide swathe of unusually dense undergrowth. Cursing, I dart frantic looks left and right. Damn! There's no easy way around it. With little alternative, I plunge headlong into it. My heart is now racing furiously, partly from excitement, but mostly from the horrible realisation that at this pace I'm simply not going to make it back in time.

After a few metres, I literally have to lunge and punch my way through the shrubbery, so thick has it become. Finally I resort to crawling on my hands and knees below the thickest branches. There are still enough of them down here, though, to snag on my clothes and scratch my face, slowing me even more. Twice I have to stop to rip myself free. As I catch my breath, I feel my phone vibrate in my pocket. It's a message from Milly.

**HURRY—LANDER HEADING BACK—
HEAD OF HOUSE SAYS FIRE ALARM IN 3 MINS!**

Christ, can I even make it in time? A ten-minute walk under normal circumstances in less than three? Only one way to find out. I shove my mobile back into my pocket and plough on through with a renewed ferocity. Finally clearing the dense ring of undergrowth, I see a path just up ahead. The moment I reach it, I break into a wholly unrestrained sprint through the woods. The trees whip past in a dizzying blur of movement and I burst out onto Big-Field about thirty seconds later.

Panting hard, I duck down and check there are no teachers about. The coast looks clear. With only two minutes to go,

I race straight across the rugby pitch. Then it's a mad, frantic dash past the trees and into the car park towards the relative safety of the back door. I lunge for the handle, just as the fire alarm goes off—and slam into it with a painful thump.

'No!' I exclaim in desperation, realising some idiot's gone and locked it.

I let out a chain of expletives and spin around, frantically thinking of any alternative way in. Nothing good comes to mind. However, one thing's for sure: I'm certainly not about to hang around out here, meekly waiting for Mr Lander and his smug grin to turn up and bust me. Not after all that effort. Then, with a jolt, an idea comes to me. It's crazy—and completely insane, but desperate times …

I run around the side of the building and stop directly below our balcony. *Ha!* I was right. Snaking all the way up the wall is an old, yet pretty sturdy-looking cast-iron drainpipe. I give it a good tug. It holds firm.

'Oh, this is so not a good idea,' I whisper as I take several deep breaths and pull myself up off the ground. My trainers find grip on the large, roughly hewn stones. Then, flinging one arm up over the other, I begin climbing the side of the building. About six feet up, I begin to realise just how much harder this is than I thought it would be, and by the first floor I'm exhausted, and there's still a floor and a half to go! Panting for breath, I glance down and a wave of vertigo hits me.

'Oh yeah, this was real smart, Heather,' I say, cursing myself. The alarm has now been going for about twenty seconds and the first of my housemates is emerging out onto the patio, just around the corner. My arms are shot, my legs are shaking and I'm really starting to worry about falling. Suddenly the thought of getting busted doesn't seem quite so bad anymore.

But, never the quitter, I resolve to push on with gritted teeth until I reach the top. My muscles are getting dangerously close to failure. My arms feel like jelly that's on fire. With a last, desperate surge, I throw one of them up over the balcony rim and then frantically scramble and heave the rest of myself over. I land, exhausted, with an unsubtle thud on the flat, shallow roof and lie there, my chest heaving like I've just run a marathon. In seconds the window above me pops opens and a startled-looking Milly peers out. Her expression says it all.

'W—Where have you *been*?' she exclaims, before pausing as a wide-eyed look of realisation hits her. She points and gasps. 'Did you just …? No way! Are you completely insane?'

I groan and sit up. 'The thought did occur to me.'

She grabs my hand and pulls me in through the window. There is no time to waste and I hurriedly pull off my filthy clothes as Milly waits, fidgeting nervously by the door.

'What took you so long?' she asks as she hurries back to remove the pillows from beneath my duvet.

'What do you mean, *so long*?' I exclaim as I tug my sodden, mud-caked jeans off, almost tripping in my haste. 'I think I did it pretty fast, all things considered. I should be asking you how *you* got back here so quickly?'

'What do you mean? We just cut across the parade ground. Oh, please tell me you didn't go back through the woods?'

I give her a peeved look and pull my dressing gown on over my underwear. Then, barefooted, we rush for the stairs, taking them two at a time. Just outside the entrance to Mr Lander's private side residence, she glances at me in the light and frowns.

'Stop, wait a sec. Honestly, where have you been?' She licks a finger and wipes several flecks of mud from my face.

'Don't ask,' I sigh as she pulls a twig and several leaves from my hair.

'Well, tell me about it later. Come on.'

Grateful, I run after her. We rush out onto the patio to find the entire house already there and Mr Lander halfway through his roll-call.

'Nice of you two to join us,' he calls sarcastically from the front. 'I do hope we aren't disturbing your beauty sleep?'

'No, Sir. Just a long way down, Sir,' I reply in as calm a voice as I can.

'Hmm,' he grunts, and goes back to his clipboard. 'Nishitani!'

'*Hai*. Sorry, yes, Sir.'

'Sonakul?'

'Sir.'

'Stigant.'

'Yes, Sir.'

'Youl?'

I let out a sigh of relief. That was way, way too close!

* * *

CHAPTER 10

MORE THAN MEETS THE EYE

I have barely emerged from Sunday Chapel early the next morning, and am in mid-yawn, when someone calls my name. I turn to see Mr Decker, the school's PE teacher, approaching. We've never spoken, so I'm a little surprised when he comes over, all friendly and the like. Rumour has it he used to be in the army. He certainly acts like it, always in a tracksuit, half-marching around. Close up, he's built like a tank, with a neck as thick as my thigh.

'Hello, Sir,' I reply warily, squinting in the sunlight.

He nods politely.

'Miss Foxton, might I have a word? But preferably somewhere a bit more private.' He gestures at the groups of pupils scattered about the lawn nearby.

Uh-huh, and where have I heard that one before?

'Err, okay ...' I say.

He beckons me to follow him over to the Combined Cadet Force parade ground. He seems relieved to find it deserted.

'Right, let me get straight to the point, then, shall I?' he says. 'As you might know there was a river party last night, which was busted by the Common Room.'

I feign ambivalence and shrug nonchalantly.

'If you say so, Sir.'

'Seriously?' he exclaims, a little too confidently. 'That's how you intend to play this?'

I sense I'm not going to like where this is going.

'How about we agree not to lie to each other, okay?'

I'm on the verge of protesting my innocence again when I stop and reconsider.

'I'm guessing in your haste to get back to SH last night you got a little lost? Needed to drop the hammer a bit, did we?'

I swallow what feels like a golf ball as a hot and prickly heat envelops me. My mind races but the best I come up with is: 'I don't know what you're talking about, Sir. I was in my bed all—'

'What did we just agree not to do? I was there, alright. Standing behind a big tree with a pair of night vision goggles, and who do I see come flying past but …?' With an emphatic look he points at me.

I hang my head in resignation.

'How much trouble am I in?'

'Depends how much you cooperate now, I suppose.'

That catches me off guard.

'Cooperate with what exactly?'

'Heather, even beyond what I saw last night, you must know that the eyewitness reports from Morocco paint a rather interesting picture to anyone willing to believe the witnesses weren't all stoned. I don't think it's too much of a stretch to suggest that there may be certain things that you're capable of which most normal people aren't. We'd just like to know what they are.'

We are suddenly into deeply uncomfortable territory. My body language does nothing to disguise my discomfort.

'Foxton, relax, alright? Just accept that you're unique, deal with it, and move on, okay?'

I stare at him, speechless. Then, pursing my lips resentfully, I thrust my hands deep into my pockets.

'Look, all I'm proposing is we go to the gym and see what your limits are. A couple of simple tests is all.'

'Sir, I never asked for any of this!' I snap, my voice rising angrily. 'Why can't people just leave me alone? I don't know how I do any of it; I just can. You think I like it? Having to be so frickin' careful all the time, just so no one sees? Do you know what that's like? I hate it! I HATE IT!' I scream. With a burst of anger, I punt a small pebble off across the parade ground and stand, breathing heavily, my pulse racing and my face flushed. With a groan, I mumble, 'All I want is to be treated like a normal person …'

Decker watches the stone bounce off and turns back to me with an annoying smirk.

'You done?'

'No!' I shout back, my chest heaving.

'Good, because I think you're looking at this all wrong.'

'Oh, I am, am *I*?'

'Yeah, and I'll tell you why. You really think abilities like these should be hidden away, do you?'

'Yes, if all they seem to do is bring you a truckload of grief every time you use them. Absolutely!'

'Well, maybe that wouldn't happen if you stopped using them in front of all the wrong people. Look, if you can do even half the things we think you can, then these are skills you shouldn't be afraid to use.'

'How exactly does everyone seem to have such a good idea of what I can do when they've never seen it?' I demand.

He ignores the questions and carries on as if I haven't spoken.

'Let me put it another way. You know what the royal marines are?'

'Yeah,' I reply huffily.

'Good, 'cause I used to be one. Then you know it means I'm a hell of a lot fitter than most guys out there. I've worked with some of the fittest, smartest, strongest and most hard-core sons of bitches you'll ever meet. But I have never seen *anyone* move the way you did last night. And in near total darkness, too!

'You say you want to be normal? Well, define that. Go on. Because I bet you, you can't. I've got mates who're pilots with better than twenty-twenty vision, and yet other friends who can't even see their hand in front of their face without glasses like ice cubes. Basketball players slam-dunk hoops ten feet in the air, but I'm betting your mate Luther couldn't get more than an inch or two off the ground ...'

That draws a smile.

'Some people do marathons in just over two hours. Olym-pians can sprint a hundred metres in under ten seconds. Chess champions take on super computers, and win. The point I'm trying to make, Heather, is that people aren't born equal. Life's a crappy lottery of good genes, a bit of luck, and not much else. So why exactly is it that you feel some kind of debt of obligation to conform to the physical limitations of those less able than yourself by denying what you can really do?'

I hate him for putting it like that. He makes it sound so simple. But worse, he's trivialising the nightmare I went through so long ago. Why do adults never understand?

'Heather, I'm not asking you to do anything you aren't comfortable with, but look me in the eye and tell me you aren't even a little bit curious to know what you can really do.'

'Right now I don't know what I want.'

'Well, go have some lunch, calm down, think it over, and if you're interested, I'll be in the old gym at fourteen hundred.'

With that, he turns and saunters off across the parade ground, leaving me to my thoughts. It's not that I don't want to know, it's just I'm not sure if I'm ready for it. Letting others into what has been, up to this point, my little secret, feels daunting and invasive. Yet despite what I said to him, deep down the thought of being different, special even, actually feels quite appealing.

*

True to his word, Mr Decker is waiting outside the gym when I arrive.

'I think you've made the right choice,' he says.

'Yeah, well that's to be seen,' I reply.

He leads me inside and flicks an 'Out of bounds' sign on the door, so we won't be disturbed. Then he takes me upstairs to where the weights and exercise machines are. After forcing me to stretch, he starts with something easy: seeing how long I can hold my breath. To my surprise he shows no reaction as the seconds, then minutes, tick by. And when I finally gasp for air, he merely nods and notes the time down on a pad. Next he puts on some music and it's onto the weight machines.

At each station he ups the load until I can't lift any more. Once done, we move on to the next exercise.

I'm not sure what I expected, but this understated reaction thing is not it. Before long, I begin to question whether what I'm doing is even that out of the ordinary after all.

We take a short break, then he gets me onto the largest treadmill they have. If there's anything that is really going to stand out, it's this, and I find I'm only half-listening as he explains how he intends to increase the speed until I hit the stop button.

Do I really want to show him? I just don't know.

He drapes a towel over the digital display and starts the machine. The tread begins to roll, slowly at first, then faster and faster. After twenty seconds, I'm at a good jog; after forty, a sprint; and after fifty, it's flat out. Yet still he ups the pace.

'Enough …' I gasp.

'Rubbish, you were faster last night.' He increases the speed. 'Move it!' he bellows, barely an inch from my ear.

Now he's being annoying. I shoot him an aggrieved look. Maybe I *should* let it off the chain, just to shut him up? Fine, I think, you want it? Well, here it is. Petulantly, I stab at the button, and leave my finger there until it maxes out. I watch with a sense of amusement as my arms and legs disappear in a blur. Only Decker isn't smiling anymore. He seems genuinely taken aback, with a look of total disbelief etched across his face.

My point made, I'm just about to hit the stop button when a sudden movement in the far corner distracts me. The door of the old wooden cupboard there bursts open and from it stumbles an equally shocked-looking Milly. With wide and uncomprehending eyes she holds my gaze for a second. Then she runs for the stairs. Flustered, I lose my focus and one of my feet clips the other. In an instant, both are torn from under me. I land hard and, with a silent scream, am violently catapulted off the back of the treadmill. The combination of the highly polished wooden floor and my hopelessly thin Lycra does little to arrest the slide before I slam into the far wall. The impact drives the wind from me and I lie there, momentarily winded. Wincing at the friction burns, I slowly pull myself to my feet and swear.

Mr Decker looks even more bewildered. Understandable, really, when I see the end-of-workout summary. With an impressed whistle at the recorded top speed, I hobble off after Milly, who's already on the other side of the gym's car park when I emerge from the building. I shout pleadingly after her.

'What?' she calls back, guardedly.

At least she doesn't run away when I approach her. I suppose that's something. Her expression is nothing short of wary, but thankfully not as hostile as I feared.

'You want to tell me what that was all about?' she demands, confrontationally pointing back at the gym. 'Because that, that wasn't normal. I know what normal is, and that wasn't it.' She leans forward and her voice drops. 'What have they got you on, some kind of weaponised steroid programme, or something?'

I can't help but laugh. Then I realise she's being serious.

'No, of course not,' I blurt. 'It's just … well, complicated.'

She shakes her head ruefully and puts her hands on her hips.

'Well, you can tell me about it later. I have something more important to tell you.'

'What? About how weird I am? Trust me, I've heard it before.'

'No. I'm not too fussed about that. Curious, but not fussed.'

I do little to hide my disbelief of that.

'Look,' she says, sighing. 'Since as far back as I can remember I have been different to everyone I know. I mean, I could tell you the number plate of every car in this car park, right now, without looking. I can tell you their make and colour. Which has a scratch on its bumper and which one has a stuffed teddy bear sitting in its back window. How? Because I just ran past them. But I didn't really even look at them. I just take this stuff in. All day. Every day. It's all just up here.' She prods the side of her head. 'You think I am going to get freaked out because of what you just did. Please, give me some credit.'

'Okay, I suppose I see your point. Fine. So what did you want to tell me?'

'It's about your mother.'

'What about her?'

'It's … complicated. Come on, walk with me. So earlier on, just before service this morning, I was in the small Lady Chapel, out the back—you know, for a little peace and quiet.'

I give her an urging look.

'I'd popped into the bathroom at the back when two people came in. All hushed whispers but I recognised the headmaster's—'

'Gambon?'

'And Decker. Right off the bat, Gambon asks him to make sure no one else is around.'

'Serious?'

'Totally. And I only just managed to hide behind the door in time. Then Gambon asks about the bust. Seems Lander tipped them off about the party. But he wasn't interested in who was there, or anything. All he wanted to know about was what Decker had seen you do. When Decker told him how fast you were going, he just laughed and muttered something about how he could well imagine.'

'Sorry, he what?'

'Would you stop interrupting! I'm trying to tell a story here.'

'Alright. Fine. But can you do it any faster?'

Milly scowls at me.

'Anyway, so then Decker tells him and asks if he can take you to the gym this afternoon. Do a few tests, that kind of thing. Gambon says okay, which is how I knew to be up there. So then the conversation turns to discussing Gambon's reservations around, and I quote, "how having an unpredictable temper like yours floating around B-School might not be in the best interests of the service".'

I'm about to exclaim in protest but her look puts a stop to it.

'Hold on, it gets weirder, because then, totally out of the blue, he says something about how he knew your mum.'

'He *what*?'

'That's what he said. He goes how, having known your mother and what she was capable of, he's concerned that things with you could end up just as they had with her.'

I stare at her in disbelief.

Milly shrugs.

'I don't know. But it gets odder because then Decker says, "Sir, all due respect, but Genesis was totally different. Unlike them, she's a child. She's young and impressionable. Mouldable even. But the point is, she's controllable." But Gambon just scoffed and called him naive. He said if you're anything like your mother, then putting you in the field would be like opening Pandora's Box all over again.'

She smiles ruefully. 'Anyway, then Decker asked what your mum was really like, and Gambon gave this long, weary sigh. He said that despite all the stories, she was actually a rather sweet and endearing woman, but, like the others, was also incredibly dangerous and unstable—'

'Was? What do you mean *was*!?'

'Shh, listen. And how she would go from calm and chilled to all out high-order-violence—just like that.' Milly clicks her fingers for effect. 'He said her nickname was Lady Tackleberry, or something. Said the rumour was she even had some kind of armoury hidden in her own home.'

'I just don't get it,' I say, my forehead furrowed in confusion. 'Are you sure he was talking about *my* mum? I mean, don't you think she'd have mentioned the fact that she used to know my new headmaster? And I don't get all that stuff about her being violent and unpredictable. I know she has her moments, given what she does. That just goes with the turf. But I've never seen her lose her rag like that. Not like he's making out.'

'What does she do?' asks Milly.

I can't be bothered with the pretence any longer. Her eyes go wide when I tell her.

'Wow, that must be exiting!'

'It has its moments, I guess. But I didn't really want anyone to know,' I say. 'I was worried you guys might only want to know me because of that. Let's just say it wouldn't have been the first time.'

Milly nods.

'Yeah, I can see how that might happen.'

I smile, grateful for her understanding. 'Anyway, the point is she isn't a violent person. And she's never been a teacher, either, so I don't see what possible connection they could have had.'

'I'm sorry, a teacher? What's that got to do with it?' Milly says with a laugh. 'What? You don't think …? Oh, H,' she exclaims, 'you're missing the point. Gambon's no teacher. Nor's he ever been. He's the former head of MI6, is what he is!'

'He's w—what?'

'Well, he was until about five years ago, when he retired. How didn't you know? That's all this place is. The GPS headmastership is basically the cushy retirement job they offer each C when he or she finally retires from the service. Seriously, Hev, the only way they could've ever know each other as well as he was making it sound is if your mum was a …'

'Was a what?'

'Well—a—a spy!'

I'm speechless. Impulse demands I tell her not to be ridiculous. But it suddenly occurs to me that, in actual fact, I really don't know any better. I curse B-School, Godolphin Park, and all the teachers here for their incessant encouragement that we question everything. Because now I find myself doing just that with all I thought I knew about my own mother, my father and pretty much my whole life. I ruefully recall Mr Lander saying how everything might change. I didn't think he was being quite so literal. Now I don't know what to believe anymore. All of a sudden I have so many questions, and so pathetically few answers.

'Okay, there are just way too many fag ends flying around here at the moment. Seriously, is this what this place does to you? Turns you into some kind of paranoid fruitcake who sees conspiracy everywhere?'

'Of course. But think about it for a moment,' says Milly. 'The theory has merit, you know.'

'Well, right now I don't know what I know. Except that Gambon seems to be in the middle of this whole damned mess. Did you know he keeps files on everyone up in his office? What I wouldn't give to see what's in mine now.'

'So why don't you?' Milly suggests with an uncharacteristically rebellious look. 'I mean, Cabal's been teaching you how to break into places for a fair while now. What's the point of all that training if you don't put it to use?'

*

The idea plays in my mind for a good few weeks. But every time I consider trying it, I lose my nerve and chicken out at the last minute. All the while my training intensifies. By the end of October, I finally suss out how to pick Yale locks, or pin tumbler mechanisms. Henri manages to get us a tour of the Chubb building in Wolverhampton as part of a Ministry of Trade and Industry inspection so we can play around with a number of new locks about to come onto the market. Quite who would actually fall for my working at the Ministry, I don't know, but the trip is interesting and it's insightful to get a handle on the next generation of locks.

At the same time, after having played things very cool at the beginning, almost to the point where I thought he simply wasn't interested, Alex begins messaging me and we quickly build up a pretty impressive chat history, texting nearly every day and speaking at least several times a week. It sounds so stupid, and I barely have the nerve to admit it to anyone other than Milly, having only met him the once, but I think I'm falling for his calm, laid-back charm.

Despite the distractions, no matter what I do, I can't shake the germ of an idea which Milly planted in my head. It's only after having spent almost all of half-term in the company of my mother—the rest with Alex, hanging out, going to the cinema, having dinners even—all the while dwelling on what Gambon had said, that I finally pluck up the nerve to go through with it.

With all my gear packed into a slimline backpack that fits snugly enough so not to snag on anything, I sneak out of SH and into the main school building. Given that it's three in the morning—the optimal time for this sort of thing, according to Henri, because it's when people's guard is at its lowest— the main building is in complete darkness and eerily silent. The soft step Five Finger Gecko booties I was given by Cabal certainly live up to their name and I dart down the corridors like a ghost. Complementing them is the complex-inducingly tight, black, IR-reducing suit I also have on. Perhaps it's overkill but I'm not taking any chances with what our crafty headmaster might have set up to protect his office. Getting caught would be deeply humiliating and something Cabal would give me no end of stick for.

As I creep up the stairs and along the corridor that leads to his office, I become aware of a faint, distant noise. The more I listen, the more it sounds like someone humming. Then comes the squeak of rubber soles on a tiled floor. I drop into a squat and wait with baited breath. Now is not a good time for this. There are few options for escape if the night porter, who I presume this is, comes up to the first floor. The headmaster's reception area offers almost nowhere to hide and I'm a little beyond trying to hide beneath his secretary's desk. To my displeasure, the whistling only gets louder. Then the dim glow of a torch illuminates the bottom of the curved stairwell.

Oh, no, no, no! This is not happening! I spin round in alarm, trapped and with no way out. And with no excuse for being here either.

I look down at my Gecko boots and matching gloves and suddenly the craziest, stupid idea pops into my head. These things are probably the coolest toy they've given me. Mimicking the little lizards after which they're named, the boots' soles and the gloves' palms are made up of row after row of gill-like lamellae, each of which is covered in microscopic synthetic setae, or elastic-like hairs. Roughly ten thousand of them per square millimetre. Each hair has a diameter of about ten micro-metres—about half a human hair. Each of these is then capped with several hundred spatula-shaped tips. What this allows is the creation of an attractive van der Waals force between the fabric and the walls. Perfect for what I have in mind now, as the elderly porter begins his laborious ascent of the stairs.

I press my hands to the wall, out either side of me, just below shoulder height. Then, with my arms braced, I heft myself up off the floor. My feet quickly come up to grip just below my hands. Then I power myself up. With no time to waste, I do this again and again until my head nudges the ceiling. Then I edge forwards and brace myself in an awkward X shape, with my bottom thrust up at an obscene angle, almost touching the ceiling.

I slot into place, not a moment too soon, just as the porter reaches the upper landing. He wheezes for a moment or two and then advances slowly along the corridor, his shaky torchlight illuminating the way ahead. He seems completely oblivious of me, spread-eagled out between the walls above him. I don't dare move for fear my grip might weaken. He's moving so slowly. Surely there is nothing to see up here. After ten seconds, my arms and legs begin to shake. After twenty, so too do my abs. And after half a minute, my face is scrunched up into a mask of agony as I bite down on my lip to stay quiet. The first trickle of sweat works its way down my nose, hangs there for a second, then falls to the ground. I pray his eyesight is as bad as his fitness.

What the hell is he up to, plodding around in the reception area like this? Just as I think my limbs will fold, collapsing me into a painful and humiliating heap on the floor, he finally reappears and ambles back down the stairs. I wait another ten agonising seconds, just to make sure he doesn't come back, and then peel away my finger tips and toes to break the seal, and drop, exhausted, to the floor. I fall back against the wall, where I rest for a minute, wringing my aching arms and legs.

Picking Gambon's lock is nothing after that close shave and I have it open in under thirty seconds. Then I pause in careful deliberation. It was all too easy. Taking a can of Evian facial spray from my pack, I empty a good burst of it into the doorway. Instantly two red beams appear refracted in the micro-droplets, one beam at knee height, the other at chest height. Smiling, I delicately slip between them and pause again. Dropping down, I gingerly lift the edge of the carpet which covers most of the floor. Sure enough, about a foot in I see the first of what I imagine are several pressure pads. Advancing on my hands and knees, I skirt around the carpet and crawl behind his sofa. Another burst of Evian mist and two more beams appear, blocking access to the desk area. However, a repeat of my gazelle-like leap from the top of the sofa's backrest lands me safely on his desk. This time my insanely grippy boots stop me from overshooting again.

From here I step over onto the sideboard below the painting that swings open to reveal his safe. A small UV black light torch and some special glasses reveal the four number pads that comprise his passcode. Thankfully they're the same ones I remember him using the last time I was in here. Once I have it open, I take a quick photo of the contents on my iSpy for comparison later, just to ensure I put everything back precisely as I found it. I carefully remove the thick pile of files and retreat back to the desk. Perched on its edge, I flick through them until I find my own. Another burst of spray tells me there are no more beams nearby, and a scan of his chair with a small electromagnetic field detector reassures me he doesn't have any wireless pressure pads in his big leather chair. Satisfied, I comfortably settle into it and begin reading.

The profile page gives all the basics. My age, date of birth, address, et cetera. One sheet over, I get a nasty surprise. A document I have never seen before, but one I have often imagined. It hits me harder than I thought it would.

Consent to Adoption
The Adoption Act 1976

Name of child: *Heather Nicola Speirs*

Before signing this form, you are advised to seek legal advice about consenting to adoption and the effect on your parental rights. Publicly funded legal advice may be available from the Community Legal Service. You can get information about this or find a solicitor by telephoning the number given below.

I, the undersigned: *Vanessa Speirs* consent to the making of a final adoption order in respect of *Heather Nicola Spears* (my child), who is the child to whom the attached Birth Certificate relates, in favour of: *John and Emily Foxton*

(the applicant(s)).

I read it again and again in the dim red glow of my head-torch. The lump in my throat gets bigger with each re-read. It's the first time I have ever seen my biological mother's real name. My parents have never said much about my past, having always claimed they know nothing of it, which merely served to create a deep sense of longing to know more. A yearning which is instantly reignited, and in a major way, upon reading this.

I turn my attention to the next document in the pack and things really start to get interesting. It looks like a deep background summary on me. Time and again the documents make mention of something called Genesis, but never with any explanation.

Every minute or so I have to tear myself away and listen intently for any sign of movement within the school block. But thankfully it's all peaceful now.

Then comes a handwritten note from the current head of MI6 to Gambon supporting my enrolment with Godolphin Park. Justification is cited as '... a clean background check, the possession of clear and obviously utilisable abilities— potentially on a par with anything seen in Genesis'—there it is again—'and as a potential lure for Athena (if speculative reports of her survival are to be believed) ...'.

I ponder those last few points with confusion. A small, nagging suspicion at the back of my mind quickly forms into an all too real possibility. If Milly was right that my real mother could have worked for MI6, then it would make sense for her to have had some kind of operational code name. Could Athena have been it? And if it was then does that mean they are really suggesting she could still be alive? The idea and its ramifications threaten to overwhelm me. It is several minutes before I can even continue, so distracted am I now by this idea.

Next comes a copy of the ballistics report from the Moroccan police. It is curiously morbid reading. From this, it seems that John Wei was killed by two shots—from two very different weapons. There was the policeman's bullet, which shattered his right shoulder. But then there was also a shot from behind us using a far larger calibre weapon. A rifle, Interpol suspect, going by fragments of the round which were later recovered. Quite possibly a British AS50 .50 BMG sniper rifle. The write-up shows it to be no insignificant piece of kit and the size of the round certainly explains how it made such a mess of my attacker's head. But it also means someone was looking out for me. That someone was watching, waiting, ready to step in the minute things got out of hand. All set up and ready to fire. But surely that also means whoever it was had to have had a heads-up that the attack was going to happen.

I turn and stare, lost in thought, out at the inky black lake. I'm missing something here. Perhaps for that reason I'm also grasping at straws. One which I can't shake is the nagging idea that perhaps it was my real mother who saved me in Morocco. Or is that as stupid as it sounds? Right now I don't know what to believe anymore. If my mother is in fact this Athena person who they keep mentioning, why would they need to use me to lure her out? And what's so special about her that would make them want to find her in the first place?

Stumped, I push the idea aside for later, and hurriedly flick through the rest of the file. I don't want to be in here any longer than I absolutely have to. But if I thought those were all the surprises the file had in store for me, I'm proved wrong when I turn the last page to find a small, handwritten note affixed to the back inside cover. My eyes go wide as I read it.

> If you are reading this then you are on the right path.
>
> Follow it.
>
> Now kindly get out of my office!
>
> Warmly,
> Doug Gambon

I can't help but laugh out loud, only to catch myself and quickly stifle it, all too aware how easily sound travels around here.

With the files returned just as I found them, I close the safe and carefully make my exit, smiling all the way back to our study. I can't believe how crafty the old man is.

Milly is fast asleep when I creep back into the room, something I wish I could do, but there is simply too much going on inside my head for me to find peace.

* * *

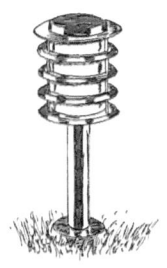

CHAPTER 11

THE PLOT THICKENS

The next day it seems Milly is even more excited about my discovery than I am. I suppose she never had the chance to find out anything about her real parents, so she is twice as thrilled to share in my journey of self-discovery.

I'm relieved to find the Oracle deserted and I watch Milly log the system on with a mixture of excited trepidation. I sit quietly behind her, fidgeting nervously with the hem of my sweatshirt as I try to suppress my growing impatience at how long it takes. Then, finally, with the room bathed in its familiar blue glow, she turns to me and grins.

'So let's see what we can find out about this Vanessa Speirs, then, shall we?'

She types the name in and hits the search command. I can barely breathe. I try going for calm and casual but my voice comes out shaky and nervous.

'So what's it actually searching?'

'More like what isn't it searching,' she replies. 'It does all the usual ones. Social Security, Inland Revenue, DVLA, NHS and national police databases. Then it does a low-level look through the MOD and Joint Intelligence databases. Okay, heads up, here we go.'

I raise my eyes to the screen as a stream of results floods onto it.

'Oh my God, this is so exciting,' I exclaim, clutching her arm tightly. Milly takes a moment to narrow the results and we scan through what remains.

'Well, it's given us all the usual things.' She circles each with a laser pen. 'Tax returns, education, early employment records. Kinda weird, though. I was expecting a bit more, I dunno, juicy stuff ...'

With a puzzled expression, she adjusts the search parameters and tries again.

'It's interesting,' she says, after a moment's reflection. 'It's all there, a normal personal history, all up to this point here. But thereafter it's like she just disappears.' She points to where the system has collated all the documents into a graphical timeline of activity. 'And she only reappears about sixteen years ago with that adoption form you also found in Gambon's file. But in between it's just one big blank.'

'What do you mean? Did she move abroad?'

'I don't think so. I mean gone gone. Like Keyser Söze gone. Poof!'

'How's that possible?'

'It isn't.'

'Then what happened?'

'Well, if you ask me, I think it just proves she went to work for MI6. But what's happened is someone's tried to clean up her file. But they weren't terribly thorough. See how they left the tax record?'

'Yeah, so what?'

'Alright, well, see ages back, one of the very first C's implemented a policy that said MI6 employees didn't have to pay taxes. Pretty sweet deal, huh? And see how her tax record disappears during this whole period? I think that's when she worked for MI6. Would also explain how Gambon knew her.'

'All because she stopped paying taxes?'

'Yes.'

'Any chance you can find a photo?' I ask.

Milly opens another file and a picture of an attractive, yet sternly determined-looking woman with short blonde hair appears. Milly flicks a comparative glance between the two of us.

'Well, I can definitely see the similarity.'

I shrug, unsure how to reply. I suppose there is. I'm just not sure what to think of this woman right now. The woman who gave me up. But why? That's what I don't get. What would possess someone to give up her own child? I can't imagine it. But whatever the reason, I am now very keen to find out what it was, if for no better reason than I think my own sanity and peace of mind demand it.

'Is there anything more on her?'

Milly's fingers dance across the touch-pad and a moment later a website for the UK Land Registry appears. In no time she has the records of ownership for a small bungalow up on the screen. The address has me out of my seat in a flash.

'Hey, hey, bring that up. What is that?'

'Just where she used to live,' Milly replies.

'No, that's ours!' I reply adamantly. 'That's our place down by the coast.'

Milly looks puzzled.

'Well, whatever it is, she used to live there. Seems the trust deeds were signed over to your parents,' she says, squinting up at the screen, 'sometime around, yeah, about sixteen years ago.'

'Okay, that is just way too big a coincidence to be chance. My parents have got to know more than they are letting on.'

'As may be,' Milly says, 'but I'd be very wary of letting them twig you're onto this until you know the whole story.'

I ponder her advice. She's right, of course. But what is the whole story? Again and again it seems to come back to whatever this Genesis thing is or was. It's the unknown elephant in the corner of the room. I ask Milly if she can try to find out more about it.

'We could, but that probably means looking in the MOD mainframe itself. Technically we're not allowed in there. But I've got something here which might help. Brace yourself. Things might be about to get interesting,' she says, rummaging through her bag. She pulls out a small gold disc, which she then inserts into the drive.

'Interesting, huh? Like they haven't already,' I mumble sarcastically. I glance at the disc. 'Do I even want to know what that is?'

'Probably not. It's an algorithm master key which I helped write to encrypt MOD files last year. To say this is breaking a tonne of rules would be a colossal understatement, but we need it to access stuff too highly classified for Oracle normally to be able to see.'

With a studious expression, her tongue just poking out between her teeth, Milly brings up the password request portal for the Ministry of Defence's mainframe repository. I edge forward on my seat and cast her a wary look.

'Okay, watch this,' she says, and presses enter. The screen floods with a myriad of windows, each full of reams of computer code. In seconds they all disappear and Milly gives a little squeak of excitement as a large 'Access granted' banner appears.

'Oh my God, we just hacked the MOD!' she squeals.

I realise we are venturing into truly uncharted waters in terms of the trouble we'll get into if they catch us. A small digital clock appears and immediately begins an erratic countdown while Milly types away furiously, looks up, and then types some more.

'So it's basically searching for any record that has both Vanessa Speirs's name and the word Genesis in it together. But at the same time it's also bouncing the signal through tonnes of different ISPs all around the world—you know, to make it harder for them to trace.'

I find myself gripping the armrest of my seat as the time remaining suddenly drops.

'Oh yeah, and that's how long we have until they trace the hack,' she notes calmly.

'Uh-huh, well not to state the bloody obvious, but there isn't exactly a whole lot of it left, you know that, right?' I ask sarcastically.

'It's fine. Relax. We only need a few more seconds.'

The countdown drops below twenty seconds. And still no results have appeared.

'Mills,' I say, edging forward nervously.

'Yeah, I know, I know,' she says, not quite so confident anymore. 'Wait, I've got another idea.' Her hands fly back to the keyboard.

'Ten seconds. Mills! It's almost—'

'Yeah, hang on … Nearly there …'

'C'mon!'

I consider hitting the escape key myself, but at the very last moment she beats me to it. A large 'Connection lost' notice flashes across the screen and she slumps back breathlessly into her chair.

'Oh my God, that was close,' she exclaims.

'Well, did it work?'

'Hmm, sort of,' she says, casting a pensive look over the results. 'There's nothing that concretely links them together, but check this out.' She points to a graphic of a flat black disc in the centre of the screen. 'See those little red dots on the far side? That's kinda what I was hoping we'd see.'

'I don't follow?'

'Okay, look. It's a huge database, right? Full of files. And every file has its own cookie with the basic details of the file's contents in it. The file name, key-words and so on. It quicker to search the cookies than the actual files themselves. But see, here's the catch. When you delete a file, the cookie usually remains. It just gets deactivated so it doesn't ping in future searches. But it's still there, if you know what to look for. Now if I unwind the timeline, you see how all those dots are clustered together around eighteen years ago?'

Suddenly it dawns on me what she's driving at. I get up slowly and approach the screen.

'So what you're saying—'

'Exactly,' she trills with a grin that stretches from ear to ear. 'Those red dots represent cookies of old files that had both our key-words in them. But someone's gone and deleted the originals.'

'Why'd they do that?'

'Well, I'm guessing that whatever Genesis was, it was so embarrassing or controversial that they decided to erase anything to do with it.'

I frown and slump back into my swivel chair.

'Alright, but there's something else which really makes no sense. Remember when you overheard Gambon and Decker discussing my mum and how they said she was rumoured to have—'

'Some kind of weapons store in her house,' Milly chimes in. 'Yeah.'

'Precisely. But if he means the place down in Selsey, well I can tell you right now, I know it back to front and there's nothing there.'

'Are you sure you've looked everywhere? I mean, it's not like she'd have them hung up on the walls, is it?'

'True,' I concede.

'And you never know, maybe your parents had it all removed ages back?'

'That's also a possibility. But suppose they didn't? Suppose they don't even know it's there? Suppose I could find it? Maybe there's something there which could cast a bit more light on all this. What do you think?'

'I guess you've got nothing to lose trying. But how are you going to get down there without anyone finding out? Especially your parents?'

I sigh.

'Yeah, I haven't really got that far yet. But I'm sure something will come to me.'

*

And it does, about a week and a half later, when, in the midst of a very lazy afternoon, slumped out in our study, Alex messages me. I sit up in excitement and, holding the phone aloft, exclaim, 'He wants to come down and see me!'

'Who?' says Nigel disinterestedly from behind his film magazine.

'Alex! Who else?'

'How should I know? It's so hard to keep up with you and your busy social life,' he says.

'Ha! What social life? I barely have one. I spend all my time with a cantankerous weirdo who thinks he's French.'

'So when did he say he'd come down?' says Milly.

'This Saturday.'

'Whit, oan his bike?' Luther says.

'That enormous Ducati of his?' Nigel adds, putting the magazine down.

'I guess,' I say, unsure and not particularly interested.

'Aye, noo that's a beastie of a bike,' Luther exclaims. Turning to Nigel, he adds, 'Noo whaur dae ye hink he got th' money tae afford somethin' loch 'at?'

'What's so special about it?' Milly asks. The looks they give her leave me in no doubt that was apparently a particularly stupid question.

'Well, only th' fact,' Luther exclaims, ''at it is a serioos limited edition model. Aw carbon fibre fram an' body. Pure custom built an'—'

'Two hundred brake horsepower,' Nigel adds.

'So it's powerful?' Anabel asks from Milly's bed, where she's reclining on a huge pile of cushions.

'Aye, an' costs jist a wee bit shy ay sixty thoosain quid.

Noo where's some eighteen-year-auld gie 'at kin' ay petty change, huh?'

'Shouldn't the question be,' says Anabel, 'how is an eighteen-year-old riding around on a bike that he isn't legally allowed to ride until he's twenty-one?'

I share a look with Milly and then suddenly exclaim, 'No, that's it! I'll ask him. And then he can take me down.'

*

My excitement at the prospect of seeing Alex again is short-lived when, first thing the next morning, Dr Gambon intercepts me halfway across the front lawn and asks me to walk a bit with him.

'I have been meaning to catch up with you for a while now, Ms Foxton,' he begins. 'But the Common Room has been rather busy trying to fend off an OFSTED inspection that some bright spark has set their mind to. Problem being, they're a rather annoying non-ministerial department under the chief inspector of schools, which means fobbing them off is not as easy as it would be were they to have a proper minister whom the PM could lean on without attracting undue attention. That is our problem, however. Now, what I meant to discuss with you is this matter relating to that Chinese chappie we did the bio on a few weeks back.'

I don't have the nerve to point out that it has, in fact, been a lot longer than that.

'The AFOTS folks came back to me the other week with some rather interesting findings from the fund trace. Apparently, after no end of difficulty, they eventually traced the bulk of the funds going into Vanguard back to a BVI shell company called Red Rock Holdings. And after an awful lot more digging they found that it is an indirectly owned subsidiary of an investment company in London called Valhalla Capital. Now what's interesting about all this is the secrecy. What don't they want anyone to know about?'

'Is there any way we can find out who's actually behind it?'

'Of course, and we already know. Their chairman and CEO is a chap called Robert Pemberton-Smythe.'

'I feel like I have heard of him.'

'I would be concerned if you hadn't.'

'Isn't he like one of the richest men in the country?'

Gambon nods matter-of-factly.

'That's the one. He's also a special advisor to the Treasury.'

'So what are you saying, that he's untouchable?'

'Now you're just being naive. No one's untouchable nowadays. Everybody can be ruined, if you know their weak spot. But that's only the half of it. It seems he, or his company, has also been very busy buying up an awful lot of retail and commercial properties recently.'

'What's so bad about that?'

'In itself, nothing. However, when you do it using forty-eight different shell companies, all in offshore tax havens like the British Virgin Islands, with funds originating from some eighty different bank accounts in thirty different countries, one does have to ask the question, what on *earth* is going on? There isn't a single transaction that we can see which could not have been done in a perfectly normal, open and transparent way without any of this cloak and dagger nonsense.'

'So what's this got to do with the men who attacked me?'

'Possibly nothing. Possibly everything. If he was involved in what happened to you, and it's a big *if*, then it opens up the possibility that he might not be as white as he paints himself to be. And that raises the possibility that he might be involved in even more nefarious activities. A man with considerable resources, such as this chap, would be someone we would definitely want to keep a very close eye on if we thought he was up to no good.'

'So can I do anything to help?'

Gambon stops and smiles in a way that tells me this is precisely what he has been waiting for.

'Well, now you mention it, there might be. I want to give you a little assignment. Keep it fairly hush-hush, won't you. Maybe enrol a couple of the others from your house, but that's it. I want you to dig around. See what you can come up with on this chap. And have some fun while you're at it. It's stuff like this which makes the Great Game so enjoyable to play.'

Dig around: I've learned that here that's just a euphemism for breaking laws without getting caught. He hands me a beige manila folder with details of the company and its chairman and then wanders off across the grass, back towards the main building. I look at the folder with mixed emotions and then decide to text Alex instead.

Persuading him to come down isn't a problem. Persuading him to collect me just after midnight on Saturday proves somewhat trickier. But in the end he agrees, intrigued with whatever hare-brained scheme he thinks I'm up to.

Come Saturday night, slipping out of the house is easy. I've done it so often since I got here. Then I jog the mile or so to the school's perimeter wall, just down from the main gates, and scale it with the aid of a nearby tree. The drop on the other side is daunting but doable and I roll upon landing, like my Parkour teacher has taught me. Then it's a short run to where I told Alex to wait. I'm thrilled to see he's already there and get the usual tingling sensation all over as I rush over and give him a kiss.

'Okay, so what's so important that you have to beg me to come all the way down here in the middle of the night?'

'Would you believe me if I said there was something in my parents' house which I want to find without them knowing about it, or anyone else seeing me come or go?'

He looks at me dubiously.

'No. But I'll play along because it sounds amusing. What are you looking for?'

'Not sure yet, but I'll know it when I see it.'

His look becomes even more disbelieving. But he's still smiling so I feel slightly better about inconveniencing him like this.

'Well, you'd better put these on,' he says, handing me a heavy bag which he had strapped behind him. 'Just in case, you know.'

Inside is a brand-spanking-new set of motorbike leathers, with gloves and boots, similar to his, and an expensive-looking red Schuberth helmet. I can't believe he got me my own set of leathers. They must have cost a fortune.

'The sizes were a guess. I hope I wasn't too far off.'

I smile cheekily.

'Only one way to find out.'

Taking the bag, I make for the side of the road, where, in the shadows near the trees, I quickly slip out of my training gear and tug on the trousers. There's something forbiddingly exciting about changing like this, standing here in the middle of the woods at night in just my underwear, with him undoubtedly sneaking the occasional voyeuristic peek while

I pull on the rest of the leathers. Done, I leave the bag, now with my school PT kit and trainers in it, concealed behind a tree, tug on the helmet and straddle the bike. I wrap my arms around his body and pull myself tightly up against him. It's a nifty helmet because I can hear him through a radio in mine and vice versa. If only my dad could see me now … dating (if that's what we're doing) a boy with a motorbike; he'd flip.

'Are you actually allowed to ride something this big before you're twenty-one?'

'Not really,' he says cheekily. 'But I made an agreement to take the police motorcyclists' advanced riding course and got an exemption.'

'You can really do that?'

'If you know the right people you can. You ready?'

'Oh yes,' I say, before screaming as I'm almost torn off the back as he twists the accelerator.

*

I'd almost forgotten how crisp the air is down here on the coast. It's only now, having not been here for a few months, that I realise how much I miss the ebb and flow of the tide over the pebbles and the noise of the seagulls overhead.

After the seat-of-our-pants, mad thrash down here on the motorway, the bumpy ride along the uneven, dark coastal road has us giggling and laughing as we bounce around on the bike.

'This is brilliant,' Alex exclaims, pointing at the breaking waves only fifty feet away to our right.

'Thought you'd like it.'

'Of course, would have been better by day, but hey, who's complaining? It's the company that counts.'

'Oh, you smooth talker,' I say with a laugh, amazed that I can feel so close to someone I know so little about. But maybe that's the appeal. I don't really want to talk too much about myself, and neither, apparently, does he.

'Hey, that's the one.' I point towards a little bungalow just up ahead. It's situated a good distance from either neighbour and, while not big, is pretty and quaint. There is a small front garden set off from the track by a low wall. A short driveway cuts across the lawn and up to a built-in garage. Along it is a series of small, blue, solar-powered lamps that nicely illuminate the front lawn.

We sneak towards the building, giggling at the unnecessary subterfuge. None of the neighbours seems to be up, but better safe than sorry. With equally unnecessary caution, I quietly unlock the front door and we slip inside. The tour is quick. It's not a big place and the moon is pretty full tonight so there's easily enough light for both of us to see where we are going without turning on the lights.

'Is all this really necessary?' Alex asks in a whisper.

'Oh yes. The neighbours are a right bunch of busybodies. They'd be straight on the phone if they saw me.'

We begin in the front room, with its unobstructed, picture-postcard view of the beach. Then we head back, past the normally light and airy kitchen, towards the two bedrooms at the rear. Beyond that, bathed in moonlight, is a nice, secluded back garden with a little fish-pond-cum-fountain, a greenhouse and a small barbeque area.

Alex sits down on the corner of my bed and bounces up and down a couple of times.

'This is nice. It's a cute place,' he says softly, staring up at me with unblinking eyes. A suggestive little smile plays across his face.

And suddenly I realise what he's obviously assuming I brought him down here for. Mortified and overcome by a flush of awkwardness, my hands fly to my mouth as a wave of apologies spills from it. In seconds I'm just digging myself in even deeper.

'Oh God, it's not that I don't want to. I mean, I do. Of course I do. I just … didn't think … wasn't ready to … you know, like so quickly. Oh, this must sound so totally lame. I'm nuts about you. I really am. And I can't think of anyone I'd like to … more, but just not …'

'Not so soon?'

I shrug and nod weakly. He must think I am so lame, or worse, just a stupid little girl who has no idea what she's doing. I want to run away and cry but am scared he'll simply walk off. I bet someone like Farabee would never find herself in this situation. How did I spend so much time focused on where this Vanessa Speirs could have possibly hidden something down here that I never stopped to think how flimsy my reason for coming would sound to him? Middle of the night. Empty house. Just him and me. You idiot, Heather! What else would he think you're bringing him down here for!

But then Alex surprises me. Perhaps because he's two years older than me and more mature? Maybe that's what I like about him. He is more mature, certainly more so than boys my age, who would probably start with the pressure and guilt trips, every effort to coerce me, almost force me to go through with it. But instead he leans back and laughs self-depreciatingly.

'You know what, no, it's absolutely fine. I'm just surprised is all, but in a good way. Until I met you my experience was that … well, how can I put this nicely, not—'

'Many girls have ever said no to you?'

'It sounds pretty bad when you put it like that, doesn't it?' I shrug.

'Depends. Not really. I'm a big girl. I get how the world works. I just wasn't ...'

'Hey, you don't need to explain,' Alex says, getting up and gently taking hold of my shoulders. 'Not to me. Look, I like you. More than that. I really like you. Probably more now, after this, than before even. So, you want to wait. That's absolutely fine. We wait.'

I look into his eyes, my own full of apology and regret.

'It's just that I'm a ... a ...' Bloody hell, I can't even say it. 'I just didn't plan to ... you know ... tonight.'

Suddenly he understands.

'Ahhhh.' He lets out a deep sigh and then, with a rueful shake of his head, smiles. 'I'm sorry. I didn't think.'

Pursing my lips, I pull him into a hug.

'I want to. I really do. But when the time is right. I want to enjoy it. For us to enjoy it. But right now I'm just way too distracted. Tonight's ...'

Alex puts a finger over my lips and casts me an endearingly understanding look.

'Then we wait. I have no problem with that. I mean,' he says pulling a comical face, 'let's not wait too long, *but* ...'

We share a laugh and it's wonderfully disarming. Then he sits back down on the bed.

'Okay, so how about you tell me why we're really here, and then maybe I can help and actually be of some use?'

'Alright,' I say, scuttling around to sit next to him. My choice now suddenly seems so clear. If I've decided that I am happy to share myself with him in the not-too-distant future, then why not share this, too? In fact, there's very little I don't think I could share with him. Okay, maybe the truth about Godolphin Park and my involvement there, because, well, frankly, I have no desire to go to prison, but this, I don't see any real problem in telling him about this. Besides, I probably do need his help.

'Now don't laugh, okay? I'm looking for some kind of secret room. I think it might help me find out more about my real mum.'

He takes it quite well, considering. Then a quizzical look appears.

'What makes you think there is one?'

'Oh, just hearsay from people who knew her. Like way back in the day.'

'Okay, how well do you know this place?'

'We come here most summers.'

'A secret room, huh? Well, I don't think any of the walls are wide enough to conceal anything.'

'Agreed.'

'What's in the attic?'

'Nothing. Just boxes and insulation.'

'So it's not inside. Unless it's under the floor?'

It only takes a few minutes to walk around, tapping the floor, to disprove that idea. We peek into the garage but it's essentially empty and the floor is a seamless concrete pour.

'Okay, so that leaves the garden.'

With my hopes of success no longer quite what they were, I agree with a half-hearted shrug.

'It would certainly be the easiest place to put something and the least likely to be discovered,' he says, now seemingly keener on this ridiculous hunt than I am.

We agree that, short of digging up the lawn, there's no good way to check under that. So we split up. He takes the shed and the patio and I the other corner and the small greenhouse. Stepping inside it, I am confronted with two very old-looking potting tables on either side with nothing but a couple of ancient flower pots on each. The floor is concrete with a light topping of gravel. I ponder for a moment and then brush the gravel aside. Kneeling down in the dark, I blow the dust away, and, using the light from my iSpy, am confronted with a very fine line in the ground. Suddenly excited, I hurriedly sweep the remaining stones and dirt aside. It's ever so subtle, but there is most definitely something here. An old, rusty coat hanger, which I find beneath one of the tables, slots down nicely into the gap.

Just at this moment Alex reappears in the doorway.

'Hey, seems you've found more than I did.'

'Hmm, we'll see,' I say with a pensive look. I wiggle the bent hanger and then pull. At first nothing happens, but then, with no warning, a whole section of flooring comes up, making us both gasp in surprise.

'What the hell?' Alex exclaims. 'I didn't think you were being serious.'

'Ha! Neither did I.' I toss my iSpy onto a potting table and grasp the trapdoor in both hands.

'Pretty neat phone you have there,' he says. 'What is it?'

'Oh, my iSp— err, I 'spose it's not out yet. My dad got a few on some banking deal he was working on. Boring stuff, but the phone's pretty cool.'

'Yeah. Same with my dad. I mean he does similar stuff.'

'You know, I don't even know what your dad does,' I say as I heft the trapdoor aside. Then, reaching into the hole, I find a light switch.

'Just boring finance stuff, like yours.'

'Uh-huh, well, come on,' I whisper daringly, as I descend the small ladder. It leads down into what looks to be some kind of concrete basement.

'Hey, you *really* need to come see this,' I shout up.

Alex doesn't hang around and is down beside me in seconds. Nothing could have prepared us for what we find. At a casual glance it resembles any normal storeroom. Until one looks properly, that is, and notices what is stacked neatly on all the shelves and racks. Guns. Lots and lots of guns. I let a long, drawn-out expletive slip from my lips.

Alex looks at me in shock.

'Sorry, this is your *parents'* place? And you say your dad's a banker. Are you *sure?*'

I laugh, still utterly astonished by what we've found. It means Milly's theory is correct. I quickly take a series of photos and send them to her using an encrypted transmission channel on my phone.

'Yeah, but it's a little more complicated than that,' I say dryly. 'I don't even know the whole story yet. That's kind of why I'm here.'

Everything is covered with a thick layer of dust. Pistols, sniper rifles, machine guns, bazookas and other more complicated-looking, tubular devices with sighting scopes and pistol grips, not to mention a myriad of other things about which I have no clue.

'It's a freaking arsenal,' I exclaim.

My eyes dart from shelf to shelf in disbelief. Even though there's a rifle range in B-School, I still haven't been allowed in there yet. In fact, few people even have firearms on their rota. Morocco aside, this is the first time I've ever seen a gun up close and in person. The movies make them look so easy, yet I feel an instant wary respect for them. There's something intrinsically malevolent about them which scares the hell out of me. One wrong move, one little mistake, and someone could get seriously injured or even die. I'm always having to watch what I do, lest I hurt someone by mistake, but these things, they're something else entirely.

Ever so delicately, I trace my finger over one of them. It has a compact metal body, a collapsible stock and a thin, curved magazine jutting out from its underside. A large, corrugated cylinder is fitted over the barrel. Taped to the rack beneath it is a small, handwritten label:

HK MP5-SD6 (Silenced)

'You could start a flipping war with all this,' Alex notes pensively as he examines the rocket launcher rack.

'Or end one,' I add, tapping the MP5 thoughtfully.

206

Alex comes over and takes it from the rack. Pressing something underneath it, he removes the magazine and checks the chamber is clear. Then he releases the cocking handle, flips it over, offs the safety and pulls the trigger. There's a soft click.

'At least they stored the magazines properly. If they're left full, the spring'll compress and it won't push the bullets up into the chamber when you eventually try to use it,' he notes, suddenly very much the expert. With a perplexed, quizzical look I take the gun from him. Seeing my expression, he hastily explains, 'Dad sent me on a course a few years back. Survival stuff with some former army guys. They taught us how to fire guns and stuff. Plus he's always got security guys around who sometimes teach me this stuff when I'm bored.'

I'd love to pry, but right now I'm more focused on seeing what there is in here. Sensing my preoccupation, and that we're likely to be here for a while, Alex offers to head into town and grab something to eat from the twenty-four-hour take-away place on the high street. It's only after I've kissed him 'bye that the horrible thought occurs to me that, after what happened earlier, and now with this on top, I might have freaked him out so badly that he could just think, sod it, and decide not to bother coming back.

Resigned to the fact that there's little I can do about it either way, I set about going through every drawer, cabinet and locker in the hope of finding something about my real mother. After twenty minutes' searching I have uncovered little of a personal nature about her, except for a black CWC diver's watch with her name engraved on the back. I slip it into my pocket.

A few minutes later, Alex returns and my spirits lift hugely. With him come two big pizzas and a bottle of Dr Pepper.

'I was worried you might have run off. You know, not exactly the night you were expecting.'

He eyes me reproachfully and passes over a folded slice of pizza.

'What, and miss all this? Please. This is the most fun I've had in ages,' he exclaims, taking a large bite of pizza. 'I've got a hot girl, guns and pizza. What more could a guy ask for?'

I laugh and give him a playful slap on the arm.

'Hey, come check these out,' I say, gently blowing the dust from a photo frame I found at the top of a box at the back. It's a picture of twenty or so people, two of whom are women, standing beside a helicopter in a remote jungle clearing. Each is armed to the teeth and their faces are all blackened with camouflage paint.

'I'm thinking one of them could be my mum.'

'Well,' he says, taking a step back to give me an appraising look. We both point to the same woman at the same moment.

Then I gasp, but for a very different reason.

'What?' he says, alarmed.

'Oh, nothing,' I reply hastily. 'Just thought I recognised someone else. But I guess not.'

But it certainly isn't nothing. For there, standing on the sidelines, is none other than Mr Abbott. The photo must be almost twenty years old, and yet he looked just as pissed off back then as he does now.

Alex gives an affirmative mumble and reaches for the next photo in the box. This one simply has a lone woman standing beside the helicopter.

'She does look oddly familiar,' he says, pointing at the woman who I now know to be my mother. I look at him in confusion.

'Sorry?'

'Maybe I'm mistaken, but she just looks vaguely familiar. Though I couldn't say from where.'

My brow furrows and I take the photo from him. Delicately, I remove the backing and take out the picture. Barely visible on the back is some writing. I tilt it into the light and just make out the words:

Genesis, Day 1.

'What do you think that means?' Alex asks.

'Your guess is as good as mine,' I say.

I take the next photo, this one taken in some sort of hospital with the same fifteen people, my mother included. Only here they have been joined by a group of doctors. Again we find more writing when we open it up. It merely says:

Genesis: the 1st 15.

'Is this what you were looking for?' Alex asks.

'I don't really know what I was looking for. Just some kind of connection to my biological mum, I suppose.'

'Well, I'd say you've found it.'

'Yeah, I guess.'

'What are you going to do about this place now?'

'Nothing, I guess. Just close it up and leave it be. Promise me you won't ever mention it to anyone. Please?'

'Okay, I promise,' he says.

I nod gratefully.

'So do you want to head back now?'

I slip the photos into my pocket, along with the watch, and turn to Alex with a smile. 'Oh, I don't think we have to rush back quite yet. I don't know when I will get to see you next. So we might as well make the most of it. Would you like to maybe go for a walk along the beach?'

'Yeah, you know what, I'd like that a lot.'

* * *

CHAPTER 12

SEEK AND YE SHALL FIND

Despite being absolutely shattered from having had so little sleep last night—we only got back around five-thirty this morning—there are simply too many things which I need to do for me to lie back and take it easy. First up is to enrol my friends into helping me with this whole Pemberton-Smythe thing that Gambon dumped on me. Even though he, or his company, now appears to have been funding the Chinese men who came for me in Morocco, I can't help but feel the hunt for my mother, if she is even still alive, is more important. Then again, if my theory about her being the one who saved my life is correct, that would also suggest she knew what was going to happen. Does that mean there's a link between her and the people behind the attack? If so, I suppose both our investigations will ultimately lead to the same place anyway.

Thankfully Luther, Anabel and Nigel keenly accept the challenge of digging up as much dirt as possible on the guy. My stressing it was a special assignment from Gambon himself, seriously hush-hush, didn't hurt my chances of persuading them. This thankfully frees Milly and me up for what I now have in mind. Finding out, once and for all, what everyone seems to have been keeping from me.

The truth …

The truth about me …

The truth about my real parents …

And the truth about why I am really here.

Milly and I find a quiet corner in B-School and I lay the pictures I took from Vanessa Speirs's basement on the table. Her reaction is as instantaneous as mine and I have to slap a quick hand over her mouth to stop her from blurting Abbott's name out in surprise.

Forewarned, she looks at me and whispers, 'Yeah, but you can't just go and ask him about it, can you?'

'I don't intend to, unless I really have to,' I say. 'No, see, I want to find out who this guy here is, or was. The scientist-looking bloke in the centre of the group photo I swiped from that basement. I'll bet if anyone can tell me what's really going on, or what my mum was really involved in, he can.'

'Well, what makes you think he'll talk to you any more than Abbott would?'

'Yeah, well, let me deal with that. All I'm asking is whether you can help me find out who this main scientist guy in the photo was, or is? You know your way around the Data-Room way better than I do. How hard could it be?'

She scoffs confidently.

'With a photo of him, it'll be a synch.'

And it is. The facial recognition software which the system runs is astonishing. Not only does it compute potential changes in his appearance since the picture was taken, but once it has identified him to a certainty of over ninety-three per cent, it then begins running a facial recognition comparison against recent footage taken and recorded by the almost two million CCTV cameras dotted across the UK.

'Well, while it does that,' Milly says, 'there's no doubt this is your guy. Dr Richard Haines.'

We quickly skim over the bio that we take from his LinkedIn page. Not even at the second line, we both stop and share a wary look. I don't like the sound of what this guy does for a living.

'Is it just me,' Milly whispers, 'or do you get a really bad feeling about this?'

I swallow uncomfortably as my own brain tries to digest what it could mean. It would certainly make sense in a twisted sort of way, but it is also deeply, horribly unsettling to think about.

'I've got to hear it from his mouth. I mean, I can't make that kind of assumption. Oh my God, can you imagine? That would be like the freakiest, sickest thing ever. Eugh!' I shiver involuntarily and wrap my arms around myself. 'I feel like I want to have a shower just thinking about it.'

'Then you have to go talk to him,' Milly urges. 'And quickly. Or it could—'

'What? Completely unravel me? I think it already is. But don't worry. I have a plan. There is someone else who I think knows the truth.'

'Gambon?'

'Precisely.'

*

But can I get in to see him? Not a chance, and by the end of the day my anger and frustration are beginning to tell. First to fall foul of my darkening mood is the SH pantry fridge. The door won't close properly, despite several calm attempts to shut it. Unable to see what's blocking it, I end up almost ripping it from its hinges in an expletive-riddled tantrum.

'Jesus, you look a state,' Milly mutters when she eventually finds me at the bottom of the house garden. 'I heard about the poor fridge. I think you owe a few people some new milk. Oh, and by the way, Lander's looking for you as well.'

'Great.'

*

By the end of the week, my sense of anxious preoccupation has become so bad that I fail my practical surveillance test. That's because I forget to charge my iSpy's battery, which promptly runs out halfway through the exercise, despite our all having been reminded to ensure they were charged. I completely give up on one of Mr Decker's cross-country runs, which earns me a scathing and unimpressed look. Most serious, however, is finding myself back in Dr Gambon's office for hitting someone. Only I'm not particularly worried because this is exactly where I wanted to end up. This time it was Augustus, who had been taking particular delight in my distracted state of mind by sending me to the mats time and again with totally unnecessary throws in CQC. So I walked up to him at the end of class and floored him.

Upon my entering his office, Gambon throws his glasses onto his desk in exasperation and scowls at me as I sit down.

'What did I tell you about exactly this kind of behaviour? You cannot go around hitting people. I was willing to let the first incident go, but now you've assaulted another member of Grey's. What on earth has got into you?'

I can't believe he's making this my fault. Common sense would say I should have waited and calmed down before coming up. Because right now, being here in a mood like this is an inherently bad idea. My temper becomes too overpowering for me to rein in anymore. I'm up on my feet in a flash and, with a loud thump, slap the photo of my mother and Dr Haines down onto his table.

'That is!' I shout at him. 'Up till now everyone's been playing a game with me and I've been willing to go along with it, just to see where it leads, but now it's got to stop. I need to know the truth. Or seriously, so help me, God, I will walk out of here and to hell with the lot of you. So, with all due respect, Sir, either you tell me what the hell this is all about, or you pick up the phone and call that doctor guy at his hospital and get him to tell me. I don't care which it is, but I need to know the truth about who I am!'

With that, I fold my arms petulantly and wait for him to decide.

'Well,' he says, leaning back in his chair with amusement. 'That's the first time a student has ever mouthed off like that in here, that's for sure.'

I'm not taken in by this deflection and continue to glare challengingly at him. With a resigned sigh, he points to the chair and beckons me to sit back down again, which I do, albeit somewhat reluctantly. He caps his fountain pen and lays it on the desk.

'None of what I am about to tell you may ever be repeated to anyone else, do you understand?'

'Yes.'

'You're lying to me already, aren't you?'

'Yes.'

'Because you'll tell Miss Butterworth, won't you?'

'Yes. Sorry.'

'No, you're not.'

'Not what?'

'Sorry.'

'No, not really.'

'Then don't pretend to be.'

'Okay, sorry.'

He sighs. 'That exception aside, this goes no further. Do you understand?'

I nod.

He doesn't seem entirely satisfied, but nonetheless flashes me a confident smile.

'Well, either way I'm fairly sure you'll keep your word. For two reasons specifically. The first, as you will soon no doubt realise, is that the ramifications should this ever get out—for you especially, let alone anyone else—could be severe.'

'Right, and the second?'

'Oh, that's simple,' he replies bluntly, with an absent-minded spin of his pen. 'Because no one would ever believe you.'

'O—kay,' I reply hesitantly. 'Fine, I promise.'

'Good, then let's start with how much you already know.'

'Alright, well, I know I was adopted and that my biological mother was involved with some group called Genesis, and that, in a roundabout sort of way, it may have something to do with why I'm—how shall I put it—different from other people.'

'Ah, yes. Now that all came as rather a shock to us as well, I must admit,' he adds gravely.

My eyes narrow and bore in to him, as though doing so might somehow glean me some greater insight into all the coded speech and half-truths around here.

'Very well,' he says, leaning back and swivelling round to gaze out of the window. 'It all began back in eighty-three. Long before you were born. It started in America, where the US Department of Energy's Office of Health and Environmental Research had just launched a global project. Their aim was to map every gene in the human body. Their hope was to establish precisely which characteristics were bestowed by which genes. I'm sure you've heard of it. It was called the Human Genome Project.'

I give a nod. But now is one of those moments in life where I realise it's wiser to shut up and listen. I edge forward keenly.

'It was a public endeavour, run out of universities and research institutes all around the world. Initially the critics panned it. Too expensive, too hard, destined to fail, et cetera, et cetera. But slowly, after a few years, they began to make some real progress.

'Before long, the Ministry of Defence approached a few of their chaps working on it on this side of the pond. We asked if they were interested in running a similar project, but for us. I suppose the prospect of unlimited funding and no public oversight was, well, quite appealing at the time. No surprise, they accepted. Now you don't need to know much about what they actually did; suffice to say that it was an experimental methodology called Genome Shotgun Technique. Truly radical. Years ahead of its time. It had its risks, but it allowed us to do the mapping considerably faster than the public project could. When they eventually presented their findings, we offered up another hypothetical. We said if the difference, genetically speaking, between a person and a chimpanzee was only one per cent—which it is, by the way—then how much would one have to change genetically within a person to, how shall I say, enhance certain "special characteristics" within them?'

For a second I want to scoff and tell him not to be ridiculous. But I can see how serious he is and this is now getting uncomfortably close to my earlier theory with Milly. With a burst of excitement, I edge even further forward on the chair. 'You're talking about genetic engineering, aren't you?'

'In layman's terms, yes,' he replies. 'But you need to understand the context of the times. This was the military's Holy Grail back then. The height of the Cold War. We knew Ivan was toying with it. The Yanks as well. Britain couldn't be seen to be left behind. The Falklands War had just finished and the public's tolerance for heavy wartime casualties wasn't what it had once been. Yet the prospect for future wars back then was as high as I ever remember it. The world was a mess, and if the Soviet threat wasn't bad enough, the Middle East wasn't getting any rosier, either.'

'Still isn't!' I mutter.

'Quite,' he chuckles. 'Something had to be done and the tactical advantage this option could have given us was well worth the investment in the government's eyes.

'All you really need to know,' he says, 'is that they used a specific type of genetic engineering called Somatic engineering. The point being it only targets specific genes within very particular tissues of a patient, rather than the sex cells, for example, like a lot of these treatments tend do. That was important because we explicitly didn't want these changes being passed on to the next generation. Gen-ESIS,' he explains, deliberately spelling out each letter, 'simply stood for Gene Experimental

Somatic Inducement Study. And I'll come back to why that's so important later.

'Not surprisingly, we ran into all manner of problems almost immediately. You see, as was explained to us in nauseating detail, one gene doesn't just control one characteristic. In reality, it may be controlled by several genes. Change one and you create knock-on effects on others. A bit like dominos: tap one and down go all the rest. Just with this, that means disrupting the existing DNA, causing all manner of complications, most of which would invariably result in the death of the subject. But a lot of time, a lot of effort and a lot of money later, and the testing eventually paid off—'

'Sorry, just a quick question, Sir, but whom exactly were they doing all these *tests* on?'

He gives me an awkward look.

'I'm afraid that's classified.'

'Yes, but surely so's the rest of it, and you're telling me that, so what's the difference here? I mean, I'm guessing it couldn't have been animals, as their DNA is different, so what was it? Homeless people or something?'

It's a flippant, ill-considered quip. Only he doesn't laugh. Instead he looks like I just slapped him.

'Whoa …' I stammer, my hands shooting to cover my mouth as it dawns on me what that means. 'Oh my God, that's it! That's why everyone's so freaked about this, isn't it? Why no one would tell me? Why all the records got deleted? Holy crap.'

'A lot of decisions were made by a lot of people, all working independently in silos. Things happened which no one is particularly proud of. It is what it is. But to your question, yes, that's why the government is so concerned should this ever leak out.'

I can't help but grimace at the images it conjures. His expression pretty much confirms my fears.

'Not exactly our finest hour,' he mutters gravely. 'But I'm digressing and I don't have long. So, eventually the boffins discovered how to safely target and insert the new genes via the use of some sort of specially developed retro virus. And, by and large, it worked, with only minor side effects reported. Headaches, mood swings, but nothing more. Of course, the MOD wasted no time in selecting fifteen volunteers from British Special Forces and the intelligence community.

'Your mother, Heather, was one of the first volunteers. As you've no doubt discovered from your relentless searching with the equally tenacious Miss Butterworth, she was MI6. Volunteering came with the offer of picking their own missions. Gold dust in that line of work, as I imagine you are slowly realising. They became the true elite of the elite. The rewards outweighed the risks, I suppose.'

There is simply no doubt in my mind anymore as to where this is going. I want to tell myself to run and preserve what little innocence and naivety I still have left. But I don't. Instead, I am pulled even closer to the flame by an impulsive desire to know everything. Perhaps I consider running away to be the *normal* thing to do. And, as I am rapidly beginning to comprehend, I am certainly not that. All I want now is simply to hear him say it.

'And so that's what we did. They introduced the physiological enhancements, we got our team and it all went rather well ... for a while.'

'Uh-huh ...' I say as my expression takes on a more concerned edge.

'And then the problems started.' He sighs gravely. 'We began to observe displays of excessively aggressive behaviour on missions. Several supposedly covert missions turned into utter bloodbaths. The boffins found their dopamine levels were spiking to alarming levels, especially in fight or flight situations. But before they could run their tests, something far more serious came to light.'

I feel a sudden, nasty pang of dread.

'What we had never had the time to do was a proper longevity study. You see, it's not unheard of in plants and animals for these kinds of modifications to just suddenly switch off under stressful conditions. And when that happens, well, sometimes the old gene regenerates and sometimes it doesn't.'

I shoot him an urgent look and find myself holding my breath.

'And ...?'

'And the integrity of the treatments began to fail.'

'I'm sorry, but what does that mean?'

'It means they started going into regression. The modifications started switching off, or, worse still, mutating into cancers. It only took a few cases and we shut the whole programme down. Just like that—three billion pounds gone. Literally everything was destroyed overnight. To my knowledge, it was the last time any of the major military powers attempted anything like it. Until, that is, the Chinese started up a few years ago.'

'Hold on,' I blurt. 'But what happened to the others? What happened to my mum?'

'Well, those who were still alive were returned to their units. The boffins went back to their institutions, and we in the intelligence community continued playing out our dangerous game with the Russians until the end of the Cold War. We soon entered the age of the smart weapon and the need for this kind of programme diminished. But at that point your mother was fine, as far as I know. The complications generally seemed to affect the men more. The women's dual X chromosomes proved far more resilient for some reason. The rumour was your mother went abroad and disappeared. That's all we know of it for certain.'

'Okay, so what do you not know for certain? For instance, what's all that in my file about me being a potential hook for Athena? I presume that is her cover name?'

Dr Gambon smiles proudly.

'So you did get into the safe. My, Henri has trained you well. It's a rumour, really, a suspicion at best that she survived and, after giving you up, went to sell her particular brand of newly acquired skills to the highest bidder. We speculate she quite enjoyed making her own missions, and once outside of the service that's precisely what she continued to do.

'Bringing you into MI13 served two goals, Heather. To train you up so you can provide much the same skills to us as your mother did, and secondly, if word of it got out to her, which we hope it might, it could potential make her break cover. Like it or not, Foxton, I'm afraid we suspect she might indeed still be alive and involved in a number of events that, for want of a better word, could be classed as terrorist acts.'

This is not what I was expecting, not by a long shot, and my mind reels with the ramifications, not only in regard to my opinion of my mother, but for me, also. There goes any interest I had in wearing her old watch.

'S—So, how do you explain all these *skills*, as you call them? I mean, you said it yourself: none of these abilities were meant to be passed on. So how come I seem to have them?'

'Well, that was the theory, certainly. I suppose it's fair to say you are living proof that the boffins got it wrong. Now, the only logical conclusion I can come up with is that your mother was romantically involved with someone on the team and that you were conceived before either of them went into regression, thereby ensuring your inheritance of their enhanced genetic material as your own genetic make-up.'

'Wow, don't make it sound too romantic, will you?' I say dryly. 'So do you also know who my real father was?'

'I'm afraid not. Fraternisation on the team was strictly prohibited, so they must have kept it quiet.'

'So why did it take so long for anyone to come after me?'

'We don't know. There is no doubt she must have realised what it might mean to be pregnant. I presume the last thing she wanted was for anyone to know about you in case anyone asked the very questions she didn't want asked. Like it or not, if you can do half of what they could, Foxton, then you are a truly unique young woman. Our initial assumption was that the Chinese had also tried and failed. Yet somehow they learned of your existence and reasoned if they could get hold of you then all they then needed to do was—'

'Clone me?'

'That's what we thought, until you brought that ID along, which led us to Robert Pemberton-Smythe. Perhaps we were wrong to assume this was the work of the Chinese government. Perhaps it's a private operation?'

As bad as knowing all of this is, there is something even more troubling on my mind. I hesitate, unsure if I even want the answer.

'Look, if everything went so badly wrong for most of them on that team, then who's to say the same thing won't just happen to me one day?'

'The regression, you mean? Oh, I highly doubt that. Trust me, I'm no expert, but the way I see it, even though they were originally engineered, these genes are your natural genetic make-up. That adds immense stability, Heather. There is nothing wrong with them on a biological level. The problems only came about when they replaced existing genes. In much the same way a body can reject a perfectly healthy donor organ. And if that is not reason enough, bear in mind that Gen-ESIS only lasted for a year or so, and you're what, sixteen?'

I nod.

'Sixteen, last February.'

'As I thought. My point exactly. If all it took was some hot weather and elevated stress levels to trigger their regressions, then I'd say the hormonal upheaval of puberty would most certainly have done it for you.'

He sounds so confident; I desperately want to believe him, but doubt is horrible once it's got its claws in.

'At the end of the day, Heather, these are your natural genes. There's nothing for them to revert back to, so I wouldn't worry too much about it.'

I nod, grateful for the reassurance, if not entirely convinced. Not much I can do about it, anyway, so why waste time dwelling on it?

'Alright then, so how does it all work? The things I can do, I mean.'

'Well, as I understood it at the time, the speed and endurance came from their having engineered a significantly higher proportion of non-fatiguing, fast-twitch muscle. Yours will also be packed a lot denser than most people's. Plus you should develop very low lactate levels, even over extended periods of exercise. Your respiratory system is larger than most and far more efficient, so your heart can beat a lot faster than normal. Your nerve impulses will also be accelerated. Enhanced senses, hearing and eyesight are exactly what they sound. And that's it, really. Of course, it wasn't *quite* so simple to achieve in practice ...'

'So what was she like? My mum?'

'Vanessa, well, she was very sharp—in many ways a lot like you, really. Professional to a tee. Never had a bad word to say about anyone. But kept to herself a lot, as I recall. She was dedicated to what she did and a true patriot. She'd do whatever was needed to get the job done. We only ever knew each other on a professional level, so I'm not sure what else I can say.'

I laugh to myself, amazed that he can explain this all so calmly. That all of them who know the truth can be so calm about it. Do they know what they are really saying. Genetic engineering. Secret government experiments. This is the stuff of science fiction. Of movies and comic books. Not real life.

Guessing the source of my amusement, Dr Gambon says, 'Heather, trust me when I say that this, strange as it may seem to you now, is nothing in comparison to some of the things people in this line of work have cooked up over the years.' He fixes me with a focused look. 'Understand, Heather, the things you can do could, with the right training, allow you to achieve things that would make some of our most highly trained operatives look positively amateur in comparison. Much like your mother did. But that's only if you want to remain involved.'

'Well, what do *you* think I should do?' I ask, unsure of myself right now.

He laughs with a mix of genuine amusement and regretful reflection.

'After what I've seen and done in my time, I am probably one of the last people you should be seeking advice from about what the right and wrong thing to do is.'

'But you know this world. You know what it's really like. You've seen it ...'

'Yes, far too much of it, I'm afraid,' he reflects sadly. 'And I'm too old and too tainted, Heather, to have any moral right to tell you what to do. I wish I could, I really do. What I do believe, though, is that we only get one shot at this ... this life, and if we can, then we should make it count. I wish I could say I've made a difference, and maybe, through some of my work, I have. But you, on the other hand, are unique. The things you can do ...' He sighs wistfully. 'What a pity it would be to squander that, don't you think? But the choice as to how best to use the gifts you have, Heather, is yours and yours alone to make.

'Now, if that is all, would you mind awfully getting out of my office? I have business to attend to.'

*

'Well?' Milly exclaims, her eyes burning with curiosity, as I stride back into the study and close the door behind me.

'Well, it worked. Just as I hoped. They must be seriously worried that I'll just up and run away.'

'Did you really need to hit Cole that hard? I almost felt sorry for him,' says Milly.

I give her a quizzical look.

'Almost,' she says with a smile.

'I figured Gambon needed to think I was coming apart. You said yourself he was worried that I'd take on my mother's temper, right? If whatever that led to was so bad, then he needed to think I was going the same way.'

'Anyway, what did he tell you?'

I can't help but crease over in laughter.

'Honestly, I don't know whether to laugh or cry.'

'Well, go on then,' she urges impatiently.

'You're probably not going to believe any of it.'

'Stop stalling!'

'Seriously, it's insane. I mean crazy insane. But then again, for a conspiracy nut like you it'll be right up your street. Alright, fine, here goes. So it all starts some time back in the eighties …'

For the next twenty minutes, I recount the story as best I can. It's surprisingly cathartic. All the while I try to gauge Milly's reaction, but her expression remains stoically neutral. Only when I finish does she betray her stunned amazement.

'Seriously? You're not winding me up?'

'Hand on heart. I swear. Told you it was deep-end stuff.'

'Oh my God … I mean. Oh. My. God!' she stammers, leaning back as it sinks in. 'They really did that! I'd wondered, for sure, after we found out about Haines specialising in genetic engineering, but never in a million years did I actually think it might be true … I mean … S—So how are you taking it?'

I purse my lips and drum my fingers on my thighs as I try to work out how best to respond. Mixed emotions flood my head.

'Yeah, okay, I guess,' I say finally. 'Nowhere near as badly as I feared I would. I'm just trying not to think about the rest of it too much, especially about what happened to everyone else on Genesis.'

For a moment we sit in silence.

'I guess it's like Nigel always says: everyone's got their role to play. I never really knew what they wanted from me or why they've been pushing me in the direction they have.'

Milly nods.

'Yeah, James Bond, watch out. Though I wouldn't hold out too much hope for anything like that,' she says, laughing. 'But is that really what you want to get involved in?'

'It's certainly a life less ordinary, isn't it? And I did ask for a bit of adventure, didn't I? Bit rich to turn it down now. And better this than some soul-destroying trudge from school to uni. and then into some boring-arse office job for the rest of my life, don't you think? Nah, to hell with that! I want to have some fun with my life. And I want to do something useful with it, like Gambon said. You know what I mean? Maybe this is it. Besides, for the first time in my life, adults actually seem to be taking me seriously, so why not stay?'

Milly nods acceptingly.

'Seriously,' I say, 'you have no idea how glad I am that you're cool with all this. I was so worried that you'd freak out. To be able to share all this is such a huge relief. I'm not even allowed to tell anyone else. Because if it ever got out ...'

'I know,' she adds solemnly. 'You don't have to tell me. There isn't a government on the planet that wouldn't—'

'Yeah okay, let's not go there.' I laugh. 'Anyway it means a lot and I love you for it.'

'Yeah, I know.' An embarrassed little laugh escapes her lips.

'No, I'm serious,' I say, taking hold of her shoulders. 'Thank you for being my friend when most people would have either run off screaming or, worse, sold me out.' I lean forward and embrace her.

With a depreciating smile, she adds, 'Isn't that what best friends are for? Taking the good with the bad?'

* * *

CHAPTER 13

THE MAN FROM VALHALLA

I t's tough to describe the change that's come over me since hearing the truth from Dr Gambon. I certainly have a newfound enthusiasm for what Cabal is teaching me. There's a spring in my step and a new, more confident cheekiness about me. And I love it.

With this change in attitude the weeks seem to fly by in a dizzying blur of activity. Days full of new classes and practical training exercises merge with evenings spent in catching up with all my overdue projects.

As it turns out, there was little need to ask my friends to help with the whole Pemberton-Smythe/Vanguard thing, but given how much I have on, I'm grateful to let them run with it.

Things only get better when Alex invites me to come to his upcoming birthday party. Only snag: it's in Switzerland at their family house there. I frown at the thought of asking my dad for the money to go.

As November rolls into December, a palpable sense of festive excitement descends upon the school. Almost overnight, courtesy of the lower fifth, the boarding houses and main public areas become festooned with Christmas trees and colourful decorations. Around the same time, the weather turns typically unpredictable and one morning we all wake to find the grounds covered in a glistening layer of frost. Winter's arrived.

Two days later, and in a comical twist to our normal status quo, I find it's me who's waiting impatiently for Milly as she fumbles around in the study, getting herself ready for the day ahead.

'Oi, are you coming, or what?' I shout, flicking an exasperated look at my watch.

She fires me an irate scowl.

'You're getting worse than me lately!'

'Yeah, right,' I say with a roll of my eyes. Taking her arm, I pull her along with me. 'I guess I've just found inner peace and a sense of direction.'

We look at each other and burst into fits of giggles.

'Uh-huh, right,' Milly snorts, pulling her arm free.

'No, seriously,' I exclaim. 'For the first time, I actually feel comfortable in myself. I'm enjoying my life and not worrying all the time. I feel fitter with all the exercise I'm doing and—'

'I don't call getting up at six o'clock every day to go for a run exercise. That's self-inflicted torture,' she teases, 'and you should probably see someone about it.'

'Ya! Well don't knock what you haven't tried,' I fire back good-humouredly. 'It's lovely at that time in the morning. Literally, there's *no one* around. I'm free to let things off the chain a little, if you know what I mean?'

'Uh-huh, well I'm quite happy in my nice, comfy bed, thank you very much. But seriously, though,' Milly says, peering down with consternation at my legs, both of which have become noticeably more toned of late, 'you might want to think about cutting back on some of that stuff. The runs, going to the gym all the time. 'Cause at this rate you'll end up more buff than some of the first fifteen,' she lectures, only half-joking, as we come out of SH to head off towards class.

'You don't think girls with a six-pack are sexy?'

'Eww, no!'

'Eh, whatever. Why can't fit be the new skinny? Besides, I like the buzz it gives me. That endorphin rush. It's like the afterglow people get after they've had sex.'

'How would you know?' Milly exclaims. 'You've never had sex.'

'Well, neither have you!' I fire back.

She shrugs ambivalently.

'I'm just saying, is all.'

Being reminded of the fact is irritating me more and more of late. I know it's a choice I consciously made, and up till now it's been one I have neither particularly liked nor regretted, but it is starting to bug me. There's simply so much peer group pressure that at times I just want to get it over and done with. But that would feel like I've fundamentally abandoned something about myself, about my morality, my standards, let alone my self-respect. There isn't much I get to control in my life. So much of what happens, where I go, what I do, is dictated by adults. But this, what happens to me and my body, that's my choice and no one is going to take that away from me. It's a small thing in the grand scheme of the world but it's important to me and who I am. Christ! Would you listen to me? I sound like my mother!

Before I can say anything, there's a shout from behind us. We turn to see Anabel waving to us.

'We've got something you'll find interesting,' she calls.

Upstairs in her pretty little study, we find Luther and Nigel hunched over a custom-built laptop. Seeing us, Nigel beckons us over.

'What have you got?' I ask.

'Only the entire inbox of Pemberton-Smythe's lawyer.'

'How the hell did you get that?' I exclaim.

'Easy,' Luther chimes. 'Weel, we got his nam frae a wiretap Mr Sparkman authorised. 'En ah jist wrote a nifty wee trojan 'at went tae wark while their nightly system back-up happened.'

'See, we buried it in an e-mail that Luther made to look like it came from his boss,' Nigel adds excitedly, 'which, when opened, instructed his mailbox to send us its entire contents. Now we know pretty much everything he was working on for this Pemberton-Smythe guy. And there's some pretty interesting stuff.'

I peer closer at all the files they pirated from the lawyer at Breneke, Leibovic and Kyriacos.

'But there's tonnes of stuff here.'

'Give them the weirdest bit,' Anabel says.

'Alright; well, Gambon was right,' Nigel says, looking up at us. 'This Pemberton-Smythe guy, or his company, has been divesting like anything over the last year or so.'

'And in a way that seems rather odd, given what their primary business has always been,' Anabel adds.

'How so?' says Milly.

'Well, besides all the property he's been buying, which seems strange enough in itself,' Anabel notes, 'he's apparently also been buying up quite a few companies. But all in just as secretive a way as the property.'

'What kind of companies?' I ask.

'All sorts,' Nigel replies. 'But we did see a weird trend.'

'Aye, take this one,' Luther says, handing us a printout. 'It's a private equity company he bought a few years back—'

'But that's not so different, is it, to what his own company does?' I point out.

'True,' Nigel says. 'But what that company specialises in is very different to what his has typically invested in.'

'How so?' Milly asks.

'Well, because the company he bought specialises in only one kind of investment. And that's investing in upstart genetics companies,' says Anabel.

Milly and I turn to each other with startled looks. Leaning in towards the screen, I point at the list of companies which Pemberton-Smythe's Valhalla has recently acquired.

'Can you send all that to my e-mail?' I say, waving my phone, before rushing from the room, with Milly hurrying to keep up.

*

Two days later, it is with a palpable sense of excitement that Milly and I charge up the escalator in Canary Wharf underground station and emerge out into the sun. This is all Dr Gambon's idea. Upon hearing our discovery—something which even AFOTS missed—he immediately got the ball rolling by calling in a favour with a contact at the Treasury to secure us a meeting with Robert Pemberton-Smythe under the guise of a university economics project.

Our mission, therefore, which I'm not sure we had a whole lot of choice but to accept, is to use a cleverly constructed set of questions designed to lure Robert Pemberton-Smythe into confessing whether these investments into the gene-bio industry were made by his company or, more worryingly, himself. Unfortunately we were told all this verbally so there was no message which then self-destructed five seconds later.

My excitement, though, is nothing compared to Milly's. She jolts to a halt and gazes up in wonder at the impressive steel and glass towers that soar high into the sky all around us. It's certainly a sight to behold, but one I'm all too familiar with, given that my parents' place—if I can still call them that—is just around the corner.

Of course, typical British weather: it was cold and miserable down in Surrey, yet it's warm and sunny here in London. We soon sling our coats over our arms and, being early, decide to meander the canyon-like roads of the Docklands financial district. As we walk, Milly keeps looking me up and down and giggling. I can barely keep a straight face myself.

Fearing that Pemberton-Smythe might recognise me, which isn't beyond the realm of possibility if he's directly involved with whatever has been going on with Morocco and the Chinese, Gambon insisted that I seek the assistance of a disguise expert from MI5. She came down this morning to give me a make-over. And a rather drastic one at that. Now my hair is jet black from a one-time washout dye and pulled back aggressively from my face into a French twist. I'm sporting a pair of black-rimmed glasses, which make me look far more academic than either of us knows to be true. But at least I don't feel out of place around here. Because whereas Milly settled on a flowing pastel gypsy skirt, a lacy cotton blouse and a small blazer, I decided it would be more appropriate, having visited my dad's office on several occasions, to go with one of my smarter pinstripe suits with a matching pencil skirt, black tights and a crisp, white, fitted shirt. And in marked contrast to Milly's more sensible ballet flats, my unashamedly high pair of patent-black heels clack noisily on the paving stones as we walk. I look a million miles from my usual self. But hopefully it's enough to fool Robert Pemberton-Smythe.

While we wait for our midday appointment, we grab a coffee and sit down by the big, round fountain in the centre of Cabot Square. One of the larger, more picturesque squares near the centre of the estate, it's surrounded on all sides by high-rise office towers. I point out the tallest one, with its pyramidal roof, as being where we ultimately need to get to. I don't think Milly's too happy at the thought of being that high up.

We take the express lift up to the fiftieth floor of the Canary Wharf tower. I don't think I'll ever get used to my ears popping inside a building as we rush skywards. We share one last wary look as the doors swish open to reveal a spectacular-looking reception lobby. Spacious and windowless, it is clad, floor to ceiling, in polished black marble. To our left, several plush leather sofas are arranged neatly around a designer glass coffee table. Numerous flat-screen televisions adorn the walls, all silently playing a variety of different financial news channels. Dozens of small recessed lights shine down to reflect up off the floor, reminiscent almost of the stars shining amidst a dark night sky.

Across the way is a long front desk with a cluster of im-maculately dressed receptionists behind it. Fixed to the wall behind them is a big gold sign.

Valhalla Capital

'Good morning, can I help you?' one of the receptionists enquires, pointedly addressing the question to me.

'Yes,' I reply cheerily. 'We have an appointment to see Mr Pemberton-Smythe at midday.'

'Ms Stephens and Ms Rogers, from the London School of Economics?'

'Yes, that's right,' Milly lies smoothly.

Gambon wisely decided to use a cover university which Pemberton-Smythe neither attended nor lectures at.

'Very well, if you'd both like to take a seat?' the receptionist says, indicating the waiting area. 'I'll inform the chairman's office that you've arrived.'

I've barely opened the first magazine when I realise I could probably do with the toilet. One of the receptionists points the way. By the time I return, Milly is already gone.

'I'm sorry,' the woman says. 'Mr Pemberton-Smythe finished his last meeting early, so he and your friend have already started. I can take you through, if you wish?'

I glance at my watch.

'Well, we only had a few minutes,' I note. 'I'm not really sure there's much point now.'

'Well, would you like something to drink perhaps, while you wait?'

Rather than fetching me a glass of water, as she might have done were I a client, she gives me a visitor's badge and leads me through a large set of double-doors and down a corridor, past a row of plush-looking offices and a long glass window, behind which lies a huge open room crammed full with row after row of desks. Each has more computer screens on it than

I would even know what to do with. A plethora of colourful and constantly changing data flits across each one. Everyone is either on the phone, shouting across the floor, or rushing around with a tangible sense of urgency or panic—I'm not quite sure which.

She leads me into their canteen and points to the food counter and its adjoining coffee bar, before saying, 'Please help yourself to whatever you want. It's all complimentary. Your friend should be done in about five minutes, so if you want to head back then.'

I nod and she leaves me to it. Armed with a large hot chocolate, I find a seat by the window with its breathtaking view out over London. The drink is still a little too hot for my liking, so I casually listen in on people's conversations as they come and go. Barely half a minute later, my ears prick up at the mention of Pemberton-Smythe's name. I look round to see two middle-aged men chatting by the coffee bar.

'Don't expect an answer till after the weekend,' one of them says. 'He'll be travelling till Monday.'

I tune out, only to be hit by a sudden, worrying realisation. What if Milly has no luck? What if Pemberton-Smythe doesn't bite as we hope he will? The whole trip will have been a total waste of time. But if I'm lucky, I've still got about five minutes before my absence is noted. Ultimately we don't need to prove Pemberton-Smythe is involved; we only need to prove his company isn't. Then, by default, we'll have our answer. I'm thinking if his company was behind the purchase of all those genetics research companies, then surely someone around here would know about it?

I open up an internet browser on my iSpy and quickly familiarise myself with some commonly used corporate acquisition terms. Given what I'm now contemplating, I'm quite relieved at my choice of clothes.

With my cup in hand, I hastily make my way out of the canteen and down the hallway towards a bank of lifts. Amazingly no one gives me so much as a second glance. If only they could hear the frantic thumping from within my chest. I half-expect to be stopped at any moment, but no one does. A decent outfit, some make-up, a pair of intimidatingly high heels, and, like a chameleon, I disappear amongst the suits.

Pausing by the lift, I turn to the shortish man waiting beside me.

'Sorry, you wouldn't happen to know what floor corporate acquisitions are on, would you?'

He peers up from his phone.

'M and A? Forty-eight, I think.'

'Cheers!' I say and press the corresponding button. He goes straight back to tapping out an e-mail.

I take the lift down two floors and glance briefly at the wall sign. Mergers and Acquisitions to the right. Beside the security door is a pass-card reader. I dare not try mine in case it sets off some sort of alarm somewhere and opt instead to wait for the next person to come through. Barely ten seconds later, a man steps from the lifts. I make a good show of fumbling in my bag whilst balancing the cup and my phone. Seeing my predicament, he smiles and runs over to open the door for me. I smile gratefully and walk straight onto another of their huge trading floors.

I tentatively head over to a nearby desk to ask the lady there where I need to go. She barely glances up as two of her phones begin ringing at once. Clearly stressed, she points towards the other side of the room before snatching up both phones. I soon find what I am looking for and approach the nearest person with as confident and authoritative a manner as I can put on. He has just put his phone down when I catch his eye.

'Hi, I'm sorry,' I begin, setting my Venti-sized cup aside. 'The chairman's office sent me down to get the files on last year's Gene-Tec purchase. Do you know who could give them to me?'

'The what?' he replies. Then he looks at me properly and, in an appraising sort of way, which I don't particularly like, says, 'I'm sorry, who are you?'

It takes me a second to remember my alias.

'Kelly Rodgers,' I say. 'I started in the chairman's office this week.'

He scowls, clearly annoyed.

'When are those muppets going to stop wasting our time with stuff like this?' He takes a deep breath. 'Alright, sorry, sweetheart, not your fault. What was it you're after again?'

'All they said was we did a purchase of a company called Gene-Tec a year or two back and they want me to get the file.'

'What are they? Like bio industry? I think someone's having a laugh with you,' he says with a cheeky, knowing smile. 'We don't do that kind of stuff here. Sorry.' And with that he swivels round and snatches up his incessantly ringing phone. 'Valhalla. Falloon. How can I help?'

I nod gratefully and head off back the way I came as fast as possible without attracting attention. I've been gone quite long enough and my heart is racing, partly from the fear of getting caught and partly from exhilaration at having found our answer.

Once I reach the lobby, I know something is wrong. I can just tell from Milly's expression. She's obviously been waiting for a good few minutes; a thick stack of brochures is clutched tightly under her arm. Seeing me, she hurriedly presses the lift summons button. The doors promptly open and she practically drags me inside. As they close again, we spin to face each other.

'Where did you get to?' she asks.

'Well, I figured if he was going to be awkward then I needed to find some other way of finding out if the company was involved. So I went to look for the people who do corporate deals here. Turns out it's all Pemberton-Smythe. They don't invest in bio companies.'

'Interesting,' Milly says, pondering that for a second. 'Well, that's good because the interview was a total waste of time. He completely dodged my questions.'

'Doesn't matter, though,' I say. 'We still got our answer.'

But rather than being happy, Milly sighs and looks at her shoes.

'Yeah, but it gets a little more complicated. There are two other things.'

'Yeah?'

'Well, you're not going to believe who came out of his office just before I went in!'

I give her a vacant, quizzical look.

'Vadim-flipping-Menyatov is who! Right here, in this very building!'

'It's funny how you say that. As if you expect me to know who that is. Is he famous?'

'Oh—my—God,' she exclaims in exasperation. 'He's only one of the most famous hackers in the world! You'd know that if you'd been listening during the GCHQ lecture earlier this term.'

I ignore the dig.

'Are you sure?'

She sighs and gives me a 'What do you think?' look.

'Okay, point taken,' I concede. 'What the hell would *he* be doing here?'

'Exactly!' she says pointedly. 'Gambon's definitely gonna want to hear about this. Let's give him a call once we're outside.'

The lift pings, announcing our arrival at the ground floor lobby.

'You said there was something else.'

'Oh yes,' she says gravely. 'You might want to find out who your boyfriend's dad really is.'

'How so?'

'Because Pemberton-Smythe has a picture of Alex on his desk.'

With that, she hurries from the lift, leaving me open-mouthed and speechless.

'W—What?' I stammer, and rush out after her. I'm barely into the lobby when I spot the first man, and freeze. A horrible gut feeling has me snap my head around. And there, just as I feared, is a second man. I don't need another look, I already know who they are, and I flee back into the lift. My brain whirrs feverishly with a combined rush of panic at the sight of the men and a blur of confusion at Milly's revelation.

* * *

CHAPTER 14

A RATHER HOT EXTRACTION

U nfortunately, the two chinese men have, rather cleverly, covered both ends of the lift bank, effectively blocking the only ways out. Their choice of suits and ties is inspired cover, as I just discovered, to blend in unnoticed around here. Miraculously, neither was looking up when I stepped from the lift. So my arrival now will hopefully come as a surprise. It had better, because it's the only advantage I have.

Though how they knew to be here concerns me. Only a handful of people were aware of our plan today. Milly peers back into the lift with an impatient look. Instantly she sees something is wrong.

'Hey, maybe it's just a horrible coincidence, them being related,' she says, almost apologetically. 'Maybe he's got nothing to do with whatever his dad's up to. I'm just saying it's a hell of a coincidence, the dad funding the company who came after you and the son ... well, you know. It just worries me, is all.' Then she stops, realising that isn't what's on my mind.

I fix her with a steely gaze and put my finger to my lips. 'Shh. Just follow me and do exactly as I say, okay?'

'Why? What's up?'

'Those mercenary guys. The ones from Morocco. Well, there are two more of them waiting in the lobby.'

She makes to speak, then stammers and goes silent as a worried look plasters itself onto her face.

'Come on,' I say, 'but we've got to move fast.' Leading the way, I stride confidently from the lift, my head down, eyes averted. Up ahead, the first man looks up briefly, but obviously sees no further than my black hair, for he immediately goes back to his paper; though only for a second. Because then, with a puzzled expression, he glances up again, does a double take, and recognises me. Permitting himself the faintest of smiles, he folds his paper and moves forward to block our path. As we near him, despite a noticeably trembling hand, I loosen the plastic lid of my still full hot chocolate.

With no warning, I fling the entire contents straight into his face. He recoils backwards, but not fast enough as I follow through and slam the iSpy into his face. Sapphire crystal screen versus human nose. The phone wins and he crashes to the floor, clutching the pumping, bloody mess that's become the centre of his face.

I grab Milly's hand and yank her towards the revolving doors. She squeals and flails for her brochures as they slip and scatter off across the floor.

'Holy crap!' she gasps as we burst through the doors. 'Now what?'

I spin round, looking for the best avenue of escape. With no idea how many of them there are, we've probably only got a few seconds before they regroup and move to plan B.

She darts a frightened look back inside.

'H—How did you know?'

'C'mon.' I pull her along behind me as I set off down the street as fast as my heels will permit. 'I dunno. Hunch, maybe. But they were both wearing those weird, lightweight urban combat boots. Just didn't feel right.'

I cast a hasty look over my shoulder, just as the second man rushes out onto the pavement. He shoots a frantic look up and down the busy road. A phone is pressed to his ear. I can't be sure if he sees us or not.

'Quick, in here,' I blurt, and drag Milly roughly in through the side door of a shopping mall. Even in my heels, we run through it and emerge out onto the adjacent street. Halfway across it, another idea pops into my head. I curse at not having thought of it sooner. Furiously, I dig into my handbag. With relief, I find the card in a side pocket, adhered to a pack of chewing gum.

'What's that?' Milly says as she hurries to keep pace with me.

'Something Abbott gave me. For situations just like this.'

We rush down a short flight of steps and dash past a couple of bars already bustling with the busy lunchtime crowd. I dial the number and a woman answers.

'EXCOM,' she says promptly. 'Your access code, please.'

I place my thumb on the biometric reader. A moment later, a number appears on the screen. I read it out to her.

'Thank you. Redirecting to Hereford four-five-six. Stand by.'

The phone rings twice before a man answers it.

'Hello?'

The voice sounds familiar.

'Hi. I was told to call this numb—'

'*Foxton?*'

The confusion in Abbott's voice is unmistakeable.

'Yeah,' I exclaim breathlessly. 'We're in the Docklands and they're here. The Vanguard people. And now they're after us.'

'Wait, back up. Who's we and what do you mean you're in the Docklands?'

'Long story. It's Milly and me. I don't know how many of them there are. We just had to leg it and are now being chased on foot.'

We run down a large flight of semi-circular steps and stop to consider our options quickly. We could go right, along the pedestrianised waterfront with its crowded bars and restaurants. Straight on would take us over the bridge to West India Quay. But I'd prefer not to lead them right to my front door. That leaves left, back towards Cabot Square.

'They'd expect us to hide in one of the bars, don't you think?' Milly gasps breathlessly.

'Agreed. Come on then.'

We hurry along the quieter path to our left. I switch the phone to speaker as Abbott loops someone else onto the call.

'MOD European theatre operations. Sergeant Barry speaking.'

'Sergeant, this is a Blue Bird emergency,' Abbott barks, all gruff and to the point. 'Authorisation code zulu-zulu-niner-niner-bravo-delta. This is not a drill. Do you understand?'

'Yes, Sir. Authorisation approved. Standing by.'

'Foxton, where exactly are you?'

'Near West India Quay. Just around the corner from Cabot Square.'

'Sergeant, give me a rundown of friendly assets in that vicinity.'

There is a brief pause, accompanied by some pretty frantic typing.

'No immediate ground assets within twenty clicks, Sir. But I have a CH-47, RAF, five clicks out, en-route to Poole. Manifest lists the cargo as M Squadron, SBS.'

Abbott swears.

'Okay, not the best. But it'll have to do. We can deal with the fallout later. Alright, listen up, you two. If I didn't think these numb nuts wouldn't follow you straight into a police station and cause a bloody mess, then that's where I'd be telling you to go. But they turned Marrakech into a warzone, so let's not assume they won't do the same thing now. Sergeant, I need you to listen very carefully ...'

Milly clasps my arm and points.

'Look!' she blurts.

I turn to see five men, all dressed like the first two, rushing down the steps. Cursing, we move faster but refrain from running, lest it catches their attention. A flight of steps take us up into a large rectangular courtyard with a pedestrianised access road that connects it to the adjacent main road, a short distance away. All around us, people are obliviously having their lunch at the collection of tables and chairs arranged nearby. Knowing we'll get little help from them, we hurry on towards the main road.

'Foxton! Butterworth!' Abbott shouts irritably. 'Did you catch what I just said?'

'Abbott—no, sorry,' I gasp. 'Now there's a whole bunch of them after us. We had to leg it up into Columbus Courtyard. Where do you want us to go?'

'Okay, keep calm. Don't get your knickers in a twist. Help's on the way. I want you to make for Cabot Square, but quickly. They'll be with you in about a minute. Do you understand?'

'We do.'

Milly casts a wary glance at her watch. I take her hand and we break into a run—just as two of the Chinese men appear at the top of the stairs. Too late, they spot us and start running, rapidly chewing into our head start. We take the corner at speed and are suddenly faced with a wide, tree-lined boulevard that leads up to Cabot Square. The pavement is crammed with office workers streaming out of the high-rise buildings which line both sides of the street.

With no time to dawdle, we push on through the crowds. As I pull Milly along, I become aware of a distant whopper-whopper-like sound that's coming from somewhere behind us. I turn to look and my eyes go wide. With stunned disbelief, I direct Milly's attention up into the sky to where a huge, twin-rotored Chinook helicopter has just begun banking hard. Then it dives towards the glass-and-steel-sided canyon in which we are. Milly's eyes are almost as wide as saucers. She can barely form the words.

'O—Oh, no way,' she stammers.

I blink my surprise away and grab her hand. 'Oh, hell yes,' I exclaim, and pull her on towards the square with renewed vigour.

Any other day, five hundred metres in under a minute would be a cinch. But now, here, today, with the pavement crammed with dawdling locals, all either on their phones, in conversations with others or reading books or newspapers, I'm not sure we'll even be able to do a hundred in that time. But with no choice, we elbow and push our way through the wall of slow-moving pedestrians, many of whom have now stopped to gawp gormlessly up at the approaching helicopter.

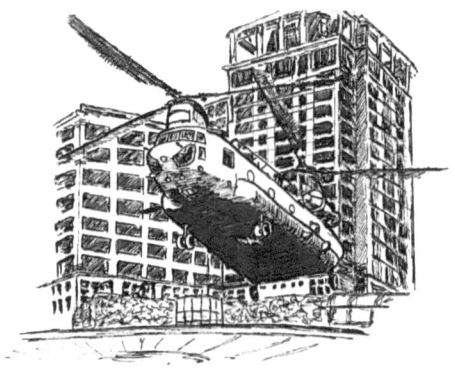

It's still some way off, but it looks huge. At least the size of a bus. Four sets of sturdy-looking undercarriage hang from beneath its flat underbelly. Up top, set in tandem, are two massive counter-rotating rotor blades. Together they thump their way aggressively through the air, beating gravity into submission. The noise as the Chinook thunders by overhead is phenomenal. And even though it's well above the buildings, the downdraft still buffets the trees and sends every piece of loose vegetation flying out from the road's central divide.

I curse as I'm brought to an abrupt halt as one of my heels catches between the paving stones. Wedged firm, I have to wrench it loose by hand, completely skinning the heel. Horrified at the sight, and not about to risk it happening again, I snatch the other shoe off and carry on in my tights. Thankfully the rubber-necking crowd is slowing the Chinese men down as much as it is us.

With a last push, we finally break free and sprint across the road towards the square—just as the helicopter comes to a hover directly overhead, casting a dark shadow over everything below. Cars and taxis honk in annoyance as we bring the traffic to a standstill.

Lunchtime on such an unexpectedly sunny day and Cabot Square is packed to near overflowing with office workers looking to make the most of it over their short lunch breaks. Their collective sense of naive curiosity falters and then completely collapses as the helicopter suddenly drops like a stone towards them.

Some make to flee, panicking and screaming, but even they aren't fast enough. No one is remotely prepared for the near gale-force wind which is whipped up when, only thirty feet from the deck, the pilot puts an aggressive halt to the descent. A sudden, unimaginable havoc is instantly unleashed on all those below it as the helicopter's monstrous downdraft wrenches everything not firmly secured and flings it violently from the square. Sandwiches, drinks, scarves, jackets, loose papers and the entire contents of the central fountain all blow out sideways in a blizzard of unmitigated carnage. Hundreds of screams are drowned out by the immense roar of the helicopter's turbines as its back wheels lightly kiss the edge of the now empty fountain.

With no time to waste, we rush forward towards the lone crewman standing on the lowered rear ramp. His eyes dart rapidly over the sea of terrified people. Waving our arms frantically, we break from the crowd and sprint for the fountain. With a leap, we're up onto its rim, and from there we jump again onto the ramp and into the safety of his outstretched arms. He shouts into his helmet microphone and grips us tightly as the engines scream, punching the helicopter back up into the air.

For a brief moment I spot one of the mercenaries down near the fountain. He appears to be shaking his head in disbelief. Resignedly he takes out his mobile phone. I laugh and flick him my middle finger.

By the time the ramp whirrs up and locks into place, Canary Wharf is far behind us. Only then, however, does the crewman release his grip, allowing us to look round for the first time. We stop abruptly. For there, seated along both sides of the fuselage, and all staring back at us, equally surprised, are around thirty fully armed soldiers. I hesitantly turn to Milly and we both burst into fits of giggles.

* * *

CHAPTER 15

LAST CALL FOR THE 4.40 TO GENEVA

By the time we are summoned to Dr Gambon's office, first thing the next morning, he has corralled together quite some audience. Several of his bookcases have been moved aside to reveal large TV screens. Frank Sable, the head of B-School's Covert Espionage programme, is in the middle of briefing everyone who's dialled into the video call on what's happened overnight. The audience consists of the most senior figures from MI5, MI6, GCHQ and COBR (the cabinet's emergency briefing room in Downing Street who will update the prime minister later).

With a wry smile, Dr Gambon beckons us in and points to another screen on which the image of a journalist standing amidst a sea of blue flashing lights is frozen. He depresses the pause button.

'... chaos descended on Canary Wharf today as a British Army helicopter on a training exercise was almost forced to make an emergency landing after suffering an on-board computer malfunction.

'Only the quick reactions of its crew averted disaster for hundreds of City workers below. A spokesperson for the Ministry of Defence praised the pilots for their swift efforts in correcting the fault and added that the aircraft's black box was being examined. However, the MOD refused to give any further details at this time. CCTV footage from the square was unavailable due to unscheduled maintenance work.

'In other news, Defence Minister Guy Forbes has launched a scathing attack against the French government's failed efforts to control the influx of illegal immigr—'

Dr Gambon mutes the TV and indicates the spaces on the sofas.

'Take a seat, girls. We'll come to you in a moment.' Then he turns to Frank and signals for him to continue.

'Right, so after the sighting of Menyatov in Pemberton-Smythe's office yesterday, Five sent a team in last night to have a sneak-and-peek around the place. Unfortunately they drew a blank, so we must proceed on the assumption that Pemberton-Smythe is keeping his cards very close to his chest.'

I shoot a loaded look at Milly. That would explain why we haven't heard anything since our return to school yesterday afternoon.

'Mmm, quite so,' mumbles Dr Gambon. 'So we should probably try his private residences. There's the place in Mayfair, the estate in Sussex, and that castle of his in Switzerland.'

Then it's the turn of the current head of MI6 to speak.

'Now Douglas,' he begins, 'didn't you say something about Pemberton-Smythe being in Switzerland over the weekend?'

'That's right,' Dr Gambon replies, flashing me an ominously knowing look as he opens a manila folder. 'Seems his youngest son—now his only son; the other died in a skiing accident last year—has a birthday tomorrow night. Pemberton-Smythe senior is expected to be in attendance. Perhaps Miss Foxton here can fill us in a bit more?'

With that, he smiles at me, obviously enjoying my discomfort. I fix him with a dirty look, but he simply nods in a way that suggests everything will be fine. I clear my throat dubiously.

'Yes, as the headmaster says, tomorrow is Alex Pemberton-Smythe's birthday.'

'And you know this how?' someone asks.

I swallow awkwardly and hesitate. Thankfully Gambon comes to my rescue.

'Miss Foxton has been cultivating a friendship with Pemberton-Smythe's son for a while now,' he says dispassionately.

Surprised silence falls over the room. First to speak is a man from MI5.

'Was this some sort of crafty plan of yours, Douglas, to get on the inside early?'

Gambon smiles tellingly and shrugs.

'Let's just move on, shall we?'

'Well, how do we know he isn't in on whatever the father's up to?' another person fires back.

Milly fixes me with a tractor beam-like stare.

'Because overnight I had GCHQ deep-dive every communication the boy has ever sent, is how,' Dr Gambon replies neutrally. 'There is no doubt in my mind that the boy has no idea what his father is potentially involved in.'

Part of me gives a huge sigh of relief. Even Milly, the ultimate cynic, seems to accept that. Despite having never been one for religion, I find myself closing my eyes and saying a little prayer of thanks.

'Good, then I think we should seriously consider sending your girl in there to have a jolly good nosey around,' the man from MI5 suggests. 'We can take the place in Mayfair. Seems Pemberton-Smythe, well, certainly the family, don't use the Sussex estate very often. If at all that we can tell. The wife seems to stay in Switzerland and he just flits back and forth between there and the London pad.'

'It's worth noting,' someone from COBR chimes in, 'that Heathrow security has him flying out early this morning with a laptop in his possession.'

'Even better,' says C. 'If it's important enough to take with him, then it's worth us having a look at to see what's on it. Internet accessible?'

'Not that we can see,' a lady from GCHQ says. 'Seems he disconnects it from the net almost permanently. There is never any bounce back from the IP address, either. Nor does he have any external back-up cloud service which we could tap.'

'Then a party should provide the ideal cover for something like this,' Dr Gambon notes dryly. 'Deborah and I had nine of William's little friends round last weekend. To say they kept us busy is an understatement. God only knows how Pemberton-Smythe intends to cope with several hundred teenagers. That's bound to keep him occupied while you sneak off, find the computer, and copy the hard-drive without being detected,' he says, looking in my direction.

I try not to laugh as they all start planning what I should do without so much as bothering to ask me what I think. They obviously have no idea what a party like this will be like. I mean, Alex is friends with the royal twins! The security is going to be ridiculous.

Ugh, typical adults.

That said, it does, however, rather nicely solve the problem of how I was going to be able to pay for my ticket. Oddly, Dad was being unusually hesitant about letting me fly to Switzerland to stay with a boy he's never met. I think his plan was to dither for so long that there'd either be no tickets left or, more likely, I'd just miss the party.

'We could always task it to Spec Ops?' says a man from the MI6 screen.

A stab of panic races through me. No! I want this. More to the point, I want to see Alex again. It's been weeks since we last saw each other. And despite whatever his father might be mixed up with, my feelings for him have only deepened, and I have found myself falling for him hopelessly. Distance of any kind between us hurts desperately and fills me with a constant dull ache. They can't take this opportunity from me. I won't let them.

'That might get a bit heavy-handed,' Dr Gambon says with a chuckle. Then he looks over at me and winks. 'No, best I think if we keep this strictly to those currently in the know.'

'Agreed,' says C.

Suddenly becoming serious, Dr Gambon pauses thoughtfully and steeples his fingers under his chin.

'If I didn't think you capable, Ms Foxton, I wouldn't bother suggesting it. But the choice to do this must be yours, and yours alone.'

I nod and try not to laugh at how often I've heard that lately. Everyone's attention is firmly fixed on me. All waiting expectantly.

'Look, I don't mind doing it,' I say. 'I was probably going to go anyway. Guess it can't hurt to slip off for a few minutes for this.'

It's barely out of my mouth before the adults all start chattering away furiously amongst themselves, drawing up all sorts of complicated plans, no longer in the least bit interested in what I have to say. I turn to Milly and we share an unspoken, weary look.

Thereafter everything accelerates into a blur. First, it's straight down to B-School using Gambon's secret lift, an antiquated birdcage-like contraption hidden behind another bookcase, and along a utilitarian maintenance tunnel in the little golf cart which he uses each day for the journey. Then, once there, with Milly also in tow, Frank Sable takes us to a huge storeroom that neither of us even knew existed.

Leaving us by the counter at the front, he disappears into the back, only to return a few minutes later with a collection of innocent looking everyday items. One is a nice little silver make-up compact.

'Right, now pay attention,' he begins, snapping his fingers in front of my face. 'This is what you'll need to access and download his hard-drive and then to send it on to us via a high-frequency burst transmission. That way, once it's done, you can dump the gear and leave the party without having anything incriminating on you.

'Now once you've found Pemberton-Smythe's computer,' he says, taking a matchbox-sized, black plastic box, 'you'll need this password decrypter. Just turn the laptop on and plug this into the USB. When the LED goes green, it'll automatically provide the password. Take it out and then plug in the compact. It's a hyper-fire-wire solid-state drive. Inside you'll find four pallets of eye shadow and some good-old-fashioned slutty red lipstick. But listen carefully.'

Milly and I lean forward for a closer look, only to be somewhat disappointed by the shades on offer.

Seeing where our focus is, Frank sighs and clicks his fingers.

'Oi, listen. Do not use them, okay? They're only about a millimetre deep. Alright, now this is important. You need to press this pallet here, and out pops a USB plug. Slot it in and press the pallet next to it to begin the download. While it's doing that, this LED will flash. When it goes out, you're done. Remove it and then get this—'

'How long will that take?' Milly asks. 'Mine takes all night when I back up my hard-drive.'

'Yeah, well our stuff's a bit better than what you'll buy on the high street,' he replies disparagingly. 'Now comes the complicated bit. Do you smoke?'

I shake my head.

'Why, should I?'

'Probably not. But for the purposes of tomorrow, you might have to appear to.' He holds up a thick yellow and black Cohiba Number 4 cigar tube.

I burst into laughter.

'Hold on. You're kidding, right? I mean, seriously, there's no way anyone my age would ever smoke something like *that*.'

'Point taken, but unless you can think of another way to smuggle a collapsible satellite dish into the party, you're just going to have to be the trendsetter of the night.'

I shrug with resigned acceptance and toy absentmindedly with a strand of unruly hair; a bemused smile plays across my face as he sets about assembling it.

'Just pull off the top, remove the dish, and crumble away the tobacco from the tip to reveal the plug. Once the download's done and you've unplugged the make-up compact, connect it to the dish and then unfold it. It's about the size of a dinner plate, so pretty easy to handle. Go to a window and aim it towards the horizon at the narrow end of the lake. Then angle it up at about forty-five degrees and just press this button to send. The LED will flash rapidly for a second or two, and then go out, and that's it. Evac time. In and out in less than three minutes.'

'Okay,' I say, scratching my head. 'Let's just do that one more time to be safe.'

Once Frank is happy that I'm happy, he sends me off with a long list of things to do. Top of it is charging my iSpy.

*

Saturday afternoon arrives in the blink of an eye. I still don't quite believe that come this evening I'm expected to break into a billionaire's castle and steal the contents of his hard-drive, all under the nose of what's likely to be some pretty serious security. That the target's also my boyfriend's dad just adds to the complication. No surprise then that I have a bad case of the butterflies as I climb into the taxi which will take me up to Heathrow Terminal Three for my flight to Switzerland. Milly comes down to see me off, which is sweet, but I can tell she's almost as nervous as I am, maybe even more so, because she just won't stop talking.

'... anyway, so then C asked if I'd like to join them up in the operations room at Legoland during the mission. Pretty cool, huh? Frank said he'd drive me up later.'

I suppose she has to stop for breath at some point. For a moment neither of us knows quite what to say. The silence doesn't last long, though, before Milly's nerves get the better of her again.

'Well, I'll see you when you get back in the morning?' she says.

'Yeah, I guess,' I say with a hopeful smile. I glance at my watch. 'Best be off then, or I'll miss the flight. How embarrassing would that be?'

We share a quick hug and I climb into the back of the cab. Milly leans in after me.

'You know I was kidding earlier, right? About the security. I'm sure it'll be a cinch. First missions always are.'

'Yeah, well, we'll see about that,' I say, hoping for the best but secretly steeling myself for the worst.

*

By the time I get to Heathrow, I'm actually beginning to get quite excited. Things only get better when I arrive at the Virgin Atlantic counter to collect my ticket. I was all set to be dumped into steerage, so am pleasantly surprised to see they had the decency to spring for a business class ticket. It'll make the trip a bit easier. Okay, a lot easier. And as I only have a small carry-on and a small dress bag slung over my arm, it's straight through immigration and into the business class lounge until they call the flight.

I have no escorts, though I've been told a car will be waiting at the other end to take me to the party. In my luggage, besides my cosmetics bag, which isn't exactly small, I have a short, strapless black satin dress, a pair of four-inch stilettos, black tights, a gun-metal chain-link belt, a pair of interlocking C-shaped silver earrings, a mid-sized quilted black-leather Chanel 2.55 handbag of mine (okay, my mother's), and a black pashmina. Topping off the outfit

I have a pair of black, three-quarter-length gloves which are really there just to keep my fingerprints off anything I touch when I find the computer.

*

Sure enough, there is an anonymous-looking driver in an anonymous-looking silver Mercedes waiting for me. Once I've changed in one of the more spacious disabled toilets at the airport, we waste no time in leaving the city and heading out into the countryside. There's no conversation, so I amuse myself by playing games on my phone.

The clock on the dashboard has just passed nine o'clock when we round a bend and catch our first glimpse of our destination. I let out a low whistle. It is simply colossal.

A few minutes later, we turn off the main road and head down a long, winding driveway through pitch-black woods towards the lake. The castle, when it appears, is even more spectacular up close. It sits, perched on its own rocky little outcrop, just off from the shore, and is illuminated all around by a ring of yellow-green lights at its base.

How I am going to find anything in there is beyond me. Not only are there several main buildings inside the high, crenulated outer walls, but there are also so many little turrets and towers topping each that I have no idea where to even *begin* looking.

The Mercedes trundles over the castle's short wooden bridge and pulls up behind a line of cars waiting to clear the security checkpoint. An efficient-looking team of humourless guards in dark-grey trench coats make their way from vehicle to vehicle, checking each guest off from their list.

Given that I know Alex there was no option of coming under an alias. We're just hoping that even though Robert Pemberton-Smythe set up and financed the people who are after me, it doesn't necessarily mean he knows what they were doing. Admittedly that's based on a pretty flimsy assumption. But the way I see it, considering the men in Canary Wharf were clearly not prepared for me to step from the lift when I did means they were not summoned by Pemberton-Smythe himself. It's more likely, then, that someone else told them I'd be there at that time. Though that's probably even more worrying as so few people knew we were going in the first place. Either way, we are about to test the theory, and if he does know who I am then this will be a pretty quick visit.

One of the guards approaches the car and taps on the glass. *'Guten Abend. Ihre Einladung, bitte?'*

I lean forward and pass over the card which Alex sent me. As I do so, I notice the tip of the guard's right index finger glove has been cut away to expose his bare skin. Now why would you do that, I wonder? Especially considering how cold it is tonight. Then it clicks. Of course! Better trigger sensitivity. The man takes one look at my invitation and passes it back without comment. A flick of his wrist and the driver buzzes the window and moves the car on.

I breathe a deep sigh of relief as we pass beneath an archway and drive into a large square courtyard which is illuminated by a ring of medieval flaming gas torches. Slowly we creep forward until it's our turn outside the main entrance. A group of photographers stand crowded behind a rope cordon, their breath instantly turning to fog as they clamour for poses from the guests as they pass by on their way inside. And each time someone obliges, their cameras erupt into a dazzling burst of flashguns and strobe bursts. Everyone is either in a tuxedo or a cocktail dress. A few brave ones remain outside, chatting in groups while they have a last cheeky cigarette before heading inside to warm up.

As I swing my legs out, the driver turns to me with a smile and says, 'You'll do fine. You look very nice by the way.'

The compliment buoys me immensely.

'Thanks,' I gush.

With a depreciating smile, I close the door and the car pulls away. And with it, I realise, goes my last bit of support. Now I am well and truly on my own. With a sense of wary unease, I turn and look up at the enormous, snow-covered castle and let out a long, deep sigh. Even the entrance is intimidating. Huge and medieval, the eighteen-feet-tall wooden double doors stand open, beckoning me into the warmth. No wonder Alex has never mentioned his family. I thought people might want to get to know me for the wrong reasons, but what must it be like for him?

'Okay, show time!' I mumble, and make my way inside, running the gauntlet of photographers and their flashes, mindful not to look at any of them.

* * *

CHAPTER 16

FOXES IN THE HEN HOUSE

The foyer is packed and the fun, rowdy atmosphere helps put me at ease. A small army of waiters, all immaculately dressed in black waistcoats and bow-ties, meander around serving champagne. I take a glass and make for the stairs. As I go, I get a pretty good sense of the type who got invited by the snatches of conversation I overhear as I pass by.

'... are you going to Cowes next year?'

'No, but I might join Papa at Henley.'

'... and I'm Rupert, by the way,' another boy drawls to the vacant-looking girl beside him. His accent is so sharp that I'm not in the least bit surprised by what comes next. 'And like Rufus, I'm also at Harrow.'

Oh, Jesus! I muse as I join the queue for the stairs. *Yeah, well, my name's Foxton, Heather Foxton. And I go to a school run by MI6 ...*

Two flights up, I come to a wide, open landing and another set of impressive double doors that lead into a colossal dining hall. There are more waiters here, this time in white tuxedos, which glow brightly in the onslaught of lasers and UV disco lights. The place looks like an Ibiza after-party. Long tables flank the walls, and all are laden with food. A band, who I can't quite place, are already playing up on the stage at the far end.

I try to push all the competing thoughts in my head aside. What I really need is to come up with a proper plan. Also probably for the best if I avoid talking to anyone who could end up missing me later when I slip off into the castle. While I focus on where to begin, I wander over to a nearby table to see what's on offer. I've barely eaten today and am absolutely starving. That said, I've been so nervous I probably wouldn't have been able to keep anything down anyway.

I've just taken a bite of a mini foie gras canapé when I sense someone hovering around behind me. I resist the temptation to turn as a little smile plays across my face.

'Hi,' he says.

My smile only gets bigger as I turn to see Alex standing before me in a very nicely cut tux, holding two glasses of champagne.

'I wasn't sure if you already had one,' he says, setting the spare one down with a playful smile. 'You look amazing.' He casts a quick look around before leaning forward to place a long, lingering kiss onto my lips. I barely manage to swallow the canapé in time.

'Are you having fun?' he whispers into my ear.

'I am now,' I say playfully. 'And the night's still young.'

The grin he flashes me is so loaded with subtext that my heart flutters.

'Yes, it is, isn't it?' He looks at his watch and smiles. There's a cockiness to him tonight which I quite like. A casual confidence which wealth such as his tends to engender, especially in regard to how calmly he deals with all the sycophants passing by.

'Hi, Alex ...'

'Great party, Alex.'

'Hey, Alex, remember me, Alex?'

He acknowledges them all, but each time his focus remains firmly on me.

'Heather,' he says, clapping his hands together enthusiastically. 'Truly, you look a vision and I am so very glad you came. Unfortunately, as much as I'd like nothing better than to stay and hang out with you, I'm afraid my parents have gone and invited far too many people. It would be rude of me not to mingle, at least a little, just to be polite. Of course, you're welcome to join me, but I will do the honourable thing now and spare you the mind-numbing boredom of having to make banal conversation with them. So look, make yourself at home. Enjoy the food. I hear it's pretty good. And I'll be back absolutely as soon as I possibly can and then I'll take you for a tour, if you like.'

Staring into my eyes, he gently takes my gloved hand and plants the softest of kisses on the black fabric. And then he's off, darting deftly through the crowd, stopping only to glance back and flash me an adoring smile, before disappearing into the sea of people.

I try to hide my sense of giddy excitement. I drain my glass and then, for good measure, empty the spare he left behind. A cheeky smile crosses my face as I feel the warmth spread through me. Maybe tonight will be more fun than I had reckoned.

I spend a while moving from group to group. I suspect Alex was just being considerate because quite a few of his friends are actually quite nice. Though a lot here don't even seem to know him personally. It seems odd to invite people you don't know to your birthday party.

*

About half an hour later, I'm near the main doors when Alex suddenly startles me by appearing out of nowhere to whisper into my ear.

'Can I get you a drink?'

The sound of his voice gives me an unusually hedonistic thrill. I turn to see he's undone his bow-tie and top button. His hair is more ruffled than it was earlier. Again he has two flutes, one of which he promptly offers to me.

Maybe it's the alcohol, or possibly the thrill of the night, but I have the sudden, irresistible urge to grab him and kiss him. He seems to sense it.

'How about a tour?' he asks, gesturing airily to the party in general. 'I think I've had about enough of this lot.'

'What, you've given up meeting and greeting the masses, have you?' I ask playfully. 'I thought they are your friends.'

'Please! I barely know half of them. Most of them my father invited because he does business with their parents.'

'Then a tour sounds perfect,' I say, gladly accepting the glass.

'That's what I was thinking,' he says with a playful chuckle as we head for the exit.

A backward glance reveals several girls staring at me with undisguised looks of envy. At the door, Alex takes a freshly opened bottle of Bollinger RD from a wine cooler. And then we wander off, arm in arm, down the corridor, leaving a dripping trail of water behind us as we go.

*

I don't even try to keep track of how long we walk for. The castle is certainly impressive. God knows what it must have been like growing up here for much of his life. Eventually we reach the more opulently decorated residential wing. Thanks to the now empty bottle of champagne, we have become noticeably more tactile with each other than normal.

'So this is basically the family wing,' he says, pointing down the long, wood-panelled corridor. 'Over there are my parents' rooms, with Dad's study at the far end. My side is over here. It's got a great view. You want to take a look?'

'Oh, I bet it does,' I reply playfully. Despite the sudden rush of excitement at the possibilities it holds, I can't help but dart a look towards the double oak doors of what I now know to be Robert Pemberton-Smythe's office. 'Do you and your dad get on well?' I ask out of curiosity.

He shrugs.

'You know, it's funny because it's not like he's a bad father or anything. It's just that his idea of parenting is more about providing financially than anything else. Which, let's face it, he does pretty well. I guess he doesn't have the chance to do much more than that. It's a shame, because I so very rarely get to see him. And being at school for such long periods doesn't exactly help, either.'

I nod sympathetically.

'Yeah, tell me about it. I guess I was just curious because that's how my parents are. Always at work and hardly ever at home.'

'Makes things kind of lonely, doesn't it?' He smiles ruefully and fixes me with an intent gaze.

The conversation dies and we stand, gazing at each other in silence. The charge between us builds. Alex cocks his head and gently pushes off from the wall. Moving slowly, he comes towards me, calm and confident. All the while, his eyes stay transfixed on mine and I feel a growing sense of excitement the closer he gets. He stops a foot away. I dare not move. My anticipation soars as he reaches out and gently brushes a loose strand of wispy hair back behind my ear. I find myself lightly licking my lips as he cradles the back of my head. I'm rapidly losing the fight to contain my excitement. Within my chest my heart is going berserk, thumping so hard it's almost impairing my breathing. I feel slightly light-headed as he moves even closer and gently presses up against me. I give a pleasurably sigh and close my eyes as his mouth finds mine and lightly kisses me. Then he pulls away. I don't even try to disguise my wanton desire as I feverishly seek out his mouth, finding only empty air. Infuriatingly he hovers playfully just out of reach, inches from my face. His mouth twitches into a teasing smile.

Aching for him, I take his lapels and pull him to me. Our mouths embrace and I offer no resistance as his tongue pushes its way inside mine. He drops the bottle to the floor and runs an urgent hand through my hair while the other glides eagerly over the contours of my dress. His touch feels delicious through the thin, silky material and my head swims, dizzy with arousal. Breathless, I press myself up against him even harder. In response, his enthusiasm grows to match mine and his caresses become even more intense. We stumble backwards into the wall, where we grind up against each other. His thigh wedges itself between mine and I press myself firmly against it with a groan. He sucks on my tongue and I roll my eyes upwards and moan out loud. That merely fuels his desire and I quickly have to reposition a somewhat overly ambitious hand a few rungs back down the ladder of progressive intimacy. But suddenly I know it feels right.

'Let's go to your room,' I whisper with breathless urgency.

'Are you sure?'

I put my finger over his lips and take his hand. He needs no further encouragement.

His room is huge. It's more like a small apartment than a bedroom. His bed is a king size and is set on a raised platform which overlooks a sunken living area with L-shaped sofas and a massive home entertainment system. Dominating the room is a large, stone, medieval-looking fireplace with a healthy wood fire burning in the grate. In front of it lies a huge, thick white rug. As he closes the door, an ugly, slobbering bulldog forces its way inside.

'Spencer, out!' Alex hisses.

Ignoring us completely, the dog rushes over to flop down in front of the fire.

With a resigned sigh, Alex dims the lights and turns to me. Suddenly my butterflies are back.

'Relax,' he whispers. 'Close your eyes.'

I do, and suddenly everything calms. I desperately want to remember every touch, every intimacy, but I lose myself almost immediately as his mouth seeks mine out. After a minute, he sinks down slowly before me. I'm shaking and suddenly find I don't know what to do with my hands as his fingers trail their way up my thighs. I take a sharp intake of breath as he slowly eases my underwear and tights down. My mind empties and I let out a small gasp as I concentrate on his fingers and tongue, circling, then invasive, but all deliriously exciting. The clandestine thrill of what's to come only adds to the heady cocktail.

Before I know it, he's leading me to the bed. There, he gently pushes me back onto it. I've never felt so exited, or so nervous. In no time, my dress is bundled up around my waist, and the top half is unzipped and pulled down. My shoes are off but the gloves remain. He seems to like that. Last to go is my bra and with it any inhibitions I had left.

Taking out a condom, Alex smiles playfully.

'Best be safe, right?'

Christ, I hadn't even thought of that!

I try to relax again as he flashes that irresistible grin of his and discards his shirt over his shoulder. Next goes the foil wrapper. For a moment my mind flitters between intense arousal and nervous trepidation. But it passes in the blink of an eye and so, too, do my worries as I suddenly feel him.

And so, just like that, I lose my virginity in a castle overlooking a lake and a range of distant snow-capped mountains, to a boy who I know I love. I close my eyes and focus intently on the sensation, hovering between sensual bliss and peals of laughter every time I open my eyes to see his ugly dog watching us with a deeply suspicious look from the chair in the corner where he's finally settled. Laughing and giggling, we wriggle off the bed and crawl over to claim his old spot on the rug in front of the fireplace.

This is probably the most vulnerable I have ever felt in my life, but Alex's touch is soft and passionate, calming and reassuring, and I trust him. It all feels even more forbidden out here in the middle of the room like this. Neither time nor my mission is of any relevance anymore as I lose myself completely in the moment. I grip the carpet tightly and let excited, guttural little cries escape my lips as he picks up the pace. Opening my eyes, I see an intense look of concentration etch itself onto his face. His thrust intensifies. So, too, do our gasps and grunts. Suddenly he elicits a loud groan and tenses, before falling forwards on top of me. Together we lie, laughing and panting, in a tangled, sweaty heap on the floor.

'Are you okay?' he gasps.

I nod vigorously and snatch a kiss before he rolls off to rest, splayed out beside me, exhausted and fulfilled.

'Oh my God,' I exclaim, finally finding my voice. Then, in a softer tone, I whisper, 'Oh my God.'

My whole body is trembling. Lifting my head, I glance across at him for a sign, any sign, that he's happy, or satisfied, or that I did okay. He looks at me and smiles. It's enough. With a sigh of relief, I sink back down to catch my breath.

A moment later, I prop myself up onto an elbow and gaze into his face, grinning like an idiot. I can't stop my eyes from occasionally wandering from his as I take all of him in. He laughs and lies back, clasping his hands behind his head. There we stay, soaking up the afterglow, talking in soft whispers, while I gently play with him in intrigued fascination. All the while my mind races, thankful beyond words that it wasn't the cringe-worthy, awkward experience I had feared it might be. That it felt natural and surprisingly effortless. That I didn't come across as a stupid girl who didn't know what she was meant to do. But mostly because it made me feel desirable.

I don't even care that I'm not his first. I'm just glad that he's mine and that I was true to myself tonight and made a decision which I won't look back on and regret for the rest of my life. With that thought in mind, and gently biting my lower lip, I snuggle contently in his arms, staring into his eyes as my mind replays everything over and over. My body tingles as he softly traces his fingers across my skin and suddenly I find myself feeling ever so grown up. Now I just want to do it again and again, but at the back of my mind, like an annoying little spark, desperately fighting for attention, is the pressing knowledge that I'm really here for a very different reason.

Our eyes suddenly dart to the door, from where a hard rapping sound comes. We both curse and scramble to our feet in a mad rush to re-dress.

'Just a moment,' Alex shouts. He frantically points to the gap on the other side of the bed. I dive into it just in time as the door opens and Robert Pemberton-Smythe steps into the room.

'What are you doing in here?' Alex's father exclaims in an exasperated and annoyed tone.

'Well, some idiot spilt red wine all down my shirt. So I'm changing,' Alex replies calmly. Almost calmly enough to beat a polygraph, I muse to myself.

His father grunts.

'Well, get a move on. The speeches are supposed to start in a minute.'

'Well, don't let me keep you,' Alex says, sauntering over to his wardrobe, from where he takes a clean shirt. 'I'll catch you up.'

Without a word his father leaves.

I poke my head up above the mattress. Alex turns to me with a sigh.

'Duty calls, I'm afraid.'

I purse my lips and nod understandingly. I can't hide my disappointment as he finishes dressing. Yet at the same time the more rational part of my brain is finally resurfacing. Probably best I got on with what I was sent here to do.

'You coming?' he says, straightening his bow-tie into place.

I nod.

'Sure, but I could really do with a freshen-up first, though.'

'Just in there,' he says, laughing and pointing to his en-suite. 'Towels are on the rail.' Then he smiles, runs over, and plants one last kiss on my lips. 'Okay, got to go,' he says. With a playful smack of my bottom, he runs off after his father.

I laugh quietly and give a pleasurable, satisfied little sigh. I wait a moment longer, just to make sure he isn't coming back again. Then I gather my clothes, albeit minus my tights, which I can't find anywhere, and slip into the bathroom.

God! I look a state.

Hurriedly, I put myself back together as best I can. Yet regardless of what I do, I can't shake the feeling that the moment I walk back into the party everyone will somehow know what we did. That somehow they'll smell it on me. With a frown, I realise there's little I can do about it now. So, with my heels in hand, I pad silently from his room, down the passage, past a small marble bathroom, and on towards the large double oak doors at the far end. I didn't think it would actually be possible for my heart to go any faster than it had been going a few minutes ago, but I'm proven wrong as I gingerly edge the door of Robert Pemberton-Smythe's study open. All that greets me is silence.

I am crossing a very big line here. *If they catch me now …*

A deep breath and I slip inside, letting the door close softly behind me. The office is large and imposing, with bare stone walls and a collection of ornate-looking furniture arranged neatly on what is quite possibly the biggest and most colourful Middle-Eastern rug I've ever seen. It fills almost the entire room, which is largely in darkness, save for a small lamp that illuminates the desk area, all the way off on the other side of the room. Behind the desk is a long row of windows which look out over the dark lake beyond, offering much the same view as from Alex's room.

I see the wall alarm box is off. That certainly makes things easier. Nonetheless, with my iSpy in hand, I hop about three feet onto the carpet and tiptoe my way towards the desk. Halfway there, I catch myself quietly humming the James Bond theme. With a reproachful scowl, I do the rest of it in silence. The desk is meticulously neat and tidy. But all I really care about is the nice shiny laptop sitting smack bang in its centre. I take a photo of the area for later reference.

A glance at a picture of Robert Pemberton-Smythe with Alex in a small boat on the lake makes me shake my head. God, what I am I like? A few minutes ago I was with . . . I bite my lower lip and resist the huge smile which is threatening to make an appearance at the thought. And yet here I am about to steal his father's most personal information. And I'm *okay* with that. *What kind of warped moral code has GPS instilled in me?* Pushing doubt aside, I turn my attention back to the task at hand, lest I lose myself in the enormity of what's just happened in my life.

With no time to waste, I open the computer and turn it on. The login screen quickly appears. Taking the small decoder, I plug it in and sit back, drumming my fingers nervously on the desk as I wait for it to work. Five seconds tick by. Then ten. After twenty, I begin to get concerned. When it's obvious the thing isn't going to work, I curse and pull it out, bang it on the desk, and try once more. Again, no luck.

With no burning desire to get caught here, like this, I quickly repack my bag. Once the computer is shut down again, I run back to the door, where I stay with my ear pressed to it for a moment. Satisfied the coast is clear, I slip out and dart back down the hallway, stopping only to put my shoes back on. Almost tripping over the empty champagne bottle, I hurriedly dump it out of sight in the little toilet, back around the corner.

The speeches have just come to an end as I re-enter the Great Hall. Everyone is in full applause as father and son make their way down from the stage. The band starts up again. With a glass from a passing waiter, I take a sip to moisten my mouth, and then make a beeline towards them. I need to get into that computer and there's only one person around here who can help me do that. From the way Robert Pemberton-Smythe is joking with Alex and his friends, one would almost think he was being genuine. But having seen how curt he was with Alex earlier, I can't help but take his current jovial public persona with a pinch of salt. I hope I'm wrong and that it was just your usual father and son conflict. Right now he looks a lot friendlier and more approachable than he sounded. He'll need to be if my plan is to have any hope of working.

'Hey, you're back!' Alex exclaims happily as he sees me approaching. 'For a minute there I thought you might have left.'

'Sorry, I kind of got a little lost,' I admit sheepishly. 'Next time you should draw me a map.'

He laughs and suddenly a dozen faces hone in their undivided attention towards me. Most are merely curious, but there are a good few who openly radiate jealousy at the prospect that anyone might know Alex better than they do. I ignore all of them and turn instead to Robert Pemberton-Smythe.

'Actually, I was hoping to speak to you, Sir.'

'Oh dear, and for a moment there I thought the lovely lady might actually be looking for you,' Robert Pemberton-Smythe says, giving Alex a conciliatory pat on the shoulder. 'Yes, and how may I help you, my dear?'

I grin at Alex as he fends off his friends' ribbing.

'Well, Sir, I promised my mum I'd let her know when I was going to be home tonight. But my phone's died. I was wondering if you might have a computer which I could use to e-mail her quickly?'

'Use my phone. Call her instead,' he says, reaching into his pocket.

I grimace.

'I'd prefer not to, if it's all the same to you, Sir. I know what she's like. She'll just start chatting and then I'll be stuck on it all night.'

'Then send her a text instead,' he offers.

'If I could remember her number,' I say apologetically. 'I only ever have her on speed dial.'

'Ah, the curse of modern technology,' Mr Pemberton-Smythe sighs wistfully. 'Of course, back in my day we used to write these things down in little address books.'

'You can always use my laptop?' Alex offers.

'Hmmm, nice try, son!' His father laughs as he sees my uncertainty. 'But I'm not about to leave this young lady with no other option than to accompany you to your room.' Then he turns to me. 'Of course you may, my dear. I have one in the study.' He gestures that I follow him. I wave to Alex but he's busy punching a friend on the arm for some sarcastic comment or other.

'So you are a friend of Alex's from Eton, are you?' Mr Pemberton-Smythe asks as we head away from the loud music. I look at him curiously, wondering if it's a test.

'Err, girls aren't allowed at Eton, Sir. I'm just a friend, really.'

'Oh yes, quite so. Do forgive me. Just rather a lot on my mind at the moment, you see.'

What's plain to see is how distracted he is now he's away from the party. We walk on in silence for a bit before he starts talking about Alex again.

'It's nice to see him having fun with all his friends again. He's a good boy, deep down,' Robert Pemberton-Smythe notes, sinking deeper into thought. 'It's been a tough few years, especially after his brother. That hit him pretty hard. But that's not really something you ever really get over, is it?' he says rhetorically, and his expression saddens all the more.

I nod sympathetically. The longer the silence lasts, the more his thin veneer of composure slips and an underlying melancholy surfaces; to the point where I almost feel guilty for what I am about to do. Instead, I try to convince myself that, in some obscure way, it might even be to his benefit. Assuming, of course, that we can figure out what he's up to with Menyatov before it happens.

'After you, my dear,' he says, holding the door open when we reach the study. He leads me over to his desk, where I hover awkwardly while he logs the computer on. He nods towards the windows as he types.

'I remember when I actually had the time to sit here and watch the sun set over the lake. But now work pretty much monopolises my life. The markets never sleep, and all of that nonsense,' he says scornfully. 'Frankly I'm amazed my wife hasn't divorced me. This monster we created has grown far too big and complicated for any of us to control anymore. Ironic, isn't it, that we've become slaves to the very financial system which we created for the betterment of our lives?'

I nod, yet remain silent, much in the hope that he might say something telling. Maybe I can nudge him in the right direction.

'Don't you like what you do anymore, Mr Pemberton-Smythe?'

He sighs.

'Well, the City certainly isn't what it used to be. That's for sure. It used to be fun, back when I first started out. But recently it's just become a slog. It occasionally still has its moments, but after all the ups and downs of late, it's changed. Now there's too much regulation, and politicians in the UK seem hell-bent on biting the hand that feeds them, and all for the sake of a cheap vote from an ignorant, don't-know-better, couldn't-care-less public. It's sad really.' He stares off into the distance, lost in thought. 'If you want my advice, young lady, don't do a job which you don't like. Do something more worthwhile with your life.'

I shrug self-consciously and smile. *If only he knew.*

Snapping out of it, he says, 'Just log it all off when you're done, won't you? My IT people are constantly nagging me about that sort of thing. The Bogeyman snooping around the web, and all that tosh.'

I hope my sudden flush of guilt doesn't show.

Once he's gone, I slump down into his plush leather chair with relief. Then I assemble all my equipment out before me and slip my iSpy's earpiece into place. Within seconds I'm through to the MI6 Control Room in London and am rapidly explaining the situation to Frank Sable. Though I can't quite make out what they are saying, my call seems to have sparked some sort of commotion in the background. From what I gather, they've all been getting a little alarmed at how long it was taking me to find the computer and were worried that something had gone horribly wrong. They calm down soon enough, though, when I tell them I am into his system and the download is already well underway.

'How? Did the decoder work?'

'Nope. I just went and asked Pemberton-Smythe if I could use his computer. So he came along and logged me on.'

Total silence.

'What? Just like that?' someone asks incredulously.

I roll my eyes as they collectively marvel at the originality of my approach.

'Alright, you guys ready?' I say to Frank, 'because from the sound of it, I'd say we're almost there.'

'We are,' comes his reply. 'Nice and easy. No need to ru—'

His voice trails off, distracted by a commotion in the background at his end. People are now shouting frantically. But nothing they are saying makes sense. Things like, 'Pull out' and, 'Abort, abort!' Then someone swears and a deathly hush falls over the London end. Suddenly Frank is back on the line, his voice is fraught and his tone urgent.

'Foxton, clear up everything you're doing and get the hell out of—'

I flinch as a loud staccato-like burst of what can only be gunfire rips through the grounds. It's immediately followed by a single loud bang. Then another burst, and silence …

Frank curses down the line. Without hesitation, I'm out of the chair and racing for the nearest window. Down below, in the wide-open rear garden, a group of guards hastily approach two fallen figures splayed out in the snow. Even from here the violent splashes of red are clear to see.

With my face pressed to the glass, I barely dare breathe as I wait for something to happen. For someone to say something.

And as the last retort rolls off across the lake, a horrible sense of dreadful realisation sinks in.

'What the hell happened?' I hiss into my headset. But I suspect I already know. I edge the window slightly open. One of the guards grabs his radio.

'*Achtung, Achtung.* Alarm!'

Cursing, I race back to the desk. Through the fog of panic I become aware of Frank calling my name. I grab my phone as if it's some kind of lifeline.

'I'm here. I'm here,' I blurt.

'Foxes in the henhouse!' he says calmly.

'What the hell happened?' I snap.

'The powers that be didn't entirely trust you to get the job done, so they green-lighted a team from Six to run back-up. When we hadn't heard from you for a while, they sent them in.'

'I was only gone a couple of hours,' I exclaim, furiously sweeping my gear into my handbag.

'Don't beat yourself up about it. It's not your fault.'

'I know that,' I hiss. 'I'm more worried about the bloody mess they've just dumped me into. You know what's going to happen now, don't you?'

'Yes, which is why you need to get out of that place pretty damned fast,' he says. 'Plan A's obviously gone to hell, so you need to get up to Geneva. We've got people at the airport there who'll help you get out of the country. But I'm afraid it's all up to you now. We don't have time to send the driver back. Remember your training. Stay sharp, focused, on the edge, where you gotta be, and everything'll be—'

'I'm already on my way,' I say, dashing for the door.

* * *

CHAPTER 17

EMERGENCY EXIT

I don't even bother checking to see if the coast is clear. I run straight out into the corridor, pausing only to collect my bearings at the end of it. Just as I'm about to head off down the hallway to my right, I hear something and stop. I listen more closely. A man's voice. But oddly garbled and crackling with static. Then sounds of people running. Several of them. Heavy boots. My eyes go wide. Guards!

Christ! With everything I have in my bag, I can't let them find me! I spin on my heel and rush back the way I came. But there's nowhere good to hide down this way, either. Worse, if they find me hiding, then that's almost as good as an admission of guilt. I'd be equally screwed. No, what I need is something subtler. Almost like they need to see me but not *see* me. Or see me but instantly discount me. So how the hell do I do that? How the hell do I do that in a fricking castle full of drunken teen—?

I come to an abrupt halt. But of course, that's it! I race into the small marble washroom to my left. Thankfully the empty champagne bottle is still where I left it. With no time to waste, I kick off one of my shoes. Then I lift the cistern and unceremoniously dump all my gear, save for the compact drive itself, into the water. The footsteps reach the main hallway. I have literally seconds, if that, before they find me. I curse, frantically looking left and right for somewhere to hide the drive. Somewhere no one will think to look—hopefully. Out of time, I latch onto the first idea that comes to mind and shove it down the front of my underpants. Then I toss my bag and pashmina onto the floor and drop to my knees in front of the toilet. Instantly I succumb to the same nauseous sensation I always get when I find myself here. Combined with my rapidly fraying nerves, I only have to retch once to feel it coming. Twice, to be in no doubt. And on the third heave, and just as the first guard rounds the corner, I bring up a hurl of champagne and half-digested finger-food.

The man takes one look at my scattered possessions, the empty bottle, and the state I'm in. He instantly relaxes and appears more amused than anything. Time, then, to reinforce his initial assessment. I slump sideways, wedging myself between the toilet and the wall, making no attempt to wipe the dribbles of vomit before they run down my chin and onto my chest. With an unsteady head, I gaze up at him, unfocused and vacant. For the icing on the cake, I sloppily smear my chin on my bare shoulder and let out a soft groan and burp.

'Yes?' I enquire with as much indignant attitude as I dare—just as the other guards appear.

'*Ha, lustig,*' one of them says with a laugh. He slaps the first one on the shoulder and whispers something. The leader nods and jabs his thumb towards Pemberton-Smythe's study. The others all follow.

They are back a minute later and all pop their heads back into the toilet to have another good laugh at my expense. I shoo them away with an uncoordinated swipe of my hand. With a last laugh, they run off deeper into the residence.

Barely able to believe my luck, I dare not move until I'm sure they are long gone. Then, just to be safe, I give them another minute. Finally, pretty confident they're done with this floor, I scramble to my feet and flush the toilet. With a moistened towel I wipe my face, chest and shoulder. As I gather my belongings, I can't help but smile to myself for having finally found a practical use for this peculiar gag reflex.

I slip out into the hallway and run on, barefooted, back towards the grand staircase. Halfway there, I only narrowly manage to avoid running headlong into another roving group of guards by diving behind the doors of an armoury, just as they round the corner up ahead. They convene outside in the corridor, firing fast bursts of German at one another. I understand nothing, but it's clear from their tone that they are not toying around.

As I wait, pressed up against the back of the door, it dawns on me that it won't be long before one of them gets round to locking the whole place down to allow for a proper search. I need an expedited exit strategy, and fast. My eyes scour the room for any kind of inspiration. The solution ultimately presents itself. Right beside me, as it turns out. I can't help but feel a stab of remorse for what I am about to do to Alex's party. My only consolation is that he didn't seem all that keen on it anyway.

With a look of grim determination, I reach out and pull the little red handle. Instantly a piercing siren sounds throughout the castle. Even in German I can tell when people swear like sailors. The guards sprint off into the residency, allowing me to slip out and dash back towards the party. I stop only to put my heels on before joining the chaotic stream that is now pouring down the stairs. The sight of armed guards merely hastens the exodus and I let myself be carried along in the frantic stampede.

When we reach the ground floor, it's to find three guards in the midst of closing the main doors. They don't stand a chance as the fleeing scrum throws them aside and surges out into the courtyard. The photographers are all gone but the torches are still burning strongly, lighting the area with their romantic, dancing light.

The temperature has dropped significantly and my breath comes out as a thick fog. Within half a minute I'm shivering. Many of the chauffeurs never left. Not that it does me much good. With a rueful look, I glance at the time. It's almost midnight, making it eleven back home. How the hell am I supposed to get a flight at this time of night? I take a few tentative steps and slip awkwardly on the icy cobbles. Cursing, I wrench the heels off again and stand barefoot on the bitingly cold stones, but it's better than breaking an ankle. Of course, there are no taxis, either. Not that I even have the money for one.

Frustratingly everyone else seems to have a car waiting, or they simply bundle into their friends'. I watch, with growing dismay, as two hopelessly drunken boys stagger past carrying a friend whose arms are draped around their shoulders. He is so drunk he can't even walk. In fact, given how his feet are dragging behind him, I'm not even sure he's still conscious. It's only when they stop beside a nearby car that I recognise him. An idea comes to mind and I quickly hurry over towards them.

'Rupert, baby,' I call out. 'What happened? You promised me you wouldn't do this tonight.'

The two only slightly less inebriated boys turn to me as Rupert, now unsupported, collapses back across the car's rear seat.

'Err, well, to put it mildly, he's … slaughtered,' one of them replies. They both find this highly amusing and burst into peals of laughter.

I try to keep a straight face myself and focus on playing the indignant girlfriend.

'And you're just going to leave him like that?' I snap, pointing at the now snoring figure.

'Yeah, you're right. We should probably buckle him in,' one of them jokes, before creasing into hysterics again.

'Oh, get out of the way!' I say and roughly push past them to clamber in next to Rupert. With feigned anger, I pull the door shut behind me. A flick of the latch and it locks. I heave Rupert's lifeless body over to the other side of the back seat. Turning to the driver, who is watching on with growing disapproval, I kindly ask him to take us to Geneva Airport, and as fast as possible.

He's not impressed.

'We have speed limits,' he says in an offhand, superior manner. The engine starts, but with no particular urgency. So it's going to be like this, is it? I turn in frustration and riffle through Rupert's pockets. Wow, I get way too little pocket money, I think to myself at the sight of the thick wad of notes in his wallet. The driver's eyes go just as wide when I wave several hundred Swiss francs in his face. It's amazing how quickly we're in gear, out of the main gates, and flying along the dark roads away from the castle.

I squirm uncomfortably as something digs into my abdomen. Wincing, I slide forward and remove the hard-drive, just as the driver flicks an inconveniently timed glance into his mirror.

'Don't ask,' I sigh as I reposition the dress and drop the compact into my handbag. With a pang of guilt, I turn to watch the castle recede into the distance. I hate to leave Alex like this, with no goodbyes or anything, especially after what we shared tonight. But the risks of staying any longer were just too great. I certainly hope he is not mad at me for running off.

Turning my mind to other, more pressing issues, I realise I need to know what I'm looking for at the airport. I find my phone and dial Milly.

To say she's relieved to hear from me is an understatement. She sounds almost hysterical and I can barely get a word in edgeways. But eventually, once I have assured her that I am fine for the fifth time and on my way to the airport, does she finally calm down and pass me over to Abbott.

'Alright, we're taking over now. Section Eight is calling the shots.'

I vaguely remember Milly telling me about Section Eight. Apparently it's the paramilitary support arm of MI13. All ex-SAS and SBS types, which fits with what I know about Abbott and Lennox.

'So what do you want me to do?' I ask.

'At the airport you'll find a man called Rohner waiting for you. He'll get you onto a plane which'll bring you to RAF Northolt. Call us on this number again when you're airborne. Five have some rather pressing questions about something that might be on that drive of yours.'

And with that the line goes dead.

'Wow. Hi, Heather! How are you, Heather?' I mumble sarcastically. 'Glad to hear you made it out of the castle full of armed guards alive.'

With a peeved sigh, I slump back into the seat and toss the phone back into my bag. But when I close my eyes, all I can see are two bleeding figures silhouetted against a bright, snowy background. Despite what I said earlier, I can't help but wonder whether, had I been faster, they might still be alive. Was I too selfish losing myself in the thrill of being with Alex? Maybe if I had just hurried up, none of this would have happened. I try to banish the nagging doubts, but combined with the fading adrenaline rush, I soon find my mascara is streaking down my cheeks.

Eventually it's the bright lights of Geneva International Airport that rouse me from my self-inflicted melancholy. A sly smile spreads across the driver's face as I hand him the thick wad of notes. It disappears the moment I climb out and run inside, leaving Rupert snoring on the back seat.

It's well gone midnight and the departures terminal is deserted. The only people still around are a couple of cleaners, a few check-in staff, chatting idly behind one of the counters, and a lone policeman. I'm not surprised. London doesn't seem to have a clue what it's doing. After an evening where everything that could have gone wrong pretty much has, why should I now be the least bit surprised that no one's here to meet me? And to cap it off, I notice the policeman is watching me far too closely for my liking. I turn and start walking towards the other end of the terminal building.

Someone calls out in German. I ignore it and keep walking. The man calls again. Frowning, I glance back to see the policeman following me. I speed up. And then so too does he.

'Miss,' he calls out, this time in English.

Reluctantly I stop and turn. What else can I do? Not like I can start running, though the thought does occur to me. It's only when he gets closer that I see his name badge. Oh great. Rohner. Yeah, good one, Abbott! Nothing like keeping me in the loop.

After a cursory introduction, he swiftly escorts me past the empty passport control desks and down a flight of steps to a waiting car. Then, with blue lights popping and flashing, we accelerate off across the airfield, racing past rows of gantry equipment and parked airliners, before heading out into the darkness beyond. Halfway across the airfield I feel my bag vibrate.

It's Abbott.

'You find him okay?' he says.

'Yeah,' I whisper, 'but you could have told me he was a policeman. I thought I was going to get nicked and almost did a runner.'

He seems to find this amusing. So, too, does Rohner.

'Alright, quick question,' says Abbott. 'Did you see Pemberton-Smythe again before you left?'

'No, not after he left me alone in the study. Why?'

'Apparently he went straight to the airport. Air traffic control has him already on his way back to the UK. But we've got nothing firm yet to hold him on, so we can't arrest him. If he's spooked, we're worried he may accelerate his timetable for whatever he's got in the works. We really need to know what's on that drive, and ASAP, yeah?'

'Okay, I think we're almost there,' I say, now seeing where we are going. Then, lowering my voice, I say, 'Abbott, who were those guys out on the lawn?'

There's an awkward pause. When he replies it's with an unusually soft tone.

'Look, we'll deal with that another time. Just hang in there for now. We'll see you in a couple of hours.'

I hang up and stare out the window as we speed across the last of the runway towards a waiting private jet. Its lights are on and the engines are already turning over.

I quickly thank Rohner and bid him farewell. Then I get out and edge my way warily up the steps to peer inside. The sumptuously luxurious cabin is empty, save for a lone steward, who proceeds to welcome me on board as if this is all completely normal. He directs me to one of the six enormous leather armchairs. Beside it is a small walnut table with a laptop all set up and ready to go.

We are airborne in minutes. Once the steward has brought me a sandwich, a cold towel and a bottle of water, he retires up in the cockpit. I kick off my shoes and set about connecting the drive up. A moment later the armrest phone rings.

'Enjoying the ride?' Abbott asks.

'Yeah, it's not too shabby.'

'Uh-huh, well, we need you to check something for us, so if you could just hook that—'

'It's already done,' I reply.

'That's my girl. Okay, open up his calendar. Five found an entry for this coming Monday which just had an X in the title. They want to know if there's any more detail on your end.'

I do as he asks and quickly find what he's talking about.

'Yeah, there's something here, too. Only he's called it "Send Black Monday 2". You know what that means?'

'No, but I know someone who might.'

Abbott wastes no time in getting the school's economics teacher, Mr Sparkman, on the line. We clearly woke him up.

'Well, of course I know what it is,' he says irritably. 'Black Monday was the stock market crash of October 1987. At the time it was the single largest one-day drop in stock market history. No one knows what really caused it. There were no bad news stories that day, or any of the other usual catalysts. There's a theory it was because of uncontrolled black-box algo-trading, but that's just speculation, really.'

'In English, Albert,' Abbott says with undisguised irritation. 'That thing you just mentioned. What is it?'

'Black-box algos? Err, well basically it's when you have a computer model doing the buying and selling of securities on a stock market. All based on algorithmic trading models. So the theory goes that someone put in a big sell order. Nothing wrong with that, per se. But then, for some reason, these pro-gramme-driven models all started selling, and, like a snowball, they sold and sold with such speed and volume that the rest of the market instantly panicked and everyone piled in and started selling as well. Add in some questionable interest rate hikes by the government that day and end result, the market dropped by twenty-five per cent. Not a good day.'

'Foxton, do a search for anything with the name Black Monday in it,' says Abbott.

I do as he asks and get two hits. The first of which is a graph.

'It's called "Projected Market Impact FTSE 100",' I say, reading from the screen. 'And it's dated for Monday. The upright axis has "Market Volume" and "Time" is along the bottom. Just after eight o'clock there is an X with the word "injection" beside it. Then the line dips a bit. Maybe a couple of minutes after that, it says "BM Active". There's another "injection" and from there on out the line just goes down like the *Titanic*. That's bad, right?'

Before anyone can answer, Abbott is back on the line.

'Albert, if you wanted to, how would you crash a stock market nowadays?'

'You wouldn't,' he exclaims, clearly amused by the stupidity of the suggestion. 'I mean, it can't be done. Occasionally you get an erroneous fat finger trade which can cause a bit of movement, but never a full-on crash. And certainly not due to one person acting alone. Doesn't matter who they are. Most markets today are too big and complex. The FTSE 100 most definitely is. And even if someone had enough stock to dump, they'd never get away with it. The exchange would simply shut them off.'

'Understood,' says Abbott. 'Well, let me ask you this. Could what happened back in eighty-seven, with those black box things of yours, happen again today?'

'Not a chance!' Mr Sparkman says emphatically. 'All the major players have far more advanced kill-switches on their programme trading systems. These things are deliberately designed to cut off before that kind of automated panic selling could happen.'

There's a commotion at the other end. Then Abbott gets Milly on the line.

'See, this is what I mean by out-of-the-box thinking, people,' Abbott says. 'Go on, Butterworth, tell them what you just told me.'

'Err, all I said was what would happen if they failed to work? The fail-safes, I mean. Who'd ever know in time?'

'Erm, I'm not quite sure how that could—' Mr Sparkman begins.

'Okay, Sir, but think about it for a second,' Milly says, interrupting him. 'We've got to consider Menyatov. I mean, just suppose he's come up with a way, say, to turn off a whole bunch of those safety systems? Like, all at the same time? What happens *then* if Pemberton-Smythe puts in his sell order …?'

The question hangs ominously in the air and for a moment no one speaks. Seeing her chance, Milly presses her point.

'I remember that lecture you gave, Sir. About those high-frequency trading systems which all the big banks use. If they can do thousands of trades a second, millions even, then it would all happen too fast for the exchange to intervene in time, wouldn't it? I mean, the damage would be done in seconds, maybe even less.

'If I understood what you meant, then by targeting the in-line direct order routing systems, he goes for everyone whose models require them to trade in-line with the market, right? So, say he trades down. The first computer then trades its pre-programmed quota. Then another and then another. All in milliseconds, right? Now the market is already moving downwards. Then come the next raft of systems, the slightly slower ones: they all now get in on it and have to trade even more to keep in line. And so it goes. Bigger and bigger sales. But fast, unbelievably fast. And by turning off the circuit breakers, Menyatov turns the stock exchange into a train wreck.'

I listen, dumbfounded, as Milly recites, virtually word for word, what Mr Sparkman must have told her class weeks, possibly even months or years ago.

'Well, I'm glad somebody was listening,' he notes dryly.

On a roll, Milly asks me to look for anything in Pemberton-Smythe's folders which could be an executable programme. With a bit of help from the tech guys on the call, I quickly find a sub-file called BM Firewall.

'Well,' one of the MI6 technicians suggests, 'it could be a wrapper to contain a virulent programme. But we'd have to examine it first to know for sure.'

'I still don't see the logic, or the motive here,' says Mr Sparkman.

'Yeah, well in this game I've come to learn to shoot first and ask questions later,' Abbott replies grimly. 'Right now I have a guy with the means and access to cause some major trouble. Add in a proven connection to a known cyber-terrorist and a calendar reference for a major financial disaster. How much more do you need? Whatever this is, I'd prefer to stop it before I have to read about the demise of my bloody pension in the damned newspaper.'

'And don't forget all that property he's been buying recently,' says Frank Sable. 'If the economy tanks, then he has about as good a hedge there as any, right, Albert?'

'I suppose,' Mr Sparkman says, still not entirely convinced.

'Okay, I've heard enough,' says Abbott. 'I don't care how great this guy is supposed to be. Unless someone can persuade me otherwise, I say we go with the theory that, for whatever reason, this Pemberton-Smythe guy intends to send our country's stock market down the toilet while he's probably laughing all the way to the bank. How's that sound?'

No one speaks.

'Fine. It's settled then. Foxton, send over those files.'

I do as he asks and it all works fine until I try to attach the actual documents themselves. Each time an error message appears. I turn back to the phone.

'It says I need a password to attach them.'

'Alright, then we need you to bring the drive to us. If we're right, and I hope to God we're not, then we don't have long. The country's in enough of a bloody mess as it is right now without this sort of thing. Albert, I take it he can't release that virus, if that's what it is, until the market opens on Monday, right?'

'Well, that depends on what it is. Not necessarily. Market participants are sending each other orders, trade confirms, settlement details and so on all day long. If you're right, he could bury a virus into any one of those, send it out now, and no one would ever know anything about it until it was all said and done tomorrow morning.'

'Well then, let's just hope he hasn't sent it yet,' says Frank.

'Foxton, get yourself some shut-eye,' Abbott orders. 'Tomorrow's likely to get a little sporty. We'll head off down towards Pemberton-Smythe's place in Sussex. That's where he looks to be going. We'll take someone from tech support with us. When you get to Northolt, you'll find a bird waiting to bring you and that hard drive down to meet us. Butterworth and her phone are coming with us. Any problems, call her number.'

Without so much as a goodbye, the line goes dead. Not that I am surprised any more by his socially retarded telephone manner. With nothing left to keep me occupied, I quickly give in to the fatigue that's finally caught up with me. I snuggle into the seat and pull the soft cashmere blanket over me. In seconds, my eyelids begin to feel heavy and my breathing slows to a peaceful rhythm. And with that, I drift off into a deep sleep.

*

The sudden jolt awakes me with a violent start. I'm instantly bolt upright, disorientated but awake and on the defensive. Only when I remember where I am do I relax and unclench my raised fists. With a yawn and a rub of my eyes, I peer out of the window to see landing lights streaking past in the darkness.

The plane eventually comes to a standstill outside a small, two-storey private terminal building. The steward reappears and has the door open again before I can even gather up all my belongings. Thanking him, I take a cautious look outside, and then head down the steps. It's not quite as cold here as it was in Switzerland, but the night air still cuts effortlessly through the thin material of my dress. I turn as a man in a dark blue RAF uniform emerges from the building.

'Good morning, Miss!' he exclaims, waving far too jovially for this time of day. 'I'm Wing Commander Bennet,' he adds, bounding over towards me. 'If you'd like to come into the Operations Building, we can wait for your connecting flight. It should be here in about seven minutes,' he says, checking his watch.

Inside it's nice and comfortable and, above all, warm! Several white sofas are arranged around a small coffee table. The walls are festooned with squadron plaques and oil paintings of historic military aircraft. I quickly excuse myself and head to the bathroom, but not before I somewhat cheekily enquire if he might happen to have anything lying around here that's a little more comfortable than my heels, which are now well on their way to crippling me.

'What size are you?' he replies with a smirk.

'UK six and a half. If you've got it?'

He says he'll see what he can do and rushes off to look. I quickly make use of the toilet and wash my face in the sink. But without proper make-up remover I end up making more of a mess than anything. By the time I re-enter the anteroom, Wing Commander Bennet is back with a large brown cardboard box and a nice thick pair of clean socks.

''Fraid they are the best I could do at such short notice,' he says, removing a pair of Oakley lightweight military desert boots from the box. 'Not as fashionable as those,' he says, pointing to my heels, 'but they should fit you nicely.'

I smile good-humouredly, and add, 'No, they're perfect. Right now, anything's better than these.' I pull the socks on and slip my feet into the snug, comfy boots with a thankful sigh. 'Oh, bliss.'

He looks relieved.

'There's a Merlin inbound from 28 Squadron, RAF Benson. Should be here in about three minutes,' he says.

I have no idea what he's talking about and frankly I'm too tired to bother asking. It's just as I'm finishing with the laces that I catch the first faint sounds of an approaching helicopter. Bennet kindly fetches me a Styrofoam cup of tea from the hot pot brewing in the corner and leads me outside.

'Here, breakfast,' he says, handing the wonderfully warm cup to me. I gladly accept.

We spot the chopper's blinking lights as it streaks across the airfield towards us. The noise grows steadily louder until the helicopter suddenly thunders out of the darkness and into view overhead. With dramatic flair, it sinks down towards the ground, before settling heavily onto its undercarriage. The blast of wind whipped up by its rotors forces us to cover our eyes. I don't even bother trying to keep my hair in place.

With a last, curious glance, Wing Commander Bennet directs me towards the helicopter's rear ramp, from where a crewman emerges. Clasping my bag, shoes, and tea, I set off towards him, trying not to laugh at how this must look. What was it Milly said about not holding out hope for anything James Bond-y? If only she could see me now ...

At about seventy-five feet in length, the Merlin is a lot smaller than the huge, twin-rotored Chinook was, but up close it's a far sleeker machine and a lot meaner-looking, too. I approach the crewman, already braced for the confused look that greets me. He fires a quizzical glance back at Bennet, who appears none the wiser and merely shrugs in reply. Not about to argue, the crewman leads me up the ramp, past the fixed machine gun placement, and along the fuselage towards the cockpit.

Like its bigger brother, the Merlin is also essentially stripped bare inside, save for a row of canvas seats running along both sides. The loadmaster hands me a large green headset and turns to speak into his own microphone. The rear ramp hums up and locks into place and the turbines rise to a muted crescendo through the ear defenders. The sudden lurch catches me off balance and I stumble and fall onto my backside as the helicopter jerks up into the air. I only just manage to keep hold of my cup and stop it from sloshing out all over the floor.

The pilot looks back and does a quick double-take. Unperturbed, I smile back cheerfully and get up, already loving every second of this.

'Well, good morning,' he says as I appear in the cockpit doorway. 'Welcome aboard RAF Airways. I'm Flight Lieutenant Will Kingdom and I'll be your pilot today. Please remember this is a non-smoking flight and photography is generally not permitted, but for you we'll make an exception. Just please avoid using the flash, okay? Any problems, alert your cabin crew.' He points teasingly at the loadmaster and flashes me a flirtatious grin.

'Yeah, yeah,' the crewman fires back dismissively.

With a chuckle, the pilot returns to his controls. We leave them to it and retreat back into the main cabin. There the loadmaster lays a large plasti-coated map out on the floor and we kneel down to examine it in the red glow of his small pen torch.

'This is where we're heading, see? We'll set you down in this field, at the top of the ridge line. It's about as close as we can safely get you,' he says, refolding the map so that the landing zone is on the front. 'You'll need to make your way down this hill to reach your RP, which is here.' He circles a small lay-by with a red china-graph pencil.

'RP?'

'Rendezvous point. Here, take the map. Best get some rest now.'

Amazingly, considering all that's happened tonight, not to mention how uncomfortable the seats are, I actually manage to doze off almost immediately.

It feels like I've only been asleep a few minutes when the loadmaster wakes me again to inform me that we are almost at our destination. I rub my eyes and double-take at the blur of green and brown streaking by on either side. We're literally flying below tree level.

'It's called nap of the earth. Quieter approach this way,' the crewman says, as he leads me towards the rear ramp. 'Now remember to stay low until we've moved off again, okay?'

I nod.

'Stand by. Sixty seconds out,' the pilot calls matter-of-factly over the intercom. 'Thank you for flying RAF and we hope to see you again soon.'

The ramp buzzes down and locks into place as the crewman takes my earphones back. After the relative peace they afforded, the sudden rush of noise comes as a shock. A siren sounds and a red light flashes on the opposite wall by the ramp controls. The ground rushes by alarmingly fast just metres below us. Without warning, the crewman takes hold of my arm to stop me from falling over again as the helicopter's nose flairs up unexpectedly, bleeding off speed at an astonishing rate. It quickly settles into a hover, only five feet above a ploughed field.

The wall light flicks to green and the loadmaster shouts for me to jump the last few feet. I land nimbly and duck into a crouch. The wind tears at me like a thousand hands all groping at once as the engines roar and the helicopter surges back up into the air. Squinting up at it through the dust storm as it passes by overhead, I'm just in time to glimpse the loadmaster emphatically pointing towards the far side of the field.

I nod gratefully and then, just like that, they're gone and I'm all alone again.

*   *   *

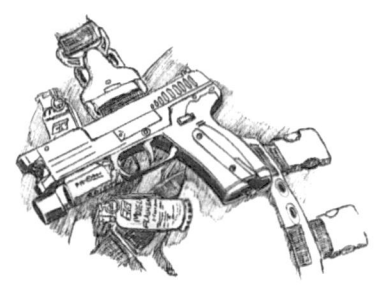

CHAPTER 18

ONCE MORE UNTO THE BREACH, DEAR FRIENDS

The first faint hints of dawn are just peeking over the horizon as I make my way across the rough, uneven field. It's enclosed on three sides by a dense belt of trees and shrubbery. The forth side, where I am now heading, is open with a wire fence stretching along its length. Beyond it, the densely wooded terrain angles down steeply into the valley below. It feels good to be on the move again, especially given the temperature and what I'm wearing.

Off to my right I finally notice a farmer standing next to his tractor, having a cigarette. He must have been there all the time. Beside him sits an obedient shaggy old sheepdog. Both watch me approach with dubious expressions. I'm not surprised. Whereas before I felt cool running for the helicopter dressed as I am, now I just feel stupid.

Oh, what the hell.

'Morning,' I call out, casually strolling towards the fence.

'Ai,' he mumbles, absentmindedly tipping his cap.

If it hadn't been for the helicopter, this might just pass for some kind of rural early-morning walk of shame after an all-nighter. Only I doubt they get too much of that happening around here.

I feel my phone vibrating in my bag. With the wireless earpiece in place, I give the screen a tap.

Typical. No hello, no chit-chat, just Abbott.

'You'll find us about a mile down the hill, through the woods. I'm sending the coordinates to your phone. Try not to get lost, yeah?' he says drolly. Then he hangs up.

I give the phone a narky look and shove it back into the bag. With an apologetic smile at the farmer, I break into a jog. There's no gate or stile, so I accelerate and hurdle the fence instead. With no one around, I'm free to break into an unrestrained sprint, weaving in and out of the trees with fast, darting strides. To say I'm grateful for the boots would be the understatement of the morning. This, in heels, doesn't bear thinking about.

I stop a couple of times to recheck my heading, and before long I spot a large silver off-roader parked in a small lay-by below.

I take the final five-foot drop slightly over-enthusiastically and stumble forwards, slamming hard into the side of the vehicle. A sure sign of tiredness, I realise. With a groan, I pull the door open and smile a weary grin at the sight of friendly faces. Abbott and Milly are up front. Quite how she persuaded them to bring her along, I'm dying to know. Occupying the back of the vehicle are Lennox and a bespectacled man I don't recognise.

For some reason I can only think to crack a big, wide grin and, in my best Irish accent, exclaim, 'Top o' the mornin' to ya!'

Milly is obviously the most horrified by my appearance and

clearly thinks I have lost my mind as I climb in. Not surprising, I suppose, given my wholly inappropriate attire for a day out in the countryside, not to mention the streaked mascara, flecks of mud and dirt all over me, and hair that looks like I've been dragged through a hedge, which isn't actually that far from the truth. The adults, I see, aren't buying my false bravado for even a second, so I quickly drop it.

Whoever customised the SUV certainly spared no expense. A bank of communications equipment covers the whole opposite wall. A near constant stream of crackled radio traffic plays from its speakers. Beneath that is a small fold-down seat. The whole central area has been cleared to give room to move about, while the rear third of the vehicle is dominated by a large, rear-facing, semi-circular computer console. On it, set on runners top and bottom, is a four-foot-long, flexible, transparent screen which can be repositioned wherever the operator wants it.

'Are you okay?' Milly asks anxiously, as she leans over the back of the passenger seat to give me a wary embrace.

'Yeah. I guess. Not quite the night I was expecting, though.'

'Yeah, tough break for your first time out,' Lennox notes gravely.

I nod. That's one way of putting it. For a moment no one speaks, each reflecting in our own private way on the unfortunate events of the last few hours. With a sigh, I slump down onto the small seat and glance past Lennox at the man who is studiously working away at the rear console.

'I guess this is for you?' I say, passing him the drive. He nods and quickly hooks it up and sets to work analysing what's on it. I get the distinct feeling no one really knows what to say. But I have no desire to relive the whole experience now and neither Abbott nor Lennox seems keen to get into an emotional discussion.

I reach for a beige manila folder lying on the console to my left. Stencilled in bold red letters across it are the words:

TOP SECRET—EYES ONLY

Inside it I find what looks like Robert Pemberton-Smythe's entire life story. In fact, it's kind of scary to see how much information they have on him.

'Do you know where he is?' I ask, laying the folder back down.

'At home,' says Lennox, pointing to the rear screen, on which a slow-moving aerial image of a large country estate is displayed. 'About a mile or two down the road. We've had a drone up for the last couple of hours and have been listening into his calls. He's definitely spooked because he's been putting in transfer orders like crazy since he arrived. But there's something else. There are a whole load of other people in there with him as well. And it looks like he has the movers in. They've been loading packing boxes all morning. Now we're just waiting for the green light from Downing Street to go in and get him.'

'What are you going to do to him then?' I ask. Even though I know Alex's dad is probably going to turn out to be a scumbag, I can't help but feel slightly conflicted and sorry for him.

'Depends on how cooperative he is,' Lennox says.

'Or uncooperative,' Abbott adds gruffly.

A phone rings somewhere at the front. Abbott answers it, grunts, and then starts the engine.

'Here we go. You two get to stay in here and listen to the radio with Brian.'

The technician gives us a quick smile as we pull out of the lay-by and accelerate off down the narrow lane. A flick of a switch on the dashboard and the windows all tint darker.

'I don't understand,' I say. 'Can't you just tap in and stop him from sending whatever it is?'

''Fraid not,' Brian replies. 'He's got what we in the trade call a closed-loop system. You have to be at the terminal itself to exercise any kind of control over it. And the hard lines are buried pretty deep around here. We won't be able to find them and cut them quickly enough. Also, he knows he's out of time, so chances are he'll just send it once he's done with his transfers.'

'Hence why we're going in now,' says Abbott.

After a few minutes, we turn off and power up a dirt track into the woods. Lennox drags a large green plastic crate out from beneath the console and begins to assemble two neat piles of tactical assault gear from it in the centre of the floor.

'I thought you said you were going to talk to him,' I enquire as he cocks, safeties, and holsters a pistol.

'After how his security guys reacted in Switzerland, we're taking no chances,' Lennox replies with grim resolve.

'Alright, this'll do,' Abbott says, bringing the SUV to a stop on a flat plateau amongst the trees. Down in the valley below, the mansion and its surrounding estate is now clear to behold. And it is huge.

When Abbott opens the side door, we startle at the sight of several men who have suddenly appeared behind him in the half-light. All are clad in black and have their faces darkened. One of them glances at me with a less-than-impressed look.

I flush, a little self-conscious, all of a sudden, of my appearance. Lennox notices and frowns.

'Cut her some slack, Giles. The girl just evaded capture by an entire platoon of German Gebirgsjägerbrigade mountain troops, yeah?'

Obviously that ranks as something worthy of respect in their circle. Giles nods dutifully and moves away, only to be replaced by another soldier.

'Morning, *ladies*,' this one says flirtatiously.

'Oh, give it a rest, will you, Oakley!' Lennox sighs wearily as he climbs out to strap on the rest of his gear. I'm glad he said it. After the night I've had the last thing I need right now is this kind of chauvinistic bollocks.

'Yes, Sir, Captain Lennox.' The soldier grins at Milly and me and then turns to Abbott, suddenly more serious. 'Boss, I really think we need to motor. Pemberton-Smythe just called in a helo. I think he's going to do a runner.'

'How long?'

'Thirty minutes ... if we're lucky.'

'Okay, Section Eight, listen up,' says Abbott.

The dozen or so soldiers all crowd around. Feeling thoroughly surplus to requirement, I edge out of the way, along with Milly. Once at the back of the group, we perch up on tiptoes to see what's going on.

Abbott begins by ensuring everyone's watch reads the same time. I take mine from my bag and strap it on over the long glove. I'm past caring about appearances and it's too nippy to do without them. What I'd give for jeans and a pullover, like Milly. We share a conspiratorial grin as we check ours are also synched.

'So, snap assault,' Abbott says, pointing at the screen with his weapon's laser sight. 'We'll work our way in through the trees, up till here. Split entry over this wall, here and here. Team One will cross the front lawn and enter the house here. Two comes in around the back of the boat shed and crosses the rear garden to this entry point, here. Synchronised assault. I want covering fire, here and here. Standard rules of engagement apply, understood? Time is of the essence, gentlemen. So no dawdling. Any signs of resistance, don't mess around. Hit 'em hard and fast. Maximum aggression, maximum surprise. Flash-Bang the room, clear it, move on. Any questions?'

There are none.

'Right, let's go,' says Lennox.

Silent and menacing, the soldiers all set off at ten second intervals behind him down the hill.

Abbott snatches up a few extra magazines and is about to head off after them when I catch his attention. He takes one look at my face and senses what I'm about to say before I even utter a word.

'Listen, I get it, alright. God knows I've been there often enough myself, and it's a sight one doesn't easily forget. But you cannot let it prey on you. It'll chew you up, and in this business distractions like that will just get you, or those around you, killed. They knew the risks. It was a tough break, that's all.'

For a moment he pauses and fixes me with such a piercing stare it feels like he's seeing right through me.

'And it wasn't your fault,' he adds. 'Doesn't matter what you were up to beforehand, all that counts is you got there in the end.'

I stare at him, aghast, as it dawns on me that he might know what I was up to in the interim. His expression confirms my worst fears.

'You think they just send one person in for something as serious as this?' He laughs. 'We don't just double up on these missions, we triple cover. You weren't the only person at that party last night. Besides, the Pemberton-Smythe boy seems a decent enough kid. No one's going to hold it against you. Let it go.' He winks teasingly at me and then jogs off to catch the others.

'What was that all about?' Milly says as we climb back into the vehicle and close the door behind us.

I look at her and smile, grateful for the weight that Abbott just lifted from my conscience. With a laugh, I launch into my story, one, which on retelling it, I barely believe myself anymore. I spare her the really intimate details, given that Brian is right behind her. She giggles and edges forward so I can whisper them to her instead.

Once I'm done, she shakes her head and mutters jokingly, 'What are you like?'

We laugh conspiratorially and I give her a playful slap on the arm. We turn as a burst of hushed radio traffic comes in, announcing the soldiers' arrival at the perimeter wall.

'I hope it's as easy as they think it'll be,' Milly says.

'C'mon, it'll be fine. The guy's a finance nerd. And he's really old. Like he's really going to give them a hard time,' I scoff.

'I suppose ...'

For a moment Milly says nothing. Then she shakes her head and smiles.

'Look at us,' she says, indicating our surroundings. 'How did we ever get mixed up in all of this?'

'Tell me about it. Not exactly a life of make-up, gossip mags and sleepovers, is it?'

As we sit in contemplative silence, my eyes settle on a chunky, pistol-like device left on the equipment pile. Absentmindedly I reach for it. It's surprisingly light. Some kind of toughened plastic. Curiously there's no magazine. Nor is there anywhere to put one, either. And where I'd have expected to see a barrel, all I find is a vertical I-like slit. On its side is a small red button, protected by a clear plastic flap.

'Careful with that,' Milly says, gently pushing it away from her.

Tentatively I press the button and it begins to emit a faint hum. At the same time the I-slit illuminates with a blue glow.

'Why? What is it? Some kind of electric pistol?'

'Yeah, I think so.' She delicately takes it from me and turns it off. 'But not one of those ones with the wires. I think it's more of an electrically charged ion-gun. It's still in testing, or so I heard. Supposedly it works to about ten or fifteen feet. Oh yeah, and best leave those alone as well,' she jokes, pointing at two green tubular canisters.

I peer more closely.

'Oh ...' I murmur, seeing the label. Flash-Bang Stun Grenade. With a nod, I sit back and laugh. 'Yeah, see what you mean.'

We sit in silence for a moment longer.

'Alrighty then,' I say, stretching and stifling a yawn. 'I think I'll just pop outside for a quick pee before it all starts. Back in a sec.'

I spot a thick clump of bushes about thirty feet away and have just bent down behind it when I hear something moving through the undergrowth. I turn and peer through the shrubbery to see a bald, stocky man creeping around the side of our vehicle. He looks like a farmer, with his Barbour jacket and green Hunter wellies. But then I see the pistol in his hand. I instinctively reach for my iSpy and curse when I remember it's in my handbag. I can only watch as he wrenches the door open. Milly looks around, probably expecting me. Instead, she finds a gun pointing at her face. My heart thumps desperately as I realise there's nothing I can do to help.

'Don't move!' the man snaps in a strong cockney accent. 'Who the bloomin' hell are you? An wot 're ya doin' up 'ere?'

No one answers. From my position I can't see Brian, but Milly looks absolutely terrified. I curse my bad timing. Perhaps had I still been in there …?

Suddenly the radio bursts to life. Even from here I can't miss Lennox's voice.

'Who the 'ell's that?' Cockney-man says to Brian. 'Oi, four eyes. Talkin' ter ya.'

Keeping his gun trained on them, the man takes a couple of steps backwards and pulls a walkie-talkie from his jacket pocket.

'Banovic. There're people up 'ere on the bloody 'ill.' He listens to the garbled reply. 'Nah, I'd say government. Sum kind of control moat-er. I can 'ear 'em over the radio. Yeah, okay, I'll brin' it daahhhn.'

A horrible realisation dawns on me that with the radio on, these people can now listen in on everything Abbott and the others are up to. Inside the SUV, the same thought must occur to Brian, for just as Cockney-man glances off towards the estate, he lunges for the radio's frequency knob.

The gunshot shatters the early morning tranquillity, sending flocks of birds rushing for the sky. The bullet tears through the back of Brian's head and throws him forward over the counter. He never makes it to the dial. Milly scrambles hysterically backwards, out of the way, as the limp body slowly slides off the console and falls to the floor, leaving a ragged, bloody smear behind it.

'Shut up,' the man hisses, jabbing the gun to the side of Milly's head.

I dare not move as the hopelessness of the situation sinks in properly. Not only am I too far away to intervene but I have no weapons. And even if I did, I wouldn't make it five paces over this dry, leaf-strewn ground. I consider drawing his attention and then legging it in the other direction. Maybe he'd chase me just long enough for Milly to get away as well? But I don't even get the chance to do that as Cockney-man binds Milly's hands behind her back with a set of plasti-cuffs. Then he sweeps all the remaining gear out onto the forest floor. With a slam of the door, he seals her inside and rounds the vehicle towards the driver's side. The SUV is already pulling away before I can even get out from behind the bush. All I can do is stare after it in horror as it accelerates off through the trees.

Then I spot the pile. My bag! Please let it be there! I rush over, but my heart sinks. The Chanel isn't here. I fall to my knees and desperately rummage through the muddle of belts, buckles, harnesses and other assorted odds-and-ends in the vain hope that my phone might have fallen out amongst them.

It's not here, either. With panic rapidly setting in, I stare off towards the mansion, on the one hand terrified for Milly, given what fate might await here there, and on the other for Lennox and the others, who're about to walk into an ambush.

I hang my head and want to scream in despair. It's the sight of the electric gun, however, which sparks a plan in my head. The stun-grenades merely bolster it. I cast another, this time more scrutinising, look at the estate. Could I get there in time? And what would I possibly hope to achieve once I'm there? I try to ignore the foolhardy stupidity of my idea as I grab the gun and slot it into a heavy-duty, rubberised thigh holster, which I then quickly strap to my right leg. Next I pull one of the smaller-looking Kevlar tactical vests on over my head. The two thickly padded Velcro side-fasteners allow me to tighten the multi-pocketed vest until it hugs me snugly. The Flash-Bangs go into two front pockets. Lastly, I grab my map and, with a deep breath, race off down the hill as fast as I can.

The thin dress and silky gloves offer scant protection. Twice I trip in my haste and fall heavily, grazing my arms, legs and shoulders. Yet, ignoring the stinging pain, I'm up and running again within seconds. By the time I reach the road, I'm covered in cuts and scratches and my delicate clothes have tears in several places. The thigh holster, which seemed a good idea at the start, is now rubbing irritatingly on my bare thigh, so I tear it off, along with its belt, and toss them into the bushes. I shove the gun into one of the vest's larger pockets and carry on across the road.

Before me stands the tall and imposing perimeter wall which runs around the whole estate. It has to be at least ten feet high. A quick check of the Ordnance Survey map reveals a point, about two hundred metres along to my left, where the house is closest to the ring of trees running along behind the wall. It's probably the best place from where I could nip across to the house without being seen.

When I reach the spot, or where I estimate it to be, I quickly psych myself up and race towards the wall. My boot finds grip about a third of the way up and I power myself up the rest. My hands snatch at the top and I haul myself onto the top. But too late, I realise I'm carrying far too much momentum, and instead of balancing there, I plunge headfirst over the other side. It's only by the grace of God that there's a thick bush to break my fall. I tumble through it, bouncing off every branch until I land, with an unsubtle grunt, in an ungainly, sprawling heap on the ground. Some cat-burglar I am.

I freeze, still half upside down, my legs somewhere inside the bush, and strain to listen for any sound of movement nearby. My pistol is clasped at the ready, but all I hear is birds singing and the wind rustling through the trees. An initial sigh of relief is followed by a string of colourful curses as I awkwardly extricate myself from the shrubbery. With nothing more than a few scratches and a rather bruised ego, I brush myself down and set off cautiously through the undergrowth until I can see the mansion through the branches.

As the map indicated, all that now separates me from the house is a thin strip of manicured lawn. But even in the early half-light it's far more exposed than I was hoping for.

Up close, the mansion is also a lot bigger than I had expected. Three storeys of massive, ivy-clad Purbeck stone topped with steeply angled roofs. It is surrounded by acres of gently undulating and wonderfully landscaped gardens. Halfway along its front, a long gravel drive leads off towards the estate's front gates. Parked outside the house are a dark-green Jaguar and two black Range Rovers. Several men, all in jeans and black leather jackets, are loitering around them. Each is carrying a machine gun.

If it wasn't for Milly, I'd gladly turn around right now and make a hasty withdrawal. But I know I can't. She wouldn't and so neither can I. Instead, I grit my teeth and decide to see if there's another way in around the back. I bear left and edge along the treeline until I reach a hedge that extends almost all the way up to the house itself. Faint voices are coming from the other side of it. I bolster my courage and slip from the undergrowth and run, bent forwards, towards a break in the hedge where a footpath transects it.

I stop just short of it and peer around the corner. My heart jumps at the sight of our SUV. The engine is still running, the side door is wide open and Cockney-man is at the comms panel. Brian's body has been callously dumped out onto the gravel. His head lies at an impossible angle and his lifeless eyes stare vacantly up into the sky. I grimace at the bloody mess that is his face and only just manage to cover my mouth as I retch at the sight.

For a moment I don't know if I can carry on. A powerful wave of self-preservation implores me to flee. What was I thinking? Abbott and the others are trained for this. They can give just as good as they get. Worse probably. It's only the thought of what might be happening to Milly that stops me from dashing for the bushes.

With a steely grimace, I peer along the rear of the house. I can just about make out a swimming pool peeking out at the far end. Looking towards the front, I see two men heave a large box up out of a cellar, before hefting it into the back of a white Transit van. With a bang on the rear doors, the van moves off towards the front entrance. As the men walk off to join those waiting by the Range Rovers, I recall what Lennox was saying about a string of vans leaving here this morning and my nervousness is suddenly replaced by a burning sense of curiosity.

Conscious not to be seen by Cockney-man, I slip over to the house and edge around it until I reach the trapdoor from where the men emerged. All seems quiet down below, so I duck down the stairs before the men by the cars see me. My heart is thumping frantically as I creep along the short, dark corridor towards a door at the end. I peer through the small peep window. It looks like an underground car park. But one that doesn't appear to have been used to store cars for quite some time. In fact, it looks distinctly like someone's been using it as a clinic or laboratory until very recently.

No one seems to be about, so I slip quietly inside. All manner of hi-tech medical equipment that they obviously didn't have time to move has been left behind. Rows and rows of empty animal cages line the walls. Several are bent and distorted, as if some incredibly powerful occupant tried its best to escape at some point.

My sense of foreboding only gets worse the more I see. Along the next wall a row of industrial fridges now stand empty and disconnected. Test tubes, pipettes, and high-power microscopes have all been abandoned on the worktops. A distinctly uncomfortable feeling ripples through me as I dwell on what the men in Morocco were after. And now I find this.

Having seen enough, I quickly make for the exit. I retrace my steps around the side of the building and stop at the sight of a small piece of brown paper fluttering across the dew-soaked lawn. Beyond it I see another lying at the foot of an old wrought-iron fire escape. And a third scrap sits on the fourth step up.

I check that Cockney-man is still occupied before darting past the gap and on towards the stairs. On examination, I recognise the card as having come from the cover of Pemberton-Smythe's file. There's only one explanation. Milly. I'm impressed she had the presence of mind to leave a trail for us like this. I'm not sure I'd have thought of it. Not that I'm exactly thrilled at the prospect of having to venture inside after what I just saw. The thought of all sorts of vicious, genetically meddled monsters roaming the grounds plays heavily on my mind.

The first two doors I come to are locked but the third-floor one rests ajar. It all seems quiet inside. Too quiet, in fact. Already unnerved, I hesitantly creep inside. The room is stacked full of cardboard packing boxes. I edge over to the door, rolling my feet softly so to make as little noise as possible, and cast a nervous glance out into the gloomy, wood-panelled corridor. It appears to stretch the entire length of the house. Small bookcases and ornamental tables line the walls between the numerous doorways feeding the hallway. Grudgingly I accept the fact that I have little choice but to scout them out, one at a time. The only real source of light seems to be coming from halfway down the corridor, where a landing is bathed in sunlight, possibly from a window or an atrium.

I take a tentative step out into the corridor and freeze as my damp boots squeak noisily on the wooden floor. My heart jumps into my throat and I step onto the corridor's central carpet runner, where I wait for a moment for my pulse to calm again before creeping on towards the nearest door.

I find only silence. The same at the next door, and the one after that. It's only when I reach the fifth door on the right that I hear something and stop. I strain, unsure even where the noise came from. Too late, I realise it's behind me. Suddenly the door there flies open. I begin to turn, only to see a peripheral blur of movement. I dart sideways, but not fast enough. The punch ploughs into the side of my face. My vision flares and I'm sent reeling across the corridor, straight into a bookcase. I flail desperately for a hold, but all I manage to do is cleave everything off the top shelf. With a groan, my knees buckle and I collapse helplessly to the floor.

* * *

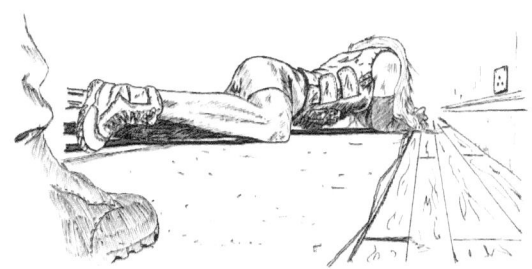

CHAPTER 19

SLEEPING BEARS

O ne punch and my balance is completely gone, coordination's shot, head's spinning like crazy, vision's flared and blurry, yet from somewhere within me I still manage to hear a voice screaming for me to get up and run, but the response just isn't there anymore. With a wave of panic I realise that I'm woefully out of my depth. A harsh, coppery bitterness floods my mouth and I reach up to find my hand comes away covered in blood. Any prospect I might have had of fighting back is already gone. My body starts to shake and the best I can manage is to half-stumble to my feet and try to run. But I don't even get the chance to do that.

My assailant looms over me, huge and terrifying, emitting aggression like a bad smell. He grabs my hair and drags me the rest of the way to my feet. I blink to clear my watery eyes, just in time to see the next punch. It ploughs into my midsection like a sledgehammer, doubling me over and nearly lifting me clean up off the floor. Even with the padded vest it's enough to drive the air from my lungs and send me staggering backwards. I hit the opposite wall with a guttural cry. My jelly-like legs wobble and then give way, collapsing me back to the floor where I lie, hacking and retching, on the verge of throwing up. Images of Candice Hardcastle and Augustus Cole pop into my head, along with dull stabs of remorse at having ever hit them, now that I know how it feels.

With no pause, the man grabs me by my vest. My arms flail hopelessly at him, but they offer up little more than half-hearted slaps. Almost effortlessly, he flings me like a rag doll across the corridor and into the other wall. My head, shoulder, and chest take the full brunt of the impact. This time my eyes simply roll upwards and I slide back down to the floor.

Despite the failure and betrayal of my body, my mind is still lucid and clear. The acknowledgment of defeat comes as a bitter shock. I am beaten, completely and utterly beaten. Despite all that training with Ms Wong. All the false confidence and groundless bravado it gave me. All for nothing. I never even got the chance to fight back.

My only response is to try to crawl away, but it's all I can manage just to heave my trembling body a few inches from the ground before my arms give way. I collapse back to the floor and take a strange comfort from the cool touch of the polished wood against my throbbing face. With resigned anticipation, I look up out of the corner of my eyes at the mountain of a man standing over me. He stares back with a cold, impenetrable gaze, but it's his sheer size which truly terrifies me. He is bulked and monstrous beneath that tight black t-shirt of his.

He turns, almost disinterested in me now, as another Slavic-looking man drags Milly out into the corridor. She stops struggling the instant she lays eyes on me, broken and bleeding on the floor. A look of horror flashes across her face. I barely have the strength anymore even to lift my head, let alone say anything. The best I can do is a weak, hopeless grimace. My shame in defeat keeps me from holding the connection for too long.

Fast, agitated footsteps reverberate through the floor, suggesting the approach of someone wearing stilettos. Something about it jogs me out of my stupor long enough to look up as a striking young woman of mixed ethnicity emerges in the hallway. She can't be much older than her mid-twenties. Her clothes are well tailored and her hair is dark and shiny and luscious. As she turns, it flicks stylishly around behind her, like something from a shampoo advert. And in that moment I realise I've seen her before. Only it was on a rooftop in Morocco, amidst a sea of lazily flapping sheets, as she ran for cover. At the time I thought the person I saw was in the middle of hanging them out to dry. But it suddenly occurs to me that wet sheets don't billow like that in the wind. Only dry ones do that. A sharp alertness comes over me as I realise she had to be the second shooter.

A million thoughts flood my mind. They range from the trivial to the profound. The most striking, and hardest to shake, is the sudden thought that maybe this is my real mother. But the dark hair, her more Mediterranean features and her age, all go against that theory. But there is an unmistakeable similarity there. I'm so confused I find I can't even think clearly as an onslaught of theories about what that would mean momentarily overwhelms me.

In her elegant, manicured hand she holds a small walkie-talkie. One glance at my attacker and he obediently steps aside.

'Don't you touch her,' Milly cries.

Her reward is a sharp slap across the face from the man holding her.

'Prop 'er up,' the young woman says in a silky French accent, pointing at me. 'I 'ave questions.'

The muscular man grabs me by my shoulder straps and slams me up against the wall, where he leaves me firmly wedged into the crook of a bookcase. Any chance of escape is now gone. I feel like I want to be sick. My chest rises and falls in great heaving movements as I struggle to get a grip on my fear of what's about to happen to us. It's only with a gritty sense of determination, and a very hard bite of my lower lip, that I manage to slow my breathing enough to prevent the paralysing effects of shock from setting in.

My thoughts rapidly become clearer and the first thing to register is that none of them have spotted my pistol yet, or thought to search me for any weapons. Today's first bit of good news. It's my only hope, but I have to pick my moment to use it very carefully indeed because I imagine I will only get one chance.

As my mind clears, I keep returning to the same question. Why attack me like that? Why not just grab me and shake some answers out of me? What kind of psycho just lamps someone in the face and then proceeds to beat the crap out of them without first having found out what they were doing here?

Unless …

A nasty thought occurs to me.

Unless he already knew I was coming!

That might also explain how Cockney-man found our SUV. But that would mean someone sold us out. And someone pretty senior, too. Because only they knew about this operation.

As my mind reels with the theories and counter-theories that distrust breeds, I become aware of a strange, warm sensation on my chin. I look down to see a trail of blood dripping from it onto my chest. The man in the tight black t-shirt grins at the sight with satisfaction. I imagine he intends for a lot more to be flowing before he's done with me. Beaten I may be, but I have no intention of giving him any more pleasure by showing it, or how afraid I am. With a hard suck, I spit a mouthful of blood defiantly at his feet.

'*Bon,*' the woman says sarcastically as she kneels down before me. Up close, she's even prettier. Despite not being physically intimidating, her eyes scare me. They are totally vacant: cold and utterly emotionless.

She looks up at the towering man and tells him to get the doctor. A moment later, a man with thinning grey hair and a haggard complexion comes out into the corridor.

The Frenchwoman points at me and says, 'Everything you need is in that.'

He nods and sets a small, black leather case down beside me. As he removes, and then unwraps, a syringe, the grotesque, muscular man grabs my left arm and tears the long black glove off. He doesn't bother with a tourniquet, but merely wraps his enormous, dinner-plate-sized hand around my upper arm and squeezes until a vein appears. A sharp prick and four quickly interchanged vials later, it's done. The doctor quickly scuttles off down the stairs.

I scowl at the woman with a look that could kill. Unfazed, she glances round as yet another person comes out to join us. I let out a quiet, hissed curse and hang my head, dreading what's to come. Instead, Robert Pemberton-Smythe turns on the other grownups.

'What the hell is going on here?' he demands. 'I will *not* have this in my house.'

It's what happens next, though, that turns everything on its head. Rather than kow-tow to him, as I expected them to, they all simply ignore him. I thought … Hold on, if *he* isn't in charge here, then what the hell's going on?

Before I can dwell on it further, the radio gives a loud hiss of static. A flash of hope bubbles through me at the sound of Sergeant Giles's voice.

'Two, be advised we've reached our go point and are now moving in. Approach looks clear. Stand by, over. Whoa, steady up. Everyone, down, down, down …'

Not for the first time tonight, the rapid burr of machine gun fire rolls across one of Robert Pemberton-Smythe's properties. And then all hell breaks loose.

'Contact! Multiple hostiles.' This time it's Lennox. 'Taking fire from the boathouse. Hodges, Bennett, engage targets at two o'clock. Anderson, you're on me.'

The early-morning silence is well and truly shattered as countless automatic weapons all begin firing at once. A moment later, the grounds reverberate to the punch of two loud explosions.

'Boathouse clear. Smoked 'em with the 203.'

'You messed up the man's boat pretty bad, dude.'

'It's insured.'

'Not against you, it ain't.'

'Yeah! Get some,' someone else calls out over the radio.

'Two. One's moving on the target. Be advised, over.'

Then comes more gunfire.

'Man down! I repeat, man down!' shouts another soldier. 'One, do you copy, over?'

'This is One. Copy that, Two. Sending Oakley to assist. Stay sharp. He's coming in flanking the boathouse with the LSW. Watch your one o'clocks, over.'

The young woman looks into my eyes with an almost bored expression. There's no reaction to what's happening outside. She stares at me as she ponders her next move. I try holding her gaze. For some reason it just seems the thing to do. Maybe I can establish a connection, girl-to-girl? But to no avail. Her mouth tightens into a cruel smile and she snaps her fingers at Robert Pemberton-Smythe.

'We don't 'ave time for zis. Send it now, while we still 'ave ze chance—'

'Don't you take that tone with me,' Pemberton-Smythe fires back, clearly annoyed. 'Or have you forgotten who's bankrolling this little venture of yours?'

'Not any more, old man,' she replies coldly. 'After zis disaster, we 'ave someone else just as willing to step in, with just as deep pockets.'

Robert Pemberton-Smythe snorts, unimpressed.

'If you mean that Irish fool then I assure you his pockets are nowhere nearly as deep as you think. I could buy him, and his joke of a bank, three times over and still have enough left over to burn your boss's arse by dumping his stock, just for the fun of it.'

Her face hardens and suddenly a small, snub-nosed pistol appears in her hand. She points it at Robert Pemberton-Smythe. He blanches at the sight.

'And you, Igor,' she says, tossing the radio to the burly man restraining Milly. 'Get your Russian friends outside to deal with whoever zey are!'

'It's Yuri,' the large Russian counters resentfully. 'My name is Yuri.'

'Do it, now!' she snaps, jabbing a well-manicured finger nail at him. 'And find out who zey are from zat one.' She gestures in irritation at Milly.

'Harrashaw,' the Russian replies, somewhat more enthusiastically.

I can only watch, powerless to intervene, as he drags Milly off down the corridor. The best I can do is to shout out after them, in as threatening a voice as I can:

'If you hurt her …'

He stops and turns. Then, without warning, he backhands Milly hard across the face and looks tauntingly at me, waiting for a response. Amused, he laughs and drags her on by her hair into a room halfway along the corridor.

The tension has suddenly ratcheted up between the adults. Only Robert Pemberton-Smythe looks down at me with any obvious remorse in his eyes.

'I wish I could say I'm surprised to see you and your friend again. But by my age not much really surprises me anymore. Especially about this government of ours, in whose employ I'd imagine you are, yes?'

I scowl defiantly up at him.

'I'll take that as a yes, then. Talking of ages, just how old are you? Because you look like you're sixteen.'

However, this I can't resist.

'I *am* sixteen!' I reply, as innocently as I can. Who knows, maybe that'll guilt trip them a bit.

But too late, I see my mistake. An unpleasant look crosses the muscular man's face, almost as if he's seeing me in an entirely new light. And not a favourable one either. I feel a dark shudder course through me and I'm gripped by a very different kind of fear. A primal one that lies hidden deep down, buried in the blackest recesses of a girl's being, in a place as terrifying as the worst kinds of nightmare. I want to get up and run, but none of my limbs respond. For the first time in my life I am truly frozen with fear, yet simultaneously all too aware of the frightened thumping coming from within my chest.

'Christ,' Pemberton-Smythe whistles rueful, oblivious to what's unfolding. 'And here I thought *we* were the ones breaking the law.'

The Frenchwoman spins around.

'You know zis girl?'

My eyes dart from one of them to the other, erratic and frightened, desperate for a way out.

'Yes, Nicole, we've met before,' he replies confrontationally.

The Frenchwoman turns to the tall Slavic man.

'Monsieur Banovic, please find out what she knows. And zen kill 'er. She 'as 'erd far too much.'

A disturbingly calculating look crosses his face and I have the horribly unsettling feeling that killing me is the last thing on his mind. For now at least. What he's thinking is far, far worse.

With an icy smile, Nicole leans closer and whispers into my ear, 'You read about zees zings in ze paper, non? But you never zink it will 'appen to you. You never imagine what it must be like. To be used and violated, like a piece of meat. *N'est pas?*' She laughs coldly. 'Well, you are about to find out.'

Holding my gaze, she drops her hand to my right knee and then delicately trails her long fingernails beneath my dress and up along my inner thigh until they graze over the thin fabric of my underpants. I flinch away. Yet despite the fear and revulsion and humiliation, I am appalled to discover that part of me is also inexplicably, wildly and hopelessly excited as well. Shame and arousal ripple through me in equal measures as she touches me there. Her smile twitches playfully as she then brings her fingers to her nose, where they linger a moment longer.

I avert my eyes and bite down hard on my tongue as tears well in my eyes.

'Pity,' she says, suddenly devoid of all emotion again. Then, all business-like, she lunges back to her feet and turns to face the Serb. 'All yours, Monsieur Banovic. Make it quick, *oui*?'

She clicks her fingers again at Pemberton-Smythe and gestures he follow her.

'Zis way, *Bobb*.'

He makes no attempt to disguise his resentment at her over-familiarity.

'Watch your tone,' he says warningly. 'You are but a puppet in this little game of thrones. So know thy place.

'And you,' he says cuttingly, turning to Banovic. 'You're an animal. Had I known it would come to this, I would never have agreed to allow any of you in here today. They are children, *for Christ's sake*!'

No longer amused, the Serb's expression hardens.

'Why you not go do what she says? Or maybe I have something happen to that other son of yours. Losing one not bad enough for you?'

In an instant, all of Robert Pemberton-Smythe's defiance and authority drains away and a terrible, haunted look dulls his face. For a second I think he's about to cry. Then, to add insult to injury, Nicole throws her head back and laughs, a cold, high-pitched exclamation, before pushing him off along the corridor.

I look up as Banovic slowly approaches.

'Please …' I cry out after them.

Robert Pemberton-Smythe tries to look round but Nicole jabs the gun into the small of his back. All my courage drains away as Banovic looms threateningly over me, patiently waiting until they disappear into a room at the far end of the hallway. I look up at him with a pleading expression. And suddenly, face-to-face with what I thought was my worst fear, I'm find that it is not panic which grips me now, nor even concern for my own wellbeing, but something else entirely. Something far more powerful. More vengeful. And it surges, stronger and stronger, purer than any emotion I have ever felt.

Anger.

At the injustice of what's about to happen.

At his presumption that he can do with me as he pleases.

But mostly at my own weakness and fear.

Never before have I better understood my own character than I do now in these final few moments of innocence. As the girl whose father calls her the personification of tenacity. Who's known for being horribly strong willed and who never gives up. From somewhere deep within me the resolve to fight on to the bitter end erupts and courses through me. That's who I am: a fighter—and that's what I will be now. With this resolve comes a firm refusal to accept this as my fate; even though I haven't quite worked out what I can possibly do to prevent it. Regardless of whatever genetic alchemy might be running through my veins, I have no hope of ever coming out on top against someone like this, not in a fair fight anyway. He is simply too big, too fast, and way too strong. I need to think of something else. I need to stall for time.

'What is that man going to do to my friend?' I ask, hating that my voice cracks mid-sentence.

'You should worry about what *I'm* going to do to *you*,' he sneers. 'But him being crazy Russian, maybe he start with fingernails. Just for fun, yes? Then maybe her teeth? But she pretty girl, so I hurry up, yes, or nothing left for me.'

I barely have time to react as he lunges forward and heaves me up off the floor. With an almost effortless ease, he flings me across the corridor. This time I am more prepared and I absorb the impact with my hands. I twist to avoid his reach but somehow he still manages to grab my vest from behind. I scream as he sends me flailing helplessly back into the opposite wall. This time I'm not fast enough. The impact jars painfully through me and I gasp as the wind is driven violently from my lungs. My legs buckle and I sink to the floor with an anguished groan. I can't take much more of this. The tank is almost empty.

I scramble backwards but my speed and agility are gone. Apparently thoroughly enjoying himself, Banovic bends low and stalks towards me, arms extended, like a predator out hunting. I realise he has no intention of asking me any questions, like the Frenchwoman instructed him to. His voice drops to a whisper.

'Now we have fun, yes?'

I stumble away and back into the wall. But then, out of the blue, with all hope of rescue or escape almost entirely gone, and the forthcoming violation looming viscerally, tangibly, before me, I recall something Ms Wong once said about watching where people shift their weight. His is all going onto his left foot. And suddenly, as clear as day, I see what's coming next.

I plunge down onto my right knee as he launches his kick. My left arm shoots out, braced before me. Simultaneously, my other hand dives into my vest pocket and finds the ion-pistol's on-button. I bend and twist to take the full force of the blow with my left shoulder. Even braced and ready, the impact drives me sideways, as if from a hammer blow, but I grimace through the sharp stab of pain and afford myself a faint smile as I hear the pistol's barely audible hum. Foiled, Banovic stumbles backwards, off balance. His arms fly out wide and I see my chance. The pistol is out in a flash. Without any hesitation, I jam it into his groin and pull the trigger.

The sudden bright burst of light is like a firework going off in the otherwise gloomy corridor and the noise akin to an electrical breaker tripping. I recoil in fright as an impossibly strong force launches Banovic off across the corridor and into a sturdy-looking bookcase. The shelves splinter and collapse under his weight, cascading their contents down around him. With a tortured cry, he sinks to the floor, his body convulsing with twitches and spasms.

Now is my chance. I hobble towards him and deliver a savage kick between his legs. With bared teeth, he howls in pain and fury and his eyes burn with hatred. One shot obviously wasn't enough and I'm not about to take any chances with this monster. With a painful grimace, I squat down and grab a fistful of his hair. Then I forcefully ram the barrel of the electric pistol into his half-open mouth. He barely has time to register what's happening, let alone react, before I pull the trigger again. A burst of bright blue light blazes through his cheeks. His head snaps backwards and punches clean through the rear of the bookcase. I'm left holding a clump of wrenched out hair, which I quickly discard before hobbling off as fast as my aching body will allow towards the room where the Russian has Milly. I just hope I'm not too late.

Thankfully the door is still half-open. The Russian's voice is unmistakeable and I'm relieved to hear he's still threatening her verbally. Fired up from the arse kicking I just handed out to the far larger Banovic, I pull a Flash-Bang from my vest and take a step back. A quick glance over the instructions, particularly at the bit about its second and a half fuse— considerably less than Hollywood has led me to expect—and I pull the pin. Clutching it tightly, I gently push the door open and, only too aware of the adrenaline-fuelled shaking of my hand, opt to throw it underarm.

Yuri glances up. His immediate reaction is one of confusion. Then his eyes narrow and refocus on the tubular green canister that's sailing end-over-end towards him. I just catch his flicker of recognition before I dart out of sight behind the doorframe and plant my hands firmly over my ears as the Flash-Bang detonates, barely a metre from him. The force of the magnesium and ammonium-nitrate pyrotechnic blasts him backwards into a glass balcony door. I'm straight into the room to snatch up the first heavy item I can find—namely a substantial, metal wastepaper bin. Before he can begin to grasp what just happened, I slam the bin into the side of his head as hard as I can. The blow sends him sprawling to the floor, where a close-range discharge from my pistol silences his pathetic mewling.

Satisfied he's not about to get up any time soon, I rush over to Milly. She's dazed and bewildered and struggles to focus on me as I give her a once over. I'm relieved to find everything is still where it's meant to be.

'Are you alright?'

'How should I know?' she yells hysterically. 'How would you feel if you'd just been kidnapped, tied up and beaten, and now, no thanks to you, I've got a fricking church bell going off inside my head! And that's saying nothing about having seen someone get shot right in front of me!' Then she looks up at me and stops abruptly. 'Oh my God!' she exclaims. 'What the hell happened to you?'

'Don't ask.'

I find a pair of scissors on the corner desk to cut the plasti-cuffs.

'Come on,' I whisper, helping her to her feet. 'Let's get out of here while we still can.' Draping her arm around my shoulder, I lead the way out into the corridor.

'How is it I'm always bailing you out of messes like this?' I say in an attempt to lighten the mood.

'Rich coming from you. Have you seen the state you're in?' she replies, far too loudly.

'If I look anything like I feel, I probably don't want to,' I say, putting my finger to my lips.

When we reach Banovic's body, I bend down and fire another discharge at the side of his head, just for good measure.

'Is he dead?' whispers Milly.

'Who cares,' I reply flippantly.

By the time we reach the packing-box room, Milly has almost fully recovered from the disorientation of the Flash-Bang. We edge out onto the fire escape and quickly race down it into the early morning sun. I gesture that she wait for me behind the hedgerow, before darting a quick peek around the corner. Assured of a clear approach, I slip through the gap and sneak towards the vehicle. Hearing the crunch of gravel, Cockney-man turns sharply. He swears and lunges for his pistol, but not fast enough. The ion-charge hits him right in the centre of his back and he collapses, twitching, to the ground. Like the others, I deliver another shot at close range. Not too long ago all of this would have horrified me, what I'm doing, but there's no holding me back now. I don't even care if I get into trouble for it. Unable to tell which button turns the radio off, I grab every cable feeding into it and rip them all out. Good luck to anyone trying to fix that.

Back at the hedge, I'm relieved to see a bit more colour in Milly's face. For a moment we share an unspoken look. An acknowledgement of just how close a call this was. Then, with relieved smiles, we round the building and run on towards the front corner of the house, nearest to the treeline. With the gunfight still raging somewhere in the grounds, the quicker we can get over that perimeter wall again, and to safety, the better.

We duck down and watch as a group of soldiers break cover, way off in the distance, and begin racing across the front lawn towards the house. The men behind the Range Rovers don't open fire until they're about halfway across the wide, open lawn. Instantly, Section Eight all fan out and go to ground, one of them noticeably harder than the rest. They then proceed to advance in two groups, one leapfrogging forward while the other provides covering fire. Then they drop down and cover the second group's advance. With this constant hail of bullets peppering the side of the vehicle, the Russians have no choice but to stay hidden.

'Time to go,' I say, but Milly grabs my arm in alarm as half of the Russians pile into the undamaged Range Rover. It quickly accelerates away, bouncing off across the lawn. At first it looks like they're making a run for it. But then, with a jolt of realisation, we see their true intention. With the soldiers still exposed in the middle of the lawn, they're essentially sitting targets for the incoming vehicle to run over at will.

Milly turns to me urgently.

'Do you know where Pemberton-Smythe went?'

'Yes. I think so.'

'Then you've got to go and stop him. The others won't make it in time.'

'What? Go back in there? After what just happened? Are you *crazy*?'

'There's no time to argue!'

'Wait! Where are you going?' I yell as she runs back the way we just came.

'To stop them,' comes her frantic reply, followed by a harried jab towards the still-accelerating Range Rover.

'But …'

'Can you drive?' she shouts rhetorically. 'Exactly! So go and do what you can, and I'll do what I can. Now go!' she screams, jumping into the driver's seat of the still-running Section Eight SUV. The vehicle slews around in a spray of gravel and ploughs straight through the side of the hedge.

For a second, I stand there, stunned and conflicted in a moment of dithering indecision. What happened to my quiet, bookish friend? Shaking my head, I snap out of it and sprint after her. But she's already long gone and I can only watch in nervous trepidation as the Range Rover continues to pick up speed, gobbling up the distance between it and the soldiers at an alarming rate. Even if Abbott and the others open fire with everything they've got, their chances of survival are thin. Their only hope, it seems, is now racing, flat out, across the grass on an intercept course. Inside their vehicle, the Russians seem so preoccupied on ducking down to avoid the incoming fire that's mincing the windscreen that they are oblivious of the far larger silver four-by-four streaking towards them like a locomotive.

Suddenly they swerve, but too late, as Milly's SUV thunders into the rear half of the Ranger Rover. The loud, unforgiving crunch of tearing metal makes me wince all the way over here. The Range Rover slews sideways. Its wheels snag the earth and the whole vehicle flips over and slams down hard onto its side. Momentum drives it on for another thirty feet, leaving a deep, ragged gouge in the otherwise immaculate lawn. When it finally comes to a rest, the nearest soldier doesn't hesitate before emptying an entire magazine through the shattered front windshield.

With my hands at my mouth, I watch in horror as our crippled SUV rolls on awkwardly, until it too comes to a ragged stop. Billows of steam gush angrily from beneath its mangled bonnet. Seconds feel like hours as I wait for a sign that Milly's okay. It's with a deep sigh of relief that the driver's door finally creaks open a few inches, before jamming, buckled within its frame. One of the soldiers runs over and forcefully wrenches it open. Miraculously Milly seems alright, though somewhat dazed and unsteady. The soldier hurriedly leads her to safety behind the wrecked Range Rover.

Cursing, I drive my own fears into a little mental box, which I then lock away as best I can, before turning and running back towards the fire escape. This time I take no chances, advancing up it and along the third-floor corridor with my electric pistol out and at the ready. Banovic hasn't moved. I ensure that stays the case by firing yet another ion-charge at his head. The same follows for Yuri.

I soon come to a well-lit landing which overlooks the entrance hall below. Suddenly a colossal explosion rocks the building and a fiery blast of hot, dusty air races up and knocks me flat onto my backside. Wide-eyed, I crawl, coughing and disorientated, to the edge and peer down at what was, only moments before, the mansion's front door. It now lies, along with a good portion of its surrounding masonry, strewn in hundreds of splintered pieces all over the atrium floor. Before the dust can even begin to settle, soldiers pour in through the ragged, gaping hole.

Without warning, a badly aimed burst of machine gun fire forces them to retreat. A second hail of bullets laces the front wall. I lean over the railing to see two men, both in the same black leather jackets as Yuri wore, lying flat on the landing below me. One is firing a large, tripoded machine gun while the other feeds an ammunition belt into it. I don't have the angle, or else I might have taken a pot shot with the pistol. But if I miss, the shooter needs only to roll onto his back and his next blizzard of bullets would plaster me all over the ceiling above. Then, with a gasp, I remember my last Flash-Bang. I wrench it free, pull the pin, and let it drop right between the two of them.

The second-floor landing disappears in a concussive blast of bright light and deafening sound. Section Eight don't hesitate. Three soldiers peer around the ruined doorway and hose the landing with a merciless stream of automatic fire. As they fall back, a forth soldier steps into the breach and takes aim with a rather cheap-looking tubular device. I've just enough time to swear and scramble away from the railing as something whooshes across the atrium towards us. I drop into a crouch, close my eyes, and jam my hands firmly over my ears as the grenade detonates, obliterating the landing below me and thumping the floor up so hard beneath me that I'm bounced an inch into the air.

Then there is only silence, albeit one tinged by a nasty, loud ringing noise in my ears. I cautiously open first one eye, then the other, and peer through the swirling haze of dust and smoke. A cursory check reveals I'm still in one piece—more or less. With a mixture of shock and wide-eyed amazement, I slowly get up and give an incredulous laugh of disbelief. How am I possibly still alive and walking after that? I run to the railing to see Abbott and Lennox enter the atrium.

'Up here,' I yell. 'He's up here!'

Obviously my presence, well ahead of them, is not what they were expecting. They share a confused look and then race up the wide staircase towards me. The second he reaches the landing, Abbott starts shouting.

'What the hell are you doing?' He stops just as quickly, aghast at my appearance.

'Jesus! What happened to you?' Lennox exclaims with more genuine concern. 'You alright?'

'I'll live. Come on. He went this way.' I run off towards the large set of double doors at the end of the corridor. A sign outside it clearly marks it as private. We stop and listen at the door.

'*Merde*, how much longer?' the Frenchwoman shouts at Robert Pemberton-Smythe. 'We need to go! Give me the bearer bonds.'

'It needs to compress first,' Pemberton-Smythe replies in irritation. Nonetheless, anxiety is apparent in his voice. 'Another forty-five seconds. And *I'll* bring the bonds, thank you very much.'

'So, it's locked, ready to go? *Oui?*'

'As I understand it, yes.'

'*Bon!*'

The soldiers must have foreseen it, but the loud retort of the gunshot makes me jump. It's followed by an ominous thud.

'Ai-yah, not cool,' Abbott groans. He reaches for the handle, but it's locked. 'Your turn,' he says to Lennox, stepping back.

'Roger that, forty seconds,' Lennox replies, calmly bracing his MP5 to his shoulder.

I look away as he puts a whole magazine through the lock in less than two and a half seconds, blitzing it into a ragged, splintery mess in the process. The savage kick which follows almost takes the left-hand door completely off its hinges. In goes a Flash-Bang. It detonates and both soldiers race in right after it, each covering a different side of the room. Two shouts of 'clear' and I dart in after them.

In contrast to the gloomy corridor, the huge study is light and airy. Like something out of a *Country Living* magazine, its high ceiling is detailed with intricate plasterwork. Everything is covered in white dustsheets. A row of tall windows stretches along the other side of the room. Below us, just beyond a shallow roof running beneath the windows, is the swimming pool which I saw earlier, with the rear gardens beyond that.

There's no sign of Nicole, but the soldiers are taking nothing for granted and they quickly clear the areas behind the sofas and chairs. A nearby door swings open in the breeze. Abbott grabs his radio and hurriedly forewarns everyone to be on the lookout for a lone female in the vicinity of the main house.

I'm the first to spot the crumpled figure of Robert Pemberton-Smythe lying at the far end of the room. I rush over and find him face down on the plush carpet between his desk and a huge aquarium that's built into the end wall. A safe sits open and empty next to him.

'Nothing we can do now,' Lennox says, rushing past me towards the desk. 'Look alive, thirty seconds.'

I struggle to comprehend how someone I was talking to only a few minutes ago can now be lying dead at my feet, bleeding out into the carpet.

Lennox's curses draw my attention to the desk. Like those at his firm, Pemberton-Smythe's desk has a bank of six screens, but all are off. Instead, Lennox stoops to examine the laptop sitting open on the desk. His expression rouses me from my melancholy and I run over to look. Some kind of trade confirms system sits open on the screen. In the centre of it, a series of message icons appears to be waiting to be sent. Floating above each is a compiler progress indicator counting down until completion.

'Twenty seconds,' I say, turning to the two men.

'Williams,' Abbott barks into his radio.

'Who?' I ask.

'Our tech-guy.'

'Oh, he's dead.'

'Damn. Okay, where's Butterworth?' Lennox calls into his.

'I'm here,' comes her reply over the radio.

'It's about to send. Any idea how we stop it?'

'Press "cancel" or "escape". Otherwise, pull out the internet cable!'

I look for one while Lennox hammers at the keys, but to no effect.

'Mills, it's wireless and he seems to have locked it somehow. What else?'

'Ten seconds,' says Lennox.

'He must have a key lock-on!'

'Let's smash it!' says Abbott, raising his assault rifle.

'It might not work,' Milly exclaims. 'Can you see the base station?'

'Five seconds.'

'No, I've got an idea!' I cry, grabbing the laptop and shoving Abbott aside. *'Move!'*

I whirl round and lunge for the massive fish tank. Lennox beats me to it. In one deft move, he tears the access panel away from the wall above it—just in time for me to plunge the machine straight in. It hits the water with a bright electrical flash and quickly sinks to the bottom. Then, almost comically, the three of us slowly lean in closer to watch as it settles on the sandy bottom.

'You think it worked?' I ask.

'Well, the lights are out, and the screen's off. So it sure looks like it,' Lennox replies. 'Bloody lucky there was nothing in there or we'd be having grilled fish for dinner tonight. Hey, boss, you don't have any shares, do you? You might want to sell them, you know, just in case.'

'On my bloody salary?' Abbott grumbles. He shakes his head and turns to me with a stony expression. 'And I thought I told you to stay in the car.'

'Well, you'd be in a right bloody mess now if I had, wouldn't you?'

Lennox laughs out loud.

'She's got you there, boss.'

Abbott fights the smile that's threatening to make an appearance.

'Don't get cocky.'

'Yeah, whatever.'

I turn my attention back to the figure sprawled at my feet. Up close, the sight is so much worse than I expected. The small, round wound above his eye and the thin trickle of blood don't even remotely prepare me for what awaits when I see the back of his head. I recoil in horror. Nearly the entire back of his skull is missing. Most of it seems to have ended up on the wall. A tatty mop of bloody hair is all that's left to ring the fist-sized mess of shattered bone and shredded tissue. A sweet, sickly smell suddenly makes me feel nauseous, and I just about make it to the wastepaper bin in time. Neither adult seems in the least bit perturbed by the sight or the smell, which I take to be either blood or brain, and both look down at me with bemusement.

'How can you be so calm about this?'

'Seen it before,' Abbott mumbles absentmindedly.

'And it doesn't bother you?'

'Not when you've seen it as often as we have,' says Lennox. 'You're best not to think about it too much or else that's all you'll see when you tuck your kids into bed at night.'

I don't really know what to say to that. Instead, I turn back to Alex's father. It seems such a waste. Alive one minute ... and then ... gone. Everything he was, everything he still had to live for, all gone, in the blink of an eye. I wonder what his last thoughts were? My own quickly turn to Alex and how he'll cope now. It's all too depressing, and I'm about to rush for the door when I stop and freeze.

'You hear that?' I cock my head and listen. 'Didn't someone say something about a helicopter coming?'

Their puzzled looks tell me they can't hear it yet. Convinced of what I heard, I rush to the nearest window.

'Damn, you're right,' says Abbott, quick to point to a small dot in the distance.

'Hey, that her?' Lennox asks, pointing to a figure just rounding the far end of the swimming pool.

I press my face to the window.

'Too right it is.'

If it wasn't for my burning desire to stab her with one of her heels, I'd almost be impressed by how fast she's moving in them now. The doctor is already waiting in the middle of the lawn.

The soldiers run for the fire escape, but I see a quicker way. Grabbing the back of one of Robert Pemberton-Smythe's expensive-looking high chairs, I fling it through the nearest window. The glass shatters and the chair falls, torn and broken, onto the gently sloping roof outside. I swipe the remaining bits of glass from the frame with a nearby table lamp and leap out onto the roof. The shallow end of the pool is directly below me. A jump from here would be suicidal, but into the deep end … that just might work.

With a harried look, Nicole glances over her shoulder.

'Oi! Come back here, you bitch!' I scream at the top of my lungs.

A faint flicker of a smile crosses her face.

Cursing, I take off, sprinting along the roof.

'Foxton, come back,' Abbott shouts. 'We'll handle this.'

I ignore him and veer right towards the edge. Abbott shouts again—but he's too late. I throw the electric pistol out over the pool towards the grass on the other side. With one last, massive stride, I launch myself off the roof after it. My limbs windmill silently as I plunge the three storeys down into the water. The impact is so much harder than I imagined it would be and it drives the air from me like one of Banovic's punches. Momentum takes me all the way to the bottom. The water's almost freezing and I make for the far side as quickly as I can.

The helicopter has already begun its descent towards the centre of the rear lawn. Nicole frantically waves for the pilot to hurry and land, as I heave myself from the pool. With grim determination, I fling my sodden hair from my face and snatch up the pistol. Turning the gun on, I set after her as fast as my squelching boots allow. I rush past a low stone wall that divides the back lawn from the neighbouring tennis courts. Two loud splashes behind me announce Abbott and Lennox's arrival. But there's no time to wait for them. A blast of cold wind announces the helicopter's touchdown. The doctor climbs in the back and Nicole rushes for the passenger side door. In goes a brown leather attaché case she's carrying. Then she grabs the doorframe and pulls herself up.

I'm still twenty feet away but it's now or never. Dropping to one knee, I take aim and fire. An arc of electric-blue light momentarily seems to connect the gun to her right leg. She screams as it buckles violently beneath her. Only lightning-quick hands and a conveniently placed grip stop her from falling to the ground.

Dangerous and wild, she flails around inside the foot well and reappears brandishing her pistol. Her first shot is way off. But it's still close enough to send me racing in terror for the low stone wall. Her second hisses past far too close to my right ear. With a scream, I launch myself over the wall and land in a painful and ungainly heap on the other side. Another shot sends splinters of stone raining down all around me.

With extreme trepidation, I snatch a quick peep through a gap in the stones. She's in and her door's closing. I can't let her get away! Flinging myself across the top of the wall, I fire off several shots at her side of the helicopter. All glance harmlessly off the Perspex. The engine pitch rises and the machine wobbles up into the air. I fire twice more, but again to no effect. With a flurry of curses, I dash after them, firing continuously until the gun runs out of charge.

By the time Abbott and Lennox open fire with their far more capable weapons, the helicopter has cleared the lawn and is already out of range. We can only watch in frustration as it disappears over the treetops and is lost from sight.

Someone calls from behind us. We turn to see Milly and several of the soldiers making their way across the lawn.

'Another time,' Lennox says, equally annoyed, as he pats me on the shoulder. I try not to wince too obviously at the sharp stab of pain. I curse and stuff the pistol petulantly back into my pocket. A few deep breaths and I manage to calm myself a little.

'Well, you guys need to check out the basement or garage,' I say. 'It looks like they had some kind of lab going down there. I think that was what they were clearing out in such a hurry.'

Lennox nods and then calls out to Milly, 'You know I'm never getting in a car with you, now that we've seen how you drive.'

With a smile, I hobble over and throw my arms around her. For a moment neither of us lets go, both just glad we made it.

'Think it's high time you two get back to that school of yours,' Abbott says, tapping his watch. 'We've got about ten minutes before the police arrive.'

'Yo, yo!' comes a shout from across the lawn. Stomping towards us with a monstrously large, belt-fed machine gun slung over his shoulder is George Oakley, Section Eight's shaven-headed, light-support gunner. 'Okay, which of you psychos made all the mess up on three? C'mon, own up!'

Milly glances at me before I can hide my sheepish grin. Lennox sees it, too, and calls to Oakley, '*Que passé?*'

'Two guys, both built like tanks. One's a former Serb Red Beret, going by his tats. Both had a can of serious whoop-ass opened up on them. Serb's had his head put through a bookcase. Other one looks like he was thrown through a window. Cuffed 'em both, but *damn*! Same with some other guy out back in the carpark.'

Abbott and Lennox turn to me with deeply curious looks.

'What!' I exclaim, as a dozen pairs of eyes all turn towards me. 'They deserved it, alright.' I pull my wet hair aside to show them the mess I'm in. Even the soldier who gave us such condescending looks earlier seems suddenly concerned. He takes a closer look and frowns.

'Serious ice-pack time, I think.'

'I'll see what I can knock up,' Oakley says, and heads back towards the mansion.

'Can I get one, too?' Milly calls after him.

Lennox slaps us both on the back and calls to one of the other soldiers.

'Spinks, go see if you can get that Range Rover out front to start. Otherwise, try to find the keys to Pemberton-Smythe's Jag and then get these two back to Godolphin Park as quickly as you can.'

'Yes, boss.'

'Oh, and Spinks,' Abbott calls after him. 'Wait for Oakley's ice-packs, yeah? The less they need to explain about why they look like they pissed off Mike Tyson, the better. And, Foxton, do everyone a favour and wash your face in the pool, will you? Else you'll scare all the other children.'

I arch an eyebrow and give him a grossly exaggerated thumbs-up. Then we laugh and run after George Oakley.

* * *

CHAPTER 20

ALL GOOD THINGS ...

To say that Corporal Spinks drives like a madman would be an understatement. Then again, Pemberton-Smythe's Jag sure can move and, given that it's just gone five in the morning, the roads are almost deserted, which allows us to get back to Godolphin Park long before anyone wakes and race upstairs without being seen. After I put the pistol on charge under my bed, we slip downstairs to take desperately needed showers and then grudgingly head off up to the san, as Oakley insisted we do, for a quick check-up.

Despite nearly running ourselves out of concealer and doing our level best to keep low profiles, it proves impossible, and before long we are literally fending off the inquisition.

'Who hit you, Hev?'

'Yeah, so where've you two been?'

'Did you get into a fight with her?'

'Who started it?'

'Oh, go on, please tell us!'

*

Just after nine o'clock that evening, Milly hurries into the study and drags me downstairs into the common room where the evening news has just come on.

'... the business world is today mourning the passing of one of its most influential figures. Valhalla Capital Chairman Robert Pemberton-Smythe, a close advisor to the Treasury, died this morning during an attempted robbery at his country estate. The sixty-seven-year-old renowned corporate raider leaves a wife and son ...'

At the back of the room, unbeknownst to the others, we exchange somewhat more knowing looks.

'Has he been in touch yet?' says Milly.

'No,' I say forlornly. 'But that could be for loads of reasons, I guess. I mean, with all this going on, I wouldn't expect to hear anything for quite some time. He's got far more important things to be dealing with. But you don't think he found out that I left with another boy, do you? And that maybe he's pissed off with me?'

I try to say it casually yet inside I feel anything but.

'I'm sure that's not the case,' Milly says. 'In all that chaos, I doubt it.'

'Well, I can only hope so, right?'

*

After the thrill of the last few days, being back at school smacks of boredom and mundane routine. We try our best, but find it's not so easy to get excited about classes and studying again. Even for Milly, who's far more academic than me, everything seems a little trivial and uninspiring.

I'd completely forgotten that our end of term marks were due out and it's only the sight of a scrum of students fighting to get to the main notice board which reminds me. I'm genuinely surprised to discover that I haven't done nearly as badly as I was expecting. Thanks in no small part, I suppose, to the positively nerdy influence of my roommate, I've managed some pretty good grades, including a B in Mobile Surveillance and, running my finger down the list, I smile to see I've scored an A in 'Geology' (otherwise known as the subtle art of Placement and Procurement).

Thoroughly buoyed, I hear a commotion and turn to see Victoria Farabee-Peacock barging her way through the crowd. She ignores me completely and hurriedly runs her spindly finger down the list. Even she can't hide the look of concern that comes over her as she takes a step back and gasps. For the first time, instead of her usually arrogant expression, I see something else. A look of genuine worry. A glance at the board tells me why.

'What are you staring at?' she snaps.

Behind her, Augustus quickly tears the sheet down, to cries of protest. His grades are probably no better than hers. He ignores everyone's annoyance.

'Nothing,' I reply and turn to walk away. Clearly flustered—mostly, I suspect, from fear of what her father will do when he finds out—she fires a barrage of ever-more offensive insults after me. But there's nothing she could say or do that would bother me anymore. It's quite liberating. Seeing her insecurities like this somehow also humanises her a bit in my eyes. I turn back and Augustus stiffens noticeably behind her.

'You know what, Farabee,' I say, calmly walking up to her. 'I get that you're a stuck-up, arrogant, racist bitch. And I don't really care. That's your problem and you're the one who has to live with it. So, fine, go on thinking what you want. But don't take your own insecurities out on my friends. You want to pick fights with someone, fine, pick them with me. But please leave my friends alone.'

Maybe it's her results playing on her mind, or something else, I don't know, but for once she has no answer. No pithy, sarcastic put-down. No vicious, catty comment. Only silence. Of course, how long it will last is another question entirely. But I intend to enjoy the peace while it does.

*

The final week of term passes in a blur of activity, and before we know it, the end is upon us. It's hard not to reflect back on what has been the most amazing three months of my life. Three short months in which my world has been folded inside out, torn to pieces, shoved into the proverbial blender, and then spat out the other end, somehow so much better than when it started. I'm almost sad that term's coming to an end. I'll miss this place. The outside world feels very different now to when I left it. But I know it's time to start trying to rebuild the mess that awaits me at home. Knowing what I do, I've come to understand my 'mother' so much better. Well, sort of … And while I know we'll probably never be the closest, that doesn't mean I can't at least try to be cordial with her, if only for my dad's sake.

*

Come breakfast on the penultimate day of term, a lower-fifth former approaches Milly and me with a note from Top Table. It requests our presence in the headmaster's office before morning prayers.

'Great, now what?' says Milly.

When the time comes, we find him waiting for us together with Frank Sable.

'Come in, girls. Take a seat,' Dr Gambon says warmly. 'This won't take long. We just wanted to congratulate you properly for last week and to let you know what has happened since then.

'But first things first. It seems the powers that be have deemed it only fitting that you both receive some form of recognition for your actions. You have, therefore, each been cited for a clandestine services medal for bravery. Might mean a trip up to London in a couple of weeks' time, but we all have to make sacrifices, don't we? Alas, once received, they'll have to stay in my safe. Need to know, and all that. I'm sure you understand. And the code's changed, by the way,' he says, looking at me.

I smile and turn to Milly with an excited look. Not because we won something, but because it means she can come and stay at mine for a few days.

'We can go Christmas shopping,' I say excitedly.

'Anyway, not to keep you,' the headmaster says, frowning. 'On to the real reason I asked you up here. As you know, Robert Pemberton-Smythe failed. But rather more alarming was what we found in that garage of his. You were right, there was some sort of laboratory down there. Equally concerning, however, is that much of the equipment left down there was of Chinese origin. And all typically of the sort found in IVF labs.

'The question that has us all rather perplexed, though, is what was Pemberton-Smythe even doing mixed up in any of this in the first place? Our initial analysis suggests this was merely part of something far bigger and more complicated than a stock market scam. But quite what, we don't yet know. From your debriefings, it sounds like he was being used as a conduit to the financial markets. We can't rule out blackmail, which is sounding ever more plausible. However, he was also scheming behind their backs. It's our guess he realised what their plan would do to his company, so, in order to protect it, he started diversifying out of the stock market and into property. But he had to do it all very quietly so not to arouse their, or anyone else's, suspicions. I imagine when they realised he had become a liability, whoever was ultimately behind this decided to tie up loose ends. Hence the Frenchwoman and the Russians.'

Gambon says nothing more, nor does he need to. His smile and little nod are sufficient.

*

An hour shy of our Christmas dinner, we all head over to B-School for the last time this term. Milly and I hang back with Frank Sable, Henri Cabal and Mr Sparkman as everyone else takes their seats on the matted area for the end of term debrief by the head of MI13, a woman called Katherine Sloan-Sinclair.

'Good evening, everyone,' she begins over the video conference set up at the front. 'I know you're all keen to get to your dinner, so I'll keep it quick. I just wanted to thank you all for another especially good term. I think we've proved, yet again, just how vital we are to this country's intelligence apparatus. I know we ask a lot from you and you should all be very proud of the role you've played, regardless of your speciality.

'This term you've assisted in some very significant wins on the gathering front. Most recently against certain Asian criminal enterprises.'

We look round for Anabel, who blushes in embarrassment and sinks lower in her seat.

'We have also had considerable success against certain home-grown jihadist groups recruiting out of British schools. For all of you who've had to spend time away from your friends in this effort, I sincerely thank you.'

This time everyone looks for a boy called Adam, who I learn has spent the term boarding at a rather prestigious school, rooming with the son of an Arab sheik who MI6 suspect of facilitating terrorist activities. In almost comical contrast to Anabel, he stands and laps up the applause.

'And to everyone in the shared services and technical support, you have demonstrated, yet again, that you are, more often than not, well ahead of the curve. Your creativity and ingenuity never ceases to amaze us, and I'm sure this is a trend that we'll continue to see throughout the rest of the year.

'So that's it. Short and sweet, like I promised. I wish you all a very happy holiday. Merry Christmas, MI13!'

The feed cuts and the screen goes blank. I look at Milly and smile surreptitiously. Some secrets, I realise, won't even be shared with the others here.

By the time we reach the dining hall, most of the school is already seated. We hurry to our tables and slip in amongst the others. For the last week, the hall has played host to a plethora of decorations and a large, brightly lit Christmas tree, towering high over by the windows. For this meal only, each place setting also has a little sprig of holly, a Christmas cracker, and a colourful napkin laid out on it. Candles burn everywhere I look, and the hall dances in their warm, flickering glow. The lights have been dimmed to give the place an even more Christmassy feel.

As the school settles down, Dr Gambon stands up at the far end and clears his throat.

'Attention, everyone,' he calls. 'Now, before we all gorge ourselves on the magnificent feast that Mr Falstaff and his catering team have prepared for us—'

The hall bursts into applause and the school's burly chef beams with pride over by the kitchen doors.

'Yes, quite so, quite so,' Dr Gambon exclaims, bringing everyone to order again. 'But first I would ask you to raise your glasses in a toast to everything that we have accomplished this term. You should all be very proud of your achievements here, and I'm not just talking about the First Fifteen's demolition of Milfield last Saturday.'

Even louder applause drowns him out again. He claps to regain our focus.

'For it is only with the sum of all our individual achievements that we make Godolphin Park the truly unique place that it is. So Merry Christmas, everyone.'

For the one time a year when we get an inch of champagne, we all raise our glasses without fear of getting busted. The school bursts into applause again as the catering staff emerges from the kitchens, laden with food for all the tables. The chatter picks up and soon we can barely hear each other. Crackers and party poppers merely add to the festive spirit.

I watch my housemates for a moment and feel quite overcome at the realisation of just how fortunate I am to be able to count them as my friends. For someone who doesn't do all that well with large groups of friends, I really couldn't have got luckier with them. I laugh as Milly goes up on tiptoes to position a paper crown onto my head. Luther wastes no time in diving straight in and loading his plate to the point of overflowing. Nigel tries to pour us all a glass of the school's oddly non-alcoholic mulled wine, yet somehow manages to get more over the tablecloth than in our glasses. Anabel rolls her eyes and takes the jug from him before he can cause even more mess.

With a happy smile, I lean back and breathe a deep sigh of contentment. Yes, life is good here. Yet I can't help think what kind of Christmas this is going to be for Alex and what remains of his family. I haven't had the nerve to call him yet and he's obviously had too much on his mind to call me. I'll give it another couple of days, and maybe then try again …

*

And suddenly the end of term is upon us. Within half an hour of lunch finishing on our final day, the grounds start filling up with cars as everyone's parents begin to arrive. Many of them join us for the last chapel service of term. After that, it's a mad rush back to our houses. Typically, having left everything to the last moment, we all drag our trunks down from the laundry room and hastily begin packing. Ten minutes is all it takes for SH to descend from its usual state of disciplined order into the same chaos and mayhem which I remember from my first day here.

It's not long before Milly's parents arrive. I'm touched. They bought me a present! With a happy grin, I agree not to open it until Christmas. Then we all help carry her stuff down to their car. As the last item is loaded, Mr Butterworth turns to me.

'Now are you sure we can't give you a lift to the station, Heather?'

'I'd really just planned to get a taxi later on, but I guess this'll save me a tenner, so why not?'

I gratefully accept and rush back upstairs for my belongings. Thankfully, as I am going home by train, the school will have my trunk sent on in the next day or two. With my backpack hefted onto my back, I cast a last look around our study, trying to think if I've forgotten anything. Then, with an exclamation, I run back to my bed and drop to the floor. With a sigh of relief, I find the electric pistol and shove it into the rucksack's side pocket, determined that from now on it's coming everywhere with me.

Twenty minutes later, we arrive at the local railway station. After thanking the Butterworths, Milly and I climb out to say our goodbyes in private.

'Now are you sure you're going to be okay with your parents?' she asks with a concerned look.

I shrug.

'I hope so. I mean we've got to live together, so I'm just going to have to make the effort, aren't I? But yeah, I think we'll be okay, one way or the other.'

'Good, I'm glad,' she says with a heartfelt smile. Then, after a final hug, she climbs back into the car. Her window buzzes down.

'So you're going to call, right?'

'Of course,' I reply. 'Say nine o'clock?'

'Perfect!' She grins at me with that huge smile of hers.

I wave goodbye and watch as they drive off, with Milly waving frantically out the back window. With a happy nod, I head inside to buy the offensively expensive ticket up to Waterloo Station. Slinging my backpack over my shoulder, I make my way along the platform towards the bench at the very end. At least I have some music on my iSpy to listen to while I wait. I pop the earphones in and scroll through my playlists until I find Feeder's 'Comfort in Sound'.

As the music fills my head, I settle back and look around. Several other pupils from school are also here and we share familiar smiles. Some are with their parents, while others, like me, are alone. With that thought in mind, I wonder whether I was completely honest with Milly. Whether I am being completely honest with myself, for that matter. In truth, I really don't know. Resisting the urge to ask my parents about what they know of my biological parents is going to be the hardest part. But one way or the other, I'm going to need to know eventually. At least I'm not dreading seeing them. Maybe that's the real genius of schools like this. The time we spend apart from our parents. Because, despite everything, I actually want to go home now.

Clearing my mind, I look off along the platform. One thing about B-School, it certainly teaches you to be more aware of your surroundings. My eye is quickly drawn to an unassuming middle-aged man sitting three benches away. I take him in within a fraction of a second. The broadsheet newspaper, the loose-fitting clothing, and the practical shoes. But something about him makes me look again. That's when I spot the well-concealed earpiece. I chuckle to myself and stare at him until he notices. It doesn't take long. Presumably he's one of MI5's watchers. When he looks up, I give him a cheekily wave.

That draws a frown and he slowly raises his cuff to his mouth, hoping no one will notice. I can't help but laugh. Chances are he isn't alone. I wonder if I can spot their whole team by the time we get to Waterloo? That'll certainly make the trip a bit more entertaining.

Just then my iSpy vibrates twice. I unlock it to see two new messages. The first is from Alex. With a burst of excitement, I rush to open it.

Miss you like crazy, babe. Sorry for not writing. World's gone to pieces. First David. Now Dad. Just want to hold you and cry. Need to see you so bad.

Like an idiot, I start blubbing in relief and hurriedly type back a reply. I know it's not going to be easy, and in all likelihood it'll be quite some time before he truly comes to terms with his dad's death, but if I can help him in any way then that's what I'll do.

With a sniff and a rub of my eyes, I give a choked, happy little laugh and open the next message from Milly. It's only three letters long—**BFF**—but it still brings a smile to my face.

Too right! I reply.

Which reminds me. I reach into my rucksack and pull out a tattered old book which she insisted I read over the holidays. I cross my legs and happily make myself as comfortable as the bench will allow. Then I turn up my music, open the book to the first page, and begin reading.

> Mr and Mrs Dursley, of number four, Privet Drive, were proud to say they were perfectly normal, thank you very much.

Oh well, I smile to myself, I guess everyone's got their role to play, haven't they?

THE END.

Heather Foxton will return in *The Hyderabad Siphon.*

THANKS

Anyone who has ever written a book, or even tried to write one, will know just how solitary an activity it can be. Hours upon hours spent sitting in a darkened room, gazing at a computer screen, tinkering, procrastinating and plotting away with dozens of ideas all up in the air at the same time. And in the knowledge that everyone else is probably out having fun in some loud, crazy bar somewhere. But that's the life of an author. I am, however, fortunate and privileged enough to be surrounded by some of the most supportive friends and family which any aspiring author could ever have wished for. For most, this must at times have felt like the odyssey that would never end.

Every one of you deserves a very big thank you for sticking with me.

To Ting, my Bella Bambina, your support and belief in this crazy project, which has been onerously time consuming and monopolising, has been so important to me and to its ultimate success. Your humorous acceptance of the 'other girl' in my life has been fabulously, awe inspiringly tolerant and I love you all for the more for it.

To my mother, who, for nearly seven years, has had a huge poster of the first cover design hanging on her wall, all my love and gratitude for everything you and Dad sacrificed to give me the best start in life that you could. I haven't been the best at saying it, but I am more grateful than you may ever know. Through thick and thin, you have stood by me and I love you very dearly for it.

To Carolyn Boyes, very much an author in her own right, my heartfelt thanks to you for your friendship, patience and company over the years, from aimlessly wandering the grounds of London's historic old houses with me as the first semblance of a cohesive plot began to take form, to the endless hours on the phone, or by e-mail, offering nothing but support. I am most grateful!

To my extended family, who have watched from the sidelines, probably with a wry, slightly perplexed smile at what must have seemed like the pipedream from Never-Never land. Thank you for tolerating it with such humour. You have embraced and welcomed me into your world most warmly.

To my friends who offered to read the book and gave me suggestions and a healthy dose of criticism, I know doing so on something as personal as a book is always tough, so I am most, most grateful. No book will ever be perfect, but this one is only where it is thanks to you. You know who you are. And to those other friends who have been particularly supportive in other ways, many of you will find yourselves within the book.

To my copy editor, Sarah Ashton, and the folks at Charlie Wilson's, my sincere thanks. The role of a good editor cannot be trivialised. Being able to combine a fastidious approach to grammar and spelling, neither of which are my strongest points, whilst letting the author's voice remain unchanged is a rare skill, a testament to professionalism, and Sarah is the embodiment of this. To my book designer, John and everyone at Chandler Book Design, my thanks for your support in making this book so much more than I could have ever done alone. To Geoff, who gave Heather a public face, you are so very talented. Thank you for all your hard work.

The decision to go solo on this as a standalone author/publisher was as much a commercial one as it was a personal one. That said, along the way I have received more than my fair share of support from people within the traditional publishing business. At certain points, possibly more so than the quality of the writing justly deserved. Therefore, my sincere thanks go to them for all their encouragement and the belief they showed in Heather and her friends.

To Blofeld, thank you for your interest. I am sad that things didn't pan out in the end.

To Tania Hurst-Brown and Jane Villiers at Sayle Screen, who supported me at a time when the book was half-baked at best and surely not worthy of the effort you invested. I thank you both for your belief.

To Becky Stradwick, formerly of Darley Anderson, it's a shame no one with your vision followed in your footsteps after you left. I hope you found fun and happiness at your next home.

Of course, I would be remiss for not acknowledging those whose professional criticism has also spurred me forward over the years. Any writer who doesn't get their share of rejection letters is either extraordinarily good or astonishingly lucky.

I rather suspect it's the latter. For me there were many, many of these rejections. But special credit has to go to Patrick Janson-Smith, now of Blue Door at HarperCollins, for those few inspirational words all the way back at the end of 2007. So much of my drive to continue is due to that e-mail, possibly the most cutting rejection I received. And, ironically, it was the first feedback I got on the book. Yet at the same time, and by a massive stretch, it was also the most inspirational feedback I received. Thank you for making me want to prove you wrong. I hope you feel I have.

The list could go on and on. And yet still there would be people I don't mention. So to everyone else who has offered their support and encouragement over the years, or who has, in some other way, helped me get here, I sincerely thank you.

Lastly, but by no means least, my thanks to you, the reader, for having taken a chance in buying this book. I really hope you enjoyed it. The fun of taking on an endeavour such as this is matched only by the enjoyment readers get from entering your imaginary world of paper and ink and escaping their own, if only for a short period. Long may the adventures of Heather Foxton continue to bring you this kind of escapist entertainment.